BLESSED
ARE THE
PEACEMAKERS

TERENCE V. HAYES

PAGE PUBLISHING, INC.
New York, NY

First originally published by Page Publishing, Inc. 2015

ISBN 978-1-63417-462-6 (pbk)
ISBN 978-1-63417-463-3 (digital)

Printed in the United States of America

I'd like to dedicate this book to all who have, are, and will carry a shield.

To Joanne Fleming, an outstanding woman, who translated
my chicken scratch into a book.

To my parents for the gift of life.

To my daughters for the choices they've made in life.

My grandsons and granddaughters especially my favorite
(you know who you are) for the joy you've brought to my life.

My brothers and sisters for their love, friendship and guidance.

My work partners past and present.

Last and certainly not least, my wife Janet for her support and love.
It's been one hellofa ride kid.

I guess I should start at the beginning. It was a beautiful day with a clear blue sky and a few puffy white clouds high up.

I was ecstatic. A whole new world was opening for me. The culmination of my childhood dreams. I was going to be sworn in as a patrolman in the New York City Police Department.

I climbed the stairs to 240 Centre Street in Manhattan. These were the very same steps that Police Commissioner Teddy Roosevelt had walked on. Countless others had mounted these same stairs and did great deeds.

I patted the statue of the lion on the paw and said a silent prayer of thanksgiving to St. Michael, the archangel, the patron saint of policemen.

I entered the awesome lobby and was immediately intimidated. The tile floors, the vaulted ceiling, the somber-faced men coming and going. All very serious and concerned.

I made my way up the marble stairs to the large room where hundreds of other young men were milling around.

Finally, four big, burly men entered and one called us to order. We sat on the straight-back folding chairs in silence. One of these monster men started to cough, and then, in a voice so loud you'd think he was using a microphone said, "All right, I'm only going to say this once. When your name is called, come to the table up here and produce all the copies of the documents you were told to bring with you. I'm gonna start with the letter Z and go to A."

Heads popped up, and quizzical looks were given. The large man semi-smiled and said, "My name is Zembowski. Anybody got a problem with me starting from Z?" Nobody said anything, and he continued, "Since I was a kid, I was always called last. Now I have the power and authority to change the rules. Seeing that no one is objecting, let's start."

My turn came, and I approached the long table in front of the stage. At the one side, you produced all your documents, in the middle you signed a bunch of papers, and at the far end was a large box containing the coveted police shields.

When my turn came, this tough-looking man looked at me. He took the stub of a cigar out of this mouth. "All right, kid, gimme your birth certificate, Social Security card, your draft card or your discharge papers, and your driver's license." I handed everything over to him, and he recorded it on a sheet bearing the title "Probationary Patrolman Daniel Stark." He gave everything back and put out a massive paw and said, "I need your driver's license." I felt as if my feet were nailed to the floor. "Driver's license, I . . . I . . . I don't have one. I live in Brooklyn. I take trains or buses or cabs. Some of the girls I date have cars. I don't need a license." He stuck the cigar in his mouth and scowled at me. "Hey, kid, no license, no shield."

It really isn't a good idea to cry in front of a room filled with men, but boy, I almost did. Walking out of Headquarters, I looked at the gargoyle statute and thought I should have patted the one on the right side too.

I didn't know what to do. It was eight-fifteen in the morning. At one o'clock, the official swearing in ceremony was to take place. My uncle Mike, the detective, my brother Jack, the detective, my grandmother, my fiancée and my other brother "Big Jim" were all planning to be there for my big moment.

"Big Jim!" It hit me. Call Big Jim; he can help. What the heck, he's an FBI agent.

I called the FBI office and got put through to his extension. It rang and rang and rang, and finally, he answered.

The words tumbled out, and there was silence. Then he let me have it. "You stupid son-of-a-bitch" was one of the gentler things he called me.

Twenty minutes later, he and his partner, Joe Phalen, pulled up to the corner of Centre and Broome Streets. Mr. Phalen opened the back door and motioned for me to get in. I did. Big Jim didn't say a word. With red lights and sirens, he wove in and out of the early-morning traffic and pulled to a screeching halt at the side of a building.

Mr. Phalen said, "Get out. Don't talk to anyone. Stay with us." We went into the building, up the stairs through a corridor, through another door, into a smelly freight elevator and got out on the sixth floor. For the first time Big Jim looked at me. "Sit here," he said, pointing to a bench, "And don't talk to anyone."

He and Mr. Phalen went into an unmarked door, and fifteen minutes later, out they came. He handed me a plain white envelope and just said, "Don't lose it," and added a few remarks about my mental capacity.

I got back on the line and gave the cigar man my name and papers. I took the envelope from my pocket and gave him the most important documents of my life. My New York State driver's license.

He looked at me and looked at the license. He looked at the license and scrubbed his gnarly fingers across it. *Oh, God, please don't let the ink smear!* I looked him in the eyes and blurted, "I forgot I had gotten it the other day. I . . . I . . ." He held up his massive paw and said, "I'm not even going to ask. Move on." I clutched the license like it was the most important piece of paper of my life. Actually, it was.

I moved down the line and got my shield number, 15945. I was in heaven. St. Michael came through for me. That was the first time, but not the last over the next twenty years.

I'm one of nine children. Big Jim is the oldest, then my other brother, Jack, Cele, Peggy, Kathleen, me, Patty Ann, and Virginia Ellen. Daddy and Momma are both dead. Daddy was an insurance agent for Metropolitan Life, and Momma, of course, was a housewife.

One September night in 1947, Daddy came home, played with me and my three younger sisters. We ate dinner and laughed. The girls, all of them, helped Momma clear the table and wash the dishes. Daddy and I went into the living room, and he turned on the radio so we could listen to the Lone Ranger. I climbed on his lap, and he made entries in his big black debit book. It was actually his client book.

You see, in those days, he not only sold the policies, but also had to collect the premiums from his customers. There were penny, nickel, dime, quarter, and dollar policies that he would have to collect.

After a day of going up and down numerous flights of stairs, he'd return to the office, count the money, put it in the safe, and then come home. Apparently, he was good at what he did because we never wanted for anything.

The dishes were finished, and so was the Lone Ranger. Daddy horsed around with my little sisters while the others were doing their homework or writing to Jimmy and Jackie who were still in the service. Momma shooed the younger girls up to bed after kisses all around and settled on the couch with her crocheting. About nine o'clock, Daddy announced that he was going to take a shower and get to bed. He gave us all kisses and went up the stairs. We could hear the water running, and then all at once, there was a sound, like someone growling. I remember Momma dropping her wool as she ran to the stairs. She called out, "Lester, Lester, what are you doing?" She was halfway up the stairs, and all you could hear was the water and the growl.

Cele and Peggy were close on her heels and Kathleen put her arm around my shoulder. Momma yelled down, "Get Mr. Mulvey. Something is wrong." Peggy came flying down the stairs, and she and Kathleen went out the back door across the alley to Mulvey's house. I ventured up the stairs and saw Momma drape a towel over Daddy's waist, and she and Cele struggled to get him out of the tub. I squeezed into the tiny bathroom and turned off the shower. Mr. And Mrs. Mulvey squeezed in, and between them, Momma, and Cele, they got Daddy out of the tub and into their bedroom.

The growling was continuous. The next thing I knew, Cele was on the phone calling Uncle Dr. Vin. He was and MD who was married to my father's sister, Aunt Marion. Peggy ran to the Mulveys to call for the priest at Our Lady of Guadeloupe. Mrs. Mulvey went in to my sisters who were crying and told me to stay with them. She left, closing the door.

Uncle Dr. Vin arrived with his little black doctor bag at the same time our neighborhood doctor, Dr. DeVito, came running from his house a block away on Seventeenth Avenue. It turns out that one of the Mulvey boys ran up to the corner and got him out of bed. Father McKinney came in through the front door, followed by Father Coyne. My mother's brother, Uncle Jack, arrived. He was a Catholic chaplain in the navy and happened to be home on leave. Her other brother, Uncle Richie, a navy chief home on leave, came with Uncle Jack.

I crept into the quickly filling bedroom. Dr. DeVito and Uncle Dr. Vin were talking to my Momma in hushed tones. The three priests were praying in Latin and anointing Daddy. Uncle Jack anointed his forehead and the growling stopped. Mrs. Mulvey put her hand on my shoulder. My sisters were huddled together in one corner of the room.

Daddy seemed to be smiling. There really wasn't any noise coming from the street. The only sound was Daddy breathing and my sisters covering their sobs. I looked up and asked Mrs. Mulvey if it would be all right if I kissed Daddy good night because I was tired. She took me by the hand, and I bent over and kissed his cheek. I know he was smiling. I kissed Momma's hand and she hugged me. For the first of many times to come, she called me her Little Man.

I went to my and Jimmy and Jackie's room and climbed into the top bunk in "the boys' room." Jackie had the bottom when he was home and Jimmy had the single bed on the other wall.

The next morning was chaotic in our house. Everybody was coming—relatives, neighbors, friends. People were bringing in platters of food. I didn't know what to do. I couldn't get close to Momma. She was in the living room in Daddy's chair. Her sisters, Aunt Kiddie and Aunt Margie, were with her along with her mother, Grandma Walsh. Pop was in the alley with Uncle Jack, Richie, Tom, and Aunt Margie's husband, Uncle Steve, the fireman. They weren't talking or laughing, and this was unusual in my family.

Mr. Mulvey joined the circle, and they all just smoked and whispered. Father Coyne came into the alleyway and joined them. Mr. LaPenna, our neighbor on the other side, came with Mr. Malloy, the super of the apartment house. Still, no laughter.

I sat by myself in the dining room off the kitchen looking out the window into the backyard. I sat there by myself for what seemed like hours.

Finally, Uncle Steve, the fireman, wandered in and asked me what I was doing. I gave him the standard nine-year-old answer, "Nothing."

"Do you mind if I do nothing with you?" he asked. I told him it would be okay. I really liked Uncle Steve.

We didn't talk for a long time. Finally, Aunt Margie opened the dining room door and called, "Danny, your mother wants you."

I went into the living room and my sisters were there. Everyone else was on the front porch or in the alley. Momma started to speak and then stopped. I said, "Where's Daddy, Momma? I looked in your room and he wasn't in bed. Did he go to work?" Dry-eyed and very calmly she said, "He went to heaven early this morning and he won't be back. God wanted him because he was so special."

The three girls cried softly. I thought that it was a good thing because God liked Daddy. Patty Ann and Mary were crying and Virginia Ellen, who was only two, was sitting on Momma's lap. I didn't think she had a clue that Daddy was one of God's favorites.

We reported to a dilapidated building on Hubert Street in Manhattan. Police sergeants and lieutenants herded us into a courtyard in the center of the four buildings. I don't think the sun ever touched the ground.

The building was circa Civil War and had been used as a jail for AWOL soldiers. It was converted after the Civil War into a school, and it eventually morphed into the New York City Police Academy. Oh yeah, it had been condemned sometime in the 1920s. The sergeants took over and formed us into the companies. Then the lieutenants took over. I was in Company18.

The tall, trim crew-cut lieutenant stood before us and introduced himself. "I'm Lieutenant Vic Rohe. I'll be your advisor, father, mother, and brother for the next five months. Any problems, you come to me through the company sergeant. Your company sergeant will be appointed by me. He will be one of you, but will obey. I mean, he will have my authority. No one comes to me without going through the company sergeant. Now, I have checked your records and I have decided that Probationary Patrolman Stark has the background necessary to be your company sergeant. Probationary Officer Stark, front and center."

I left the rank I was in and approached the lieutenant. I came to a halt directly in front of him and giving him a snappy military salute, which he promptly returned.

We had all been issued our revolvers, but were told to leave them in the box. We were dressed in gray shirts and gray trousers with our silver shields pinned on our shirts, a blue uniform regulation police hat with a cap device minus the numbers. The cap device has the same numbers as your shield, and upon graduation, you are entitled to affix it to your hat.

Lieutenant Rohe handed me a roster with all the names of the members of Recruit Company 18. "You will know every name on this list and be able to pronounce it properly. People like to hear their names pronounced properly. As company sergeant, you will be handling a lot of administrative work that will make it easier for me to teach your people how to be cops. Don't disappoint me, Stark. When you get to know the company, you can choose an assistant company sergeant."

I really couldn't understand why I was picked, and I wanted to ask, but Rowe's no-nonsense approach threw me.

Momma died when I was seventeen. We were all devastated. She had cancer and really suffered. They took one of her breasts, but in 1955, the doctors really didn't have the knowledge to properly treat her. She had radiation, which burned her terribly, but the cancer spread into her bones and it was impossible to operate. They just tried to make her comfortable. I never heard Momma complain.

Cele had gotten married to Hank before Momma got sick. Jackie and Jimmy also were married. I was at home with Peggy, Kathleen, Patty Ann, Mary, Virginia Ellen, and of course, the glue that held us all together, Momma.

Jackie had been recalled to the navy when the Korean War started and Jimmy was appointed to the F.B.I. This was three years after Daddy died. Life was going on, but it was tough. Not for me or the girls, but for Momma, but she never let on.

Ever since I can remember, we had a summer bungalow in Mountain View, New Jersey. Everybody in the neighborhood thought we were rich, and I never did anything to correct the notion. In reality, it was right next to the Lackawanna railroad tracks, no running water, no windows, just screens and shutters, and an outhouse. But, to us, it was paradise.

I mean, what the heck would we have done with nine kids for the entire summer in Bensonhurst, Brooklyn? How could Momma keep track of us? (Really, I mean me.)

The summers were filled with swimming, ball playing, hanging out, and more swimming. Mountain View was a collection of bungalows of various sizes and shapes. When the river would overflow, everyone would pitch in and put up each other's furniture on hooks high up on the bungalow walls.

Canoes and rowboats would ferry people in and out, and as a kid, I prayed for rain. It was like a big party. Those that had cars would take them out of our area, which was called Hoffman Grove. Pop and Gram had a two-room bungalow, two doors up Brookside Road from us.

Across the swamp area and through someone's yard was River Road. About a quarter of a mile up River Road was High Dock, and going another quarter mile west was Lock Dock.

Low Dock was in the west end and we were in Hoffman Grove. Really, it was just one summer community made up of people from Manhattan, Brooklyn, Queens, Jersey City, and Newark. Everyone knew everyone, and for the most part, we were all in the same boat with regards to socioeconomic standing.

We looked forward to the weekly softball games. The Hoffman Grove men and the bigger boys against the dreaded West Enders. This was every Sunday. The rivalry was fierce, almost as bad as the Brooklyn Dodgers and the New York Giants.

After the games, no matter who won, everyone would go to Arnie's. Arnie's was a general store that supplied us with everything from soup to noodles. For the big order, you would have to go into Mountain View itself to really stock up.

Next to Arnie's was the bar, up four steps to a platform and then up four more into the dark. Inside was the longest bar my young eyes had ever seen. Once inside, there was the stale beer and cigarette smell coupled with the sawdust on the floor. From the bar area you could reach the dance hall by going up three steps. In the dance hall, all the activities happened. Not just theme dances like the barn dance where everyone wore overalls and straw hats and stuff like that, but they also had meetings pertaining to things that affected the whole community.

The Hoffman Grove Association, as it was called, owned the land, but you owned the home. Dues were assessed and taxes were paid.

On Wednesday evenings, a movie was shown in the dance hall. There were cartoons, travelogue newsreel, and the feature movie. When it was all over, the bigger kids hung out on Arnie's porch until it was time to go home.

Hardly anyone had a phone. So if someone needed to call you, they'd call to Arnie's, and he'd send one of the porch people to your house and tell you that so and so would be calling back in five or ten or fifteen minutes, depending how far away you were from Arnie's. It was a pretty good system.

Twice a summer all the men and boys would get together to fill in the potholes in the roads. Since the roads were dirt and the place always flooded, this was a big job. Then there was the footbridge leading to Hoffman Grove, through the woods, into the town of Mountain View. I used to love when they'd repair the bridge. Most of the time there was a trickle of water into this little brook, and it flowed from somewhere up in the mountains and came through the woods, emptying into the Passaic River. After a heavy rain, it would fill and rush wildly under the footbridge. There were times when a group of us would work up the nerve to hang from the bottom of the railroad trestle and see if you had the nerve to drop into the swollen brook.

Across the river was a little sandy beach in Lincoln Park. During the week, Daddy would stay in Brooklyn. He'd take the train up on Friday afternoons and sometimes he would leave early on Tuesday morning.

He and the other working men and women would walk the tracks in their business clothes, and, I guess depending on where they worked, some would continue to the Lackawanna Station or where the tracks crossed. They'd go to the Erie R. R. Station.

When he was in the city, Momma would pack all sorts of sandwiches and make some mystery fruit drink in a gallon glass jug and she'd row all of us across the river to the beach.

This was done only after I took the big bucket that was used by my sisters during the night as a toilet and emptied it down the outhouse hole.

Then I'd wash out the bucket and put it in the sun to dry. Momma didn't want the girls going to the outhouse in the dark because there might be hobos walking the tracks. I didn't understand why hobos would bother my sisters. I mean, every once in a while, some men would come off the tracks and Momma or Grandma or Mrs. Offner next door would give them a sandwich and water or soda or something.

Anyway, my next job was to fill the water jugs from the common well pipe up near Arnie's. I'd get our jugs, Gram and Pop's and the Keegan's, and pull my wagon up to the well and fill them all and deliver them.

After a year or two after Daddy died, the people across the road, the Pratts, dug their own well and that was the one we used. It was a lot closer.

We had a hand pump in the kitchen that had to be primed, and an ice box that had a drip pan underneath that had to be emptied. I'd take a cup and use the drip pan water to prime the pump and then throw the rest of the water in the yard.

The kitchen pump water was only used for cooking and washing clothes. You weren't supposed to drink it. Pop Walsh told me that, if I ever drank it, my ears would fall off. So I never did.

Now there was a character, Pop Walsh. He developed an infection in one of his toes from walking barefoot and he cared for it at home. During one winter, he had to have the lower half of his left leg cut off because of gangrene. It seems that a pebble got under his skin and Pop kept digging at it with his pen knife. In order to save him, they cut off the leg. I used to sit on his stoop and he'd tell me stories about his days in the New York City Fire Department. He told me that before WWI, he was on a fire boat and they were called to assist the Jersey Fire Department. It seems there was a fire on an island on the Jersey side of the harbor. The island was called Black Tom Island. It was used to store ammunition for the army. As he told it, some German spies had set fire to it and there were shells blowing up all over the place. He got blown off the fireboat and swam to Jersey City. He was presumed dead. Some of his brothers and sisters lived in Jersey City, and Pop being Pop and the Walsh's being the Walsh's, they partied for three or four days before he decided to find a phone and notify Grandma and the Fire Department. Back then, phones were rare. So he told the Fire Department that he had amnesia and just remembered who he was. They fell for it, but Maggie (Grandma) was suspicious. If he had amnesia, how come his Fire Department uniform was washed and pressed, and who did it? She knew the truth, but he stuck to the story.

Then there was the time when Jackie Robinson broke the color barrier in baseball. Pop had me convinced that Jackie Robinson was related to me on the Stark side of the family. I believed him.

He used to ask me to scratch his foot, and I'd naturally scratch it, but he'd insist the one that wasn't there was itchy. So I'd lean down to scratch the phantom foot, and up he'd come and hit me in the chin with his stump. He'd laugh and laugh. I fell for it every time.

The training was intense. The first two weeks were dedicated to the laws of arrest and the use of deadly physical force. We'd go to the PD range in Rodman's Neck in the Bronx. The instructors would drill us and quiz us on the laws all morning. Then we'd go to the range after lunch, or as the PD called it, meal. After two weeks of law and safety and live firing exercises, we were allowed to wear our guns to and from work. Everyone in the city knew you were a rookie cop by the gray uniform and the newness of the leather of your holster, handcuff case, and your youth. If all that wasn't enough, you had a large black bag with a nightstick protruding from it, and it was crammed with law books, police rules and regulations books, traffic regulations and your PT gear, sneakers, shorts, T-shirt, jock, sweat socks, and mouthpiece for when they taught us boxing and judo.

Despite the fact that you were obviously a rookie, people would ask you directions. "How do you get to such and such?" When you politely told them you didn't know didn't know how to get to such and such, they'd seem annoyed.

One day I was on the West End subway going from my house to the academy, and a guy in a suit came up to me and asked if I knew how to get somewhere—I don't remember where—but I didn't know how to tell him to get there. He asked me if I could tell him how to get to another location and I didn't know that answer either. In a loud voice, the suit says, "Are all New York City cops this stupid? I mean, I'm lost, and I don't know how to get to where I want to go and you don't know how to tell me to get there?" I looked at him and remembered the punch line from one of Pop Walsh's jokes. So I said to the guy, "Well, sir, maybe I am stupid, but at least I'm not lost. I know how to get to where I want to go." This evoked laughter, and the guy turned red in the face and got off at the next stop. Oh yeah, when the train doors closed, he gave me the finger.

The physical and the range were easy for me, but the academic part was a doozie. I didn't realize, for instance, how hard it was just to fill out a traffic summons. I really hadn't had any contact with traffic tickets, if you know what I mean.

The laws of arrest, the forms for aided cases, the traffic accident forms. Forms, forms, forms. The Police Department had a form for every situation known to God and man. Then there was the Rules and Procedures. This was a thick book in green loose-leaf binder. I think they really expected me to memorize it. In a nutshell, it was a book of do's and don'ts. Mostly don'ts.

Toward the middle of our training, I started staying on weekends at my fiancée's house. The rule was, as long as you were home by midnight, you were okay. This included weekends. There was only one problem. My fiancée, Jennifer, lived in North Arlington, New Jersey. I rationalized that it was all right because it took me less time to get to her home than it did to get to Brooklyn from the Police Academy.

I'd get the Hudson Tubes train, to Journal Square in Jersey City, walk through an alleyway at the back of the Stanley Movie and onto the street where Jennifer or her brother Georgie would be waiting in their car, and in fifteen minutes, I would be in her house with her mother, her sister, and Georgie. If we went to a movie or for pizza or anything, I'd be in the house before midnight and I'd go to sleep in Grandpa Norton's room. Well, it wasn't his room anymore, because he was dead.

So I figured, what's the harm, right? Wrong.

One Friday night toward the middle of October 1961, I got off the train, and as usual, I put my police bat in the big bag, took out a raincoat, and forced the butt of the nightstick into the bag. With the raincoat covering my shield and gun belt, I looked like a college kid going home for the weekend with a bag full of dirty clothes. Anyway, I was walking through the dark alley and I heard the sounds of a struggle. I saw two guys struggling with a third. Then I saw that the third guy was a uniformed Jersey City patrolman. They were fighting over his gun. They were trying to take it from his holster and he was trying to stop them.

"Hey, I'm a cop." Well, almost. So I took out my revolver and yelled something about police, break it up, or something like that, and I got no response. So I did what I figured my brother Jackie or Uncle Mike would do. I fired a shot.

Uncle Mike, Momma's brother, was a detective in Queens when Daddy died. I remember him coming into our kitchen after Daddy was buried and he and Momma sitting at the table talking.

When he married Aunt Ann, his family wanted nothing to do with her or him. They had money and Uncle Mike was "just a milkman." They really didn't have much, so Momma and Daddy told them to move into our house until they got on their feet. This was long before I was born, but this is how the story goes. Anyway, they lived with my parents and, I guess, Jimmy, Jackie, and Cele. Along came my cousin, Virginia, who was promptly called Dolly.

Momma and Daddy must have been incredibly generous to Uncle Mike and Aunt Ann because he handed Momma an envelope and told her that there was $8,000 in it. I heard him say that he and Annie were saving it to repay them for all they did for them. Momma took the envelope and all she said was, "Michael, you didn't do anything wrong for this, did you?"

"Absolutely not. Annie and I figured you could use the money now." In 1947, $8,000 was a lot of cash. I saw tears in Momma's eyes, and she leaned over and kissed him on the cheek. He got up, patted her shoulder, and left.

I didn't realize growing up without a father was that bad because I had a lot of good men in my life. I mean, I had my brothers, my mother's brothers, my father's brother, Uncle Frannie, Uncle Bill Lane, Uncle Steve, Pop Walsh, and of course, Daddy's friends.

There were two bachelors that lived in the Bronx, Mr. "Hick" Irmay and Mr. Bill Curran. Then there was Mr. Tom and Miss Bess Thorton. They were married, but we all called her Miss Bess.

Then there was Mr. Abe Freeman and his wife. Mr. Abe and his wife would drop in on a regular basis to check on Momma and us. Mr. Abe was a long-time friend of Daddy's, going back to their days as executives with the Eureka Vacuum Cleaner Company. He was now an insurance agent for Met Life. He handled all of the insurance for Momma and made sure that she received all of Daddy's benefits. He'd always show up with a paper sack filled with candy and lollipops.

While Momma and the older girls would sit with Mrs. Freeman and their daughter, Paula, Mr. Abe would fix little things around the house. There was a light fixture in the hall that would spark once in a while for no reason. Mr. Abe took it down using a kitchen knife to unscrew it, taped the offending worn wires, put it back up, and it worked perfectly. What amazed me was that he didn't turn off the electricity.

He told me Daddy and he formed a group that opposed the communists back before the Depression. After the stock market crashed in 1929, they lost all their stock in Eureka and their positions. Both started at entry level jobs with Met Life and both rose to be in the Million Dollar Sales Club.

He'd tell me about the war years, how Daddy tried to enlist in the navy. He'd served in WWI, and at the age of forty-one, he was rejected. It might have had something to do with the fact that he had eight kids.

He told me that when Daddy would patrol the neighborhood as an air raid warden, that Momma would shine a flashlight at him just to get his goat. He'd make believe he was annoyed, but he'd laugh about it at work the next day.

The alley quickly filled with uniformed cops and they swiftly took away the two perps. A lieutenant came over to me with his hand extended and thanked me numerous times. The cop was finished with the paramedics. They had wiped away the blood and bandaged his head. They were trying to pull him toward the ambulance, but he insisted on talking to me. He gave me a big bear-like hug and thanked me.

Two captains, and I guess a chief, all thanked me. The lieutenant wanted my name, and he read my shield number and wrote it down. A chill ran through me when he said, "Officer, we're gonna send a letter to your commanding officer to thank you. You deserve a medal." I actually begged him not to do that. I explained that I wasn't supposed to leave the city and I would get into trouble. I might as well have been talking to a wall. All the cops and detectives were shaking my hand and patting me on the back.

Finally, I got out of the alley and saw my future brother-in-law Georgie sitting on the hood of his car smoking a cigarette. "Hey, Tip, where the hell have you been? I have been waiting a half hour!" I threw my bag in the back of the car and got into the passenger seat.

Most of the time I'd drive when either Jennifer or Georgie picked me up just so I could practice. Tonight, I couldn't have driven a block.

As Georgie swung around the corner, Journal Square was still jammed with police cars. "Geez, I wonder what happened." I didn't reply. I took out a cigar and flamed it up. As we neared Park Avenue, North Arlington, Georgie said, "Oh, I forgot to tell you, Jennifer and Eileen went to Newark to shop. They'll be back around nine. Wanna stop at Wilson's for a beer?"

While on probation you are not supposed to go any place that sells alcohol. But I figured that would be the least of my problems.

The following Tuesday Lt. Rohe called me into his office and I knew I was in trouble when he smiled. "Well, you've been a busy boy, I see. What the hell were you doing in Jersey? Don't answer. I expected more from a marine. I picked you over guys in your company that were higher ranks than you, but they were in the navy and even one was a goddamn officer in the friggin' army. What were you thinking? I'm a former marine and I figured you had common sense. Don't answer. In a few minutes the CO of the academy will be here, so this is what you told me. Just look scared." He didn't have to tell me that twice.

"You were exhausted. You got on the wrong train. You got on the Hudson Tubes. You were sleepy. You weren't paying attention. You had a slight fever. You realized you were in Jersey City. You went upstairs from the station to look for a phone to call me at home." He took a breath. "You do have that paper with all my contact day and night numbers?" I tried to speak and he handed me the paper with the numbers on it. "Put this in your memo book. So," he continued, "while you were looking for a phone, you saw the uniformed cop fighting for his life, and without thinking, you took action. Don't mention you were wearing a civilian raincoat and don't mention you were gonna stay at your girlfriend's house." How he knew that, I still don't know. "Just look contrite and don't volunteer anything. Just yes, sir and no, sir. Got it?" Before I could answer, the door opened and Chief "Big" Georgie McManus came in. Man, was he big!

"Probationary Patrolman Stark, I'm Chief McManus." Like I didn't know. "I'm the CO of the academy." No fooling, I thought. "Lieutenant Rohe told me your excuse that you had a fever and got on the wrong train." He went on and on with the story Rohe concocted. I stood there mute waiting for him to tell me I was fired.

Finally, after what seemed like an eternity, he said, "This won't happen again, I trust. I don't mean helping a brother officer. I mean, being involved in an incident in New Jersey." I numbly nodded my head in the affirmative. "I don't ever want to hear about another incident in Jersey." He turned to walk away and then abruptly turned back and stood about two feet from me. Oh boy, here it comes. He changed his mind. "Listen, kid, I shouldn't tell you this, but you did one helluva job. If it wasn't for the fact that it was in Jersey, I'd put you in for a citation." I think I mumbled something that was meant to sound like "thank you, sir", but I'm not sure how it came out.

The Chief left and Lieutenant Rohe looked at me and winked. "Relax, it's over. The bad news is that you owe me one hundred push-ups. Oh yeah, the letter from the Jersey cop will not be in your folder. Do you want to read it before I rip it up?" I declined the offer and went back to class.

On Labor Day weekend, 1961, we were all sent out on the street to observe and assist a traffic patrolman. I was to meet the officer I was assigned to on the corner of Thirty-Second Street and First Avenue in Manhattan.

In those days, both Thirty-Second Street and First Avenue were two ways. I got there about three-thirty and traffic was at a standstill. People were trying to get out of the city through the Queens Mid-Town Tunnel and people were trying to get into the city from the tunnel.

I looked around for the real policeman and didn't see him. Hey, I'm a cop. I can do this. I'll unsnarl this mess.

I went into the middle of the street and held up my hands. The cars inched through the intersection and it finally cleared. I reached for my brand-new police whistle and placed it in my mouth. Scared and dry-mouthed, I tried to blow the whistle. Instead of a sound emanating from my lips, the whistle flew out about three feet, making an arc in the air. Well, that was all the hot and harried drivers and passengers had to see. The horns were blaring and the people were laughing. I wanted to crawl into the sewer at the corner.

The real policeman appeared out of nowhere and took me by the elbow and led me to the sidewalk. The pedestrians and motorists all applauded and the real cop took a deep bow. Traffic started to inch forward and an eighteen-wheeler rolled right over my whistle that had never made a sound. I think he did it on purpose. The real cop took me into the florist shop on the corner. "Listen, kid, and remember, traffic takes care of itself. You being out there is an annoyance to the public. They're gonna do what they want anyway. We're only window dressing. They see us standing there and maybe they'll slowdown or not go through the light, but they know you really can't chase them. I mean, they're in a car and you're on foot. Who wins?" I couldn't argue with logic like that. I mean, who would listen to me? I didn't even have a whistle.

About three weeks before graduation, I was staying at Jennifer's house for the weekend. Her mother, sister, Eileen, Georgie, Jennifer and I decided we'd get pizza for dinner, and Jennifer and I volunteered to go to Guido's on River Road in the next town over, Kearney. Georgie insisted they had the best pizza in the world.

Since the Journal Square incident I changed my routine somewhat. I'd leave the academy in the rookie gray uniform and walk to the subway. I would make sure I wasn't being followed, come out of the subway at the far end and walk to Cortland Street and the Hudson Tubes station. I'd go into the men's room, change into street clothes, stuff the uniform into my bag, and go to Jersey City were Jennifer and Georgie would be waiting for me.

Anyway, Jennifer and I got into the car to go pick up the pizza. I drove down the Bellville Pike and swung a left onto River Road. It is a winding, turning, dark road. The river on one side, hence the name, and woods with some houses on the other. It's about a ten-minute ride. I'm driving, we're chatting, and out of the blue, this pickup truck comes within inches of my bumper and the driver is leaning on the horn. I guess he didn't know I was a new driver because he kept flashing his high beams, and he and the passenger were screaming at me to speed up. They pulled alongside and let out a stream of ungentlemanly remarks. The truck pulled in front and the passenger flipped a can of beer at the windshield. It hit the hood and bounced off. I hit the high beams just to be a pain.

The driveway to Guido's was about ten yards up. I hooked a right into the parking lot and parked nose to the river on the side of Guido's. I went in, paid for the order and came out to see the two jerks on either side of Georgie's car. Jennifer had wisely locked the doors. I approached the guy on the passenger's side and tried to reason with him. He came at me and the other mutt slid across the hood. I dropped the pizza box and backed up. The first clown came at me in a rush. I used my academy training. I side-stepped, put my foot out, grabbed his hair, and slammed him into the black top. The other mutt ran to the back of the pickup and came at me with a tire iron. He was running full speed with the iron over his head. Again, I side-stepped and kicked him right in the stomach. He fell to his knees and I rammed his head into the ground. Both were screaming in pain when a black four-door Ford with a whip antenna came into the parking lot. It was then that I realized that I had my service revolver on my hip. Here I go again.

There was a bungalow at the end of Brookside Road, our road, that was called the Cat's Meow. A bunch of vets got together and bought the place. They were all from Clifton, New Jersey. Some had jobs and others were still collecting government benefits. I kinda latched onto them and they adopted me as a sort of mascot. They were great fun.

One in particular took a shine to my sister, Cele. This was Hank Van Winkle. Hank had been an officer in the Merchant Marines and was in both the Atlantic and Pacific theaters. He was built like a bull. Hank also played semi-pro football for the Clifton Rams.

All the girls in Hoffman Grove were gaga over all these single guys. The Cat's Meow was like a big fraternity house. This was especially true on weekends. They played ball at the ball field on the other side of the railroad tracks. They maintained the field by cutting the grass on the weekends and putting down the chalk baselines. They repaired the back stop by replacing the rusted chicken wire. They brought to life the whole grove.

Hank was always around our bungalow, just a few houses up from the Cat's Meow. He would cut the grass, patch the screens, replace the broken steps on the front and back porch. He even built an outdoor cinderblock barbecue pit. We also used that to burn our garbage.

One day, Momma and Grandma and some of us were sitting on the front steps of our place when a whole group of guys and girls came down Brookside Road. On top of Hank's shoulders was Cele, surrounded by everyone else. Grandma tsked and told Momma that Cele should be told that it was inappropriate behavior. Momma just waved back to Cele as they all went to the Cat's Meow. A few minutes later, a carload of the guys and girls drove past us. Everyone was waving. Momma looked concerned.

A couple of hours later, the car came back and pulled off the road into our yard. Hank opened the door and lifted Cele out of the car and carried her into the bungalow. Her foot was wrapped up in gauze. Momma, naturally, asked what happened. Cele explained that she had cut her foot open up at High Dock. Someone had carelessly thrown a broken glass jug into the river and she stepped on it. That was why they carried her home. They wanted to get her to the hospital to be stitched. She explained that they didn't want to upset Momma, so they wanted to get her stitched up and then tell her. I thought that was nice because it was not even a year yet that Daddy had died.

In Mountain View there was a stable where you could rent horses and ride the trail through the woods, cross the brook under the train trestle, skirt the ball field, and cross the road into the fields on the other side.

I had been hanging around the stable since I was about seven or eight. Daddy would take us once a summer and we'd ride through the woods to the brook and let the horses drink. We never crossed the brook, but we'd just meander through the woods.

The year he died, he took us riding. It was Patty Ann, Mary, Kathleen, and me. Something scared Mary's horse and he bolted. Daddy had dismounted and I was on a parallel trail to where Mary was. The horse was heading back to the stable. Although it was just a hack horse, it was moving. Mary was about six and I was nine. I pulled up on the reins, and as they say in the movies, I headed her off at the pass. Actually, I just moved my horse in front of hers and the old nag stopped.

Mary was crying because she was scared. I felt like Tom Mix, Red Ryder, the Lone Ranger, and John Wayne all in one. We went back to the stable and Daddy told the man what I had done. He seemed proud. Then he took us over to Mr. and Mrs. Collins' Soda Fountain and bought us all ice cream sundaes. Then we walked the tracks back to the bungalow.

After I finished all the morning chores, I'd run through the woods to the stable to clean out the manure and the owner would have a string of about ten or twelve horses hooked together on a rope. I'd ride the lead horse and would hold or tie the rope around the saddle horn and walk them through the woods to the brook. I'd let them all drink and then walk them back to the stable where they'd be ready for the paying customers. It was a dream job for a ten-year-old. I got paid two dollars a week.

It turned out that the man in the black Ford with the whip antenna was the captain in charge of detectives in Kearney. He called for back-up and a couple of marked radio cars arrived. Before they got there, though, the mouth with the tire iron got to his feet, picked up a rock, and was about to hit me. I gave him a short left in the throat and down he went again, gagging and gurgling.

I identified myself as a cop to the captain and he told me to drive to the Kearney Police Headquarters. The two mouths were put into the back of one radio car and the recorder drove the pick-up to Headquarters. I got the pizza and put it on the backseat. I took off my gun and emptied it. I put the gun and the holster in the glove box and locked it. I put the bullets in my pocket.

We went into the detectives' room and Jennifer was shown a chair in a little room crammed with desks and Wanted posters all over the wall. The captain took me into his office. "Now, let me see that shield again," he said, and I showed it to him. "You didn't tell me you are New York. You know you're in New Jersey. Where are you assigned?"

"I'm still in the academy," was my reply. "Oh shit," was his.

Thinking quickly I asked him if he knew Major Bill Burke of the State Police. I knew he did because there was a picture of Bill and the captain hanging on the wall. Bill lived next door to Jennifer on Park Avenue.

"You know the major?"

"Yes, sir. My fiancée lives next door to him. He can vouch for me that I'm not a wise guy."

"All right, tell me how all this happened."

I started from the beginning and brought him up to the point where he came into the parking lot. He left the room and brought in two cups of coffee. I asked him if I could see if Jennifer was all right. He said she was fine and she had a female officer with her. I didn't realize Jennifer was giving a statement of the incident.

About five minutes later, Bill Burke came in and I went through the story again. Bill and the captain left the room. St. Michael, the archangel, was again called into action by me.

Bill and the captain came back in, and Bill sat next to me. "You don't have your gun on you, do you, Dan?" I stood up and opened my jacket. Bill looked at the captain and the captain nodded.

The bullets in my pocket weighed about two hundred pounds. Burke didn't ask where the gun was, and I didn't say. A uniformed cop came into the room and whispered something to the captain. "Are you positive?"

"Yes, sir."

"Great," said the captain. He walked over to me and put his hand out and shook mine. "Great job, Dan. These two clowns have multiple warrants outstanding down in Atlantic City, Tom's River, and Little Egg Harbor. They're for assault on a couple of cops and burglary."

Thank you, St. Michael.

"I'll need the name of your commanding officer. I'm gonna drop him a note."

"Oh boy." I quickly blurted out the Journal Square incident story to both of them, and the captain agreed that maybe a congratulatory note would not be a benefit to my career.

Finally, with handshakes all around, Jennifer, Bill, and I left. We got home to her mother's house and Jennifer relayed the story. Her mother was annoyed, Georgie wished he had gone with us, and Eileen said the pizza was cold.

I went back to the academy on Monday with great trepidation. Lieutenant Rohe, who seemed to know everything, didn't mention the incident to me. I didn't report it because Chief McManus did tell me that he didn't want to hear about anymore incidents in New Jersey.

Finals for both academic and physical training were completed. We then got measured for our blue uniforms. A week later, we all went, by company, and picked them up. Then we just rehearsed for the ceremony.

The big day arrived, and we all assembled at the armory on Sixty-Seventh Street between Lexington and Park Avenues. The mayor gave a talk, the PC (Police Commissioner), Steve Kennedy, gave us a pep talk and it was over. We had received our assignments to precincts. I was going to the Six-One in Sheepshead Bay, Brooklyn.

Just before we were about to be released, the PC announced that we were all to assemble on Seventy-Second Street because President John F. Kennedy's motorcade was coming and he agreed to review the November 1961 graduating class of the NYPD.

Jennifer, Grandma, Big Jim, Jackie and Uncle Mike, Peggy, Cele and my brother-in-law, Hank, were all there for the ceremony. They walked over to Seventy-Second Street and over fourteen hundred newly minted patrolmen marched in formation up Park Avenue with me calling cadence and Lieutenant Rohe and his assistant, Sergeant Bosco, leading over our company. Rohe looked as proud as a new father.

We all fell in, and it just so happened that Company 18 was at the corner of Park and Seventy-Second just where the motorcade would be turning north onto Park.

The motorcycles, with American flags on their wind screen and lights flashing, were followed by Secret Service vehicles and then came the President's open limo. God, he was handsome. The limo stopped right in front of our company. The president smiled and waved.

Lieutenant Rohe rendered a snappy salute and President Kennedy returned it. The president then put his hand out and Rohe shook it. Sergeant Bosco did the same and the president shook his hand too.

I was about four paces behind them. I marched up to the limo, gave my best Marine Corps salute, waited until the president returned it and broke the salute. He offered me his hand and looked me right in the eyes as we shook. "You guys look great," he said. I thanked him and I said, "You were my first presidential vote, Mr. President." He said, "Thanks." Then he added, "I'd appreciate it if you'd do it again next time." I promised I would. Unfortunately, that was one promise I couldn't keep.

Finally we were dismissed. Well, not all of us. I was held up by Sergeant Bosco. He started to chew me out, but Lieutenant Rohe intervened, saying, "John, no harm done. When the hell is he gonna be able to shake the president's hand? Besides, he's not our worry anymore."

I arrived at the Six-One Precinct on Avenue U and Sixty-First Street with two other rookies. We were assigned lockers and given a tour of the station house, from the basement to the roof. We were told to sit in the, appropriately enough, Sitting Room. This was a huge room with an enormous table in the center. Mix-and match chairs were somewhat arranged around the table.

There was a floor-to-ceiling mirror, a closet with brooms and mops, and on the other side, was a men's room. In one corner, there was an automatic shoe shine machine. The walls were covered with pictures of Wanted people behind glass. One wall had shades pulled down covering the photos.

I raised the shade and saw an assortment of faces looking back at me. Next to each name, on an index card, was a description of their transgression with the initial K.G. stamped in big letters. Not wanting to sound, look, or act stupid, I just grunted "uh" as if I knew what it meant.

Finally, after sitting in the Sitting Room for what seemed like hours, actually, it was hours now that I think of it. I mean, I must have brushed off my shoes at the machine fifty times. Anyway, we finally got in to see the captain.

Steve Walsh, a thin, serious-looking man with gray hair, welcomed us to the Six-One. He told us that he expected us to make some mistakes, but we shouldn't hesitate to ask questions of our fellow officers or any of the bosses. Everyone was there to help us. For a second I was tempted to ask what a KG was, but I thought better of it. I'd figure it out.

Captain Walsh assigned us to our duty squads and dismissed us. Halfway out of his office he called me back. "I see your mother's maiden name was Walsh. Where'd she grow up?"

"It was in Manhattan, on the lower west and east sides. She was one of ten children, sir." "Well, I'm sure we're not related, but just the same, I want you to uphold the name of Walsh. I'm gonna keep my eye on you."

Great, I'm not even on the street yet and I got the captain looking over my shoulder. I went up to the locker room and changed and went to the house on Sixty-Ninth Street.

In 1954, Momma was diagnosed with cancer. She was supposed to go into the hospital the week before Christmas, but she didn't want to spoil our holiday. I really wasn't aware of how serious the illness was. I was into my own thing between St. Francis Prep High School, the swimming team, my friends and my after-school job. I was always going somewhere or someplace.

No matter where I was or what I was doing, I always called Momma at least once a day. The conversation was basically the same, but it was important to me just to hear her voice. I guess that's what I miss the most about Momma being dead. I can't talk to her anymore. She was a great mom and a good pal.

Don't get me wrong; she wasn't a pushover. I mean, if you got her angry, you better watch out. There was the time Junior Mazzio and I got into a fistfight. This was about a year or so after Daddy died. Junior lived in the apartment house down the street from our house. His father, Mr. Mazzio, drove a truck for a meat packing firm in Manhattan. So Junior and I got into this stupid kid fistfight about who the heck knows. I caught Junior with a lucky shot in the nose and it started to bleed. Mrs. Mazzio came flying out of the apartment house door and started screaming at me in Italian. I didn't know what she was saying so I started to walk away. Come on, I mean, it was a little stupid fight. No reason to go bonkers over it. It wasn't like Junior was gonna need a transfusion or something. Anyway, I got as far as La Penna's house when Mrs. Mazzio, still screaming in Italian, grabbed me by the hair and threw me down onto the sidewalk.

It just happened that Momma was looking out her bedroom window and saw the action. Well, she came flying off the front stoop like she had wings. For a large woman, she could move. Mrs. Mazzio saw her coming; she turned and took off back into the apartment house and slammed the door just as Momma got into the hallway. Lucky for Mrs. Mazzio, Momma didn't catch her.

I don't know how that incident played out, but I do know that Junior Mazzio and I were playing ball in the street the next day. Momma would say, "Anyone who fights over children is foolish because they'll make up and you lost an adult as a friend." I guess she forgot that little tidbit when she went after Junior's mom.

My sisters had the annoying habit of biffing me in the head when they would walk past me. Peggy, Cele, and Kathleen were the offenders. It didn't hurt. It was just a little finger biff to the back of the head. It was annoying. Anytime I'd go back at them, I'd get caught by Momma. Then she'd give me the lecture: "I don't care what they do. You never hit a girl. It doesn't matter who she is or what she does. You never raise your hand to a girl."

One morning, I was waiting to get into the bathroom and Kathleen biffed me in the back of the head. I turned around and Patty Ann slipped in front of me. I shoved her out of the way and Momma was just coming out of her room. All she saw was me shoving Patty Ann. Well, she took a swing at me and I ducked. She hit her finger into the door frame with a sickening thwack. Her middle finger immediately blew up like a balloon. She looked at me and then very slowly held up her swollen hand in front of my face and said, "Look what you did to your mother's hand."

When she died and was in the coffin, I couldn't take my eyes off her hand. I just wondered how much other pain I had caused her.

My first night on patrol was uneventful. I walked Emmons Avenue on the four-to-twelve tour from Nostrand Avenue to Sheepshead Bay and back. Most of the people I encountered were friendly enough. They'd say "Hello" or "Good evening, Officer." Officer. That was nice. In order not to look like a rookie, I borrowed my brother Jackie's winter blouse. He had been promoted to detective in the prestigious Safe and Loft Squad. They were the ones that went after the major league burglars, jewel thieves, car thieves. They handled all the top-notch crooks.

I was still living on Sixty-Ninth Street with Jackie, his wife, Muriel, and their kids. After Momma died, Jackie bought the house from the rest of us. Kathleen married Frank in June of '56. I had joined the Marine Corps Reserve while in high school with an eye to going on active duty when I graduated. Jackie said I came with the woodwork.

Peggy was working for the FBI, as was Kathleen. They were both clerical employees. Jimmy had transferred from the Florida FBI office to the NYC office when Momma was diagnosed with cancer. Peggy and the other younger girls moved over the Clifton, New Jersey, to be closer to Cele and Hank.

Financially, it wasn't working out. So Cele and Hank enlarged their house on Barberry Lane and they all moved in with them. Cele and Hank didn't have any children then so it worked out for everyone.

Peggy announced one day that she was going to enter the convent to become a Dominican sister. She explained that she'd been thinking about dedicating her life to the service of the Lord since she was in St. Brendan's High School. And now that the girls had a stable environment to grow up in, it was time to follow her calling. And she did.

About a week after coming to the Six-One Precinct, I was doing a four-to-twelve tour and I noticed a bunch of unmarked cars parked near a jewelry store next to a bank on Kings Highway and Coney Island Avenue. There were two cops sitting in the marked radio car. I asked what was going on and was told that burglars had gotten into the jewelry store during the night and that Safe and Loft detectives were processing the crime scene.

I wondered if Jackie was there, so into the store I went. I talked to a few of the detectives and made myself at home as I watched them go about their work.

I sat on one of the counters, I leaned against the wall, I used the bathroom. Finally, I went back out to my foot post and had an otherwise uneventful evening. I went to work the next afternoon, and although I was an hour early, the lieutenant on the desk told me to immediately see Captain Walsh. I knocked and was told to enter. Inside were three men in suits and the captain. He pointed to a chair and I sat. One man, I wouldn't say glared at me, but it wasn't a friendly look either. "I'm Inspector McGuire from Safe and Loft." I was tempted to ask him if he knew Jackie, but I thought better of it. "Did they teach you anything about crime scenes in the academy? Your fingerprints were all over that jewelry store. Yours and nobody else's. Just yours. If you didn't have the foot post, you'd be our main suspect. Next time you want to rubberneck at a crime scene, keep your hands in your pockets. Do you understand me?"

"Yes, sir, I do," was all I could say.

I went to work that evening thinking what else could go wrong. I didn't have very long to wait.

It got really cold out when the sun went down and I was again assigned to Emmons Avenue right on Sheepshead Bay. Around 10:00 p.m., most of the stores closed and the Avenue was fairly deserted. I was standing in the doorway of a shoeshine shop trying to get out of the wind. For the lack of something to do, I started to twirl my nightstick. Yup, you guess it. I broke the front door window of the store. I thought the whole world heard the sound. I peeked out of the doorway and there wasn't a soul on the street. I didn't have a clue what I should do.

Across Emmons Avenue there was a Harbor Unit. The Harbor Police Launch was secured to a pier and up on stilts was the Harbor Unit's quarters.

I was told that they weren't very friendly guys, but I figured I'd take a chance. After all, I was a rookie.

With great trepidation, I knocked on the door. A guy in a T-shirt answered. I could feel the warmth coming from the room. I told the cop what had happened and he just shook his head. He held up a finger and closed the door. A few minutes later, he came out, walked across the street, and inspected the damaged door. He never said a word, but went straight to the corner and emptied the wire litter basket onto the street. He held it over his head and threw it through the remaining glass into the store.

He turned and walked away. Over his shoulder he said, "Go to the call box and notify the sergeant that someone broke a window on your post. In case you don't know it, the call box is on the next block." He went back into the warmth of the Harbor shanty and I stood frozen in place.

The sergeant and his driver arrived and they both examined the scene. The sergeant, Dave Joyce, didn't ask any questions. The fact of the matter was, he actually complimented me on preventing a burglary. "You know, kid, if you didn't hear the noise and come running, the burglar would have found Mr. Minelli's cash box and taken it. Minelli is a hard-working man."

He dispatched his driver to Mr. Minelli's house, about two blocks away, to bring him to the store. As the radio car pulled away, Sergeant Joyce looked at me and, like the Harbor cop, just shook his head. "Listen, kid, if you're gonna practice twirling your nightstick, make sure you don't do it in front of glass." Another outstanding night of crime fighting came, mercifully, to an end.

The Korean War started on June 25, 1950, and we were in Mountain View. Jackie was married to Muriel Keegan. Mr. Keegan drove Momma, Patty Ann, Mary, Virginia Ellen, and me up to the bungalow. He worked for Con Edison and also coached basketball and baseball at St. Francis Prep in Brooklyn. He and Mrs. Keegan lived up the road from us across from Gram and Pop's bungalow.

After a few weeks and we were settled in, Jackie came down the road with Mr. Keegan and Muriel. They all looked sad. It didn't take long for Momma to realize that Jackie had been called back to active duty in navy. He had a month before he had to report at the Brooklyn Navy Yard. Everyone was sad.

Me, I thought it was great. I'd write to him. I'd go to the store for Muriel. Hey, I'm twelve. I can do anything.

Jackie left with a big party behind him and the good wishes and prayers of all of Hoffman Grove singing in his ears. The Mulveys came up from Brooklyn, Uncle Mike and Aunt Ann, Uncle Tom and Aunt Gert, Aunt Margie and Uncle Steve, Aunt Kiddie and Uncle Bill, Uncle Frannie and Aunt Helen, Aunt Marion and Uncle Dr. Vin, Uncle Pat and Aunt Mary and Aunt Joe, Uncle Richie's wife. Uncle Jack, the priest, was a commander in the navy and Uncle Richie was a chief in the navy. Both were away at sea.

The party was held on the ball field. It was bigger and better than the July 4 fireworks or the Labor Day baby parade. There was corn on the cob, hot dogs, hamburgers, kegs of Birch Beer, bottles of orange soda, games, pony and horse rides, three-legged races, and on the railroad side of the ball field, the beer was set up. They even had some man with an accordion playing all sorts of songs. Yup, it was a great send-off for Jackie who was going to war again. It was a heck of a party.

So, here I am again, this time walking a foot post on Sheepshead Bay Road about a week before Christmas 1961. It was cold. Around nine-thirty some of the businesses started closing. The street was crowded and the Sheepshead Bay train station was discharging workers who had been celebrating the holidays, full of adult beverages.

Three large black men came from the station and started bumping into people on purpose. The biggest of the trio knocked some man's hat off, and when the guy bent to pick it up, the black guy kicked him in the rear. I walked up to them, and in my most official voice, ordered them to cease and desist. One of the trio was carrying a large brown paper bag, and he swung it at me and knocked my uniform hat onto Sheepshead Bay Road. I didn't know what was in the bag, but man, it hurt like hell. I grabbed him by the coat and we started to struggle. We did this little struggle dance all around the sidewalk until I was pinned up against a shoe store display window. The other two tried to help their friend and, in doing so, succeeded in pushing us through the plate glass window. The bag man was on top of me.

I looked up and saw this jagged piece of glass hanging about four feet above his back. He was trying to get up and I was trying to keep him on top of me. Hey, I figure, if this thing falls, it's gonna hit him, not me. Hell, it looked so sharp, it probably would have cut him in half.

Two men in suits grabbed the guy off me and two others were holding each side of the menacing plate glass. Somebody pulled me out from the tangle of tassled loafers, sneakers, wing tips and boots. As soon as I got to my feet, the two glass holders let go and the thing came down like a guillotine.

I handcuffed the bag man, but his two friends split. Somebody called the police and radio cars started streaming onto the street. Sergeant Joyce pulled up and told his driver to tell the Central Dispatch to tell all the cars to slow down. Sergeant Joyce asked if I was all right and then asked what happened. I told him as best I could. He then had a cop, Eddie Quigly, get the names and info from the two men that helped me and the other two that held the guillotine.

Sergeant Joyce retrieved the offending bag and opened it. Frozen chicken parts! I was assaulted by a guy with a bag full of frozen chicken parts. I started to look for my hat and saw it sticking out from under the wheel of Quigly's radio car, squashed.

Back at the station house, I learned that making an arrest was the easy part. It was all the attendant paperwork that made it hard. Plus, Sergeant Joyce had to make out a line of duty (LOD) report. After a lot of good-naturing ribbing from the desk officer down to the civilian cleaner, all chicken jokes, somebody decided I should go to the hospital to get checked out.

Richie McPartland drove me to Coney Island Hospital where, once again, chicken jokes abounded. I was fine, just a little headache. The doctor gave me aspirin and released me.

I got back to the house and was sent up to the detectives who were fingerprinting the bag man. More chicken jokes. I finally lodged him in the cell in the back of the precinct for the night. I was told to be back for an 8:00 a.m. to 4:00 p.m. tour the next day. I contemplated stopping for a beer, but my head did hurt so I went home and told Muriel and Jackie what happened. More chicken jokes.

I was back at the station house at 7:15 a.m. with a throbbing headache. The procedure was that you waited for the patrol wagon to make the rounds to the precinct to pick up prisoners to be transported to the photo unit at the Seven-Eight Precinct on Bergen Street. From there, you and your prisoner climbed back into the wagon for the trip to court.

At court, you off-loaded and signed the prisoner into the Corrections Department holding pen area. Then, we went to the complaint room where a whole bunch of guys sat behind a counter typing out the affidavits. Once you got to the typist, you told him the facts of the incident, the bad guy's name, address, age, location of crime. Then you gave him your information, name, rank, shield command. A lot more chicken jokes.

Finally, when it was all typed, you read the affidavit, and if it was correct, you signed it and got onto another line in a different room. This is where you got the court docket number. Then you proceeded to the court.

There, you wait and wait and wait for your name to be called. I saw cops who came in after me getting their names called right away. This being my first time in court, I figured that this is the way the system worked.

The judge took a break and I went out into the large lobby of the courthouse in search of a men's room. I heard somebody call my name, and to my surprise, it was my sister Kathleen's husband, Frank Horohoe. He was a court officer.

After the pleasantries, he explained that the court he was normally assigned to was closed and he was going to be in the arraignment part, the part where my prisoner was waiting to face the judge. I told him about the bag full of chicken and the arrest and all the ribbing I'd been getting.

He promised not to laugh, but he couldn't help himself. I asked him how some guys who came in after me got out before me. He explained that, over the years, the court officers and the cops developed a bit of a friendship. Once in a while, the more active cops would bring in donuts and coffee for the typists in the complaint room and for the bridge man. "Okay, Frank, what the heck is the bridge man," I asked. "He's the guy that picks the cases to be called." he explained. Once your case was called, the arresting officer was finished in court and was to immediately return to his precinct to be re-assigned until the end of the tour.

Some guys wanted to get back to their command. Others like to hang out at the court and get their case called near the end of the day. While at court, they could go and get some coffee or just hang out. This way they didn't have to go back to work.

I thought that that was wrong. Why wouldn't you want to get back out onto the street? Little did I realize that sometimes you were better off not being on the street.

The summer of 1954 wasn't all that good for Momma. She really wasn't well, but she put a good face on it. She did everything she always did, but the twinkle had left her eyes and her beautiful smile didn't come as often. She was sick and on medicine. She never complained about the pain and tried to make everything as normal as possible.

I got a job as a lifeguard three days a week at a place called Laguna Beach Club on Route 23 in Mountain View. I also worked as a gofer at Doc Gordon's Drug Store, also in town. I stocked shelves and waited on customers. Doc Gordon was a nice man. The people at the beach club were pretty nice, but some of the members treated the help as if we were their personal slaves. "Get this or get that for me. I left my towel on that chair. What did you do with it? I have to go back to the room, you watch my kids." No "please," "thank you," "would you mind." They were obnoxious.

But through it all, it wasn't a bad summer for me. I left for the club early on Tuesday morning and helped clean up the area around the beach and the little cabanas. I emptied garbage cans, cleaned the cement walks leading to the beach, and just before 10:00 a.m., I drove, yes, I drove, a stick shift old Ford truck, with a bed spring tied to the back, all around the sand to make it look nice and to collect any cans or glass that had been buried.

I even made two water rescues that summer. I was on the St. Francis Prep swimming team and was a pretty strong swimmer. Not fast, but strong.

I'd come back to the bungalow and Momma would be sitting on the side under a tree. Grandma would be there, as well as Pop and two or three of the girls. I couldn't wait to tell her about my day. She'd sit and listen like I was the only one there.

I'd tell her about how the people treated the staff, and she'd just nod and say that I should learn a lesson. "You should always treat people the way you'd want to be treated. You should never look down on anyone because of what they looked like or how they spoke of where they came from. Make sure you always look for the best in people. Eventually, you will find it." Momma was so smart. But I didn't fully realize it until after she died.

My brother-in-law Frank, gave me a crash course in the nuances of the court procedures, and when the judge came back on the bench, my case was the first one called. It didn't even cost me a cup of coffee.

I went back to the station house and Captain Walsh was there. He called me into his office and told me to sit down. He asked about the arrest and I gave him the details. He grunted and then asked how I felt. He wanted to know if I could identify the chicken bag man's buddies. I told him I couldn't because it all happened so fast. He told me that I'd done a good job and told me to get changed into my street clothes and go home. He was giving me three hours off early. He didn't once laugh or make a chicken joke.

On Christmas Day, I was scheduled to work from midnight Christmas morning until 8:00 a.m. Jennifer was disappointed, but she understood. My brother Jackie told me that I should go in early and volunteer to work so that one of the cops working the four-to-twelve midnight shift, who had a bunch of kids, could go home early, and help his wife get the presents ready for the kids.

I reported to the desk officer, Lieutenant Joe Ravalga, better known as Joe the Boss. I told him why I was early and what I wanted to do. Joe the Boss was from Italy and still had a very pronounced Italian accent. "Gooda boy, Stark, whose agonna get picked?" I told him I didn't care as long as he had a lot of kids. He called one of the guys in off patrol and told him to go home.

I got hooked up with a veteran, Steve Risley, and I got in the car with him. The first thing he said was, "Listen, kid, what happens in this radio car stays in this radio car. You got it?" I told him I did. In reality, I didn't know what the heck he was talking about. "A lot of the store owners like us. They like to see the radio car parked in front of their store. It gives them a sense of security. Take an all-night diner, for example. If you owned the place, wouldn't you like it if a cop came in at three or four in the morning when all the bars are closing and the drunks crave their bacon and eggs? You walk in and sit and have a cup of coffee or even breakfast. You just being there will give some mutt second thoughts about harassing the waitress or the counter-man, right?" I agreed because it made sense. He continued, "Now, you have breakfast, you eat slow, you look around at the customers. You'll know who you have to keep an eye on. Use your common sense. The counterman and the waitresses are relying on you. Always make sure you offer to pay. If the cashier tells you it's on the house, thank him but make sure you get him to change a bill. This way it looks to the other customers like you paid. Got it?" I said yes.

He pulled out a cigarette and lit it up. I asked him if I could smoke a cigar. "Listen, kid, between now and midnight, you and I are partners, equals if you know what I mean. I rely on you and you rely on me. Smoke whatever you want as long as it's legal." He let out a little chuckle.

I flamed my cigar. Relaxing a little, I thought I was in heaven. I'm really a cop, something I'd only dreamt about since I was about five or six. I mean, I'm riding in a police car in New York City! I started to say something and then stopped. Risley looked at me. "Go ahead, kid, ask me anything."

"Well, I don't really want to take a free meal or a cup of coffee. I'm single. Well, I'm engaged actually, but I don't want to . . ." He interrupted me. "Listen, are you gonna arm wrestle with the cashier over a buck and half worth of ham and eggs? Come on! You leave the waitress or the counterman a buck and a half tip. See, you never go into any place expecting a free meal or a free anything. Never order anything you can't afford to pay for. If people want to treat you because you're possibly preventing some jerk from being a pain in the ass, then that's their business. You never, ever expect to get anything on the arm. If you demand or expect it, you're wrong."

I'll have to ask my brother Jackie about this, I thought.

On December 26, 1954, Momma finally went into the hospital for her operation. She was supposed to go in before Christmas, but put if off so me, Patty Ann, Mary, Virginia Ellen, and she would have a Merry Christmas. The older ones knew how serious it was, but they kept it from us. I just figured it was some, as Momma said, "A woman thing." I didn't know it was cancer. They removed one of her breasts, but apparently there was a lot of follow-ups. I don't really remember New Year's Eve except for the usual routine of banging the pots and pans on the front steps of our house at midnight.

Pop and Gram were there as well as Uncle Mike and Aunt Ann. Mr. Abe and Miss Freeman were there along with Uncle Frannie and Aunt Helen, Uncle Doctor Vin and Aunt Marion, Aunt Peggy and Uncle Toddy and Daddy's other sister, Aunt Essie and Uncle Hermie. After midnight, Uncle Pat and Aunt Mary came with Aunt Kiddie and Uncle Bill. It was a party, but not like it usually was when the Stark and Walsh families got together. I knew something was wrong, but I didn't know just how wrong it was. Momma was really sick.

Risley and I got a call at about a quarter to eleven. We responded to Tappans Restaurant on Ocean Avenue near Emmons Avenue. A woman was having labor pains. We pulled up and were greeted by two men and two women. The younger one was obviously pregnant. The older, her mother, was holding her hand and the younger one sat in a chair in the lobby area. Risley asked her how she felt and she said that she thought the baby was about to be born any minute.

I really didn't know much about babies or birth or things like that, so I turned to my partner and gave him a questioning look. He shrugged and outstretched his palms. The woman started to moan and her mother looked at me.

I bent down and lifted, very gently, her into my arms. The older man, turns out it was her father, opened the door. Risley went to the radio car and opened the back door. I placed her on the backseat and she put a death grip on my arm. "Don't leave me, stay back here with me." Her husband, who was in shock, got into the front seat, the recorder's seat, and Risley jumped behind the wheel.

It had snowed all through the week and another light snow had just started making the roads very slippery. Risley told us he was heading to Coney Island Hospital, which was only a few blocks away. A mighty "Nooooooo" came from this tiny woman. "My doctor is going to be at Sister Elizabeth Kenny Hospital on Fourth Avenue and Forty-Sixth Street. I will only go there."

"Lady, you need a doctor now. Do you know how long it will take us to get you to Sister Elizabeth?"

"I don't give a—" and she let out a stream of curses that made the veteran and the rookie cringe.

Down the Belt Parkway we headed, slipping and sliding in spite of the snow chains. Just passed C.I.H., when she let out this God-awful howl. "Pull over, pull over, the baby's coming." Steve pulled the car on to the snow-covered grass shoulder and got out. I ran around to the back passenger side and opened the door. Her head was on that side and her feet were right in front of me. I was scrunched behind the driver's seat.

I opened my door and looked to Steve for guidance. He looked at me and I looked at him. Finally he said to me, "Go ahead." I asked him where I should go. "You just saw the films in the academy. You know what to do."

"Hey, I'm single. You have two kids. I don't know what to do." The words from the backseat, laced with profanity, came in a rush. "I don't care who knows what, just help me." "You!" She looked at me. "Pull my panties down."

Now, most of my experience with women was relegated to above the waist. I mean, I have never been in the backseat with a girl who told me pull her panties off. I was embarrassed.

Suddenly, she was calm. She told Risley that she thought she would be able to hold off until he got us to the hospital. Through it all, her husband sat in the recorder's seat looking straight ahead with his hands pressed in the dashboard.

She said she was cold, so I took my uniform blouse off and put it over her. Risley tried to push the heater up and almost went off the road. The husband was no help. He just sat there looking straight ahead. She was calm, so I figured I'd get some information for the card I'd have to make out. It was a salmon-colored index card called a U.F. 6 (Uniform Force) Aided Card. She gave me the necessary info and I wrote it down. To get her mind off her condition, I asked her her religion. She told me she was Roman Catholic. I reached into my trouser pocket and removed a little black pouch containing Daddy's Rosary beads for her to hold. Then I figured I'd make her laugh, so I said, "You know, this being Christmas morning, if the baby is a boy, why not name him Jesus?"

"Yeah, that would go over big," she said. "I could see it now, Jesus O'Brien. That would be a . . . a . . ." She stopped and grimaced and let out a big howl.

Risley got off the Belt Parkway and was speeding down Fourth Avenue, lights and sirens. We were well out of our precinct. As a matter of fact, we were out of our division. So our radio was not compatible to the ones in the Six-Eight Precinct where the maternity hospital was located.

Fortunately, Risley had told Central Communications where we were going and they called the hospital to tell them to expect us.

Risley pulled down the block just as this tiny little body leaped into my hands. I lifted up my winter blouse just as Steven stopped the car and placed the baby, cord and all, onto the new mother's stomach. Waiting doctors and nurses took over. They got her out of the car onto a stretcher and rushed her inside. Risley lit a cigarette and the husband just looked straight ahead. I opened his door and shook him a few times. "Is everything all right? Are we there?" I informed him that his wife and new daughter were inside and fine. He straightened his tie, buttoned his overcoat, and walked into the hospital. I wanted to get Daddy's Rosary, so Steve and I went into the hospital. He called the desk officer in the Six-One. I was glad that Steve called because I didn't know if we were in trouble or not. Not only did we not take the woman to the nearest hospital, but we were four precincts away from ours and not even in our division. I figured we were in trouble. St. Michael, please help!

As it turned out, the woman's uncle was a deputy inspector in the PC's office and her father was a retired lieutenant of detectives. Talk about dumb luck on our parts. But then, I thought about St. Michael. Maybe it wasn't luck after all.

There was this big tree in front of our house on Sixty-Ninth Street, and ever since I was old enough to climb, I'd been doing just that, climbing into the tree and watching the world of Sixty-Ninth Street parade by me.

Momma liked to sit on the cedar chest in her room and watch the street scene too. I'd be in the tree, and she'd be in the window and we'd talk or make faces at one another. She never told me that I shouldn't climb higher. In fact, she sort of encouraged me to go to the next limb.

In 1955, my whole world would change forever. After her operation, Momma tried to keep things as normal as ever. She tried to be her usual bubbly self, but you could tell it was an act. She spent more and more time in bed or just sitting in a chair by the window.

My brother-in-law Hank and Cele were constantly at the house. Hank moved the heavy chest to the far wall and put a straight-back chair by the window for Momma.

Eventually Cele spent a couple of nights a week and Hank would come over from Clifton on his days off from the post office. I tried to spend as much time with Momma as I could. I was working after school, a couple of days a week, delivering radio-grams for R.C.A. I would go to different offices in Manhattan. I didn't realize it, but I was getting an education on how to travel around the city.

One day I had to deliver a radio-gram to an apartment above Carnegie Hall. I knocked and announced who I was. This scruffy-looking guy in an old sweatshirt and torn dungarees opened the door. Geez, this guy looks familiar, I thought. He didn't say a word, but tore open the cable-gram. I was about to walk away, and he called out to me. "Hey, young man, wait a minute." He went into the apartment, and when he came back, he handed me a $10 bill. I looked at the signature on the receipt; it was Marlon Brando.

I couldn't wait to get home to tell everyone. My sisters said, "Yeah, right." But when I told Momma, she wanted to know every detail. How tall was he, did he look tan, what color eyes he had, and everything else I could remember. She was extremely interested. But, then again, she was always interested in everything that each of us told her.

As the winter gave way to spring, she spent more and more time in her room. She was either in bed or sitting in the chair by the front window. She had a steady stream of visitors. Mrs. Mulvey was there every day. Mrs. Malley from the apartment was regular. Dr. De Vito would come almost every night after he finished his office hours and house calls. Mr. and Mrs. Keegan would visit at least once a week. Mrs. Keegan would make her famous veal cutlets for us for dinner.

Our parish priest, Father Tom Coyne, was a regular guest, as were all my aunts and uncles. Grandma Walsh was another constant along with Pop. When Father Coyne came, he and Momma would just sit by her window and talk for hours. He'd be in a folding chair and she would be in her chair.

When they'd be talking, nobody else went up to see her. I'd go outside and climb the tree and just watch the two of them talking. Every once in a while, she'd look at me and wink or make a face.

After Father Coyne's visits, she'd perk up, and even sometimes come downstairs and sit in the living room with us. On those occasions, she would talk about us. Never about her condition. She liked to re-tell the story of the food fight she walked in on one night.

She used to keep Virginia Ellen out of school and take her downtown to A&S's Department Store. They'd shop all day and then take the train home with whatever she bought. Before she and Virginia Ellen left, she'd have dinner and dessert prepared in case they were late coming home.

One night we finished eating and there was a huge bowl of chocolate pudding with whipped cream. Kathleen put a little bit on her spoon and flicked it at me. I took a little more and flicked it at her. She took a lot more and flicked at me. Peggy and Cele protested, so Kathleen and I flicked some at them. Patty Ann and Mary laughed, so Cele and Peggy flicked them. Now it was on, hand in the bowl, mushing faces with the pudding, everyone laughing.

Enter Momma!

It just so happened that the squad I was assigned to was off on New Year's Eve and New Year's Day. I packed a little bag and went to Jennifer's house to spend the holiday.

Her brother, Jack, and his wife, Margaret, had come home for the holiday. Jack was a salesman and was living in Kansas until he could transfer back to the New York/New Jersey area. Jennifer's aunts and uncles were there along with various neighbors. Midnight came and went, and the family partied on.

About 3:00 a.m., I ran out of gas and snuck up to the spare room where I promptly fell asleep. I awoke about 8:30 a.m. to the smell of bacon and eggs. Jennifer's mother, Mrs. McDermott, was in the kitchen cooking. I took a quick shower and shave and headed to the kitchen.

Mrs. McDermott was widowed when Jennifer was fifteen. Jack was the oldest, then Jennifer, then Georgie, followed by Betty-Ann and Eileen. She reminded me so much of my own mother. She greeted me with a big smile and pointed to the coffee pot. "Sit down. How many eggs to you want?"

Little by little the others straggled in, some looking worse than the others. After breakfast, I helped with the dishes and we all got ready to go to Mass. New Year's Day is a holy day of obligation. In those days, it was known as the Feast of the Circumcision of the Baby Jesus. It conformed to the Jewish tradition for male children.

After Mass we all just sat around and watched the football games. That night, Mrs. McDermott had another big meal prepared and on the table. After the dishes were done, we all just kinda did nothing.

I went back to work the following afternoon for a four-to-twelve shift. When I went into the station house, Joe the Boss called me to the desks. "Hey, Stark, I hear you did agooda job with the baby. You gotta the foota post on Emmons Avenue tonight, but itsa gonna snow. So, I'm gonna putta you in a car. You be by you self. You no answer the radio for no jobs. You justa patrola the post. You understand? You no leavea you post. The only time you leavea you post is if I needa help in the house here. You understand? Then you come running."

I thanked him and told him I understood his instructions. I really didn't relish the thought of walking along Sheepshead Bay what with the wind and the snow. Lieutenant Ravalga did me a big favor.

About eight o'clock it started to snow hard. I was riding up and down Emmons Avenue thinking I was really hot stuff. Then I saw a bit of a flicker in a window above a row of stores. I backed the car up and looked again. Yeah, I was right. Something was flickering in the third floor window. I couldn't figure out what it was. All of a sudden, the curtains caught fire and the window blew out.

About six feet from me was a fire alarm box on the corner. I ran to it to pull the alarm, but hesitated. You know how it is when you're a little kid. You get it drummed into your head to never pull the fire alarm box or you'll get in trouble.

This all went through my mind in a flash. I pulled the alarm and ran across the street and started banging on the door to the apartments above the stores. I couldn't get the door opened.

In what seemed like seconds, the first fire engine pulled up, and two firemen just kicked open the door and went upstairs. It looked like controlled confusion. As more trucks pulled up and the rubber-suited men jumped off, everyone knew exactly what to do and they did it.

Someone yelled to me go get out of the way or I'd get wet. I moved back to the radio car where it was warm and dry. A fire lieutenant came over and sat in the recorder seat. "Did you turn in the alarm?" I still thought I'd get in trouble. Shows you how smart I am. "Yes, I did. I saw flames and—"

"You did good, son. We got people out from the second and third floors and contained the fire to one room. A space heater malfunctioned and lit the curtains." He asked how long I'd been on the job and I told him. He took my memo book from the seat and wrote his name and the company that responded on the backside of one of the pages. "Call the station house and tell them you want the sergeant here. Tell the T.S. [telephone switchboard] sergeant what happened and stay here unless we need you for traffic control. Oh yeah, put on the bubble light so people can see the car." I flicked on the dome-shaped exterior roof light and went to the call box. I notified the T.S. sergeant and asked him to send the patrol sergeant. He asked me what truck and ladder responded and the name of the ranking officer. I flipped to the page with the lieutenant's info and rattled it off. "Good job, kid. The sergeant is on the way."

At the end of the tour, Joe the Boss and Lieutenant Priola were talking behind the front desk. They beckoned me, and Lieutenant Priola, smiling, said, "Nice work, Chicken Head." They laughed. I signed out, changed, and went home. More chicken jokes!

Spring was ending and so was school. We weren't sure if we were going to go to Mountain View, but Momma insisted that we were. She said the fresh air would do her more good than sweltering in Brooklyn all summer.

So the girls and my sisters-in-law Muriel, Jackie's wife, and Barbara, Jim's wife, all helped. Mr. Keegan drove some of us, and Jimmy drove Momma and the rest. Hank and his brothers, Dutch and Nardi, actually Bernard, and Mr. Van Winkle, Hank's father, were waiting to move us in. Hank had already driven Grandma and Pop up, a week before. The move-in went fast.

There was one huge room that had navy style bunk beds fastened to the wall that you could lift up and latch to the wall itself. There were seven bunks above and below one another. Also in the room was a huge bed that my sisters would use when they got older.

I had turned seventeen, so I slept on the front porch on a couch. Behind that was Momma's room with her bed and some wicker chairs and table. Then the bunk room. Then the huge kitchen, and in the backyard was the outhouse and the railroad tracks.

Jackie and Jimmy and Hank cut a hole in the side of the house where Momma's room was and they rigged up a shower for her using the water from the pump in the kitchen. To this day, I don't know how it worked, but it did.

When Momma took her daily bath, I would pump the pump in the kitchen, and through some (Rube Goldberg) contraptions, the water would flow up a drain pipe type of thing along the house and into the shower platform.

It was cold water, but Momma never complained. Almost everyone in Hoffman Grove took their morning bath in the river. She could never have done that due to her condition, so she was glad to have this little luxury of her own.

I got a job on the ice truck two days a week, and for three, days I'd life-guard at the Laguna Beach Club. Every penny I made I'd give to Momma to hold for me. Any time I wanted to buy anything, she always gave me money. I'm sure I received more from her than I gave her, but she never discussed the family finances (or lack of them) with me.

Since I could remember, every Saturday we'd all walk about two miles along the train tracks into Mountain View to Holy Child Church and go to Confession. Then the trek back home. On Sundays the trek was repeated and we'd go to Mass.

Father Scully would say the Mass and give his sermon. The church was small, crowded, and hot. Even with the windows open and these four huge fans with blades that looked like airplane propellers, it was hot. I always dozed off, and depending on who was next to me, I'd be rudely awakened with either a finger biff to the head (one of my sisters) or a pull on my ear (Momma)or an elbow in the ribs (Grandma Walsh).

This summer it was different. Momma rarely came to church. It was just too much for her. Even if Mr. Keegan, Hank, or Jimmy offered to drive her, she'd decline.

Father Scully, now a monsignor, would come to visit her every other Sunday afternoon and bring her Holy Communion. They'd sit and talk and we'd all just do whatever.

Normally, I wanted the summer to last forever, but this year, I couldn't wait to get home so Momma would be able to be comfortable and have a nice hot bath. Looking back, Mountain View was a paradise, but pretty primitive.

I was assigned to a foot post on Avenue X, from Ocean Parkway to MacDonald Avenue. It was a residential and commercial mixed area. Near MacDonald Avenue there was a bar called Ro-Sal, and across the street on the other corner was a no-name luncheonette where the wise guys and wannabe wise guys hung out until they filtered into the Ro-Sal.

The captain turned us out and told us to give double-parking summonses and hydrants. He explained (I think for my benefit) that fire trucks and ambulances had a hard time getting through to emergencies if the streets were blocked.

So I got to the post and did a walk up and down. One of the cops, Manny Bogen, had taken me on the side and told me that there were a bunch of nasty bastards on the post and I shouldn't take any crap from them as they'd walk all over me if I let them. He told me to be firm, but fair. In the case of giving out a summons, I should knock on the store windows where the car was parked. This would give the owner a chance to move and I'd be the good guy. But if they didn't move the car in a reasonable amount of time, I'd give them tickets.

Armed with those words of advice, I did just that. It worked for the first couple of tours. People thanked me for the courtesy and some of the store owners thanked me too. Finally, on the last four-to-twelve, it came to an abrupt end.

One day in early October 1955, I was sitting at the foot of Momma's bed just talking to her and trying to make her laugh. She told me to come closer, so I inched up toward her pillow. "Put your hand out and take this." She had taken her wedding ring off her terribly swollen finger. "Momma, why are you giving this to me?"

"I want you to give this to the girl you choose to be your wife." I started to protest, but with great difficulty she held up her hand to silence me.

I held the silver band in my hand and looked at the inscription. It was the date that Momma and Daddy got married. "Mom, what if she doesn't want it?" She looked at me with her beautiful blue eyes and just softly said, "Then don't marry her!"

I went to bed one night after going in to say good night to Momma. Her condition had worsened, so we had a nurse come in between 11:00 p.m. and 7:00 a.m. This gave my older sisters and sisters-in-law a little break in the daily routine of helping Momma.

I bent down to give her a kiss and she opened her eyes. The twinkle was gone, but her smile was the same. She gripped my hand and pulled me close to her. I knelt down next to her bed. She took a deep breath and very slowly and clearly started talking to me. The nurse, a very kind and nice woman by the name of Bertha N. Bright, started to get up from her chair. Momma motioned with her hand and Miss Bertha sat back down.

Momma said to me, "Always be a good man! Never intentionally hurt anyone, but if someone is trying to hurt you or your family, you can stop them. Always stay close to your faith and your brothers and sisters. Love them and help them." She hesitated and took another breath, gripping my hand tighter. "I love you, son! You've given me a lot to be proud of and I thank you. Remember, if the girl you choose to marry you doesn't want my ring"—she sighed and continued— "then don't marry her. Now, go to bed. You have to look good for your picture tomorrow." She released my hand and sank back into the pillow. Miss Bertha came over and placed her hand on my shoulder. She smiled and ushered me outside into the hall. "She needs her sleep. You go to bed now, boy. I'll be with her if she wants anything."

I went to sleep, but it was an uneasy sleep, if you know what I mean. My mind was racing with a hundred different thoughts. I was graduating from high school in a few months and I was scheduled to go to Seton Hall University. I didn't want to go, but Big Jim had somehow gotten me in. I wasn't the sharpest knife in the drawer when it came to academics, so I guess he used up a few favors.

I told you I was a good swimmer, so I was accepted to the swim team, and I also had a job waiting on tables and washing dishes in the school cafeteria. That would cover my room and board and some tuition, and Jimmy and Barbara would pay for the remainder.

I kept tossing and turning all night long. I kept hearing Momma's words and seeing her smile.

About five in the morning, my brother Jackie turned on the light in my room. I sat up and saw the look on his face. He looked so sad. I felt sorry for him. He started to speak and he just couldn't. I put a robe on, and he put his arm around me and we went into Momma's room. My sisters, Jimmy, Barbara, and Muriel were all around the bed. Sitting next to Momma was Miss Bertha. She was holding Momma's hand and I saw big tears on her full ebony cheeks.

I looked at Momma and she actually had a smile on her face, or so it seemed to me. I noticed that in her right hand were her Rosary beads. Miss Bertha must have given them to her.

Nobody was crying or anything like that. The nine of us just stood together holding hands or arms around each other. Looking back, we were like links in a chain never to be broken.

Momma was dead. Now it was up to us to keep the family together. Peggy started and we all joined in, "Eternal rest grant unto her, oh Lord, and may the perpetual light shine upon her. May her soul and the souls of all the faithful departed through mercy of God rest in peace. Amen."

I was walking the post and saying hello to people and knocking on windows to move the double parkers. I worked my way to the end of the post and right outside the no-name luncheonette was this big Cadillac Fleetwood double-parked.

There were plenty of curb spaces, but this boat was right out there in the street. Cars and buses had to maneuver around it going into the oncoming traffic lane. I knocked on the luncheonette window with my nightstick and motioned toward the car.

A couple of heads turned and promptly looked away. I waited a couple of minutes and knocked again. One of the group at the counter flashed me a signal which, even I knew, he didn't mean that he thought I was number one.

I took out the summons book and proceeded to start the ticket. I heard someone calling me, I guessed. "Hey, you, whadda ya think you're doing'? I'm talking to you, cop. Do you know who I am?" I didn't, and what's more, I really didn't care. I looked at him and he was the guy who had flashed me the number one sign. He was tall and well-built with a black leather jacket, black silk shirt, black pants, and black hair. He kept yelling and people started gathering on the sidewalk. I placed the summons on the car and turned to him just as he threw a punch. I blocked it with the nightstick and hit him square in the face as hard as I could. The crowd started getting bigger and they started yelling at me. As he was holding his bloody face, I kneed him in the groin. He went down to his knees and I quickly cuffed him.

I pulled him to his feet by his hair, and he let out a scream of curses and threats. I gave him a quick pat-down for weapons. *Damn*, I thought. I wished he had a gun or knife. If he had, I would have shown it to the growing crowd to show them what kind of a mutt they had for a hero, that they were backing a punk with a gun. But alas, no gun, no knife.

I found his car keys and threw them on the hood of the Caddy. Well, I actually, accidentally, scratched the paint with the bottom of the key causing about a two-inch gash in the hood. Now, you have to realize that we didn't have any portable radios in those days. If you needed help, you relied on the good citizens of the neighborhood to phone the police. I didn't know who this guy was, but the people either loved him or were scared shitless of him. I jerked him upright and proceeded to walk to the call box about five blocks away. The wise guy bar, Ro-Sal, emptied out and all the petty thieves and the bookmakers and their sycophants were milling around. There was a lot of finger pointing, shoulder shrugs, Italian curses, and, oh yeah, the famous forefinger and pinky sign. You know the one I mean. You cup your thumb and the middle and ring fingers and you extend the forefinger and pinky straight out.

I knew from growing up in Bensonhurst that I was having the horns put on me. I had so many horns on me, I should have dropped dead at least one hundred times. There was one fat slob who was giving me a double whammy. This a-hole, like the others, was all in black, but what struck me was that although it was dark, he had sunglasses on.

Crossing the street, I held the clown by the hand cufflinks. I had his arms back and up, forcing him to bend forward. Just the way I was taught in the academy. We were about two blocks away from the crowd when I heard a sound behind me. I lifted my prisoner's arms up, forcing him to bend even more. I crouched and saw the fat slob with a baseball bat above his head. I realized that he wasn't going to donate the bat to the P.A.L., so I dropped to one knee and pushed the prisoner down onto the sidewalk. I could tell that it hurt. Anyway, this fat slob kinda, sorta, stopped in mid-swing when he saw the.38 revolver appear about a foot and a half from his private parts. Oops. I guess he thought better of it because he turned and half-waddled and half-ran back to the sanctuary of the Ro-Sal. The noise I heard, originally, was the glasses hitting the sidewalk. So we, my "don't you know who I am," prisoner and I continued our trek to the call box. I told the sergeant on the switch-board that I needed transportation to the station house with a prisoner. "Hey, kid, whadda ya think this is, a taxi service? Hoof it." He then added, "By the way, are you okay?" I assured him that I was and told him I'd see him soon.

Well, I finally got to find out what K.G. meant. The man in black with the terribly scrapped and swollen face was a K.G. or made-man in the Colombo crime family. Joseph Broccelo. Ooooh, was I scared. This piece of crap sitting in the cell was supposedly a tough guy. I wondered, if he was so tough, how come he pissed his pants? Oh yeah, a K.G. is a Known Gambler.

I brought the tough guy upstairs to the squad to be fingerprinted by the detectives. Frank Healey was the detective that was up to doing the fingerprints. Healey printed him and helped me fill out the arrest cards. He introduced me to another man, Big Bill Shea. Shea was tall and distinguished looking. Frank Healey was average height, but squat like a lineman on a football team.

After I lodged Broccelo in the holding cell, Healey grabbed me and took me into the coffee area of the squad room. "Tell me what the guy with the bat looked like." Well, to me, he looked like a two-hundred-and fifty–pound wallet with his black leather knee-length jacket. He had a big nose and his eyes looked like a ferret. Real good-looking fella."

Healey laughed and then turned serious.

Momma's body was still upstairs waiting for Mr. Cosgrove, the funeral director, to take her out. The house was jammed with people. Uncle Jack, Father Coyne and Father McKinney came and said prayers and anointed Momma. I know she didn't need it, but it was nice.

Jackie took me up to my room and told me to get ready to go to school to have my yearbook picture taken. I protested and he listened. Jackie was always a good listener. So, after he listened and I finished having my say, he just gave me a couple of bucks and told me to go to school. I did.

I got to St. Francis Prep about nine o'clock and got online in the gym for the senior pictures. A bunch of brothers came over to me and gave me their condolences. The lay teachers came over and did the same. I was especially touched by the sincerity of Mr. Boras, my swimming coach. He had tears in his eyes. Mr. Keegan, the basketball and baseball coach, was really upset. As I told you, my sister-in-law, Muriel, was his daughter.

The guys in the class were terrific to me. I'll tell you, and I mean it, if it wasn't for my family, brothers, sisters, aunts, uncles, the Franciscan brothers, and the lay teachers, I probably would have been in jail.

After the picture taking, I rushed back home and found the house filled with relatives and neighbors. I wandered from room to room. Occasionally, someone would stop me and say something nice about Momma and then give me some type of adult wisdom that I guess was meant to console me.

I went outside and climbed the tree. I know, I know, what the heck was a big goon like me doing in a tree? Well, the old tree was comfortable and I had time to be with my memories. I mean, everyone had someone. Kathleen and Frank, Jackie and Muriel, Jimmy and Barbara, Cele and Hank, Peggy and God, and my little sisters had each other. I had my tree and my memories.

I sat there for I don't know how long. I kept looking at Momma's window, waiting for her to raise the shade and make a face at me. I swear that I saw her. To this day, I honestly believe that she opened the window and said to me, "Don't worry, my little man. I'm fine and you will be too." I swear she closed the window, pulled the shade down, and that was that.

One of the Mulvey boys was calling up to me from the sidewalk. I snapped back to reality. "What are you looking at?" I didn't reply, but I said to myself, "Something I'll never see again, my mother."

About a week after I arrested Broccelo, I was doing a day tour, walking up and down Emmons Avenue along Sheepshead Bay. A radio car pulled up to the curb, and the driver leaned over. "Hey, kid, hop in. The captain wants you at the house." Manny Bogen was the cop. A heck of a nice guy. He had about six years on the job.

Driving me back to the station house, he asked me all sorts of questions about myself—are you married, relatives on the job, brothers, sisters, just pleasant chit-chat. Meanwhile, my heart was racing a mile a minute. Why did the captain send a radio car to drive me to the station house? Was I in trouble for the arrest? You know, dumb thoughts as to why the commanding officer of the precinct wanted to see me. Me, a lowly rookie.

I went into the house, and there was Frank Healey, the captain, Sergeant Dave Joyce, and a bunch of other guys. The captain motioned to me and he walked toward his office. "Go into the sitting room and tell me if you recognize anyone."

I was a little bewildered, but being a good soldier. I walked to the sitting room and looked in. There were about thirty guys in the room lounging all around, under the watchful eyes of ten detectives and plainclothes men.

In the far corner of the room, near the shoeshine machine, there was the fat slob with the bat. I don't mean he still had the bat, but he was the same guy—oh hell, you know what I mean. I walked up to him and he was backing up into the men's room. I said, "Hey, fatso, you want your sunglasses?" I reached into the inside pocket of my uniform overcoat and held them out to him. He went into the men's room. That was his mistake. I followed and proceeded to punch the shit out of him.

I rear-cuffed him and pushed him back into the sitting room. I spotted Broccelo in the group, and in a loud voice asked him if he'd pissed in his pants again since I arrested him. He didn't look happy, but some of his fellow city guests laughed.

Healey and the plainclothes men knew who the guy with the bat was, and they waited until the weekly wise guy crap game was in progress and raided it. I learned that my prisoner was a low-level mongrel named Joseph Prestiotti.

I started to walk Prestiotti upstairs, and Captain Walsh looked at me, and in his dry sense of humor, just said, "I take it that you recognized someone, Officer? Take him upstairs and have him printed."

My uncle Mike was a first-grade detective in the Queens DA's office and the advice he gave me was now my mantra. "You never put a prisoner in hungry or broke. You never hit a handcuffed prisoner, and when it's over, it's over." In the years to come, I tried my best to adhere to Mike Walsh's law.

It's a funny thing about cops; they make you earn their trust and respect. I guess I earned it because I wasn't getting the rookie treatment any longer. At least once a tour, one of the sector car teams would pull up to my foot post on a cold winter night and open the back door and tell me to sit down. They'd give me a cup of coffee and we'd talk about the conditions on the post I was assigned to. It really made me feel great.

In November 1955, I joined the Marine Corps Reserve. I had full intentions of going on active duty right after I graduated in January. But, as I told you, Big Jim had gotten me into Seton Hall. So that's what I was going to do.

The time came for my prom and I didn't really want to go, but my sister Kathleen kept pushing and pushing, and yeah, pushing me to go. So, I went. I asked a girl from Mountain View. She wasn't really from Mountain View. She was from Manhattan, but, like us, her family went there for the summer. The prom was fun, and with all the guys that I hung out with, I kinda had a good time.

Peggy came to the graduation and then she took me to the Automat Restaurant to celebrate. I don't think there are many Automats left anymore. You'd go in, and there were rows and rows of glass windows where you'd look and find what you wanted to eat. You'd put a coin in the slot and the window would pop open, and you'd take your sandwich or soup or pie and sit and eat.

The girls were moving to New Jersey, and Jackie and Muriel were moving into the house on Sixty-Ninth Street. I was moving to Seton Hall. Jimmy and Jackie drove me to the campus in South Orange and helped me get settled. It was a two-man room on the third floor of Boylan Hall. Right down from the chapel.

My new roommate, Jack Perez, was already in the room. He was premed and was going to be a doctor. His father and mother were with him. After the pleasantries were exchanged, Jack's father, a doctor, asked me my goal. I told him I want to be a New York City cop. Geez, you'd think I farted. He looked at me like I had stepped in something and didn't clean my shoe. I sensed that this was not going to be the place for me. I was right.

Jack was a good guy, but very serious. I, on the other hand, was a clown. I tried to fit in, but all the other guys had money and friends and I just felt like I didn't belong.

I read the student regs and noticed that the floors in the dorm had to be washed and waxed once a week. Bonanza! There were at least forty rooms with two guys per room. I charged them one buck each, every two weeks. That was a hundred sixty dollars a month.

I enlisted the aid of one of the maintenance men, a man named Mr. Rodney. I'd bring him left-over pie and fruit from the kitchen, and every two weeks he'd let me use the mop, the wax and the buffer machine. I mean, the food was just gonna be thrown out. So, as Momma used to say, "Waste not, want not," right?

The first couple of months were okay, but I really didn't fit in. These guys had cars and clothes, and I don't know, I just didn't fit in.

I'd spend every other Friday night mopping and waxing when most of the students went home for the weekend. I made sure I got the money upfront, mind you. Then, I'd do some school work. I practically had the whole campus to myself.

There was a lovely woman, Mrs. Davies, who ran the kitchen, and she sort of took care of me. She'd let me eat whatever I wanted and she'd give me a bag with the leftovers. I think she knew about my deal with Mr. Rodney, but she never let on.

I'd call home and talk to Jackie or Muriel. The girls would write me letters and that was a cheerer upper. Don't get me wrong, it wasn't like I was a thousand miles away. It was a bus ride to Newark, take the Hudson Tubes to the city and take the subway home. It was about a two-hour ride.

The hardest part for me was when I'd go into the chapel and look through the stained glass windows onto South Orange Avenue. I'd see men coming home from work being greeted at the door by their wife and kids. It just reminded me of our house when Momma and Daddy were alive.

The swim team was another story. Good group of guys and coaches. About two months after the semester started, I was practicing for a meet and went to do a flip turn. I was a lot closer to the wall than I thought. Instead of just brushing the wall and flip for the return lap, I barreled into the wall and broke my hand. Have you ever seen a one-handed dishwasher/swimmer?

They let me finish the semester, and in June, I joined the regular Marine Corps for two years. After boot camp, I was promoted to P.F.C. and went to the Infantry Training Regiment in Camp LeJeune, North Carolina. Instead of going to another assignment, the C.O. asked me to stay as a junior instructor. I got an extra stripe and was now a corporal.

The C.O. was from Brooklyn, a career Marine, and his X.O. was from Queens. I guess the New York connection was enough for them to request my assignment.

Nothing spectacular happened, just the usual. Training, rifle range, drill, and field problems. I'll tell you, I was in some shape physically.

Well, there was an incident that almost cost me a stripe. The commanding general of Camp LeJeune was going to inspect my company. We're all out on the company street near our squad boys and directly in front of the mess hall. The captain comes up with the general and XO. The captain starts telling the general about me and the potential he believed I had. I had my rifle at port arms ready for inspection. The general grabs the rifle in the prescribed military manner and I snapped to attention.

He looks at the rifle, spins it around, looks down the barrel and then, with a very heavy duty Southern accent, asks me, "Boy, what ya'll do case of a mess fire?" So being bright and quick witted, I responded in my best military voice, "Sir, I'd call the fire brigade, sir.

He threw the rifle back to me and proceeded down the line. After the inspection, the Company Sergeant grabbed me and told me the captain wanted me ASAP.

I knocked and entered and stood at attention in front of the captain and the XO. "What the hell is the matter with you, answering the general like that? I never pinned you as a wise guy. I have to tell you, I am furious with you."

I requested to speak and he gave me permission. "Captain, I don't know what I did wrong, sir." You always have to add "sir." "You don't know what, what you . . ." He was starting to turn purple and sputter. "What the hell do you think the general asked you?"

"Sir, he asked me what I would do in case of a mess fire, sir."

The captain and XO just looked at each other. "You . . . you're serious, aren't you?"

"Sir, yes, sir." The captain jumped up from behind his desk and came to attention as did the XO. I didn't, 'cause I was already there. The general came into my view. "Boy, are y'all tellin' me you don't unnerstan Merican? What the hell kinda schoolin' y'all get up north? Ah asked you what would you do in case of a mis-fire from your rifle. Now boy, was that Yankee enough?" He then laughed, as did the skipper and the XO. I was dismissed.

The only thing I can say about my service to the country is that nobody, and I mean nobody, tried to invade North Carolina while I was stationed there.

When I came home, I got a job as an executive trainee with First National City Bank. The idea was that I'd eventually be one of those people that you go to when you wanted to take out a loan at your local bank. I started dating a girl I had met at a St. Francis College dance. I went there with a couple of my high school buddies, Tommy Nelson and Jim (Dutch) Leonard. Thanks to my sister Kathleen, I knew how to dance. Her name was Pat Dowd. She was pretty, cute, intelligent, and could do a mean Lindy as well as a foxtrot. She lived in Bay Ridge and her family had a summerhouse in Breezy Point, Queens, right on the beach. She was attending St. John's University in Brooklyn. To say we hit it off would be an understatement.

Her father and younger brother liked me all right. But I always had the feeling that her mother and older sister didn't care for me all that much.

When I was with her, I had a lot of fun, whether we were bowling or at a movie or just having a beer and pizza after a dance or a ball game. We'd talk, vaguely, about our future once she graduated from college.

Things were going pretty good for me at the bank. I was making a cool $8,900 a year at the age of twenty. In 1958, that wasn't bad money, especially since I was living practically rent free with Jackie and Muriel and their six kids on Sixty-Ninth Street. As Jackie liked to say, "When we bought the house, he [me] came with the woodwork."

One night I was walking Pat home to her house in Breezy and I asked her what she would think if (and I emphasized *if*) we were ever to get married and I asked her to wear my mother's wedding ring. She didn't miss a step. "Oh, no, I'd want mine. Why would I want to wear someone else's ring?" I just said, "Oh," and I walked her home.

I went to work for a four-by-twelve tour, and Captain Walsh was still talking about all the complaints he was getting about the double-parkers and people on hydrants, and he wanted everyone to write summonses for the violations. After my encounter with the two jerks from Avenue X, I wasn't the least bit concerned about writing summonses.

Any time I had the Avenue X Post, after the arrests, I didn't even have to knock on the store windows. The word went out and people either moved on or just found legal spots. I wasn't being obnoxious or anything, but it was my post and I wanted to keep it orderly. With the exception of a few of the younger gangster wannabes giving me dirty looks, Avenue X was kind of boring. I even went into the no-name luncheonette for a cup of coffee now and then. I did watch to make sure I didn't get an extra helping of phlegm in the cup, though.

I ambled from one end of the post to another, stopping to chat with some of the store owners or some of the teenagers on one of the corners. Nothing big, just good old letting people know that they could talk to the cop on the post, come to me if they needed help or anything, they thought I could do for them.

Along about ten thirty, I was walking toward the Ro-Sal and this Lincoln Continental pulled up in front of the place and double-parked. Some greasy-looking guy gets out and glances at me and starts to go into the bar. "Hey, mister, could you park it at the curb? There's plenty of—"

"F—— you," comes his reply to my sensitive ears. And into the bar he goes.

Being very mild-mannered and calm, I went to the car and wrote a summons. The greasy-looking jerk looked out the window and gave me the Italian salute. So I walked to the front of the car and ripped his antenna off and threw it at the bar window. Much to his chagrin.

I still can't understand what makes people have such disregard to a cop in uniform. They don't hesitate to put up their hands and fingers. I don't mean I was offended personally, but who the hell were they to take on a cop in uniform? I guess it was a culture thing. Maybe they weren't loved when they were kids. Or maybe they were just punks who think they can do whatever they wanted and get away with it. In the case of the owner of the Lincoln, he learned that sometimes you can't.

About a block away from Ro-Sal, I saw this figure in the doorway, and in hushed tones, he was calling me. I walked over, and he said, "Kid, I used to be on the job. I got jammed up and they kicked me out. That doesn't mean I don't like cops. I was wrong and I got caught, but that's ancient history."

I could smell the odor of booze on his breath. I asked him if I could do anything for him. "No, but I want to tell you about the guy with that car. He's a made man. He's really bad. He's done some hard time. When he was a kid, he beat a guy to death over two dollars. He's done stick-ups, assaults, and just got out after four years for bringing a shit-load of drugs up from Miami."

I thanked him for the information and started to walk away, but he continued, "Kid, he ain't got no conscience. You insulted him and he won't forget. He's a sneaky bastard. Just be careful." I reached in my pocket and shook his hand with a five-dollar bill folded in my palm. He didn't even look at it. He just bent his head and mumbled thanks.

Pat and I went to a dance at the Hotel St. George in Brooklyn. We were at a table with Tommy Nelson, Dutch Leonard, Rick Cross and Herbie Rourke. With the exception of Rick, the other guys and I went to high school together.

Rick was dating a girl from New Jersey named Betty Ann. Betty Ann's sister was there with her boyfriend, John. We all pulled our chairs together and took over this big table. Jokes and conversations were flying all night.

Every once in a while, I'd look at Betty Ann's sister, Jennifer. Man, I thought, she was beautiful. She had blonde hair and beautiful blue eyes. She was about five foot five inches and one hundred and thirty pounds of great-looking body.

She didn't even pay attention to me when I tried to talk to her. Every time I tried to start a conversation with her, she'd smile and start talking to her date or sister or someone else. Oh, well!

The next time I saw her was when her cousin Maryann graduated from St. Vincent's School of Nursing. After the ceremony, Dutch, Rick, Herbie, and I took the subway up to the Bronx to Maryann's house for a little party. Little, my foot. There were relatives and friends all over the place. And she was there.

I tried to talk to her, but everybody was laughing and singing and talking. Tommy Nelson (we called him Nellie) and I went on a beer run. I asked Nellie all about her and he filled me in.

She had been going with this guy, John, and apparently he had recently dumped her. They'd been going together for about three years, and all of a sudden, he decided that he didn't want to go out exclusively with her. They did have their ups and downs, and he was prone to arguing with her.

We came back from the beer run and the party was in full swing. Her aunt Rose was singing an old song, so I joined in. I then segued into a song that I made a point of dedicating to Jennifer. Talk about getting off on the wrong foot.

The song was "You're the Kind of a Girl that Men Forget," and I sang it right to her without taking my eyes off of her. I knew she was beautiful. She thought I was an a-hole.

About four months later, Pat and I went to a party for one of my buddies' birthdays and there she was. Pat saw me talking to her. (Actually, it was a one-sided conversation). And Pat suddenly developed a headache and wanted to go home. So we left and I walked her home.

I guess I shouldn't have, but I went back to the party. I saw her sitting in a corner all by herself. I asked her to dance and she said no. I asked her again and again and again. Finally, and reluctantly, she agreed. Boy, oh, boy, what a dancer. I asked her for her phone number and she reminded me that I was dating Pat. I reminded her that I wasn't married or even engaged. No sale on the phone number.

I was doing an eight-to-four tour on foot along Sheepshead Bay. I stepped off the curb and this car came speeding right toward me. The front fender missed me by inches, scaring the hell out of me.

The car was going so fast I couldn't even get the plate number. The car did look familiar to me. I shrugged it off as just another jerk that didn't know how to drive (I should talk). Along about three o'clock, I saw the car parked on a fire hydrant. It was the car that narrowly missed me, but, more importantly, it was the car without its antenna.

So I whipped out my handy-dandy summons book and proceeded to ticket the car. As Yogi Berra once said, "It was déjà vu all over again." The greasy mutt came at me in a rage. No need to go into detail, but I felt good after the encounter and he didn't.

When I dragged him into the station house, he was humble. Frank Healey was up in the detective squad and he was salivating. "Come here after you throw him in the cage." So I took him. Literally un-cuffed him and threw him in the cell.

Lieutenant McCarthy came out of his office when he heard the commotion. He took one look in the cell and grinned. Healey and I went into the lieutenant's office and sat. McCarthy asked me what happened and I told him about the Ro-Sal incident (without the bit about the antenna). McCarthy nodded and finally gave me the run-down on my prisoner. It turns out that Pasquale Gerati (call me Patsy) was indeed a bad boy. The Six-One Squad liked him for two armed robberies and a homicide. The investigations were still in their early stages, but they needed time to work on the witnesses because they were terrified of Pascal (call me Patsy)Gerati.

McCarthy explained that he was on parole and this arrest, for felonious assault on a police officer, was just what they needed to have his parole violated and put him in jail. This would give them time to convince the witnesses that this piece of crap wasn't invincible.

McCarthy explained that I shouldn't be too surprised if the DA knocked the charges down to attempted assault because I was okay and Call Me Patsy wasn't.

Frank Healey came up with the idea that maybe it was our responsibility to safeguard his car. McCarthy agreed and he called for a department tow truck to bring it to the stationhouse.

Healey and I went through the car, and what to my wondering eyes should appear, but a.45 caliber, loaded, under the driver's seat. Bingo, and bye-bye, Patsy.

Hey, this cop business was fun!

In late 1960, Pat Dowd and I were still dating, BUT I guess it was more out of habit than anything else. We were still having fun and we were interested in each other, but I don't know, it was just a BUT. She was getting ready to graduate and I was just biding my time waiting to be called by the Police Department. That seemed to be a bone of contention between us too. She wanted me to finish college and stay with the bank. "You'll have a very respectable job. You'll be somebody, not just another civil servant." Once in a while, our conversations went that way.

Speaking of the bank, I gotta tell you this one. As part of the Executive Trainee Program, you were sent to different parts of the city for a week at a time.

I was in one of the branches on Park Avenue in Manhattan working a teller window. So on a Wednesday, I showed up with a pair of khaki trousers, blue button-down collar shirt, red tie, Madrass jacket, looking like a picture of colored lines and shapes and whatever, all in squares. Looking back, I looked kinda like a jacket that a circus clown wears.

So I go into the bank, and the snooty branch manager eyes me up and down and crooking his finger, motions me into his office. "Mr. Stark, in this branch, all the men wear business suits."

"Yes, sir, I know, but the tailor hasn't finished putting the cuffs on the trousers and all my suits are in the dry cleaners."

"Are you telling me that . . . that . . . that jacket is part of a suit?"

"Oh, yes, sir. I got a good deal on it at Macy's."

Needless to say, the manager gave me a wide berth for the next couple of days. I'll tell you, though, the rest of the staff and the customers complimented me on the way I looked.

Pat and I were, more frequently, disagreeing about me going into the Police Department. I couldn't get her to understand that being a cop was all I really ever wanted to do. So I decided that the best thing to do was to go our separate ways and still be friends.

I took her to one of our favorite places, a German restaurant in Manhattan that we'd been to many times. They had a piano player and rounds of sing-a-longs and pretty good food.

On the way home, I sort of hinted that maybe we should cool the dating and maybe see other people. She didn't cry or protest or anything, but she did ask if I was already seeing anyone. I told her I wasn't, and as we stood on her stoop saying goodnight/goodbye, she said, and I quote, "Watch out for that McDermott girl. She has her hooks out for you."

I began to protest that that wasn't so, but she simply kissed me on the cheek, turned, and went into her house.

I found out later that I had beaten Pat to the punch because she was seeing other guys. She was planning to tell me the same thing I had told her. So much for knowing your girl.

A few months later, Tommy Nelson and Maryann were getting married. I was in the wedding party and so was Jennifer. She didn't have a date and neither did I. Everyone was out on the dance floor except me. She was being semi-nice to me. Well, at least she was answering my chit-chat conversation. I asked her to dance and she accepted. We danced and danced and I even had her laughing. About halfway through the reception, I asked her, "If you were to ever get married and the guy asked you to wear his mother's wedding ring on your wedding day, what would you say?" Before she could answer, the new bride and groom were about to cut the cake, so my question went unanswered.

The reception was ending and everyone was milling around, so I asked her if she'd like a drink at the hotel bar. About ten of us went to the bar. I got her a seat and we both ordered drinks. Before they got there, she turned to me and said, "In answer to your question, I think it would be a honor to wear the wedding ring of my husband's mother." Six weeks later, I asked her to marry me. A year and a half later, May of 1962, we got married.

After the Avenue X arrests, I got more and more chances to ride on patrol. I made more arrests, and I was comfortable hearing and watching how the veterans conducted themselves and handled the myriad of situations that a cop faces daily.

I learned that at the scene of a simple finder-bender, people react differently. Some are thankful that no one was injured. Others take it as a personal assault on themselves and go nuts. Some people haven't a clue as to what information they need to report to their insurance companies. I learned how to calm them down, communicate with them, help them by getting the info they needed. I was impressed with the way the older cops handled every situation that came up.

I was riding with a good guy, Manny Bogen, when the radio ordered us to meet the sergeant at an apartment house on Sheepshead Bay. We arrived and the sergeant told us we have a DOA on the top floor. "Hey, kid, you ever see a dead body before?"

"Plenty of times, Sarge," was my somewhat cavalier reply. "Good, 'cause you have to sit with him until the squad and the ME respond." With that, we all trudged to the top floor and into the apartment.

The sergeant motioned toward the bathroom door. "In there." Opening the door, I saw a guy with his head back, sitting on the bowl with a shotgun resting on the bathtub in front of his knees. I noticed black marks around his mouth. "What happened?"

"He shot himself by pulling the trigger with his toe."

"I don't see any blood." The sergeant pointed, with his clipboard, to the ceiling. There, on the ceiling, was the entire brain of this poor guy sitting on the bowl. One look up, and breakfast and lunch made a quick exit. That was bad enough, but I barfed all over the DOA, the shotgun, and the bathtub. "So much for safeguarding the scene," said the sergeant. Everybody's a comedian. "Hey, kid, I thought you were used to dead bodies." Wiping my lips, I admitted that the only dead bodies I had seen were in funeral parlors. He just looked at me and sort of smiled. "Unfortunately, kid, you will get used to it." Manny Bogen put a hand on my shoulder and walked me into the hallway. "Sarge, I'll stay. Let him get some air." As I said, Manny was a really good guy.

We set the date for May 5, 1962. So long about the beginning of April, my brother Jackie asked me if I had put the UF-28 in with the roll call man requesting the vacation time. I hadn't.

I filled out the Leave Request Form and gave it to the roll call cop. He took it, looked at it, and laughed. "You gotta be kidding me. You're only a rookie and you expect to get those two weeks off? You gotta be kidding me." I told him I was very serious, and indeed, I wasn't kidding. More laughter. "This will not happen," he said. I explained that I was getting married and that we had booked the plane and hotel. Not to mention the church and the reception hall.

He didn't laugh as hard, but laugh he did. I started to do a slow burn. I leaned over his desk, and in my best Brooklynese, explained to him that if I didn't get the time, I would throw him out of his office window. "Take it up with the captain," was all he said, but I know I got to him because he was a pale as a sheet.

Snatching the slip, I went downstairs to the captain's office. He wasn't in. Sergeant Dave Joyce asked what was up, so I told him. He took the form, signed it and went up to roll call. About two minutes later, Sergeant Joyce came down the stairs and gave me a thumbs-up signal. I was happy, but I knew that the roll call man would not be very friendly toward me. Oh, well, you win some; you lose some.

Finally the big day came and the wedding went off without a snag. Uncle Jack said the Mass, and my cousin Father Donald Riley assisted. Everyone was in a festive mood. The reception was great. My brothers and some friends were in the wedding party. My relatives and neighbors from Brooklyn quickly joined into conversations with my new New Jersey relatives and friends. Jennifer and I danced and danced and danced.

After the reception, it seemed like the whole party went from the hall to Jennifer's mother's house. Her mother was a bit overwhelmed by the crowd, so my sisters and sisters-in-law pitched in with getting drinks and sandwiches for all the party animals.

We have invited Lieutenant Rohe and his wife. They came and they stayed. Bill Burke inadvertently told him the story of my encounter in Kearney and Rohe laughed. When he asked me why I didn't tell him, I replied that the CO of the academy didn't want to hear anymore stories about New Jersey, so I figured, neither did he. He laughed some more and smacked me on the back.

Jennifer and I went upstairs to Grandpa's room and sat on the bed and opened the envelopes that the guests had given us. Her mother had written a check for the reception, so we had to give her the money to cover the check. I'll tell you, I was worried that we wouldn't have enough to cover the check. Between our families and friends, we made out just fine. Along about seven o'clock, she and I started to leave the party. About a quarter to eight, we finally made it outside. Grandma Walsh came over to us and gave us her blessing. "If he doesn't behave, you just call me, I'll straighten him out for you." She then gave me the all too familiar tap in the back of the head and winked. My new brother-in-law, Georgie, had volunteered to drive us to Idlewild Airport where we were to spend our first night of wedded bliss. We pulled up in front of the International Hotel with Georgie helping us with the baggage. I went to the desk and timidly said, "We have a reservation."

The bellhop took our bags up to the room, and when he left, we both just stood there looking at each other. Finally, I spoke, "Are you happy?" We went down to the restaurant and had club sandwiches. We were both talking at once. No, it was more like babbling.

Finally, hand in hand, we went up to the room. Jennifer went into the bathroom to change and I stood there wondering what I should do. When she finally came out, I held her close. She was a vision in her brand-new peignoir. I held her, and finally, we both, tentatively, moved toward the bed.

I stopped and knelt next to the bed. She did the same. Blessing ourselves, we both said prayers that God would protect us and help us in the years to come. Silently I thanked St. Michael the Archangel. The next morning, we went to Mass at the airport chapel, Our Lord of the Skies.

Florida was great, sunny but not too hot. We both had a ball. Swimming, shows at the hotel. We even went to a movie, *West Side Story*, one day that it was cloudy.

Big Jim somehow got us into the Met Life owned apartment complex, Stuyvesant Town, in Manhattan. But, there's always a "but," we couldn't get into the apartment until August. I was damned if I was going to live in Brooklyn while Jennifer lived in New Jersey, so we moved into Grandpa's room. The NYPD frowns upon its members living out of the city limits. But she was worth the risk. Besides, Jackie and Muriel had already put two of their daughters in my room and I didn't want to sleep in the cellar.

We were home a few days, and Muriel and my sisters were having a bridal shower for Patty Ann who was getting married in a month. I drove Jennifer to the shower and the car radio announced that two detectives had been shot while breaking up a robbery at Cigarette and Cigar Wholesale. More news to follow.

Finally, the news guy announced that preliminary reports are that two detectives have been shot while breaking up an armed robbery at a wholesale tobacco store on Forty-Eighth Street and New Utrecht Avenue in Brooklyn. Details are sketchy, but an alarm has been sent for two white males seen fleeing the scene. This, according to police sources. More news on this breaking story as soon as it becomes available.

I knew Jackie was working, and, naturally, I was concerned that he might have been involved in the shooting. The Safe and Loft Squad went after some pretty bad guys.

After I dropped Jennifer off, I went to the shooting scene. I had to park about five blocks away. There were marked and unmarked police vehicles all over the place.

I got to the store just as they were putting bodies in an ambulance. I recognized one of the detectives immediately. It was Mr. Luke Fallon. Mr. Fallon was a friend of my grandfather, Pop Walsh. They used to sit on the stoop in front of Pop and Gram's apartment and drink beer and argue about politics and sports.

The other detective was John Finnegan, a handsome young detective with a young wife. It was obvious to me that both were dead. I said a prayer to St. Michael. I saw Lieutenant McCarthy from the Six-One Squad pull up to the scene with three detectives. I made my way over to him and asked if there was any way I could be of assistance. The block was filling up with off-duty cops and retired cops. We all had the same intention. We just wanted to help catch the rotten bastards that killed two great men.

A captain of detectives announced that all off-duty personnel assemble on the corner and he pointed to the corner. Once assembled, a sergeant with a clipboard came and took our names, shield numbers, and command. Then we were paired off with a detective to do a canvass.

I had no clue what the heck a canvass was. The guy I was with had about fourteen years on the job, a sharp Italian guy named Joe Banetta. Banetta and I were assigned to go and knock on doors and see if anybody saw people running, or a car racing away, or anything out of the ordinary. The light bulb went on in my head. That's what a canvass is, I deduced.

Banetta and I went to an assigned block and started the canvass. Joe told me that he'd knock on doors and take statements, and I should look under cars for anything unusual, including a gun. I did as I was told, but added a twist. I started looking into the garbage cans in people's yards or by the curb. About three houses from Fifteenth Avenue on Forty-Eighth Street, I hit pay dirt. Using a stick to lift the lid on the metal can, I saw a hat, sunglasses, and a towel with what appeared to be blood on it. The description of one of the mutts was a white male, wearing sunglasses and a brown fedora-type hat. I whistled to Banetta who was across the street. He looked in the can and nodded, "Stay here, don't let anyone touch anything around here. You got it?" *What do you think, I'm stupid or something? Do you think I'd mess up a crime scene?* Oops, been there done that! What was I thinking? I just nodded.

About three minutes later, everyone and his brother was crowding around the garbage can. Finally, a detective came and carefully we lifted the can off the ground using tree twigs through the handles. Another detective placed a very large paper bag packing under the bottom, and they lowered the can into the opening while the guy with the bag unrolled it until the can was completely covered and sealed.

The bag was loaded into an unmarked car and whisked off to the police lab for examination. I saw a whole gaggle of cops, detectives, and brass all smacking Banetta on the back. It seems that Joey Baby forgot to mention that I was the one who discovered the items.

I wasn't sure how to feel. Was I angry, ticked off, hurt, disillusioned? The answer was, yes. Walking back to my car, I bumped into Frank Healey. I guess I looked like something was on my mind. "What's the matter with you, kid?" So I told him.

We buried the two brave detectives and the hunt was on for their killers. I learned the sequence of events that led up to the shootings. Finnegan and Fallon spotted the two guys going into the cigar place. Apparently, Mr. Fallon recognized them as local stick-up punks that he'd had previous dealings with.

The two detectives were in an unmarked taxicab doing a roving robbery patrol with special attention to commercial establishments. According to witnesses, the cab pulled to the curb and the two occupants just sat there focusing on the storefront.

Three witnesses heard a shot and saw the two detectives rush to the doorway. The older man was in the front with the younger man directly behind him. The witnesses saw them open the store door.

One of the clerks picks up the story from inside the store. One of the stick-up men was behind the counter facing the door. He saw the detectives, guns in hand, and yelled, "Luke, don't shoot, Luke," and he put his gun on the countertop. At that point, the second mutt comes out of an office to Fallon's left and fires a shot. Fallon falls, probably dead before he hit the floor.

The guy behind the counter picks up his gun and fires rounds in Finnegan, killing him. The two bastards bolt from the store and run in different directions. About that time, a late-model Pontiac peels away from a spot on New Utrecht Avenue.

Through great detective work and cooperation from legitimate citizens, as well as informers, three arrests were made, Rosenberg, DeLearnia, and Portelli. Rosenberg and Portelli were the shooters and DeLearnia was the get-away driver.

The garbage can contents were a help because Rosenberg's fingerprints were on the lid and also on the sunglasses. The towel with the red on it was red ink from the cigarette sales tax machine. Rosenberg used it to wipe his fingerprints off the safe in the manager's office.

This meant that Rosenberg couldn't deny being in the vicinity of the shootings and that would be a big plus in the prosecutor's case.

A few days later, I returned to work and saw a note on the chalkboard directing me to see the roll call man. I knocked on the wall of the open office and he looked up with a big smile on his face. "Come in, my friend, and sit down. I've got great news for you. You've been assigned a summer plainclothes detail in Coney Island. It's a great move. You've been personally selected." I made a mental note to thank Captain Walsh.

I was thrilled. A whole summer of chasing drug dealers, stick-up men, purse-snatchers. That was police work. It would be better than walking a post and fighting with every skell who objected to getting a parking ticket. Right? Wrong.

It seems that Captain Walsh had been on vacation and he didn't know about the assignment. Sergeant Joyce was also unaware. My good buddy, the roll call man, had assigned me on his own. The Division and Borough brass didn't care who was assigned. They just needed a body to fill the summer coverage in Coney Island.

Unbeknownst to many people, there was an investigation going on into possible corruption of big members of the Beach Plainclothes Detail. The duty of the men assigned was to stalk and summons peddlers. Yeah, I said peddlers. You know, the guys that trudge up and down the block selling knishes, soda, water, and ice cream to all the hungry and thirsty sunbathers. Oh yeah, I forgot, they also sold those big pretzels.

This was to be crime-fighting at its highest level. I surely would make detective if I gave the most tickets in the history of the "Beach Squad."

I guess this was the way the roll call man was getting back at me for having the audacity of wanting time off to get married. It turns out, he had a friend at Headquarters who tipped him off about the investigation. So, they say, payback is a, well, you know.

I honestly believed then, as I do now, that except for a few, (and I emphasize few), people in the police department, organized corruption is not a problem. Sure, you read every ten years or so about this unit or that unit being indicted or disbanded because of corruption. But, looking at the bigger picture, the majority of the men and women are clean. They do their job, take their meager city salary and take care of their families.

This is not to say that some individuals, or even groups of individuals, didn't band together and shake people down for money. They are the ones that the papers like to headline. They are the ones that give the black eye to the thousands of honest men and women who, daily, put their lives on the line and literally go unnoticed by the press and the public.

This was the focus of the Beach Squad investigation. It seems that in previous summers, allegations had been made that a regular schedule of payments had been set up to have the Beach Squad members look the other way to allow the beach peddlers to sell their wares unhindered.

Jennifer and I set up housekeeping in North Arlington, New Jersey. We bought a big old tank of a Pontiac from Aunt Rose. It had a push-button transmission. The damn thing was indestructible. There was only one problem: it was registered in New Jersey. Why, you ask. Because we didn't have a New York residence. That's why.

It was fun living with her mother, Georgie, and her sister Eileen. After the honeymoon, Jennifer returned to her secretarial job at an insurance company in Manhattan. On my days off, I'd drive her into work and sometimes, depending on traffic, even have breakfast with her. Life was almost the same as it was when we were dating except now we share the same bed.

We'd go to the movies or the Newark shopping or sometimes visit her sister Betty Ann and her husband, Rick. Oh, didn't I mention that they got married? Yes, they did, and they lived in a garden apartment complex right in North Arlington.

They already had one baby and she was expecting another. So we'd have dinner there or we'd babysit so Rick and Betty Ann could go to a movie or something. I really enjoyed those days. Georgie was always around on his days off and he'd have a new girl with him every couple of months. Eileen was now working for the FBI in the Newark office with my youngest sister, Virginia Ellen. Jack and Margaret were in the process of moving back to New Jersey. Jennifer's mom, Mrs. McDermott, was happy to be surrounded by all her family. Now, that included me.

I walked into the Six-O Precinct station house two days before Memorial Day 1962. I asked the desk officer where the Beach Squad could be found, and he nodded toward a door on the other side of the room. After I knocked, I opened the door and saw a very tiny room crammed with desks and men. The desks were typical city-issued, tin with some type of Formica top. A few others were wooden types, probably been there since the turn of the century. The room was windowless and smelled like the inside of an outhouse.

I looked around for a familiar face and spotted Bill Metcalf. Bill worked in the Six-Four Precinct and had worked with my brother Jackie, when he was assigned to the Six-Four. He crossed the room (that took about three steps) with his hand outstretched. He then started to introduce me to the rest of the squad. Some old-timers, some kids like me.

The door opened and a dark, heavyset man entered. Most of the guys in the room nodded or said hello. "For those of you that don't know me, I'm Charlie Arcuri. I'll be the squad sergeant for the summer. We are going to have one group but six teams. Some of you guys I know, others only by reputation." Did I imagine it, or was he looking at me? Did I imagine it, or was everyone looking at me? He continued, "You'll be divided into teams, two to a team. You will have, pretty much, free reign as to where you want to be. We have all of Coney Island, Brighton Beach, and Manhattan Beach. All you have to do is let me know who's going to cover each area."

"Listen to me, this isn't a vacation, but it isn't going to be hard either. You bang out summonses for park regs and then you patrol. Remember, we are still cops and writing up peddlers is just a very small part of this detail. We look for crime. We don't start incidents. [*Is he looking at me again?*] We prevent crime. All right, here's the assignments." He paired us off and I was paired with Metcalf. One of the other guys patted him on the shoulder and said, "I guess you got the short straw," and then he winked at me.

I was getting the feeling that some of these people thought I was a troublemaker. I didn't know what they had heard about me, but whatever it was, it couldn't have been all that good. I'd love to just set them straight. I'm one of the good guys.

We left the station house to take a tour of the Six-O Precinct. Metcalf drove. In those days, we used our own cars when you worked a plainclothes detail. Only the detectives had department autos. So we were tooling around Coney Island in a non-descript Chevy station wagon.

Bill had been in the detail the summer before, as was Charlie Higgins. The rest of us were newcomers from all different commands. He pulled into the parking lot at Manhattan Beach and showed his shield and was waved ahead. After parking, we found a bench and made ourselves comfortable.

I asked him a million questions. Well, maybe not a million, but I inquired about if I was right when I thought Sergeant Arcuri was eyeballing me when he gave his talk. Bill simply nodded yes. "Aw, come on, he doesn't even know me, and another thing, what did that guy mean that you got the short straw? What the hell does that mean?"

I really wished I hadn't asked him, but he told me that someone spread the word that I was too quick with my hands and that I ratted on a cop and got him transferred.

Collar by collar, I walked through every arrest where I had to use force. He sat and he listened. Once in a while, he'd nod his head, or other times, he'd make some kind of grunt noise. After I finished my soliloquy, he simply said that he would have done the same thing. That made me feel better.

"What about the cop thing?"

"Bill, I have no idea what that's about or how something like that got started." He then said that he had asked to be partners with me because of my brother John, (who the hell . . . oh yeah, Jackie.) So I shouldn't worry about the short straw remark. He told me he'd tell the other guys that I was okay and that someone was spreading bullshit. But he never answered that rat thing.

As we stared across the white sand at the ocean, he shifted and was almost in my lap. In a low voice he asked, "Do you take money?" "What?" I nearly yelled out loud.

"If a peddler wants to give you money because you didn't give him summonses for a week, would you take it?"

"Would you?"

"I asked you first."

"Well, I asked you second."

This was reminding me of two little boys in a schoolyard. "Did too, did not, did too." I looked him right in the eye and said, "No."

"Good, I wouldn't either. Now I don't have to worry about you if you're ever out of my sight." He got up and slapped me on the shoulder. "Let's go to work." And work, we did. We'd start at the Six-O station house at ten o'clock in the morning and the squad would fan out across Coney Island, Brighton, and Manhattan beaches. Clouds or shine, the peddlers would be out hawking their sodas, pretzels, knishes, and Yoo-Hoos. Some even had ice cream.

They were tricky devils. They'd have young kids in front of the station house to identify the Beach Squad members and the cars we were using. Then the kids would jump on their bikes and tell the peddlers. It was a kinda silly but amusing game. But sometimes it worked for them to know what we were wearing. Bill and I would bang out about five summonses each before lunch and prowl the boardwalk looking for any other violations of Park Department regulations. Although we were dressed in beach clothes, people seemed to know who we were.

For example, you'd see some bozo on a bike weaving in and out of the strollers on the boardwalk causing some people to jump out of the way, or some kid fall and get hurt. Usually, the bozo was a muscle head who didn't have a shirt on. Bingo, two summonses for the price of one bozo.

Bill and I would block his path and the conversation would go something like, "Hey, whatsamatta wit youse guys, I ain't doin' nuttin'."

"Let's see some ID."

"Ain't you got nuttin' better to do?"

"ID, please."

"I forgot my wallet at home."

Either Bill or I would produce our handcuffs and bozo would produce proper ID. It never failed. We'd escort him off the boardwalk and give him one summons for riding the bike and the other for no shirt. I think the no shirt rule came from the Puritans. I mean, you are at the beach and it's eighty degrees. Who wears a shirt at the beach? Well, that's what the people of the city of New York were paying us for, so that's what we did. My heart really wasn't in it. Yeah, I know the guy on the bike could hurt one of the strollers but, well, my heart wasn't in it. After about a week and a half of peddlers and topless muscle heads, I told Metcalf how I felt. He felt the same way. Daily, we'd go into the station house and check all the reports of crimes from the previous day.

Bill decided to check the locations where most of the crimes were reported from and then he'd catalogued the type. A lot were missing property taken from blankets left unattended while the owners were frolicking in the surf.

He broke the crimes into locations, times, description of suspects and amount of physical force used. With thousands and thousands of people using the beach daily, it was a piece of cake for the perps to just blend in with the other sun worshipers. This made ID almost impossible.

Under the boardwalk was a whole other world. You had your summer residents who actually lived under the boards. You had your perverts who would walk under the boards looking up through the cracks to see what women were wearing underwear and who wasn't. You had your young lovers who would put a blanket over them and go at it in the sand. They didn't care about the families coming from the street walking to the beach. The young mother was left to explain to her kids why that man and woman were jumping up and down under the blanket making all that noise.

We decided to concentrate in the area where most of the property was reported missing. What would happen was that people would ditch their street clothes on a blanket and already have their bathing suit on. Then, they'd spread the blanket, tune in their portable radio, sunscreen up, open their book and enjoy. When the dreaded peddler would show up, they'd buy their soda or whatever. They would, mostly, put their wallet and jewelry in one of their shoes under the blanket.

The young perps would zero in on likely prospects and just sit in the area and wait for them to leave the blankets unattended. Then they would cause a commotion by pushing and shoving one another, kicking sand around until one would fall, reach under the blanket, take the shoe and then casually dissolve into the sea of humanity.

Quick and easy score and nobody hurt. The only problem was that, according to Bill's plotting, five or six of these thefts took place all around the same time. And from the questions that the uniformed cops asked, from the sun lovers near the blankets, they all described three or four boys and girls in the rowdy group. The ages went anywhere from thirteen to nineteen years of age.

Now this Beach Squad business started getting interesting. The way Sergeant Arcuri had the schedule made out, every other Saturday and Sunday was our days off. Jennifer worked and I'd only see her when I got home to her mother's house. We'd eat, watch a little TV, and go to bed. Most mornings I'd drive her to work in Manhattan and then go to the Island of Coney for another fun-filled day in the sun catching felonious peddlers.

On weekends, she and I would walk all over town window shopping for furniture and things we'd need for our apartment. We we moved into the apartment in Stuyvesant Town in Manhattan. We had checked apartments in Brooklyn, but I just couldn't see leaving her in a strange neighborhood while I was out doing a four-to-twelve, or, worse yet, a midnight to 8:00 a.m. shift. I mean, it was bad enough taking her from the bucolic setting of North Arlington and then leaving her, as I said, in a strange neighborhood.

Big Jim, again, through his connections, got us bumped up on the list for a one-bedroom apartment. Stuyvesant Town was owned and operated by Metropolitan Life Insurance Company. It was a huge apartment house complex that went from First Avenue to Avenue C and from East Fourteenth Street to Twenty-Third Street. Also included was Peter Cooper Village.

Peter Cooper Village was more exclusive than "Stuy" Town, allegedly. Personally, I couldn't see any difference. Both complexes had parks and walking paths, benches, kiddie areas, and just well-kept facilities. So, we put money down at Mr. Bill Mace's furniture store on Ridge Road in North Arlington. Every payday, Jennifer and I would go to the store and give Mr. Mace money to pay down the bill. We'd stop and have pizza or she'd go to Newark with her mother and sisters or her Aunt Rose. I think that's where the expression "Shop til you drop" came from.

I never knew you needed so much stuff to furnish a small kitchen, dining area, living room and bedroom. Jennifer had gotten a lot of household stuff during the bridal shower, but you can never have enough of, oh, say, napkin holders, eggtimers, spatulas, towels. I swear. Where the heck are we gonna put all this stuff?

Her mother and Aunt Rose told us to pick out a bedroom set and they'd buy it for us. I said no. Her mother couldn't afford it and Aunt Rose was a widow who was still working. I didn't think it was fair to them. They protested. I protested. Then they protested. This went back and forth, so Jennifer and I decided we'd tell them the one we wanted was half the price that it really was. So, we let them pay. They were happy and I was satisfied that we weren't taking advantage of them.

Meanwhile, back on the Island of Coney, Metcalf and I were doing our thing. We'd get peddler summonses, but we also were making collars for guns, drugs, and people who were throwing fireworks at other people just trying to enjoy the beach. All the while, we kept an eye on the missing property reports to come up with a pattern.

We'd stand at the rail on the boardwalk with mini binoculars just trying to see who would be a likely victim and who would be possible perps. Bill had narrowed down the area where most of the thefts were taking place to a section called Bay 13.

Then one day we hit pay dirt. I was focusing on the beach and Bill was scanning the entranceway from under the boardwalk. Just as the reports indicated, three separate groups came from under the boards. Bill nudged me and pointed. They meandered toward the water and then squatted on the sand. We kept the groups under watch as we walked toward the stairs leading to the beach.

In the blink of an eye, the groups started playing grab-ass and spinning all around three different areas, but close to one another. The beach crowds were distracted and didn't see the snatch. Three young kids casually walked toward the boardwalk, each with towels under their arms. Wrapped in the towels were the shoes of the unsuspecting victims.

I went under the boards at the foot of the stairs and Bill continued about twenty yards further where he ducked under the boards. We both took up spots behind the concrete support pillars holding up the boards.

The three went to a wall and were met by two guys about eighteen or nineteen years old. The decoy group filtered under the boards and gathered around their pals. There were fourteen of them and two of us in a secluded area under the boards. Now, you have to realize that we didn't have any walkie-talkies, cell phones, or any other means of communication to call for help. The nearest Police Call Box was about one hundred yards from us up on the boardwalk.

The youngsters were unwrapping the towels and looking at the two older guys as a puppy looks at its master. The two older men were scowling and posturing. I looked at Bill and nodded. We got about four feet from them, and one of the snot-nose teeny-boppers yelled out, "Cops!" The group turned as one to face us. I pulled out my gun and Bill pulled out his." Face the wall, on your knees." Most complied, but one of the older ones sneered and started to casually walk away. As he tried to pass by me, I kicked him right in the nuts. Down he went, trying to catch his breath. "Get up, bozo, and get with the rest of them." He crawled over and went face down in the sand.

I turned to Bill. "Give me your gun. I'll hold them here and you call the cavalry." So, there I am, two-gun Dan, with fourteen young mutts on their knees or on their stomachs. The second older guy started mouthing off and was giving the younger ones ideas about splitting.

"Anyone moves and you're gonna get shot." I told him to shut his mouth or he'd be the first one. "You ain't got the balls to shoot!" So I did.

Jennifer, Georgie, Eileen, the mother, and I were walking out from Our Lady Queens of Peace on Ridge Road when I suddenly felt like a louse. Everybody was saying hello to them and some even said hello to me. I felt like why should I take her away from this beautiful, friendly town and plop her in an apartment in Manhattan? Did I have that right?

I loved being a cop in New York. It was exciting and fulfilling (excluding hassling the peddlers.) Georgie must have sensed something. "What's the matter, Tip? You look like you've got something on your mind."

"No, I'm all right."

"Come on, kid, don't lie to me."

We went out in the backyard and cracked open a couple of cans of beer. Georgie was filling the cinderblock barbecue pit with charcoal. Betty Ann and Rick were coming over with their kids and we were gonna cook up some steaks and drink some beer and listen to the Yankees.

"I don't know if I'm being fair to Jennifer, taking her away from here," I blurted to Georgie.

"Whadda you mean? She's looking forward to New York. You two deserve to have a place of your own. You like what you do. As a matter of fact, I know you love what you do. Listen, I only know you about three years, but I consider you one of my best friends. I am telling you that she'll be happier in her own place. I know, because she told me so. Manhattan is, what, a half hour from here? Give me a break. It's not the moon you're moving to. Trust me. I wouldn't lie." I nodded, lit up a cigar, and handed him a beer. Bill Burke came into his yard and I threw him a beer and the opener. "Dan's got second thoughts about leaving North Arlington, Bill, talk to him."

I walked over to the fence, and Bill and I talked while Georgie put on burgers and dogs just as Betty Ann and Rick and the kids came up the alleyway and into the yard. The kids ate first, then the steaks went on and the yard filled up, and I kinda snapped out of my funk.

That night in bed in Grandpa's room, I told Jennifer how I felt. She listened, and then held me and whispered that she understood that because of the Police Department rules, I had to live in the city and she didn't care. She said she'd go anywhere with me. I think I slept all night with a smile on my face.

The shot scared the hell out of all of my prisoners. "Now, the next one goes into you, bozo. Face the wall and get on your knees and shut up." He did.

Metcalf came running back and I handed him his gun. I could hear the sirens getting closer. So with Bill covering them, I cuffed the two older ones together. One cuff on one and one on the other. I think the loud mouth soiled his shorts because he stunk. The wagon came and after we searched them—well, not the teeny boppers, since they couldn't have hidden anything if they tried—we cuffed them and put them in the wagon and took them to the station house.

We recovered a bunch of jewelry, about four transistor radios, about ten wallets, and over a thousand dollars cash from Bozo squashed nuts and Bozo dirty drawers. The detectives took over questioning the group while Bill and I filled out the arrest cards and the juvenile forms. Three of the fourteen were under sixteen, so they would be released to their parents to appear at a future date in Family Court.

It turned out that the bozos were brothers, one nineteen and one eighteen. The Brunti boys. The detectives got one kid to give up the deal. The Brunti would send the younger ones out to make the grab and they'd get, depending on the take, five dollars a head for the distraction team and ten dollars for the ones who actually snatched the shoe or the purse or whatever the valuables were hidden in.

The Bozo Brunti brothers called home, and their big sister came charging into the station house all indignant and huffy like we were the bad guys. She was about twenty-four and had a mouth on her like a Marine Corps drill instructor. Brother Bozo two whispered to her that I tried to kill him. He said that I shot at him. She threw a fit.

Along about this time, all the others joined in saying I shot at them. Captain Ray McDermott (no relation to Jennifer) came into the house, along with our boss, Charlie Arcuri. McDermott looked at me and asked for my gun. I opened the cylinder and presented the weapon in the prescribed PD manner.

McDermott dumped the cartridges into his hand and counted five rounds. He smelled the barrel of the snub-nose thirty-eight. He called big sister Brunti into his office. "Smell this." She sniffed the barrel of the gun the captain was holding. "I don't smell anything."

"Exactly. If it was recently fired, you would smell gunpowder." Contritely, she asked, "Do you think they are lying?"

"Yes," was the captain's reply.

Bill and I followed the patrol wagon downtown to photo and court. I was driving and I reached into my pocket, handed him a bullet. He took out his thirty-eight, opened the cylinder, removed the empty cartridge, and placed the new round in the cylinder. I pulled over to the curb right by a storm sewer grate. He opened the door and dropped the shell into the river.

We processed the gang and then had them in the courtroom waiting for the case to be arraigned. Bill looked over at me and smiled. "You know, that was a pretty neat trick using my gun. But what would you have told the captain if he asked if you had a second gun?"

"I don't know." I really didn't think he cared. We made a great collar and closed out a lot of cases. He looks good and we look good."

"All the same, it was a good idea." Being very modest, I said, "Yeah, I know."

Work was really getting to be interesting. The whole squad was getting into the act. Collars were being made for everything and anything. Previously, the Beach Squad just gave out summonses for peddler violations. Now, besides the peddlers and other park regulation summonses, the guys were actively looking for crimes.

The boardwalk stand vendors would tell us what was going on on the boardwalk. The concession owners under the boards were doing the same. Bill and I even cultivated some of the peddlers for information. Every day at the beach was a new adventure

Then, one Sunday morning, I was making a ring to the station house just to let them know we were alive and in the area we were supposed to be. The way the call box worked was that each post for the foot men had a call box on a pole, and when you picked up the receiver, it rang to a switchboard complete with the plug-in wires.

"Six-O Precinct."

"Yeah, this is Stark and Metcalf Beach Squad. We're just making a ring."

"Hold on, the Sarge wants to talk to you."

"Yeah, who's this?"

"Officer Stark, Sarge. I'm with Metcalf."

"Where are you?" "On the boards by the Half Moon Hotel, Box 34."

"Yeah, yeah . . . hold on, Stark." So I stood there holding the receiver listening to the background noise of the station house. I could hear voices that seemed to be raised. I could hear the station house base radio and all the other noises. "Yeah, Stark, you still there?"

"Yes, sir."

"Good. You and your partner come into the house forthwith." Then he whispered, "Make sure your books are up-to-date." Then I heard a click.

I told Bill the conversation as we walked toward my car on Surf Avenue. He didn't comment, but he took out his memo book and started to write. I did the same.

The memo book is carried by everyone on patrol in the PD. You record all your activity with the time, location and results. At the end of the day, you sign off with the words "nothing to report," and sign your name and shield number.

Nothing to report. What the hell does that mean? I had stuff to report. That is why I wrote all this crap before signing off. I thought it should say "Nothing further to report." "I could have found out who killed the Lindbergh baby or who snatched Judge Crater, or for that matter, who really helped the gangster/witness, Abe Rellis, out the window of the Half Moon Hotel from the seventh floor front. I'd put all that in the memo book and still have to write "Nothing to report."It didn't make sense.

I stopped my car near the station house and parked. "Look at those cars over there, Bill. Something's up." They were all new black vehicles and clean. No seagull poop on the roof or hood. Bill looked and nodded. There were a couple of guys in suits lounging around a car with more antennae than a spy ship.

We nodded to them, but they didn't acknowledge us. "They got to be from Headquarters," was all Bill said. We walked into the house, and as we approached the desk officer, some guy with sandals, khaki pants, a loud Hawaiian shirt, bald head, and an obnoxious face, approached us. "Who are you two?" he asked. I ignored him and tried to walk around him. He grabbed my arm. "I asked who you were."

"Mister, if you don't take your hand off me, I'm gonna break your big nose." I pulled from his grip and approached the desk Sarge. "Officer Stark, Sarge, what's up?"

"Go into the sitting room. Most of the guys are there."

I walked past the big nose, baldy guy, and he was giving me the murder one look. I smiled and kept on walking. Most of the Beach Squad were assembled in the sitting room just talking and speculating as to what was going on. Finally, Ed Carey and Bob Sprague, the last two squad members, arrived.

Captain McDermott, Sergeant Arcuri, and the guy with the big nose came into the sitting room. "Everyone, give the Sarge your memo book and stand by." Big nose didn't say a word, but just stared at me. After the books were collected, McDermott and company left. I asked Bill who the big nose was, and Charlie Higgins said, "That's Sidney Cooper from the PCCIU. He's an inspector."

"First of all, how was I supposed to know, and secondly, what the hell was the PCCIU?" Charlie continued, "I forget you're still a rookie. The PCCIU is the Police Commissioner Confidential Investigating Unit. They handle all the sensitive investigations in the job as well as corruption allegations. Somebody must think that the peddlers are paying us off. Joey Giacalone said that he heard something about an investigation last summer, but it didn't go anywhere."

Higgins, Carey, Sprague, and most of the others started to speculate about what that had to do with us. Finally Bill said, "You know, for years I wanted to get into this detail just to get out of uniform for the summer, but you needed a hook or a phone call to get it. I mean, for years.

The guys on the detail all had fathers or uncles or a neighbor who was a big boss in the job. Now, this year, almost everyone here is new. No hooks. We were just told that we were assigned. Don't you guys think it's a little strange? I mean, I'm not saying the guys in the past took any money, but even if there was an allegation, it wouldn't look good on the record of some chief's son that he'd been the subject of a corruption allegation."

"So what do the bosses care about us? We don't have any hooks. They put a whole new crew here for the summer. They do their Mickey Mouse investigation, maybe get a few of us for improper memo book entries and give us a complaint. Maybe we lose a few vacation days or a couple of days pay. The investigation is closed with results and the relatives or friends of the brass aren't involved. Goddamn! These people in Headquarters take care of their own."

Well, we didn't have long to wait. The captain and Sarge came back into the sitting room and we all went silent. McDermott gave us the scoop on the investigation. It turned out that Bill was right on the money. The allegation had been made that the Beach Squad members were taking weekly payments from the peddlers to cut back on the amount of tickets they would hand out weekly.

McDermott told us that we all had to report to police Headquarters on Monday. He told us to expect to be there the entire day or more. Expect to sit in a hallway and periodically have someone walk past us with a boss or two. The unknown someone would look us up and down and then nod his or her head and, loud enough for us to hear, the unknown person would say, "Yeah, that is him!"

"Don't let this bother you. It's all bullshit. That is the way Cooper plays the game. By the way, Stark, I guess you know now who inspector Sidney Cooper is." He laughed a little. I started to say something and he held up his hand, "I know, I saw the whole thing. He never told you who he was and he never showed you his shield. I told him that in my office, but he said, 'Even if he was a private citizen, you shouldn't have called him big nose and threatened to punch him.' I told him that a private citizen is fair game for anything that happens when he grabs someone's arm for no apparent reason. Don't worry about him. He's full of . . . never mind. If anyone wants to have a beer with me, I'll be at the Atlantic on the boardwalk in about half an hour. If you don't, just take the rest of the day off on me. I just ask one favor for tomorrow. Dress appropriately. You know, like what they call business attire. Thanks, fellas. I have full confidence in all of you so I know no one is going to be arrested for taking money. Those of you that want to, let's get a beer."

The whole squad sat in the back of the Atlantic out of the blinding sun and heat. The back room had an air-conditioner, circa 1928, but there were cross-breezes through the windows and the ceiling fans moved the air around. But the beer was cold and the captain was very generous with the buying.

After a few rounds, I went over to Sergeant Arcuri. "Sarge, the first day I met you, there was a remark made about me being some type of rat. Bill said that I had ratted out some detective for something. I want to clear the air. I have no idea what that was all about. Can you tell me?"

He looked me in the eye and then picked up the beer pitcher and topped off our mugs. "Look, kid, I wasn't there, but this is what I heard. When Finnegan and Fallon were shot, you went to the captain in charge of the detectives and told him that one of his men was a liar and didn't find some crucial evidence but it was you that found it. So the captain, Al Siedman's his name, checked a bit and confronted the detective. He didn't like the answers he got, so he transferred him to steady nights out of the squad. That's all I heard about you except that you are fast with your hands, or, more recently, your feet. Now, that's all I heard. You wanna know what I think?" I nodded and he continued. "I think I don't know you yet. But by the end of the summer, I guess I'll have an opinion. Now, it's your turn to talk if you want."

I told him about the canvass and told him about how I felt Banetta had screwed me, or, more to the point, had disillusioned me. I told him that I didn't know that the guy with Frank Healey was a boss. I just thought he was another detective. I told him that if I even thought he was a boss, I never would have told Healey.

He passed more beer, took a long swallow, wiped his mouth with the back of his hand. "Banetta? You mean Joe Banetta? He's a snake. If he thought it would help him, he'd lock up his own mother. Don't worry, kid, I'll spread the word. The rumor will stop right now."

True to his word, he went around to every one of the squad members and told them my side of the story. I just sat there, alone, at the table, smoking my cigar and drinking the captain's beer.

After awhile, one by one, the group started coming over. Some knew Banetta and some had heard about him. The consensus was that he had screwed me. I tried to explain that I wasn't looking to get ahead using the death of two great men, but I felt disappointed that Banetta was using their murders for his own purposes. I couldn't explain how I felt or even what I meant. It sounded sophomoric to say I was I disillusioned or hurt, but that was the way I felt.

The social broke up and we all went our different ways, each of us thinking about tomorrow.

I went back to North Arlington with my head swimming. I couldn't believe the job would try to whitewash a corrupt investigation that was supposed to have been conducted a year ago.

If Bill was right, we were sacrificial lambs. We were to be scrutinized by the PCCIU to cover possible wrong-doing by cops that had big connections in the PD.

Jennifer had a great meal waiting for me, but I really didn't feel like eating. I did eat, though, and felt better. She wanted to go up to Ridge Road to see a movie. So we did. I forget what it was, but she liked it and that made me feel much better. The morning came, and I drove her into work and she chatted all the way into the city. I had on a nice summer suit, and she said, "I guess you are going to court today. You look really nice." I just smiled and changed the subject.

After I dropped her off, I found a parking spot on Baxter Street off Grand Street and walked back to Headquarters. I was early, so I stood outside just thinking about what the heck was going to happen to me. Suddenly, I realized that only one year had passed since I bounced up the stairs with my new driver's license in hand. It was June 29, 1962, one year to the day. Boy, a hell of a lot had happened in one year. Up until today, it was all good.

Bill, Charlie, Eddie, Sergeant Arcuri, and the others all came and we entered the building. I stopped and patted the lion, still standing guard on the steps. Sergeant Arcuri asked, "What's that for?" I smiled and just said, "Just for luck." Then I sent a plea to St. Michael.

We were all seated in a corridor on long church-like benches. We sat and sat and sat. Every once in a while, a door would open and somebody would peek out, shake his head up and down, and the door would close.

This silly exercise went on and we all sat there just looking at each other not saying anything. About four o'clock, some guy in a suit came out and announced, "You're dismissed for today. Be here tomorrow morning at eight." He turned on his heel and disappeared into one of the offices.

We stood outside not saying anything until Charlie Arcuri suggested we all stop for a beer. He didn't think it was a good idea to go to a bar near Headquarters, so he suggested a place on Mulberry Street behind the Criminal Courts building called Giambone's.

I drove Bill down to the bar and parked. It was a small but homey place. You know the type. A little bar, about fifteen tables, of course, with the red-and-white tablecloths and a huge sailfish on the wall. Sinatra music came from the jukebox and the smell of Italian food just hung in the air.

I liked this place immediately. I figured that when Jennifer and I moved into Sty Town, we could walk to it and have dinner from time to time.

Sergeant Arcuri bought the first pitcher and we ordered some bar pizza squares. In a hushed tone, Arcuri told us that the investigation was all BS. Captain McDermott has the utmost confidence in our integrity and that we shouldn't be fooled by the doors opening or the faces looking out at us. McDermott did his own investigation and we all came up clean.

That was the good news. The bad news was that they, meaning the PCCIU, would be looking for any minor infractions they could find and then they'd bring charges against us. They, meaning the PCCIU, would close out the investigation with results.

We all began to grumble and he held up his big hand. "That's the way it works. You're all over twenty-one. You're not kids. So take what comes like men. Hell, they might even give me a complaint. You know, it's tough being the boss of a bunch of crooks." The last remark got a laugh. So we finished the beer and we all went home.

"So how was court?" I smiled and said that I had to go back tomorrow. "I'll press a shirt for you." "Thanks, that would be nice."

The next day was the same and so was the following. But then, on the fourth day, things got better. I saw this little man walking down the corridor pushing a shopping cart. It was filled with belts, socks, shoes, pants, razor blades, flashlights, batteries, etcetera. He stopped at every office door, opened it, yelled in, "I'm here, come and get it." And the suits appeared and made their purchases. He worked his way up to us. "So whaddaya need?" We all looked at each other with one thought. A felonious peddler right in the bowels of PCCIU. Sergeant Arcuri looked at me and must have read my mind. He slowly shook his head from side to side. I got off the bench and went over to the cart. "So whaddaya want?"

"I want to see your peddler's license."

"What license? I don't have a license. I don't need one. I got special permission from Mr. Cooper."

Arcuri was still shaking his head, but a smile was creeping across his broad face. "May I see some identification, please, sir?"

"What? What for?"

"Some ID, please, sir," and I put my hand out. He produced his driver's license and I wrote him a summons for peddling without a license. After he took the summons and I gave him back his license, I took my seat on the bench and continued to read.

The little peddler went straight into Cooper's office. No knock. No, "may I please come in." Nothing. He just barreled in like he owned the place. He was livid. You could probably hear him yelling on Coney Island.

About twenty minutes later, some suit appeared and, after clearing his throat, announced that we should, "Return to your commands."

That was it! No big apology or fanfare. No nothing. Just a "Return to your commands." So we did.

Captain McDermott greeted us at the front door of the house. "Hey, kid, are you nuts? Are you on drugs? Do you have another job I don't know about?" I simply said that I was tired of sitting there, tired of reading, and besides, my tan was starting to fade. He and everyone else laughed, and McDermott said we could either go home, or seeing as it was lunch time, he'd buy at the Atlantic. We all went to the Atlantic and then went home.

The next day we all went back to work and resumed doing what the people of the city of New York wanted us to do. We gave peddler's summonses. Oh yeah, the squad also made some great robbery, drug, and assault arrests too. Big Jim called Jennifer at work and told her that we'd be getting our apartment in the first week of August. She was thrilled. I was happy, but I still didn't want to take her from North Arlington. But rules were rules, and we both knew that we'd have to live in one of the five boroughs of New York City. I told her we'd spend at much time as she wanted in NA. But, again, she smiled and just said she'd be fine in Manhattan. What a girl!

The department chaplain, Monsignor Joe Dunne, addressed our recruit class at the academy. During his talk about ethics and morality, he said, addressing the single guys, "Remember, in the garden of love, don't pick a lemon." I picked a peach!

I was still driving the car we bought from Jennifer's Aunt Rose back and forth from North Arlington. The car didn't have N.Y. plates because we really didn't have an address in New York yet. When we got married, I just left all the records with my brother, Jackie's, address. I mean, I couldn't very well tell the department., "Well, it's only temporary that I'm going to live in Jersey.

You know, just until we get the apartment in Stuyvesant Town. I'm sure you understand."

No, that's not the way of the job. So I tried every night after work to take a different route to the Holland Tunnel just in case someone noticed the Jersey plates on the car and decided to tell the PCCIU. Paranoid? Who, me?

One night, in the beginning of July, I swore I was being followed. It was more a feeling than a visual thing. I stopped at a phone booth and called my sister-in-law, Muriel. I asked her if I could stay the night. I filled her in on my suspicions, and, being a cop's wife, she understood.

I walked around the corner from the phone booth and went into the candy store. I checked everyone outside on the street while, ostensibly, buying cigars. There they were! One on foot and one in a car, just sticking out far enough to keep an eye on his partner and on the store.

There was a phone booth in the store so I called Jennifer at work. I told her what I thought was going on and why. I told her that this was probably in retaliation for the summons at Headquarters. (I had told her about the investigation after we went back to work.) I told her I was going to spend the night at Jackie's just to be on the safe side.

The guy on foot was trying to be inconspicuous while just standing in front of the candy store. I mean, who wears a suit in July, two blocks from Coney Island Beach, unless you're a cop? Not just a cop, but a Headquarters cop. Gimme a break.

I saw that the back door of the store was open to let the ocean breeze flow through the store. The rear yard was closed by a Cyclone fence that had a space big enough for me to squeeze through. I paid for the cigars, squeezed through the fence, walked down the block to the avenue and approached the suit still standing in front of the store. Putting a fresh cigar in my mouth, I went up to the suit and tapped him on the shoulder." Excuse me, pal, but do you have a match?"

I wouldn't say he was startled, but that's a kind way of describing the way he looked. He fumbled for the matches and told me to keep them. He walked away from me, but the guy in the car on the avenue stayed just watching.

Hey, what the hell? If you're gonna be a wise guy, why not go all the way? I went back into the candy store, called Muriel, called Jennifer and told them both to disregard my previous calls as I was going to go to North Arlington.

I looked out the window and saw the two totally confused suits sitting in the car looking like maybe I was twins or something. They were in a very animated discussion with each other and the passenger was on the radio talking to his dispatcher or his office directly.

I repeated the drill by going out the back door through the fence to the car. Instead of crossing in front of them onto the avenue, I made a U-turn and took off for North Arlington. I watched for another car, but didn't see any tail. Home I went.

I wasn't too worried about them finding out about Park Avenue 'cause that didn't show on my PD records. I wasn't worried about Aunt Rose telling the cops where the car was 'cause she wasn't home, she was in the Catskills with her sister. Plus, the car was registered to Rose Flad in Iselin, New Jersey. Iselin was about thirty miles south of North Arlington.

I was off the weekend so I was lounging in bed when Jennifer called from downstairs. "Your brother, Jackie, is on the phone." I threw on a robe and bounded down the stairs. "What's up?"

"Two suits were here looking for you."

"Really? What did they want?"

"You."

"Well, what'd you tell them?"

"That you weren't here. That I thought you and Jennifer went down to the shore for the weekend. I asked them what it was all about. You know what they said? They said it was police business. I told them that I was a detective and I wanted to know what they wanted. I have a department car right in front of the house and they didn't even make it. Two sharp guys. Who did you piss off?"

I gave him the Reader's Digest version of the past goings-on and he grunted. He continued. "Well, after I told him I was on the job, they asked me, just between you and me, where does he live? So I told them."

Now, you have to know Jackie. He's the kinda guy that would make the spitballs and get somebody else to throw them, if you know what I mean.

"What? What? Where did you tell them?" "I told them the truth. I mean, I'm not going to risk my job and my security and my family for the likes of you." This was followed by silence on both parts. "Aw, come on, Jackie, what did you tell them?"

"I told them the truth, that you and Jennifer lived here. What did you think I told them? You always have to tell the downtown suits the truth." And he hung up.

July 4 was a scorcher. Bill and I were up and under the boards just looking for anything that was amiss. I gave out a few peddler summonses, as did Bill. Man, it was hot. He and I were looking out onto the beach from the boards. There was wall-to-wall people. I mean, not a space to even put a towel down.

We heard what sounded like shots coming from the beach. Straining to see where they came from, we saw two cops in uniform heading out from under the boards. They made their way between the beachers and were in the process of grabbing some mutt when they got surrounded.

Metcalf ran to the call box on the pole by the steps and I vaulted the rail onto the beach in a dead run. Bill did the same and was right on my heels. The battle was on. It wasn't gunfire, but fireworks being thrown around by some of our citizens from the commonwealth. The two uniformed men were trying to fend off the horde while holding onto two buff half naked savages.

We reached the two cops and proceeded to join in the fray. Not having a command of their language, I just assumed they thought my name was "Marty Cohen." Well, for what seemed like an hour, we were kicking and punching and dodging bottles, all the while trying to take the two firework clowns off the beach.

In reality, it was about three minutes when we heard the clatter of hooves on the cobblestone street. That, coupled with the sound of sirens in the background, gave me new-found strength.

The Mounties came onto the beach at full gallop. I had one clown and Bill had the other. We cuffed them to an overflowing wire litter basket and got back in action. One of the uniformed guys had gotten smashed in the head with a bottle and was down on one knee holding his head to stop the blood. Bill leaned over him, protecting him with his own body.

Seeing as I was in civilian clothes (get this, Bermuda shorts, Marine Corps T-shirt, and a black Robin Hood hat with a long feather, with "I am with the Mafia" emblazoned on the front), I went back to back with the other uniformed cop.

The Mounties came out from under the boards, and in an equestrian type of ballet, just kept circling us, pushing the crowd away from Bill, the injured cop and the trash can twins, the other cop and me. One jackass tried to stab one of their horses with a broken quart beer bottle. Man, it was beautiful! The Mountie hit this guy with a shot with his nightstick and he folded like an empty sack, landing right on the jagged edge of the bottle. Talk about justice!

Finally, we got off the beach and threw the mutts into the back of a radio car. Another car took the injured cop, red lights and sirens, to Coney Island Hospital. Order was restored and we headed into the station house to do the paperwork. Paper, paper, and more paper. About four o'clock, we finished and were summoned into the captain's office. "Sit," and he motioned to the wooden chairs in front of his desk.

He opened one of the desk drawers and tossed a can of Rheingold to Bill and then one to me. He opened his and then threw the church key to open ours. "You guys did great out there today. I really mean that. I went up to the boards and talked to witnesses. I'm really glad you two are working here."

Bill and I looked at each other and grinned. You really don't get a precinct commander giving you such high praise very often. "How's the cop that got hit?" I asked. "He took twelve stitches, but besides a headache, he'll be fine. The medics are gonna keep him overnight, but it looks like he'll be okay." Together, Bill and I said, "Thank God." McDermott smiled and continued, "Yeah, thank God and you two."

After another round of beers, we shook hands with the captain and signed off duty. "Well, whaddaya say, Dan, you wanna have a few more?" He didn't have to twist my arm.

August was finally approaching and Jennifer was arranging our move. I was off the weekend, so I suggested we take a ride into Manhattan to see our new neighborhood. We knew the address and the apartment number, so we went. We were right on the corner of Avenue C and East Fourteenth Street. I drove all through the complex, watching older people and young parents watching their kids play in the numerous play areas dotted all around Stuyvesant Town.

The area of south of Fourteenth Street wasn't all that attractive, but it was a slice of "Old New York." Tenement walk-up buildings had some old Irish, Polish, and Italian families but with a majority of the "new" immigrants from Puerto Rico and South America rapidly taking over the area.

After a few hours, we were hungry. So I drove down to Giambone's Bar and Restaurant. We went in and Jennifer immediately liked it. I hadn't told her I'd been there previously 'cause I didn't want to color her impression of the place. She really liked it on her own.

We sat at the table by the front window and watched all the parents in the park across the way watching their kids on the swings, in the spray pool, and climbing the monkey bars. They weren't much different than the kids we saw in Stuyvesant Town except the majority were Asians.

At one time, Giambone's was considered to be in "Little Italy," but the influx of Asian immigrants was shrinking "Little Italy" and enlarging "Chinatown."

Jennifer looked at the young mothers and just smiled. She had the same look on her face as she did while walking around Sty Town. I reached across the checkered tablecloth and held her hand. "Someday we'll be doing that." I gestured to a couple pushing a little kid on a swing. She smiled and nodded.

August 1 came and we were excited. I still felt like a louse for taking her away from her mother, sisters, and brother. It didn't seem to bother her. She was full of enthusiasm. Her brother, Georgie, took the day off and helped us load all of our clothes into his car and our car. Betty Ann and Eileen, her mother, Aunt Rose, and my sisters Kathleen and Cele went over to the apartment first thing in the morning. My brothers Jackie and Jimmy met Georgie and me and helped us carry everything into the apartment.

When we got there, the bedroom furniture delivery guys had just left. Jimmy and Georgie set about putting the bed together. Jackie and I lugged a big TV set out of Aunt Rose's car and into the elevator. Aunt Rose had generously given us the set. It was a beautiful piece of furniture, but it looked lost in the living room. We had the bedroom set, the dining room table with four chairs, and a rocking chair for the living room. No couch. The place looked empty.

The ladies put curtains up and fixed up the tiny kitchen, putting the towels in the proper drawers and silverware in others, the shower curtain in the bathroom, and the cloth on the table in the little dining area.

About five o'clock, everyone was leaving, so I asked Jennifer what we were going to eat for dinner. She looked at me and shrugged. "I forgot to get any food!"

"I'll go to the deli on the corner and get us two sandwiches and some potato salad," I volunteered. She just smiled, took me by the hand, and walked me into the small kitchen. She opened the cabinets, which were chock-full of cans and boxes. She opened the refrigerator, which was chock-full of food. She opened the oven and showed me a pan of baked ziti. "All I have to do is heat it up and we'll eat." I gave her a kiss on the cheek and told her I had to go out and get something. She looked puzzled but didn't ask. On Fourteenth Street, across from the apartment, there was a liquor store halfway up the block. I went and bought a bottle of red wine. You know the type, wrapped in straw. Anyway, I was back in our sixth-floor home in less than ten minutes.

I helped her set the table, and while she dished out the ziti, I opened the wine. "To the future," I said, as I touched her glass with mine. She nodded and repeated, "To the future, whatever it brings."

The next day, Sunday, we went to Mass in a little church off Avenue C and East Eleventh Street; it was called St. Emerick's. After Mass, we walked all over the area. There were antique stores that we browsed in and didn't buy anything. We stopped and had lunch in a greasy spoon diner on Avenue B and East Houston Street, walked and talked. Talked and walked. Finally, we found ourselves in front of Giambone's. We ate and talked while splitting a bottle of red wine. I tell you, I had a good time. At long about eight, I hailed a cab and we went "home." The next morning, I dropped Jennifer off at the insurance firm she worked at and headed to Brooklyn and the Island of Coney.

Bill and I paired up and he spotted a car following us. I was driving and I saw it too in the rear-view mirror. Yeah, it was the suits. I made a quick left down a one-way street and we lost them. I headed back to the station house where I parked my car a couple of blocks away.

Once in Bill's car, I asked him to take me to the Department of Motor Vehicles. I headed out and found a worker who understood that I needed to register the car in New York and I needed to do it in a hurry. I gave the guy a thumbnail of why I believed the suits wanted to bring me up on charges for driving a Jersey registered car. He had two brothers on the job and he knew what I was talking about.

He rushed the paperwork and back-dated it to the previous Friday. I got the plates and we went back to my car and switched the Jersey plates for the New York ones.

(This might sound a little silly to you, but once you step on the toes of the PCCIU, they go out of their way to get you, and that's the truth.) Leaving Bill's car a few blocks away, we drove back to the station house and parked. I went up the stairs to the second-floor clerical office. Again, I lucked out. The clerical man was a buddy of the cop that got hit with the bottle. So when I asked him to back-date the change of address forms, he didn't hesitate.

I filled out this form, that form, the other form, and then the other, other form. They were sent to the personnel section that morning with a note explaining that they should have gone to Headquarters on Friday. So sorry.

Now that I had all the bases covered, Bill and I proceeded to take a bite out of crime. We gave five summonses each. What a day. About five-thirty, we parked and went into the Six-O to sign out. Oh boy. There were two suits waiting in the captain's office. "Where's your auto, Officer?"

"Who are you?" I politely asked.

"Who am I? I'll tell you who I am. I'm . . . are you purposely trying to be a wise guy or are you just stupid?"

"No, I'm not stupid, but I have a right to know who I'm talking to and I don't think I am being a wise guy."(Actually, I was but I wasn't gonna admit it.)

"I'm Lieutenant . . ." (I don't know what he said.) "And this is Sergeant . . ." (I don't care who he said.) "We're from the PCCIU."

"Hi. My car is right outside." I looked to Captain McDermott and said, "Can I ask what this is all about, sir?"

"Yeah, Dan. They seem to believe that you live in Jersey and are driving a car with Jersey plates. Do you, and are you?"

"No, sir, I don't and I'm not. I moved from Brooklyn to Manhattan on Saturday and my car has New York plates."

McDermott looked at me and gave an imperceptible nod of his head. Lieutenant suit glared at me. "Let's see the car and the registration." While we were walking out, I handed him the reg and showed him the car. Grunting, he handed me back the reg. "Were you driving this car this morning?"

"Yes, sir, I was." He continued, "Well, two of my best men said it had Jersey plates on it when you left the station house. What do you say about that?"

"Beats the heck outta me, Lieutenant. They must have been mistaken. As you can plainly see, there are New York tags and they match the reg."

Silence reigned as the Lieutenant and Sergeant Whatshispuss looked at each other. Clearing his throat, McDermott spoke. "Well, I'm satisfied. Are you?" Sergeant Whatshispuss spoke for the first time. "Did you put in the change of residence forms?" McDermott held up his hand. "He has thirty days to do that."

"Captain, I put the form in on Friday afternoon."

"Good. Now, if you and the sergeant haven't anything better to do, I do, and these officers have to sign out and go home." They stormed away.

Once they left the station house, McDermott motioned for us to go into his office. "Close the door and sit down." He threw us both a can of beer and he had one himself. I appreciate it when someone steps in dog dirt and wipes it off before he steps on my rug. "I don't know how you did it and I don't want to know. But take my advice, kid. These guys don't like getting jerked around, especially by a rookie. Be careful. After that stunt you pulled with the peddler in Headquarters, you made their top-ten list. So just be careful. Even when the summer is over and you go back to the Six-One, be careful, 'cause they have long memories. Now, finish your beers and go home. Oh, by the way, is the commute shorter now that you're not in North Arlington?" I started to say something, but he just held up his hand and smiled. Good old St. Michael came through again.

Jennifer and I settled into a kind of routine. After work on Friday nights, she'd take the Hudson Tubes from Cortlandt Street to Journal Square in Jersey City. Georgie would pick her up and I'd drive there when I got off duty. Just to be on the safe side, I'd lock my gun in my locker at the station house. I didn't want *them* to catch me carrying a concealed weapon in Jersey.

When I worked Saturdays and Sundays, Jennifer would hang out with her family. She'd go to church with them, and Bill and I would go to Mass at Our Lady of Solace in Coney Island. More often than not, we'd see the captain at Mass. He was truly a good man.

August was coming to a close in a hurry. A few more weeks and I'd be back in the Six-One walking a foot post, chasing double-parkers and fire hydrant violators. Bill would go back to the Six-Four in Bay Ridge and be put back in a sector car. Oh well, the bad part was that I'd probably lose my tan.

On the last day of August, Bill and I were doing our usual boardwalk act when we heard sirens wailing out on the street. Two uniformed cops were at the rail watching the radio cars race along Surf Avenue. Nick Panico spoke. "That must be a heavy one. It's gotta be a ten-thirteen. Can you imagine, the end of the summer and some cop needs help just when the detail is about over?"

We introduced ourselves to the other uniformed cop. He wasn't a regular on the summer detail. "I'm Byrnes from the Nine-Four. The regular guy had a wedding or something to go to, so they sent me just for the day. This isn't a bad detail. You get plenty of fresh air and the sun feels good." We continued to watch the parade of radio cars and a couple of ambulances fly up the avenue for a few more minutes. "Well, we'll see you around. Take care, fellas." With that, Bill and I continued along the boards. We came off the boards and were heading toward Nathan's Famous on the corner of Surf and Stillwell when Bill decided to make a ring to the stationhouse. He hung up the call box phone and motioned for me to head to his car.

"What's up?"

"It looks like some guy killed a girl and one of the cops might have been shot, too. They want us to go to the scene and help with the search for the perp." We got stuck in the jam of police cars and ambulances, so we continued to West Thirty-Sixth Street and Surf on foot. Captain McDermott was getting everything organized with the help of Sergeant Arcuri. "Dan, pair off I with a uniform guy. Bill, you do the same. We don't want anyone to mistake who you guys are." The other Beach Squad guys were arriving and they did the same.

Arcuri gave us specific buildings to search. "I want every corner looked into. This guy is bad. He shot a young girl and a guy dead." Charlie Higgins asked, "Sarge, we heard he shot a cop." "Not true! The guy we're looking for is a colored guy by the name of Puck Ballard. Some of you might know him. He plays a guitar by the station at Surf and Stillwell. He's a bum that panhandles. We don't know just what set him off, but he's always fighting with someone.

Be very careful. The witnesses tell us he has two guns. All right, let's check these houses."

We all fanned out going into the tenement cellars, backyards, rooftops, all over the place. Later on we found out that after the shootings, he headed for the boardwalk.

Meanwhile, Panico, and Byrnes were still looking over the rail and never saw this human piece of garbage come up behind them. He shot Nick once in the head, and as Byrnes turned, Ballard shot him twice in the head. Nick, thankfully, didn't suffer. He was dead when he hit the boards. Ballard took the guns from the mortally wounded officers and disappeared under the boardwalk.

One of the guys from the Parks Department saw what happened, but couldn't prevent it. It happened so fast. He put a call into the police, told the situation and tried to comfort the dying officer, Byrnes. The first radio car on the scene hauled Byrnes into the back seat with one cop trying to staunch the flow of blood. The second car put Panico in the back and the cop in the back tried to pump his chest while both cars raced to Coney Island Hospital.

Nick was pronounced dead on arrival, but Byrnes, the guy who was only there for the day, lingered until September 4. Then, sadly, he died too.

We found out later that our cellar, roof, yard search was in vain, but some of the guys did find some good eyewitnesses. They supplied a good description of the clothes the mutt was wearing. As soon as another piece of information was developed, it was put over the radio by the Communications Bureau. C. B. would instruct the radio cars to disseminate the info to the guys on foot.

The media vultures were all over the place. They broadcasted that two cops had been shot. Bill and I found a payphone and called home to let them know we were safe. Then, we got back in the hunt. Darkness came quickly, but it didn't stop the searchers. Charlie Arcuri came up with flashlights for us and we all went looking for this animal that shot four people, so far, two in uniform. The search party grew as off-duty cops came flooding into the island. About eight o'clock, they found him.

Bill and I were with McDermott and Arcuri, so we jumped into the captain's car with Arcuri driving. The son of a bitch was behind a huge, low fire hydrant. He had been flushed out from his hole under the boards and was shooting up the street and down under the boards. The only problem was that some of the guys up were shooting down and the guys on the sand were shooting up. McDermott grabbed a megaphone and called a ceasefire. CEASE FIRE. And they did.

We hunkered down behind McDermott's car. The skipper picked up the megaphone. "Ballard, Puck Ballard, it's me, Ray McDermott. Puck, listen to me. The people that got hurt are going to be all right. Put the gun down. We don't want you to get hurt."

The reflection of the dome lights of the radio cars, mixed with the head-lights and multiple flashlights, trained on the hydrant cast an eerie light.

McDermott again activated the megaphone. "Come on, Puck, what-ever is bothering you, I can help change it. Listen to me. I'm gonna walk over to you. I'll put my gun on the hood of the car. Are you watching me, Puck? Look, there's the gun on the hood." Then, addressing the cops up and down the street, he said, "Men, don't shoot. I know this man. Don't shoot."

McDermott started to rise and Charlie Arcuri put a massive hand on his shoulder. "Ray, do you know what you're doing? This guy is nuts. He'll shoot you!"

"No, he won't. If we don't talk him out, some of our guys are gonna get hurt. I don't want that, Charlie. Let me give it a try."

Standing up, he walked around the car lit up in the headlights. Ballard lowered his guns from either side of the large hydrant. Ray started toward him and a shot rang out.

For a big man, Sergeant Arcuri moved like a flash. He was up around the car, grabbed the boss by the collar, and flung him back to the semi-safety on the side of the radio car. The big Emergency Service truck was parked near us, so I suggested to the group, "Why don't I just start that monster up and ram it right into the hydrant?" The truck itself was formidable. I mean, it was big, dark green, with all sorts of lights and sirens with emergency equip-ment stacked inside. Included in the equipment were rifles, shotguns and Thompson submachine guns. The front bumper was an inverted V that was used to break down doors at warehouses. I'm not one to criticize the depart-ment, but this truck was used during prohibition to break into the liquor warehouses. Talk about being old.

Anyway, McDermott looked at me, and for a split-second, I thought he was going to go for it. Before he could say no or yes, out of the truck came a figure encased in a full suite of body armor.

This had to be the gutsiest thing I'd ever seen (besides the captain standing and talking to the mutt.) The Emergency Service cop, walking into the street, looked like some type of alien creature. He had a thirty-eight in each hand. Ballard popped his head up and started firing at this apparition. The cop furnished fire from both weapons.

Sparks could be seen where the bullets hit the cobblestones all around the cop. Ballard was screaming obscenities and the cop was slowly moving to the hydrant returning fire. Then, all was quiet. Except for the whining of the dome lights and the purring of the idling cars. I was surprised by the silence. It was unearthly.

Then all hell broke loose. Everybody ran to the hydrant. Ballard was lying there in a pool of blood. Cops were all over the Emergency Service cop, helping him take off the body armor. McDermott took the two guns from the dying man's hands and handed them to Bill.

Charlie Arcuri bent over Ballard and took the two police revolvers from his waistband and handed them to me. The captain went over to the Emergency Service cop and shook his hand. Now that he was out of the armor, I recognized him as Herbie Nolan from 6 Truck.

Detectives were trying to preserve the scene from being destroyed. Everyone wanted to look in the face of the dying cop killer. Everyone wanted to spit in the face of a dying cop killer. But nobody did.

Someone suggested that the street be cleared so the ambulance could transport Ballard to the hospital. Nobody moved. Finally, McDermott grabbed the bullhorn and ordered everyone back onto the sidewalk. The ambulance proceeded to the body and, taking their time, got the stretcher out and rolled him onto it.

As the attendants rolled him over, you could see a neat round hole in his back, just below the left shoulder blade. He had holes in the front that exited out the back, but this was an entry wound, nice and neat. "It must have been a ricochet."

"Nah, it's too neat," the ambulance attendants mused. "Hey, fellas, let us do the thinking. Just get this hump to the hospital before he bleeds to death," one of the sergeants said. "Oh, yeah. Okay." But they took their time anyway.

Finally, with a groan and a shudder, Ballard went to that special hell for cop killers. I said a prayer to St. Michael to welcome Nick Panico into heaven and to prepare for Officer Byrnes. I couldn't bring myself to pray for the soul of the mutt bastard Ballard. But I did thank God that no other cops were killed or injured.

Later that night, when all the reports and notifications were made, McDermott addressed the midnight shift. He told them that Ballard had been hit ten times. Nine in the front and once in the back. It seems that a young sergeant climbed up onto the roof of the building behind Ballard, and, while he was busy exchanging shots and getting shot by Herbie Nolan, the sergeant fired once and got Ballard in the back. Well, at least that mystery was cleared up.

McDermott added to the assembled troops that, "Although the ambulance was on the scene immediately after the last shot was fired, unfortunately, the perp bled to death before he could be transported to the hospital." The assembled cops looked at each other, and everyone smiled, smacked backs, and went to work.

Labor Day came and went and the summer detail was ended. McDermott invited us all out to Gargulio's Restaurant for a thank-you/farewell dinner. I'll tell you, he was one class act. He went around to all of us, individually, and thanked us for our work. Work? I felt that I should be paying the city for letting me be a cop. All the violence and sadness aside, it is a great job. Now it was time to get back in uniform and walk the streets of Sheepshead Bay once more.

My first scheduled tour of duty was a Wednesday afternoon from four to midnight. I got to the station house about a quarter to three. I marched right upstairs to the roll call officer, slammed the door, and grabbed the roll call man by the arms. "If you ever put me in a position like you did, I'll throw you out this window." His eyes were bulging out. He started to say something, but I explained to him that anything he said could be hazardous to his health.

I let him know that I knew that he knew about the investigation of the Beach Squad. I explained that he was very lucky, and for his own safety, he should never, ever, mess with me again. Tightening my grip on his chicken bone arms, I asked him if he understood me and he shook his head in the affirmative. Mission accomplished.

We were getting used to the routine of married life, but Jennifer couldn't get used to the week when I worked the midnight to eight. I completely understood. Just being alone in a fifteen-story apartment house all by herself, in a strange city, was nerve-wracking for her. So we agreed that when the midnights came around, we'd go to her mother's house and I'd leave for work from there. Talk about a good move. She was happy. Her mother, sister and Georgie were happy, and so was I.

When I was working, I totally immersed myself in the "job." When I was off, I was off. Settling back into the routine of a foot man was a little difficult after the freedom I had from May to September, but I knew I couldn't just wander the streets of Sheepshead Bay the way I did Coney Island.

Sergeant Dave Joyce took me aside and told me that I was part of a large team and that just the presence of a man in uniform is enough to stop a criminal from doing a stick-up, pocketbook snatch or even a rape. He continued to explain that the foot posts were designed to give the residents and merchants a feeling of security and to have someone that they could rely on to help them.

I listened, agreed and believed that what he had explained was right on the money. I hadn't done anything to warrant the lecture from Sergeant Joyce, but he explained that when you comeback from a detail such as I, one might have a tendency to stretch the rules and wander off post. I assured him that I wouldn't and that I'd be on post at all times. I'd be visible and available, and I was true to that.

About a week after returning to the Six-One, the captain asked all of the foot men if they wanted a steady post. I requested Avenue X, and I got it. The wanna be gangsters and the full-fledged gangsters weren't too happy to see my smiling face, but the legitimate business owners and a lot of residents were. Cautiously, they told me so.

On the midnights, I concentrated on giving special attention to the Ro-Sal Bar. The gold chain, pinky ring set seemed to love the bar and they still didn't care where or how they parked their Caddys, Lincolns, and Olds.

I set out to correct that condition and I ticked off a lot of the pinky ring wearers. Captain Walsh loved it because my summons activity was high, complaints about the parking were low, and the information as to what car was there on any given night was used by the detectives and plainclothes cops to track the KGs and other hoods.

On the side of the Ro-Sal on McDonald Avenue was a parking area where "special customers" and two of the owners parked. The only problem was that there wasn't any curb cut to allow the cars into this little area. So they improvised by cutting down a parking meter and cutting the curb to allow access to this little lot.

By doing this, they eliminated a legitimate parking spot on McDonald Avenue and screwed up traffic when they entered or left the area. In the grand scheme of things, it really isn't such a big deal. But, when you have the post, you, not the gangsters, run it. So I was standing in the shadows one night, and this guy comes out of the bar, heads to the side lot, starts his big V-8 engine, backs out and is just about to cross the sidewalk down the illegal curb cut into the street. Emerging from the shadows, I gave a quick nightstick rap on the driver's window. "May I see your license and registration please?"

"Look, Officer, I'm one of the owners here. I know you don't like some of the customers, but I can't control who comes in here. I'm like you, I'm only a working stiff."

"Okay, but may I see your license and registration, please?" So he continues, "I just got a call from my wife. My little boy is sick and the doctor just left. I have to pick up medicine for him. He was born with a bad heart. My wallet is home with everything in it. Would you give me a break this time?"

Well, I guess even the owner of a sleazy saloon can have family problems. "Okay, this time. Go ahead. I hope your little boy feels better."

"Thank you. Thanks a lot. I really appreciate this."

Captain Walsh was turning us out for a four-to-twelve tour and was giving the complaints he'd received from the residents. One of the biggest was about private ambulance service. They'd blast through the streets with lights and sirens. Now, that's okay when you're going to an emergency or taking someone to the hospital. Some of the drivers were using the siren just to go and get their dinner, the newspaper, or some other non-emergency.

Well, I was working Avenue X and this ambulance is tearing across McDonald Avenue. I was about five blocks up, so I positioned myself in the street, and with my flashlight, I signaled the ambulance to pull to the curb. The ambulance braked to a semi-screeching halt and I approached the driver's side. I looked inside and saw an older woman on a stretcher with an oxygen mask on her face. The driver, looking slightly annoyed, started to explain that he was on his way to Coney Island Hospital. He kinda emphasized that he was on an emergency call. "Go ahead, pal," was all I could think to say as he soared off with his patient.

So much for picking the right ambulance to stop. Needless to say, I didn't stop any more ambulances.

My next set of late tours (midnight to eight), I was walking near the Ro-Sal when a voice called from the shadows. "Hey, kid, over here." It was the ex-cop who tipped me off about Gerati. You know, the guy whose car antenna I ripped off?

"Evening, sir. How's it going?"

"I like you, kid! You don't treat me like I'm a bum." I could smell the booze on his breath. "The other night you let a guy go 'cause his kid was sick, remember?" I nodded. "Well," he continued, "he ain't got no sick kid. He ain't even got a license either. That's Archie Lombardi. He is a KG, a real wise guy. He's been yucking it up in the bar telling anyone who would listen about what an ass he made out of you.

"I like you, kid. So that's why I'm telling you. Archie and his brother Tommy are real bad actors. They got a lot of juice. You can't be nice to those guys. They'll eat ya alive. They're into everything, bookmaking, loan-sharking. They fence anything that's stolen, ya know, like suits, shoes, furs, everything."

I thanked him for the information and put my hand in my pocket and pulled out a ten. "Kid, I'm not looking for a handout. I just wanted to let you know."

I pressed the money in his palm and thanked him again. He looked at the bill, lowered his head, and wobbled away. He turned and looked back at me, and I swear I saw tears in his eyes. Then he just walked away into the night. I wondered where he lived.

The following night, I hung around Ro-Sal most of the tour. I was banging out summons after summons to the "boys." Around two, I left and walked up to the far end of the post. I checked the stores to make sure they were locked and that nobody was trying to burglarize them. I checked alleyways and went down the steps into the cellar ways. All was quiet.

About three-thirty, I went past the bar and saw my quarry sitting at the far end with some other pinky ring. Finally, the pinky ring left and my quarry was locking up. I crept up behind him and stuck the nightstick into his back. I grabbed his coat collar. Pushing him ahead of me, I took him into the alley between the bar and a pork store, out of sight from the street.

I spun him around and hit him with my fist right in the stomach. He went down to his knees. I then kneed him in the face. He let out a gulp. I pulled him to his feet and threw him against the wall. "Kid, whaddaya doing?"

"I cut you a break and now you and all your goombah friends are laughing at me?" I hit him another shot in the kidneys. Then, all of a sudden it dawned on me that maybe I should see if he was carrying a gun or a knife. He wasn't. I guess I should have done that first. Oh well!

He collapsed to his knees and in a pleading, gasping tone of voice said, "Listen to me, you got the wrong guy. I'm Tommy. You want me brother, Archie. Archie's the one that got over on you, not me."

I pulled him to his feet and dragged him to the front of the alley toward a sliver of street light. Oops, he was right. But damn, he did look like his brother. "First of all, don't call me, kid, you punk. Secondly, you tell Archie I don't like his sense of humor. Now get outta here. If you or your buddies start with me, I'll burn this dump to the ground with all of you in it. [I must say that I have no idea where that came from. Maybe Bogart or Cagney used it in a movie.] Do you understand?"

"Listen, kid, I mean, Officer, I got no quarrel with you. Let's just be friends." He put his hand in his pocket and took out a wad of cash. I hit him full in the face, left him slumped in the alley, and continued my foot patrol.

The next night, I got to the Six-One at about quarter to eleven for the midnight tour. I went up the stairs to the locker room. As I passed the detectives office, I heard someone call my name. I looked in and saw Captain Walsh, Lieutenant John McCarthy, and Frank Healey. Frank motioned for me to go into the lieutenant's office and the three followed with Walsh closing the door.

I figured I best keep my mouth shut until someone asked me a question. Captain Walsh nodded to McCarthy who looked up from behind his desk and pointed to a chair. I sat still, not saying a word. "Listen, kid, we know what you did last night and why. I recommended to the captain that he take you off the post. Just for a little while." I started to say something, but McCarthy held up his hand. "This is for your own protection. These guys play rough. They play for keeps. You messed up a made man, and God knows how many others you've made a monkey out of. They don't take too kindly to that. I don't want to see you get hurt."

"Lieutenant, I can take care of myself. I'm not worried about those clowns. I run the post. I'm fair to everyone there. These mutts think they own the post, and the good people, the shop owners, and even the kids, are bullied by them. That's just not right." I continued, "You told us when we first got here, Captain, that we had a responsibility to keep our post clean and not have anyone be afraid to walk the streets."

Walsh nodded. "You're right, but I've made up my mind and—" I interrupted, "Captain, this is my last late tour. Do me a favor, please, just let me have the post for tonight. I don't want those bums to think that they had me put off the post. I feel that I'd been letting the good people down. I guess if you know what happened and why, and I'm not getting chewed out, I did the right thing. Well, maybe not the right thing, but I was right in the way I did it. Maybe not the PD way, but the street way. Look, Captain, if you know, I'm sure the word is out on the street too. Just let me work it for my last tour." I was going to add "please," but I didn't want to sound as if I was begging. It was just, I guess, a matter of pride.

Healey was the first to speak. "Nobody asked me, but I know what the kid means. It really isn't pride. It's . . . well, it's hard to explain, but I know what he means." McCarthy and Walsh looked at each other. Finally, Walsh shrugged. "All right, son, but if there's any trouble, call the station house before you get involved. Do you understand?"

"Yes, sir, and thank you, sir."

We turned out and I hurried to the post. It was quiet. People were sitting on their stoops smoking and talking. The night was warm with no breeze. People were all over the street, but it was quiet. Some greeted me with smiles and others with looks of disgust. Some had a kind . . . I don't know . . . a look of sympathy for me, is the only way I remember it.

I made my way to the end of the post going toward the Ro-Sal. I watched the people going inside their houses and some of the shopkeepers closing up for the night. All of a sudden, I was the only one on the street. At least I thought I was.

I started thinking about the previous weekend when Jennifer and her family and I went up to a lake near Mountain View for a family picnic. All of her nieces and nephews were there, along with assorted cousins and their kids. Jennifer and I swam out to a raft in the middle of the lake and climbed up on it. We were watching the goings-on on the beach without saying a word.

Finally I turned to her and said that someday we'd be chasing after our little ones. I told her that and I believed it. She just smiled and squeezed my hand.

Along about three in the morning, my new best friend called out to me from an alleyway about six or seven buildings up from the Ro-Sal. "Psstt, Psstt! Don't turn around, just listen. Be very careful tonight. They got something planned. I dunno what, but it can't be good," he slurred. "Just be careful. Don't go into any alleys or buildings. I dunno what, but they wanna hurt you."

A car drove by very slowly and I reached for my gun. There were two guys in the front seat and one in the rear. They just slowed and then picked up speed. Paranoid? Who me? Without turning around, I asked my new best friend, "What exactly did you hear?" No answer. "Are you still there?" No answer.

The squealing of tires got my attention and I flattened against the wall of the apartment house and ducked down. Two shots rang out and splattered brick chips onto my hat. Now, I have to be very honest about this, I was scared shitless. I crab-walked or, more appropriately, ran into the darkened alley. After what seemed to be an hour and a half, I stuck my head out and cautiously looked up and down the street. Actually, it was more like a minute and a half, but hey, when you're scared shitless, time is irrelevant. I made my way up the avenue to the call box three blocks away. I was very cautious, sticking close to the walls and out of the light from the street lamps. I'm sure that I looked like one of those cartoon characters whose head does a three-sixty turn because I was looking everywhere at once.

I got to the box and called. I told the sergeant that I needed the patrol sergeant to meet me. "Whaddaya got, kid?"

"Sarge, I just need the sergeant to meet me. It's no big deal."

"I'll ask ya one more time. Whaddaya got, kid?"

"Well, sir, I just got shot at."

"Shit, kid, why dinnya say so? Are you okay?"

"I'm fine, Sarge, just a bit shook."

"Okay, help is on the way."

"Sarge, I really don't need—" He disconnected the call box phone.

I could hear the sirens coming. Aw, damn, all I wanted was the sergeant and now every cop that heard the radio call would be racing to my aid. When a cop's in trouble, the call is made and the Central radio dispatcher issues a ten-thirteen message. That means an officer needs assistance. Aw, damn, I didn't need assistance. I just wanted to report what happened to the sergeant.

Well, everybody came. The captain included. "Are you okay, son? What happened?" The noise from the sirens drowned me out. Finally, somebody called Central to tell everyone to slow down; no further assistance was necessary. But cops being cops, they kept coming to make sure for themselves that a brother officer didn't need their help. Really, when you think about it, it's a pretty good club to belong to. I mean, we do take care of each other.

Anyway, we went back to where I was when the shots were fired and you could see the spots on the front of the building where the bullets hit. The impact was about ten feet up the wall. Now, I'm six foot. Were they lousy shots or was there a message? I mean, if they were trying to scare me, well, they succeeded. But if they were trying to hit me, the shooter needed some quality range time.

Healey, McCarthy, Bill Shea, and Wally Gannon pulled up in two detective cars. They asked what happened. Did I get a look at the car? Could I recognize anyone in the car? Was I all right? I told them about the squealing tires and the shots. It was a dark, four-door, either Lincoln or Olds. I didn't recognize anyone in the car, and yes, I was fine.

I stood leaning against a radio car, and absentmindedly, I reached into my jacket, took out a cigar and stuck it in my mouth. I saw Captain Walsh say something to Sergeant Joyce and I pulled the cigar from my mouth. Joyce came over and lit a match. "Go ahead, kid, the boss says it's okay."

The area was lit up brighter than Rockefeller Center at Christmastime, but I noticed something odd. Nobody was looking out their windows. No lights went on in the private homes or the apartments. I realized that, despite my efforts, the mutts did run my post, not me.

Something had to be done about that!

After my last late tour, I went home to Stuyvesant Town. I called Jennifer at work to ask her if she wanted to go to dinner that evening. "How was work? Are you tired? Anything interesting happen?" "Nah, just a routine night. Actually, it was very uneventful." I guess in some cultures that would be considered a lie, but in police culture, that's just protecting your wife from extra worry. So I didn't feel bad. I felt protective.

I went to sleep and didn't wake up until 6:00 p.m. I smelled food and I heard the TV. I grabbed a robe and went into the little kitchen. There she was by the stove frying some veal cutlets. "I thought we were going out to eat."

"Well, when you didn't answer the phone, I figured you were tired so I picked up some cutlets and figured we'd eat in, okay?"

"Okay," I said.

After my swing (cop speak for days off), I went back to work. I had to go to traffic court where I testified about some summonses that drivers had pled not guilty to. After testifying, I drove back to the station house and Lieutenant Priola pointed toward the captain's office and made a knocking motion. I knocked and Captain Walsh called for me to come in.

Inside was Lieutenant McCarthy and two other men I didn't recognize. It turns out they were the division inspector and the borough commander. A chief, no less. McCarthy pointed to a chair and I sat. They all first looked at me for what seemed like a long time.

Finally, the borough commander asked how I was doing. I answered that I was fine. He then said that that was good. The inspector asked how my wife was doing. I answered that she was fine. He then said that that was good. This was followed by more silence. So I kept silent.

Lieutenant McCarthy finally said, "Listen, when we investigate a cop being shot at, we also look to see if it could be family related. You know, maybe your brother-in-law or your wife's father or an old jealous boyfriend she might have had, stuff like that." I nodded that I understood. Even though I really didn't. I said, "Okay. Well, my one brother-in-law, Georgie, is in Hawaii with his new wife. He's been there since last Monday and is scheduled to come home next Wednesday. My other brother-in-law lives in Kansas City, Kansas, and I spoke to him the day before yesterday. The last guy my wife went out with before me is married and right now lives in Paris. I never met him and I know my wife hasn't seen him since they stopped dating about three and a half years ago."

The borough commander interrupted. "How come you know he's in Paris?"

"Because his mother and father told me." The chief said, "Wait a minute, how do you know this guy's parents?"

"I met them at my wedding. They live in the same town that my wife lived in before we got married. The both families are neighbors."

"Continue," the chief said. "What about the father?"

"Oh yeah, well, he died in 1957." I was tempted to add "I guess you can rule him out" but I didn't. "Listen, Chief, I get on great with all my wife's relatives and with all of my family. The ones we should be looking for are the mutts on Avenue X." McCarthy nodded, the captain nodded, the inspector nodded, and the chief nodded. So, naturally, I nodded. For the most part, I was still a foot man. But on the four-to-twelve and the twelve-to-eight, I rode more than I walked. I guess "they" thought I should have a chaperone after dark. I learned a lot riding in the radio car with old timers. I learned how to listen to people without interrupting with dumb questions. I learned to cut to the facts without making the victim feel as if I was not interested in their problem.

I'll tell you something, the cops on the street are the greatest when it comes to interacting with people with problems. They are also the greatest when it comes to a dangerous situation. With the exception of the punks, wannabes, and "made men," the precinct was home to good, solid, hard-working men and women. Men and women who just wanted to go to work, raise their families, go to their House of Worship, and enjoy life.

The job of the cops on the street was to ensure that they were protected and safe. Protected and safe to come and go as they pleased. This is what the cops everywhere do. Day in and day out.

One sunny day, I came back from traffic court and was assigned a post on Avenue U for the remainder of the tour. So I'm walking along enjoying the early November sunshine, just moping along, when I heard what sounded like glass breaking. I looked around and nothing seemed out of place. I glanced down a side street and I see a woman pushing a baby carriage craning her neck to the opposite side of the street. On a hunch, I walked off the avenue and onto the side street, perking my ears up like a dog, listening for any sound out of the ordinary. Out of the corner of my eye, I saw the woman with the baby carriage point to a driveway about three houses off the corner.

Quickening my pace, I went into the alleyway and saw the side storm door open with the pane of glass broken. Glass shards were on the concrete.

It was then I heard a scream from inside the house. I felt my heart beat faster, and I felt like I could hear the blood rushing to my brain. Entering the house, I went up three stairs to a nice, cozy kitchen and peeked through the doorway into the living room area. I heard muffled sounds coming from the second floor. Cautiously, I took the stairs two at a time. The only sound I heard was my beating heart. I got to the top of the stairs and my hearing came back. At the end of the hallway was the master bedroom. Off to my left were two kids rooms. I went toward the end of the hall and could clearly hear the sounds of a struggle.

The first thing I saw was a guy on top of a struggling woman pinned under him on the bed. Geez, I wish I had my nightstick. I grabbed a handful of this guy's long stringy hair and yanked as hard as I could. I pulled him off the struggling young woman and slammed him to the floor.

The woman rolled off the bed and, clutching her blouse to cover herself, tore out of the room. The clown on the floor gave me a kick in the kneecap and I let go of his hair. Out of nowhere, he hit me with a shot in the forehead, knocking me on my ass.

The clown then jumped to his feet and started down the hallway. I could hear the faint sound of sirens. Jumping to my feet, I leapt on the guy's back at the top of the stairs. I gotta tell you, I was so happy that the home owner had carpet on the stairs. He and I, in a jumble of swinging arms and legs, bounced down the stairs for what seemed like an eternity. Fortunately, I wound up on top and just kept punching anyplace I saw skin. I even punched my own hand. Smart, huh? He got in a few good shots at me and I could feel blood going into my mouth. I was reaching for my handcuffs that were usually on the left side of my gun belt. In the fight, the belt shifted and nothing was where it was supposed to be.

A fleeting thought went through my mind. Why didn't I just stick my gun in his ear when we were in the bedroom? Oh well, live and learn. Anyway, I got one cuff on him and he was still fighting me. Not really having a sense of humor when I'm bleeding and in full uniform, I punched him right in the throat.

He gurgled and stopped struggling. Oh boy, now I did it. The I think I-killed-him-thought rushed through my mind. I rolled him over and got the other cuff on him behind his back.

The first uniform through the door was Sergeant Dave Joyce. I was sitting on my can trying to assess the damage to me and trying to figure out how much trouble I was gonna be in for being off my post.

Joyce and Manny Bogen grabbed the clown and got him to his feet. Thank you, St. Michael. I hadn't killed him. He was coughing and trying to curse me at the same time.

Eddie Quigley and McPartland lifted me to my feet on which I was a little unsteady. McPartland sat me in a chair and Quigley gave me some paper towels from the kitchen. The house was filled with so many cops it look like a PBA meeting.

Quigley was fussin' around with the back and side of my head and McPartland was putting a towel with ice cubes in my hand. "Put this on your nose." I did and it stung, but it stopped the bleeding. Quigley was trying to get Joyce's attention, but he was busy trying to get the other cops back on patrol. Manny Bogen had the young woman in the kitchen trying to calm her down.

Joyce ordered Frank Wright and Steve Risley to get the prisoner into the station house and get him some medical attention. Lieutenant McCarthy, Shea, Healey, Gannon, and Captain Walsh arrived. After asking if I was alright, they went into the kitchen to talk to the young woman.

I looked in and saw Manny Bogen handing her a cup of tea he had just made for her. Healey had his notepad out and gently started the interview. Sergeant Joyce told me I'd better get to the hospital just as an ambulance pulled up. The two medics looked me over and put some sting stuff on the side and top of my head. "No stitches required," was their medical finding. Quigley told me that it looked like he got me with the ratchets from one of the handcuffs.

The woman was not sexually assaulted. She was just shook. Gee, I wonder why. I mean, she's only cleaning her house. You know, making the beds, picking up after the kids, waiting for them to come home. Probably expecting a call from her husband. When she hears glass break and this mangy bozo comes into her home. I would say she had a right to be shook.

I called Jennifer when I got to the station house and told her I'd be home late because I'd made an arrest. "Was it exciting?"

"No, just routine, no big deal."

"You sound funny, like you have a cold or something. Are you all right?"

"I'm fine. I think I might have allergies."

"Do you think you might want to eat when you get home?"

"No, thanks, honey, I'll eat at court."

An old time foot cop, Hugo Pulzone, was standing near me just looking at me. "You know, kid, you sounded like you had a nose full of snot when you were on the phone. Your beak is broke. You know that, right?" Actually, I didn't. He continued, "What is it with you? Trouble has a way of reaching out and just grabbing onto you. You gotta get that beak of yours into the books. Study. Become a boss. It's a lot safer." I went upstairs to the squad room to see how the arrest processing procedure was coming along. Frank Healey was the first to greet me. "Hey, kid, how ya doing?" I smiled and I realized that my face hurt as well as my head. "Listen, kid, do you know what you got here? You got not only a house burglar, but a guy that's wanted for at least seven other burglaries, three rapes, and four attempts. That is one hell of a collar. You gotta write this one up. You'll get another citation." Healey had written up the gun collar we made when I locked up Patsy boy. You know, the guy whose antenna I ripped from his car.

McCarthy came out of his office with a stack of DD-5s. These are the follow-up reports that detectives file during their investigations. "Hey, kid, good job. Come in here." He motioned to his office. I was starting to feel a little queasy and light-headed at this point. I sat without being told to.

McCarthy went around behind his desk and sat. He looked at me for a long second, cleared his throat and began. "Before I forget, here's your cuffs. You did an outstanding job out there." I could sense there was a large *but* coming. I wasn't disappointed.

He didn't look at me and appeared to be studying some paper on his desk. "How's your brother Jim? You know, he and I are friends." This was a surprise to me. "I also know your brother, John, in Safe and Loft Squad." Another surprise to me. "They're both fine, thanks." "Look, there's no easy way to tell you this, but Bill Shea is taking this arrest to court and I'll tell you why, okay?" Before I could compute what he was saying, he continued. "This guy is wanted in three precincts. Detectives all over Brooklyn have been looking for him for about a year. How would it look, downtown, if a rookie cop caught him and the *detectives* didn't? I'm sure you understand."

I really didn't. This seemed to be a repeat of what happened when I found the evidence in the garbage can at the scene of the murder of Mr. Fallon and Detective Finnegan. Suddenly, a wave of anger came over me. I pushed the wooden chair back and it tipped over loudly. Without a word, I got up and stormed out, slamming the door, rattling the windows to the point where they shook just short of breaking.

Shea looked at me and just shrugged his shoulders. He pointed his chin in the direction of the Lieutenant's office. He had one of those "It's not my fault" looks. Healey started to say something, but stopped. Gannon looked at his shoes. I just kept walking downstairs.

I went to the desk officer, Lieutenant Block. "I'm going sick, Lieu, line of duty." The Lieutenant reached in a drawer and gave me the forms to fill out. Sergeant Joyce pulled me into the clerical office and closed the door. "Listen, kid, I know you're upset, but calm down and I'll tell you why. Both with that, he opened a desk drawer and flipped me a cold can of Bud. I popped the top and listened as he proceeded. "First, you have to go to the hospital and get a tetanus shot. When the four-to-twelve guys come in, I'll have a car run you there. Those cuts on your head came from your cuffs and . . ." I started to protest, but he just held up his hand to silence me. "I'm not gonna let you get screwed, but we have to do this by the numbers. Finish your beer, go to your locker and get changed. Then come back here. Don't go near the squad, get it?" I nodded, finished the beer and went to the locker room and got changed.

When I got to the first floor, the door of the clerical room was closed, but I could hear the typewriter noise. Patrolman Al Berger called to me, "C'mon, kid, we'll take you to Coney Island Hospital. Joyce called the head nurse. You'll be in and out. By the way, the captain told us about the col- lar . . . good job." I nodded my thanks.

When I got back to the station house, Sergeant Joyce motioned for me to follow him into the clerical office. He reached in the drawer and threw me another Bud. He pushed a stack of department forms toward me. "Just sign where I have the X." I did and slid the papers back to Joyce. He signed. "Stay here." He got up and said over his shoulder, "In the bottom drawer, help yourself." He came back in and handed me an envelope stuffed with carbon copies of all the different reports. I started to read them and took out a cigar. Joyce made a go-ahead-and-light-it-up motion. So, I did.

Now, I told you earlier that the PD has a form for everything, and they do. Aided and accident card, line of duty record (the LOD is about the size of a small phone book), and the unusual occurrence report, a U.F.-49. That's typed on official department letterhead. There was a second U.F.-49 addressed to the captain with a request for a departmental recognition award. It was signed by the supervisor, sent to the captain for his endorsement, forwarded to the division inspector, and, if he signs it, it goes to the borough office where the borough commander either endorses it or rejects it. If it's endorsed by the borough commander, it then gets sent to police Headquarters and then you get called to the Honor Board.

The Honor Board convenes when it's convenient. Once I got less than a day's notice that I was to be at the Honor Board at eight in the morning. This was for an arrest that Bill Metcalf and I made when we locked up the gang of punks stealing from the beach blankets.

I remember that day. I was so nervous. I mean, I'm only a rookie and here I am in Headquarters about to be grilled by the Honor Board. Bill and I met for coffee and then went into Headquarters, passed the benches, where we sat because of the peddler investigation. We went up the stairs to the second floor and checked in with the cop at the desk. "Grab a seat on the bench, they haven't started yet."

Bill was as calm as could be. He'd been there before. I was nervous. I wanted a multi-colored bar to put over my shield. That would show that I was a street hardened vet. Or so I thought.

Finally, at about quarter to ten, the bosses came in, one red face after another and enough white hair to give you snow blindness. Now, the drill is, you tell what tour you were doing, your assignment and what led you to make the arrest. Did you get a radio run, or was it on your observation, or some civilian alerted you?

Next to the door there were two guys from a Harlem precinct who, between them, must have had seventy citations. Their story was that they were on patrol and saw two guys backing out of a liquor store. One had a sawed off shotgun and the other had a forty-five automatic. They turned and opened fire at the two cops, hitting one in the shoulder. The cops returned fire, dropping the two mutts where they stood. The uninjured cop called for assistance, pushed his partner into the radio car, grabbed the two guns from off the sidewalk and drove, like hell, to Harlem Hospital to have his partner taken care of. This, according to witnesses, took less than two minutes.

The two Harlem cops were called into the board. The door to the room was ajar so you could hear the procedure from where we sat. The big chief, a three star, was the chair of the board. He didn't introduce himself or the other men. He told the cops, "Look, we're in a bit of a hurry this morning. Dispense with the formalities and cut right to the incident. We have the recognition request in front of us. Now, who's gonna do the talking?" One of them said, "I will." The chief said, "Be brief. What happened?" The cop said, "They did it and we got 'em." A few stifled coughs and I know I heard a snicker, and the big chief said, "Thank you, you're dismissed." God, how I love cop humor.

Sergeant Joyce lit up a cigarette and I continued to puff on my cigar. "Okay, I gave the request to the captain and he endorsed it. It's already on the way to the division. The skipper sent it to the inspector and he's gonna sign it. The inspector's gonna personally take it to the chief who, in all probability, will sign it without even reading it and it'll be in Headquarters in the morning. We did this because it was the right thing to do. McCarthy is right in having the squad take the collar. This will not only make them look good, but also the precinct. I know that you want to process the arrest, but you gotta look at the bigger picture. This way, everybody looks good. You alright with that, kid?" Before I could answer, he threw me another Bud and we sat there for another hour just shooting the breeze about life, the job and how to balance work and home.

When I left the station house for the ride home, I felt okay. Sore all over my body, but okay with the job. Joyce had explained that, naturally, I'd have to testify at the grand jury about the facts of the case, and if there was a trial, I would be an important witness for the District Attorney's Office. He explained that it didn't matter what name was on the arrest report. What mattered was that a burglar/rapist was off the street and hopefully would be for a long time.

I entered our apartment and she took one look at me and tears came to her eyes. I hugged her and told her it wasn't as bad as it looked. We sat in the living room and I told her exactly what happened. I left out the part about storming out of McCarthy's office, but included how Sergeant Joyce took care of all the reports and how he and I spoke about everything. I told her that his advice was never to bring home the sadness you saw. Bring home the good things you saw and did. Find the rare humorous sites and happenings. Share them with your wife and family."

"I'd like to meet him some day." I said she would, at the precinct Christmas party in about a month. We then went to bed. The next morning, I got up before Jennifer. It was early, about six-thirty. I took a nice, hot shower and the aches and pains from the day before left me for a time. I was standing in front of the mirror just about to shave and I saw what I looked like. I had two of the most beautiful shiners I'd ever seen. I looked like a raccoon.

I heard her in the kitchen starting to make coffee. I walked in backward with the bath towel around my waist. When I turned around, she just looked at me and laughed. I'm not small in the nose area to begin with, but it was about three sizes bigger. That, coupled with the Rocky Raccoon eyes, were cause to laugh.

About eight o'clock, she called work and said she was taking a vacation day, and if it was all right, she was going to take off on Monday too. She was the confidential secretary to a vice-president at Aetna insurance company. I was making $5,200 a year and she was making $9,200 and the worst hurt she ever got was a paper cut. Somehow, the economics of our careers was a little out of kilter, if you know what I mean.

The weather was still nice and mild for November, so we decided to go for a walk along the FDR Drive. We got ready and were just about to leave the apartment when there was a hard knock on the door. I whipped it open, a bit annoyed at the hardness of the knock.

Standing there was a sergeant and a cop. The conversation went something like this. "You Stark?"

"Yes, Sarge."

"Good. How ya feel?"

"Lousy."

"That's how you look."

"Thanks."

"See ya."

"Okay, boss."

"When can I expect you back?"

"You goin' somewhere?"

"I'd like to."

"When do you want another visit?"

"Tuesday morning."

"See you then."

"Thanks, Sarge."

"Okay, if this is going to be our life, where do I get the secret decoder ring?" I laughed. "What ? You couldn't follow the conversation?"

I haven't the foggiest idea what just went on, let alone what was said."

"Well, it goes like this: When you go on sick report, you're not supposed to leave your residence. The medical unit has what they call the sick desk, and the sick desk keeps track of all the cops that are on sick leave. Whether it is a guy with a fever or if you're recovering from an operation or if you've been hurt, the sick desk notifies your resident precinct and they send a boss over to your place to make sure you're home. If you're not, there are only a few places you should be. One is your doctor and you need a note saying you were there. A trip to the drugstore is okay, but you need a receipt with a date and time stamp got it."

"You get hurt making an arrest and now you're the prisoner? It doesn't make sense. I mean, look at how you look. Anyone can tell you shouldn't be at work. You're stiff, you're sore, and your eyes are almost shut closed. What do they want from you?"

I explained that there are some guys that might take advantage of the unlimited sick leave policy to grab a few days off to go to the track or something. So in order to preclude that, the sick desk sends the local precinct boss to verify that you're sick or hurt and are where you're supposed to be. It's something like being in the military."

"Okay," she said, "But what was all that code about going somewhere and when he was coming back?"

"I don't have to go to the police doctor until Tuesday afternoon. So I figured you and I could hang out with your mother. I mean, Georgie and Jeannie are coming back from their trip tomorrow, right? So maybe we can meet them at the airport." (Georgie and Jeannie liked to travel. He only had to pay the tax.) She smiled. "That's nice of you to offer our services." I made a face and she smiled again. "No, it really is nice. But what about the sergeant coming back on Tuesday? I mean, why would he let you out of the house? I don't understand."

"Well, he knows that I'm not faking. I mean, even you think I look like a gargoyle, right?" Then I quickly said, "Don't answer that." We both laughed and started to throw some weekend clothes into a valise. "Are you gonna call your mother or are we just gonna barge in?"

"Let's surprise her." And we did.

The next morning after breakfast, we headed to Newark Airport to wait for Georgie and Jeannie. They had planned to take a taxi from the airport to their apartment in North Arlington. When they saw us at the walkway, they were thrilled.

"Hey, Trunk, who the hell tattooed you? Jan, did you hit him with a pot or something?" We all hugged, and while he and I went for the luggage, the two girls talked. Georgie worked at Newark loading and unloading planes for United Airlines. The alarm at the carousel sounded and the red light start revolving and out came six pieces of various sized luggage. All belonging to Georgie and Jeannie. The alarm stopped and the light went off. We picked up the luggage and left about two hundred people standing and grumbling around the carousel. Georgie winked at me and shrugged. He whispered, "It's nice to have a little clout."

On the way out of the airport, he went to the newsstand and bought the *Daily News*. "I gotta keep up on what's happening. I miss my news. Where did you park?"

"I'm right at the curb." I winked at him and said, "It's nice to have a little clout." The Port Authority cop was standing there and I waved my thanks. He smiled and nodded. We put the luggage in the trunk, piled in the car, and I pointed it toward North Arlington.

"Hey, Trunk, you know a detective named Bill Shea?"

"Yeah, he's in my precinct." Georgie said, "He made some arrest. Look at the picture." I stopped for a light, and there on page three was Shea and McCarthy with my collar. Shea on one side, McCarthy on the other and Ronnie DiCortenza in the middle. He looked worse than I felt, but that was little consolation. The essence of the article was that "Through surveillance and dogged detective work, the prisoner was apprehended by a squad of detectives who had been following him and apprehended him as he entered a one-family residence by breaking through a side door. The prisoner put up a brief, but fierce, struggle and was subdued. One police officer received a minor injury during the arrest."

"A minor injury, my ass. The mutt broke my nose." I was ticked. I mean, really ticked. Georgie continued, "Police confirmed that DiCortenza was a suspect in seven other break-ins and had attempted to rape four women and had succeeded in three others. The names of the victims are being withheld to protect their identities."

I forgot the talk I had with Sergeant Joyce. I was mad. I called my brother, Jackie, and told him what had happened and how I felt. He listened, in his patient way, and when I was finished, all he said was, "You made a great observation collar. You did a good job. You really didn't get hurt and the only thing that's bugging you is you didn't get your face in the paper." I started to say something, but he continued. "It's just your pride. This bum is off the street. You did what you get paid to do. If you wanted applause, you should have gone into show business."

"Yeah, but . . ."

"But nothing. Everyone that matters knows that you collared him. That's why Sergeant Joyce pushed the recognition papers. You'll get the proper award. Go back to work and do your job."

I hung up the phone and thought about what he had said. He was right. I guess I just wanted to be a hero. It was pride and recognition. Recognition from the guys I worked with. The bigger picture became clear to me. If the article in the paper brought good publicity to the department, then it would reflect on thirty-two thousand members, not just me. As usual, Jackie was right. So was Sergeant Joyce.

The raccoon eyes healed, as did my swollen nose, and I went back to work. Guys came up to me and shook my hand, patted me on the back and I felt good. I wasn't being treated as a rookie any longer. Even the Captain gave me two days off for "good work." These could be taken any time I wanted. "Depending upon the exigencies of the service." The days off form was put in my folder with a form from the Captain. I guess it wasn't a bad deal after all.

I had finished working a day tour, and Jimmy Canavan and a few of the other guys were stopping for a couple of beers. Jimmy asked me if I wanted to stop with them. So I did. There was this little hole in the wall bar on Avenue U under the El-station, about a block from the station house. In we went. I remember that it was cold out and the place was toasty warm. There, in the middle of the bar, was Lieutenant McCarthy and Bill Shea sipping their beers. I, briefly, thought about leaving, but Canavan and Manny Bogen pushed me toward them.

McCarthy stood, looked at me and smiled. "You do have a temper, kid, don't you?" Shea stood and put out his hand. Wordlessly, I shook it, and McCarthy offered his hand, and I shook his, too. "You did a good job, kid. Lemme buy you a beer." I looked at Canavan. "Jim, was this a setup? Did you know they'd be here?"

"Of course." Look, we all have to work together. We have to depend on them and they on us. That's what it means to be a cop." I was glad I stopped.

Thanksgiving passed and New York was gearing up for the Christmas season. Captain Walsh was turning us out and told us to be mindful that this was the prime time for robberies. He told us to keep an eye on all the stores on our post. Look for anyone who he might be casing a store. Note anything out of the ordinary. Go into the stores if anything didn't look right to us. Talk to the storekeepers. Keep a high profile on the post.

I was working four-to-twelve and I had the foot post on Sheepshead Bay Road. This was the first time I'd had the post since the frozen chicken caper. I should have known something would happen. I got to the post, and it was busy with shoppers and people coming from the train station. I walked up and down, smiling and nodding to the pedestrians.

About four hours into the tour, I was starting to feel the cold. The temperature had gone down and the wind off the bay wasn't helping. Another thing that didn't help was the huge uniform overcoat I was wearing. The thing felt like it weighed fifty pounds. It went from my neck to below my shins. But it did look good.

Along about eight o'clock, the pedestrian traffic had lightened up considerably and I was hungry. I didn't have a meal period until eight-thirty. I went into the train station to get warm. There was a pot-bellied stove inside the turnstiles, so I waved to the token attendant, opened the gate and stood near the stove. I took off my gloves and jammed them into the overcoat pockets.

I heard a train come in and looked up the stairs to see a guy come bustling down the stairs. In one hand he had a large canvass bag with "Property of the Transit Authority" printed on the side. I don't know about you, but certain people have certain traits. When a guy is on the clock, he really doesn't hurry to get from point A to point B. He takes his time. I might be wrong, but in this case, I wasn't. I don't know why, but this kid did not look like he should be holding a Transit Authority money bag.

Another reason it caught my eye was that whenever money is being transported, a uniformed Transit police officer is with the money man. So, using my burgeoning detective skills, I thought something was amiss.

Oh yeah. In his other hand, he had a gun. He saw me and started to raise the gun hand. I jammed my hand into the overcoat pocket, grabbed a handful of glove and screamed, "Drop it or you're dead." (Another line from a movie? I can't be that original.)

Then a funny thing happened. He did it! He dropped the gun! I quickly scooped up the gun (after it bounced down about twelve steps.) He came down, placed the money bag on the floor, turned around and put his hands behind his back. So I said to myself, "Maybe it would be a good idea to cuff him." So I did.

I looked over at the token clerk and he was on the phone. I said to myself, "Here we go again." The clerk did what he thought was right, but I really didn't need assistance. I could hear the sirens before the clerk hung up the phone.

I put the compliant stick-up man on the bench and sat next to him. The street doors opened and I yelled to Al Beyer to "call it off, no further assistance necessary. No further." But they still came. The brotherhood in action.

When we got to the station house, I found out that the prisoner had held up the token booth man at the Neck Road station just before the Sheepshead Bay stop. I went up to the squad room with my prisoner in tow. This one wasn't going to get away from me.

The detectives couldn't have been nicer to me. They sent a car to pick up the clerk who was stuck up, they fingerprinted the guy, called the TA police boss, gave me a cup of coffee, let me give the prisoner a cup. One of them asked me why I didn't shoot him. I simply said that he dropped the gun.

I really didn't want anyone to know that the gun belt moved and the holster was resting on the right cheek of my behind. The overcoat has a pocket and a slit where you can reach into it and get at your gun. But, when the gun belt moves and everything shifts, it's hard to get at the gun in a hurry.

A few days later, I was telling my brother, Jackie, about the collar. "Look, here's what you do. Buy an off-duty holster for the service revolver, and when you're on foot patrol, you put the gun in the overcoat pocket. That way you don't have to go fumbling looking for it. Listen to me now, and I'm serious, you have to calm down out there. For a new guy, you're getting into a lot of stuff."

I could tell by his tone that he was worried about me. It was a nice feeling. "But, Jackie, I'm not creating these situations. They just seem to find me."

"I know, but the business on Avenue X you started." I started to protest. "I know, it's your post, but you can't take on the Mafia all by yourself. These guys don't care if you're a cop. They'll do you in a blink. All I'm saying is, just be careful. I don't want you hurt."

The paperwork was done and I lodged the prisoner in the cell. I gave him a pack of cigarettes and a sandwich and soda. "Let me ask you a question," I said. "How come you didn't shoot me?"

"Whaddaya crazy? You kill a cop, they give you the chair," was his simple answer.

The holidays were fast approaching, and Jennifer and I were making plans on how to spend them. My sisters didn't have anything concrete that they were doing together. "Big Jim" was way down in South Jersey, so that was out. "Why can't you come down for Christmas Eve?" "Aw, Jim, it's a long ride and I don't want to be on the road with people coming from Christmas parties. Besides, I'm working an eight-by-four on Christmas morning." He agreed. So we went to Jackie and Muriel's on Christmas Eve.

Jackie and I are about as mechanically inclined as the Disney character Goofy. So he and I stayed out of the way as Jennifer and Muriel put the toys together. I saw the look in Jennifer's eyes as she put the stroller, tike bike, and dollhouse together. I felt kind of guilty that she wasn't getting pregnant. I thought maybe it was me. I promised myself that I'd go to Dr. DeVito and have him check me out.

I went in for the eight-by-four at about six o'clock. The desk officer called in one of the guys from the late tour that lived about twenty minutes from the station house. "Hey, kid, thanks a lot. I really appreciate the early blow. I have six kids. The wife will be glad. Someday I'll return the favor."

Nothing happened the next two hours. So, at a few minutes before eight o'clock, I went into the station house to start my tour. Lieutenant Miltie Block had the desk and he assigned me to ride with Eddie Quigley.

Now, there's a story about Lieutenant Block. He had steel gray hair and stood straight as a rod. He was just about my height and had the looks of the movie actor, Jeff Chandler. Above his shield he had a rack of ribbons signifying the various awards he had received. He was a great boss and a better cop.

During the summer, he volunteered to go to Coney Island as the patrol supervisor. You'd see him all over the place. He'd talk to the rookies (me included) and give advice. If someone screwed up (me included), he'd take you on the side and explain the proper way to handle the situation.

One day, Bill Metcalf and I saw a crowd gathered around some woman who had collapsed on the beach. We saw this cop, McKinney, I think his name was, walking toward the supine woman. McKinney was carrying two plastic cups of water. Lieutenant Block was about ten yards behind him going through the sand. They revived the woman, helped her off of the beach and put her in the ambulance to Coney Island Hospital. Block took McKinney on the side. "Listen, kid," he said in his fatherly voice. "You're not Gunga Din. You tell, and I emphasize 'tell,' one of the civilians to get the water. You stay with the victim. You render first aid or at least look like you are. You don't leave them alone. Someone could take her belongings. I know you want to help, but the best way is to delegate. The people will help. Even those that aren't that nice will help. But you have to take command. You got it, son?"

"Yes, sir, and thanks," was McKinney's reply.

That was good old Lieutenant Milton Block.

Anyway, back to Quigley and me. Well, along about nine o'clock, Quigley pulled into the parking lot at St. Mark's Church on Ocean Avenue. "Listen, I'm going to go into Mass."

"Well, I have to go too."

"Okay, let me get another sector to cover us if we get a radio run."

What that means is, if you get a call, the adjoining sector car will handle the run until you get back on the air. Using precinct code words over the air is the normal way to do it. I'll give you an example. "Pizza man. We're going to see the man. Cover."

"Ten-four," comes back the reply. "Pizza man" was a cop by the name of Peter Brancato. He liked to eat pizza. Ergo, "pizza man." Got it?

The church was warm and beautifully decorated for the birth of Christ. Eddie and I stood in the rear, both of us lost in our own private thoughts. Father Brady gave his usual great sermon and we received Communion. The other church goers nodded at us and smiled. I guess it looked good to the people to see two uniformed policemen receiving the Eucharist.

After Mass, we resumed patrol. "Pizza man" let us know we didn't miss any calls, so we just drove randomly through the streets of the sector. About three-forty, the radio crackled, and the voice coming from the speaker announced sixty-one—car2107—report of a dispute at . . . I wrote down the address on the clipboard and Quigley headed to it.

It was cold, but not bitter. There was snow piled at the curbs, but the streets were clear. When we got to the address, the first thing I noticed was a big hole in the front window and a vacuum cleaner with a red bow on it lying on the grass patch in front of the house.

We knocked and a middle-aged woman in a flannel bathrobe opened the door. "Whaddaya want?" Quigley told her we received a call about a disturbance. "Nah, no disturbance here." I saw a skinny man seated on the couch in the living room. "Sir, are you okay?" No response. "Ma'am, how did the window get broken?"

"I threw that goddamn vacuum cleaner through it. That's how."

"Why?"

"What the hell kinda Christmas present is that? A friggin' vacuum cleaner? What am I, a slob or something? Is the house dirty?" Actually, it was clean. I went over to the man on the couch and we walked into another room. "What happened?"

"It was on sale. It's lightweight and it's got a whole bunch of features. I thought she'd like it." (What a romantic.) I asked him to stay in the other room. Eddie had the woman calmed down, so I went outside and brought the vacuum back.

By the time I got inside, Quigley had the two of them hugging. He gave them a phone number of a glazier from the neighborhood and left. We got in the car, he lit a cigarette, and I fished a cigar out and lit it up. "Okay, what did you do? What did you say?"

"Well, it turns out that she's on some medicine 'cause she's going through the change of life. She didn't take it today and she gets moody." (Moody! I'll say.) "I told her that the gift was heartfelt and not an indication that the husband was complaining about her housekeeping. I had spotted some boxes near the tree with her name on it, so I figured he got her something more personal. He came in with her pills, and well, you saw the rest."

"If that glazier doesn't come through, they're gonna be cold." Quigley smiled. "Not her so much, she gets hot flashes." The two of us laughed.

The tour ended and I headed for North Arlington for Christmas dinner. Jennifer and I had exchanged our gifts when we got back to the apartment, but I had a trunk full of stuff for her family. They had a tradition that they didn't open their presents until Christmas evening. They started this when Eileen, the youngest, hit ten or eleven. We had a wonderful meal. We cleared the dishes and spread all the presents in piles in the living room. Jennifer and I made out like bandits. I got ties, sweaters, a dozen pair of socks, Old Spice shaving mug (with brush), and Old Spice after-shave. She got a ton of stuff too. Georgie and Jeannie gave us a fifty-dollar gift certificate to Pete's Tavern on Irving Place. As I said, quite a haul.

New Year's Eve in Times Square! Oh, boy, I can't wait. I was assigned to report to Forty-Second Street and Broadway for an 8:00 p.m. to 4:00 a.m. tour at the "Crossroads of the World." I was actually excited about being there. I wasn't happy about not being in North Arlington with Jennifer and her family, but I'm a cop, and I go where I'm assigned. We were given areas to stand. I was told to stay on the sidewalk at Forty-Third Street and Broadway on the west side of the street. Because of my uncanny knowledge of the city, I knew which side was west, which was east and I knew north from south. Damn, I'm smart.

Some sergeant told us (there were three other cops and me) to stay against the building line about ten feet apart. Now, that was a good idea at about eight-thirty, but as Times Square started filling up with people, I found myself backed up against a plate glass window. Déjà vu?

The Sergeant came through the crowd and I grabbed him by the sleeve. "Hey, Sarge, I'm not too comfortable being pressed into this window. How about you let us stand by the curb? I mean, this crowd's just gonna get bigger and I've already had the pleasure of going through a glass window."

He looked at me and looked at the crowd. He looked at me again and just walked away. So I did the same thing. I motioned to the cop ten feet from me and pantomimed getting pushed through the window. He knew what I meant, and he motioned to the cop ten feet from him and so on up the line. We were all at the curb line when the ball came down starting 1963.

About two minutes after midnight, I heard a crack. I looked back to the sidewalk and saw two drunken fools falling against "my window." Thank God for some sober revelers. They pulled the jerks away from the window just before it splintered into pieces. I realized then and there that unless I was assigned there, I'd never be in Times Square on another New Year's Eve. That's what television is for!

Things were going good for me at work. I rode in the radio car more frequently. I wasn't getting into any situations where I had to deal with the "wise guy" element. I was just doing normal patrol duties. I'll give you a for instance. On a day tour (8:00 a.m. to 4:00 p.m.) during the week, you'd be assigned to a school crossing. That meant that usually, from about eight-twenty to nine-thirty, you'd be on the corner crossing the kids. Now, if school starts at nine o'clock, wouldn't you think that the little darlings should be there by nine o'clock? Well, the answer is yes. But the school people reasoned that "what if a student is tardy" (when I was a kid, that meant late), but anyway, "if a student is tardy" (I like that word), he or she should be safely guided across the street." I guess they had a point. But what about . . . look both ways, wait for the green light, or if you were real small, how about your mother or father or neighbor crossing you? Why the heck should two cops have to sit there and wait for some little bozo or bozette who is late?

Then you had the afternoon crossing. "You will be there no later than eleven-twenty and you will stay until 1:45 p.m., okay?"

"Okay." Lunch is from noon till one, so why eleven-twenty? What? Some bozo or bozette is gonna sneak out early to have a three-martini lunch? Come on, give me a break.

Now you come to the excusal time crossing. That went from two-thirty to three-forty. Now, school ended at three o'clock. I don't know about you, but I was outta there before the echo of the dismissal bell had stopped bouncing off the walls.

But they were the rules, and God forbid, the Sarge came around and you weren't at the crossing. Man, you'd be in big trouble.

Now, if you got a radio run, one stayed at the crossing and the other responded to the job. It really wasn't safe for your partner, but that's the way it was. Nothing you could do about it. Somewhere in between the crossings, you and your partner had to find time to wolf down a quick sandwich and a soda. If you got a radio run in your sector, the sandwich and soda were thrown into a litter basket and you handled the job. Most cops hated school crossings. They were boring. No action. No excitement. Unless, yes, you were me. I felt like I had that "trouble" cloud over my head. I mean, I'm on the crossing.

Quigley got a call, so he left. I'm in the middle of the street, and from out of nowhere, this big black Lincoln makes a screaming turn from the side street onto Avenue U. It looked like it was coming straight at me. I froze right there. At the last second, the car veered away and sped down Avenue U. What to do? What to do? I did recognize the driver, though.

Jennifer was getting a little sad due to the fact that she wasn't getting pregnant. I had gone to visit Dr. DeVito and he gave me all the male tests. Even though I hadn't studied for them, I passed. So half the equation was solved.

Big Jim had a friend, a former FBI guy, who worked for a large container shipping firm. It seems that they had an apartment in a hotel in San Juan, Puerto Rico that was not going to be used for the first two weeks in February. "You get yourself down there and the apartment is yours for ten days." That was the message Jim relayed to me.

We made plans to leave on the first Monday in February on the two o'clock plane to Puerto Rico. (Sun and fun time.) I put in the requisite vacation form, a U.F.-28. The captain signed it and I hand carried it to my friend, the roll call man. He logged it in and even told me to have a nice vacation. (Nice man . . . yeah, righht!)

I was still steaming about the school crossing incident and I kept looking for the driver. Alas, it was to no avail. Until, yes, until the day we were leaving. Well, it was the morning of the afternoon we were leaving. I was just finishing my late tour (12:00 p.m. by 8:00 a.m.) and was walking back to the station house. It was a dreary, cold, damp, February morning. I had just spent the entire night shaking hands with doorknobs up and down Avenue U. I was thinking about how nice it was going to be in Puerto Rico. I stopped to wait for the light on Avenue U and Ocean Parkway, and I just glanced around and spotted a cab who was waiting for the light to change. In the back of the cab was a dozing Nunzio DiCostanzo, the brother of the rapist. Also the driver of the large black Lincoln from the school crossing.

I motioned to the cab driver to stay put and he complied. Opening the back door of the cab, I reached in and pulled Nunzio "the startled" out onto the street.

"Hey, who's gonna pay for the fare?" the cabby asked. "How much?" was my query. "Buck and a quarter." I threw two onto his lap. "Keep the change," and Maxi the Taxi sped away.

"Whaddaya crazy? I didn't do nuttin'." I had his arm twisted behind his back so far that his hairy knuckles were touching his head. He was screaming and squirming. I marched him in that position to the side entrance of the station house. I opened the garage door and released my hold on him. "Okay, tough guy, let's see what you have."

He kind of stammered a bit and then said, "Yeah, but you got the badge and the gun."

"It didn't stop you from scaring the hell outta me when you had the car." I didn't see it coming, but he threw a left that got me on the shoulder. Now the dance was on.

The side inside doors of the station house were swinging types. You know the kind. They swing in and out. I dragged Nunzio from the garage and used his head to open the doors inward. This caused him great pain and embarrassment and he fell forward onto the floor.

Lieutenant Priola and Lieutenant Block were at the desk. "Whaddaya got, kid?" Then I remembered, Puerto Rico! "Jaywalking, Lieu."

"Take him in the back and give him a summons and then throw him the hell outta here."

"Hey, Nunzio, how you doing?"

"Nunzio, you look like crap."

"Yo, Nunzio, man, you don't look too happy."

"Nunzio, did you fall or something?" The cops didn't let up on poor Nunzio until I showed him the front door of the station house.

We arrived in Puerto Rico and it was great. I got the luggage from the carousel and we headed toward the exit. Jennifer tugged on my arm. "Look," and she pointed to a man holding a sign with our name.

I walked over to him and told him who we were. He reached down, took the suitcases, and, with a nod of his head, gave us the "follow me" sign. We got in the back of the car, and after he put the luggage in the trunk, he wordlessly got in and drove us to the Hotel Pierre in San Juan.

On the side of the road, I noticed the deplorable condition of the shacks along the highway. Rusted trucks and cars on the grassy area in front of their corrugated tin huts, shacks, lean-tos or whatever they were. You couldn't call them houses. Kids, kids, and more kids playing in and around all the clutter and dirty puddles that dotted the area. These poor kids.

Once we passed the area near the airport, things picked up as far as the houses and the surrounding area. We drove through San Juan and it looked like any other urban area except for the palm trees. The driver stopped in front of the hotel, got the luggage, and handed it to the bellhop. I reached in my pocket to give him a tip. He held up his hand. "No se gracias, Señor." Huh? He turned, got back in the car, and drove off.

Jennifer and I approached the desk. I gave him our names and he nearly snapped to attention. He waved his arms and three bellhops arrived to take us up to the room. I mean, like, if he just gave me the key and told me the room number, I could find my own way. But why fight when you're being treated like royalty?

So the royal couple and our entourage go skyward to the floor marked PH! PH? Wait a minute, doesn't that mean *penthouse*? Man, I hope we can afford this. I hope Big Jim's FBI friend wasn't mistaken.

Well, we're in the living room (which was the size of the deck of a battleship) and I'm thinking that we're going to be sleeping on pull-out couches until the "prime minister of the royal couple" asks us to follow him. He opens two side-by-side doors (floor to ceiling, mind you) and we go into a room the size of a flight deck on an aircraft carrier.

The rest of our entourage follows with our luggage. One of them opened a walk-in closet to hang up our garment bags. In the closet, I spied a few sport jackets, some trousers, and a few casual shirts. All in clear dry cleaning bags. I knew it! It's all a mistake.

I turned to the "prime minister" and inquired. "Whose are they?" A bit of a pause and then the toothy smile. "Mr. Maloney's. He leaves them here so he doesn't have to travel with them. You know Mr. Maloney! Right?" I looked at Jennifer who was studying the large bouquet of flowers on this huge table.

"Mr. Maloney? Er. Which Mr. Maloney?" I thought that might be a good come back. "John, Señor, Mr. John Maloney."

"Oh, good old John. Jennifer, you know John. Well, actually I call him Jack. That's a great idea, leaving extra clothes here. Very smart, good move. Makes sense." I was babbling.

"Señor, if there is anything you or the Señora need, just ask. Sign for anything you want and the bills will be sent to the home office after you leave." I put my hand in my pocket to give the royal entourage a pittance. They politely refused and backed off the aircraft carrier deck and closed the doors.

Jennifer looked at me with that "are you sure we belong here" look. I just smiled, gave her a big hug, and (as if I believed it) said, "Boy, this is great. Why don't we get changed and hit the beach?" She started to unpack and I told her I had to go to the lobby because I forgot to pack razorblades. I got to the lobby and looked for a pay phone.

After talking to Big Jim, I felt a lot better. It seems that the shipping firm let its employees and their relatives use the hotel when it isn't being used for business. The company had a twelve-year lease on the penthouse. The retired FBI friend was now my cousin.

I returned to the room and Jennifer was already in her swimsuit. Boy, did she look great. The days went flying by. We swam, shopped, made love, had lovely dinners, and danced a lot.

Along about the sixth day, I rented a car to do some exploring on the island of Puerto Rico. We called room service and asked to have a picnic basket ready. The desk clerk gave us explicit directions on how to get to the fabled rain forest (that's El Yunque, to those of you who aren't world travelers) and the beautiful Luquillo Beach.

So off we go. I'll tell you this, the rain forest was beautiful. Fruit trees, palm trees, and a lot of other trees. Birds of every color, all squawking at the same time. Waterfalls that cascaded into deep blue pools that would radiate rainbows as the falls hit bottom.

I remember that I guess this is what Adam and Eve must have had every day before she found the cursed apple. We found a leafy clearing on the far side of the pool, away from the falls. We spread the blanket and Jennifer opened the picnic basket, reached in, and handed me an apple. What went on for the next few hours is really none of anybody's business. But, well, it was one of, and I emphasize, one of, my favorite memories of our time in Puerto Rico.

We got back to the hotel, showered, and went to dinner. We went right to the room and *almost* went right to sleep.

The next morning we started out early to see the famous Luquillo Beach. With another basket and blanket in tow, off we went. The beach was everything the hotel man said it was and then some. Around two in the afternoon, we started back, but I took a wrong turn and somehow we found ourselves in the "back" country. Finally we spotted a general store in the middle of nowhere. Inside I asked the young boy behind the counter where we were. "You are here."

"I know. But where is 'here'?"

"Well, it's here." After about two or three minutes of the Abbott and Costello routine, a rather large, scary, and hairy man came from the rear of the store. Jennifer was just moping around looking around at souvenirs and getting some film and sunblock.

The large scary and hairy man was busy making a map of "here" to where we wanted to go. Jennifer placed the souvenirs and other stuff on the counter. I started wandering around the small but neat store. One large glass display case caught my eye. The boy was packaging the items, and the large, scary, and hairy man came over to the display case. "Señor, where you come from you can't have any of them." It was a display of handguns. He continued, "But maybe *you* can." He emphasized "you." "Why do you say that?" I queried. "Because you are a cop from New York." I heard a quick intake of air from Jennifer.

"Er, what makes you think that?"

"I know a cop when I see one. Your accent is New York. Your eyes never stop looking around. Yes, you're a cop." Another intake of air, only this time it was from me. The large, scary, hairy man smiled.

Okay, okay, no more suspense. We made it home to the hotel in one piece. It seems that he had owned a *bodega* (Spanish grocery store for the un-initiated) in Spanish Harlem and took illegal numbers while ("I no sell drugs") selling his Goya beans. He had been arrested many times by the plainclothes cops who always treated him with respect. No rough stuff, no name-calling, and they always got him "right."

His American dream was to make enough money (legal and illegal) to come back to Puerto Rico and open a general store "here." He considered himself a success. His family (which was large) considered him a success. He insisted that we have a little lunch with his family, and we did.

I guess looking back on it, he was a success. I mean, who'd he hurt? People wanted to gamble, so he let them. What the heck, the state of New York is in the numbers business too. Where is all that money going? It sure as heck isn't going to upgrade the school system. That is what the politicians told us the money was going to be used for. But that's another story.

The next morning, we headed out again. But this time I had an official map so I could get back from "there to here." It was really a hot morning, but the hotel clerk informed us that "on the island, this is considered to be a winter day." I looked at the temperature clock on a bank across the street. It read eighty degrees. I guess he'd never been in New York City in February.

We drove toward the beach and Jennifer was looking at the map. "Up ahead is a little inlet. Why don't we just pull in there and see what it's like?" I like to explore and we weren't in a hurry to get to the beach. Besides, there had to be a beach if there's an inlet, right? I pulled off the main road and drove along a path guarded, on both sides, by large palm trees and palm bushes. At the risk of being redundant, what went on for the next few hours, at this secluded inlet, is nobody's business. But this, too, is one of my favorite memories of Puerto Rico.

Sadly, it was time to return to reality. We flew home totally refreshed, in love, and deeply tanned. All I can say is, what a trip. Oh yeah, I forgot, we also won a thousand dollars in the hotel casino. Not a bad trip at all. I went back to work on the four-by-twelve shift, and man, I froze. I had the foot post on Emmons Avenue right off the bay. Why anyone would leave that beautiful island to come to the city was beyond me. I'm not a sociologist, but it didn't make sense to leave year-round nice weather to come to New York, live in a crowded, dirty neighborhood and freeze in the winter.

We continued our routine. When I worked eight-by-four, I'd shoot home and we'd go out to dinner in our neighborhood. If I made an arrest, Jennifer would meet me at night court, and when I was finished, we'd have a late dinner in Little Italy and go back to Stuyvesant Town. On the twelve-by-eight tour, Jennifer would go to her mother's house and I'd be there when she got home from work. We'd eat, watch some TV and I'd go to work. Not a bad life so far. Only one thing was missing, kids.

Although she didn't say anything, I could tell she was disappointed when she knew she wasn't pregnant. Her mother told her that in due time we'd have a family and not let it get to her. I told her the same thing. Meanwhile, my sisters were having one right after the other, as was her sister Betty Ann. C'mon, St. Michael, come through for us.

I was starting to ride in the radio car more frequently. Sometimes I'd be picked to drive the sergeant, or when Lieutenant Miltie Block was working, I'd drive him. He was an interesting man.

He would talk about growing up in a predominately Jewish and Negro (yes, that is what black people were called then) neighborhood in Brooklyn. He'd talk about the prejudice he experienced and the prejudice he saw from his own people toward the Negroes. He talked about being in the army and how the people he served with picked on him because of his faith. He wasn't bitter about it. He just strove to be the best soldier he could be. Gradually, the harassment stopped and he was "accepted" by everyone. He took the younger men under his wing, both colored (yes, that was another acceptable term) and white.

He was sent to Korea where he "fought like hell to have his squad survive."

"Ya know, kid, when the bullets are flying, it doesn't mean a damn thing what color or religion the guy next to you is. All that matters, that you protect him and vice-a-versa. It's the same with the job. You look out for your partner and he looks out for you. Got it?"

"Yes, sir, I got it." I learned a lot from Lieutenant Block. Not only about the job, but life in general.

One night I was driving him and he asked about my life. I told him all about Daddy and Momma, my sisters and brothers. Then, I guess, because he was Jewish, I told him about Mr. Abe Freeman and how he and Mrs. Freeman were so good to Momma and the rest of us after Daddy died. "Do you still keep in contact with him? I mean, did you ever tell him just what you told me?"

"Well . . ." And I paused. "No," I kind of said a little sheepishly.

"Do it. He deserves to know what you think of him and so does she. Make a point to at least call him and thank him. I know for a fact that it would mean a lot to them."

"I will, boss, I promise." I didn't say it, but I thought, how could he "know for a fact?"

After my "jaywalking" encounter with Nunzio, I didn't have any problems when I stopped to give a "pinky ring" type's car a double-parker. It was kind of weird, actually. I'd pull up in front of the Ro-Sal and the usual cast of characters would be inside. A few of the mutts would be looking out the window. I'd point to the offending vehicles and out they'd come to move them. Once in a while one car would still be there, so I'd ticket it. The window watchers would just nod and have a benign smile on their ugly mugs. But no problems. Maybe I was getting through to them. Or maybe they knew something I didn't.

We kept our routine and all seemed well. When I had a weekend off, I'd take off the last tour and my first one back to work and we'd string four or five days together. We'd jump in the car and headed anywhere we wanted. No plans, just . . . I'll give you a for instance. We got in the car and all I said was "Let's go to DC."

"Okay."

About five hours later, we were in the Nation's capital. No plans and no place to lay down our heads. Along about four in the afternoon, as dusk was starting, I said, "Maybe we should look for a room." We asked a DC cop and he suggested Georgetown. With explicit directions, that Jennifer wrote down, in shorthand, I might add, we found this beautiful hotel. So in we went and there we stayed. With no thought of the cost.

Jennifer was making twice what I was making. I mean, give me a break! Every day guys are on the job doing things to help people. In some, not a lot of cases, risking their very lives to save strangers. You take the Emergency Service cops. They climb to the top of bridges to save some sick soul who wants to kill himself because his girl left him. Or for some equally irrational reason. Detectives going after armed killers who have vowed not to be taken alive. The guys on patrol, the backbone of the Police Department. They have to be father, mother, big brother and, in some cases, clergyman. All depending on the circumstances. Now you have a secretary making twice the money a cop does? Hey, don't get me wrong, secretaries do their jobs the same as all the people in the workforce. But! After a day tour, it was actually a treat when Jennifer would say, "Let's not eat out, I'll cook." It really was a treat. Did I tell you before that she's a good cook? Well, if I didn't, she is. We could travel and eat out all because we didn't have any money problems.

I went into work for a twelve-by-eight tour and on the roll call I saw I was in a sector car with Manny Bogen. Manny was smiling when he saw me. "I asked to have you fill in while my partner is out sick." "Great." I smiled back. I knew I'd learn a lot from Manny, and because he had a reputation as a worker, I knew we'd be handling a lot of jobs. Not! For five nights, we just drove around. Not one single radio call in our sector. I think there were two jobs in the precinct all week. So much for learning!

I did have a good time with him. He had just been elected as president of the Shomrin Society. The Shomrin Society is an organization of Jewish cops. It's basically a fraternal organization, the same as the Columbian Society for the Italian American cops and the Emerald Society for the Irish Americans.

I joined the Emeralds and the Holy Name Society, but if the truth be known, I'm really against the divisions that these fraternal groups engender. I mean, we're all Americans. Sure, I'm proud of my Irish heritage, the same as Rocco Mandille (one of our sergeants) is proud of his Italian heritage. But, I mean, we all do the same job, and presumably, we all have the same values. So why not have one big group, open to all, with the goal to support all cops and their families when the need arrives?

Anyway, Manny was happy about his election and I was happy for him. We talked about everything and anything the entire week. He told me that his partner wouldn't be coming back for at least three weeks and did I want him to "tell your pal, the roll call man," to put me in a car with him?"

"Sure, I do." I wondered how he knew about my run-in with him.

"Everybody knows about it and nobody thinks you were wrong." He went on to explain that "inside men or the Palace Guard think they run the precinct. Sometimes they lose sight of the fact that they're still cops. They assume the mantle of boss. All the roll call guy wants is to make sure that the radio cars are manned and the foot posts are covered. If you break their routine or complain, they can really make life miserable for you. So don't worry, you did the right thing." He paused and then smiled. "Ya know, he really believed you were going to throw him out the window." I just sat there and didn't say a word. Work was going well, as was married life. I tried to adhere to my brother Jackie's admonitions about calming down at work. I did my job when I was on foot or the times I rode. I kept a high-visibility profile when I was on my post. When I was in the radio car, we answered all the runs and backed up the other sectors on their jobs. But I didn't go out of my way to look for problems.

I was walking along Kings Highway on my last twelve-by-eight tour. It was the beginning of April, but there was still a winter chill in the air. Jennifer had made me a nice, navy blue wool sweater, and that, plus the overcoat, was enough to ward off the chill. I was just ambling along looking and listening. The streets were virtually deserted. Then I started hearing sounds. I don't know if you've ever been on a deserted street at three in the morning, but sound is magnified. It's hard to tell from whence it comes.

I stopped and so did the sound. Occasionally a bus or car would pass and the sound diminished. I'm asking myself, "What the heck is that noise and where's it coming from?" I heard it again and I knew what it was, finally. Did you ever hear the sound of metal tearing wood? I mean, like a crowbar pulling at a big piece of wood? That was the sound. It took me a few more minutes to isolate where the sound was coming from. I went off Kings Highway and around the corner to East Seventeenth. There was an alleyway behind the stores from East Seventeenth to East Eighteenth.

I noticed that the street light next to the alley was out. I thought that was unusual. I cautiously peeked into the alley and spotted a dark van parked behind a fur store. Now what do I do? The nearest call boxes were four blocks away from the alley in either direction. The burglars would be long gone by the time I went, called, and got back.

I crept into the alley, hugging the wall and bending low so I'd be a smaller target. I backed into the doorway next to the fur store. I saw two guys, all in dark clothes, coming out of the ripped open doorway. I could have sworn that they could hear my heart thumping inside my chest cavity. Come on, St. Michael, help me out . . . again.

They dumped their cargo into the back of the van and went back into the store. My hands were shaking and I was starting to sweat. Oh, boy, am I nervous? Out they came again, and as they dumped their load, I stepped out of the adjoining doorway. The next voice I heard wasn't mine but it came from my mouth. In a slow, measured tone, not loud, and not soft, I said, "Stay where you are. Don't turn around or I'll blow your heads off. You're under arrest." Ever since I had my first run-in on Avenue X with Bruccolleri and Prezziotti, I took to carrying two sets of handcuffs. (All right, all right, my uncle Mike and my brother Jackie told me to do it.)

Anyway, they threw the furs into the van but I knew what they were thinking. The open van doors blocked their exit out to East Eighteenth, so the only way to escape was through me. "Put your hands behind your back *now!*" No compliance. So I took the nightstick in my left hand and hit the taller one right across the back of the neck and then the other one across the back of his legs. I put the gun in my pocket holster, grabbed the cuffs, pulled the big guy's head back by pulling his hair. I cuffed him and threw him face first into the van.

The smaller one had his own ideas. He straightened up and spun around. He tried to bum rush me. I stepped aside and stuck out my foot and clunked him with the nightstick full force on the back. I knelt on his back and cuffed him too. I got him to his feet and hauled him into the back of the van. I pushed the tall guy all the way in and slammed the doors closed. I had taken their belts off and secured their legs together. The keys were in the ignition, so I took them and locked the van.

I turned on my flashlight and went into the store, still scared, and with the thumping heart. Before I went in, I saw the burglar alarm box on the rear wall. It had been by-passed by putting alligator clips onto the lead wires and connecting the other end to a ground wire. Pretty smart! I felt along the wall and found a switch and lit the place up. I was hoping that I won't find anyone else because I didn't have any more handcuffs. I searched the place and it was clean. I spotted the phone on a desk and called the station house. Lieutenant Miltie Block was on the desk, so I told him what I had. I asked him to send a sergeant and could he have someone notify the owner to respond and secure the premises. He grunted and asked if I was all right. (He really is a nice guy.)

So the sergeant and his driver pulled up in about a minute after I hung the phone up. The standard question, "Whaddaya got, kid?" was asked.

"A rear break, Sarge."

"Didya get anybody?"

"Yes, sir, they're in the van." I unlocked it and there they were, all neatly packaged. "Hey, kid, you know what you got?"

"Two burglars," was my reply.

"No, no, you got two pros. These two clowns are real pros." "

Okay," was my reply.

He called for another car to meet us, and when it arrived, he directed one of the cops, Steve Risley, to ride in the van with me and the other to follow the van. The sergeant led the little caravan while his driver stayed at the store to await the owner.

We pulled into the driveway and one of the cops opened the garage doors. Lieutenant Block was standing there. "You got some great collar here, kid. I mean it. You got Tommy Logan and his uncle Mikey Taranto. These guys only steal high-end merchandise. They're good, but we're better, 'cause they get caught a lot."

We counted the fur coats and put them away for safekeeping. There were sixty-two mink jackets and full-length coats. The lieutenant told Risley to watch the two guys because we left them in the van still tied up and cuffed. "No sense in having to watch them in the House when we have to voucher the evidence. I don't need to listen to them yapping."

After the property was vouchered and Polaroids taken, they were put in the Property Room. From there, they'd be collected and stored in the Main Property Clerk's Office in the Seventy-Eight Precinct. Bloch explained that I should hang onto the photos so there wouldn't be any necessity to lug the sixty-two coats back and forth for to court for every appearance. I thought that that was a pretty good idea. I mean, how does one carry sixty-two fur coats? The lieutenant told me that I should, as soon as possible, request a Property Release for the coats from the Assistant District Attorney (ADA) assigned to the case. This way they could be returned to Mr. Levy, the furrier.

We unbuckled the two unhappy passengers and Risley and I took them up to the squad room. The detectives working that night were at the scene of a suicide. We had no idea when they'd come back, so Steve pulled out the fingerprint cards and started to print Logan. They both were complaining about police brutality. "We were only passing the alley. We weren't taking the coats out." They were bringing them in. They chased the guys away, and "we were trying to save the old Jew's" stuff. We live in this neighborhood. We were just being good guys and then this stupid Irish cop, he starts hitting and kicking" and on and on and on. I was busy filling out the arrest cards when the detectives came into the squad room.

Frank Healy and Bill Shea were working the night duty. Bill took over the printing and Frank went to a filing cabinet and took out some folder. He nodded tome to follow him and we went into the lieutenant's office. "I don't know how you do it but you sure have a knack of being in the right place at the right time. Bloch sent the crowbar over to BCI (Bureau of Criminal Identification) and they dusted it for prints. Both of these mutts' prints were on it. Bloch vouchered it and it's in the property room." "You got them cold."

"Now listen to me." And he was looking me right in the eyes. "You have to be very careful from now on. These are two really bad guys. Do you know anything about their background?" I shook my head. "Well, Mikey Toronto is the son of Mikey "No Nose" Toronto and Logan is his grandson. Tommy's mother is No Nose's daughter. His father is half-Italian and Irish. The whole family is in the mob. No Nose is a made man so is his son. Tommy can't be made because he's not full Italian. They make him an associate but they treat him like he's made because of his grandfather."

"The grandfather is a murdering son-of-a-bitch, so is his son-in-law and so are Mikey and Logan. Are you getting the picture? Now, Mikey and Logan have never been arrested for homicide, but they both look good for a couple of mob hits against the Bonanno family. I felt it was more like a public service when the two Bonanno guys got whacked but that's another story. Anyway, these two are a team and they are big earners for the family pulling high-end burglaries. That is when they're not killing people. Are you getting the picture? I just want you to be aware of who they are and who they associated with. You got any questions?"

"Yeah, why'd they call him 'No Nose'?" Healy shook his head and smirked.

I finished the paperwork and the lieutenant told me to go up to the locker room and close my eyes. My two friends were lodged in the cells and the cop on cell duty would keep an eye on them. "Remember, kid, you gotta take them to photo, then over to Headquarters to put them in the daily line-up, the wagon driver will tell you what to do. Now try to get a little rest. Be back here at a quarter to eight in uniform."

I climbed the stairs to the top floor locker room, pushed two benches together, put a roll of toilet paper under my head and put the overcoat over me as a blanket. It seemed as though I had just closed my eyes when Manny Bogen started shaking me. "Hey Sleeping Beauty, you gotta get up. It's time to hit the floor." He handed me a container of coffee. "I'm going with you to the line-up. Bloch cleared it with Lieutenant Ravalgi, you know just to show you the ropes. I've been there before, okay?"

"Sure, Manny, and thanks for the coffee."

Now I'd heard about the line-ups but didn't know what they were like or what the procedure was or what I did. I'd seen line-ups in the detective movies and a couple of cop TV shows but this wasn't showbiz.

The way you got your prisoner to the line-up was this way: Each Boro had a designated precinct where you went, in the Paddy Wagon, to have him photo'd and where you'd pick up your "yellow sheet." The yellow sheet was the chronological history of your perp's run-ins with the law. It was called a yellow sheet because it was printed on, guess. Right! Yellow paper.

Anyway, the lieutenant assigned there would determine if a collar was good enough or important enough to go to the line-up in Police Headquarters. Lieutenant Bloch had called ahead and told his counterpart that this collar should go to the line-up. Detectives and bosses from all over the city attended to see if any similar crimes in their precincts were linked to the ones brought in during the past twenty-four hours.

They looked over the arrest reports for any similarity to their unsolved burglaries, robberies, assaults, rapes, homicides, etc. I'll give you an example: Say, for instance, the cops in Coney Island arrest a guy or guys pulling a stick-up and all the perps are wearing Halloween masks. Now you got a detective from the north end of Queens or the Bronx and they had a spate of similar robberies, one could conclude that their miscreants might be the same ones from their command. Are you with me so far? Good. So the detectives could get all the info on the new arrest and try to connect these perps with their cases. That's the overall reason for the line-up.

Manny and I got my two guys photo'd and I collected their yellow sheets. We got back into the "Paddy" Wagon and headed to Manhattan. The wagon stopped on Centre Market Place, the rear of Headquarters. I climbed out the back and helped Toronto out and it seemed like a hundred flashbulbs exploded at once. Manny called to me, from inside the wagon, to wait for Logan. I had the two of them on either side of me. Logan was trying to kick on the of photographers and Toronto was cursing and spitting at a few others.

I grabbed the links of the cuffs and applied upward pressure. That calmed them down.

We went down the metal steps and into the, dungeon like atmosphere, of the basement. From there, we made our way up to the line-up room where I put them in a cage-like cell near the stage. A couple of uniformed officers took over, and Manny and I went into the main room.

This is where it all started, I thought to myself. The fabled line-up room was the auditorium where I was sworn in a few short years ago. We found seats among the throng of men. The place had a blue hue to it from all the cigars and cigarette smoke. I took out a cigar and was about to light up when I felt a hand on my shoulder. I turned and there was Uncle Mike. Don't even think about it when you're in uniform." I put it back inside my overcoat pocket.

After the introduction to Manny and inquiries about Jennifer, he sat next to me. The side door opened and Inspector Ray McGuire went to the podium to begin the line-up. It seemed that I wasn't the only Stark boy who had been busy last night.

McGuire made the requisite opening remarks, then told the officer on the stage to begin. Out came four guys who looked like they were just off the boat from Ireland. McGuire explained that his squad, the Safe, Loft, and Truck Squad, had apprehended the quartet as they were torching a safe at a diamond importers' showroom in mid-town Manhattan. As the detectives closed in on them, one of them pulled out a military style .45 and started shooting. (I was wondering why the one guy's head was wrapped in blood-stained bandages.) McGuire went on, "These guys are the top of the line when it comes to safe-crackers. John Stark [hey, that's my brother Jackie], Tom Swift, Ray Hoyt, and Tommy Kinnone made the events after a long month of surveillance and at great personal sacrifice and work." Leaning against the wall was Jackie with his three partners.

I kinda waved to him and he, nonchalantly, nodded. Damn, I was proud. I poked Uncle Mike in the ribs and he just smiled. McGuire continued bringing out solo and multiple perps and enumerating their MOs for the assemblage.

Then it was my turn. Well, not my turn but Logan and Toronto's turn. It really wasn't a turn, of course, but they were the next to be brought out. McGuire read their yellow sheets, described their MO and then went into the circumstances of the arrest. As he was ending he added, "The officer who got these two is the brother of John Stark who got the 'Dummy' Taylor crew." Jackie looked over at me, smiling. Uncle mike smacked me on the back with his big paw. "Good job."

I look back now and I think how proud I was, proud of Jackie and proud to be with Uncle Mike and mostly just damn proud to be a cop. The only thing missing, at that moment, was Daddy being able to see his sons. Oh, well, whatta gonna do?

Uncle Mike, Jackie, and I were standing together when Inspector McGuire walked over to us. "Hi ya, Mike, how's things in Queens?" He and Uncle Mike started talking about the old days when suddenly Uncle Mike said, "I'm getting out, Ray. I put my retirement papers in today. I figure the city is safe enough with these two out there." McGuire pointed a thumb at Jackie and said, "Yeah, well at least this one doesn't leave his prints all over a crime scene." Although he was smiling, I turned red.

Our family reunion broke up when Manny Bogen came over and told me we had to get the two mutts over to Brooklyn for arraignment. Uncle Mike told Manny to hold on and he, Jackie, and McGuire took me into a corner. "Listen, these guys are very well connected and are big earners for the family. You have to grow eyes in the back of your head. I don't want you to get paranoid but just be careful." McGuire and Jackie just nodded. I thought to myself, *What the hell did I get into?*

We left the dungeon of Headquarters. Ran past the gauntlet of photographers and got into the wagon. We off-loaded the prisoners in the basement of the Brooklyn Criminal Court building and then went to draw up the complaint affidavit. After I got it docketed, I found my brother-in-law Frank and asked him if he could put my case on the top of the list. I was really starting to get tired.

Manny and I went to the coffee shop and had a little light lunch. Along about one thirty we went back to the court and waited for the court officers to unlock the door. Manny tugged on my sleeve. "What?"

"Come with me," and he headed for the police sign-in room. "What's up, Manny, we signed in already?" Then I saw them.

If you were ever casting a movie about the mob, here was your cast. All of them with the leather coats, pinky rings, the gold chains, and wrist bracelets. They looked, well, they looked stupid. Stupid but in an intimidating way. I recognized a few of the faces but then I saw a short man in a suit that probably cost a couple of hundred dollars. He was sandwiched in between two huge guys with no necks. One no-necker was holding the suit man's overcoat and the other his hat.

They saw me about the same time. The second no-necker whispered something to the suit man, and as he turned, full face, to look at me, I immediately knew who he was. He was Mikey (No Nose) Toronto. Now, you might wonder how I recognized him, so I'll tell you. Where his nose should have been, he had a little flap of skin and two pig slits where his nostrils should have been.

I turned to Manny and I said, "That's No Nose, right?"

"Yup."

"Geez, Manny, I hope he has good eyesight."

"What the hell are you talking about?"

"Well, how the heck is he gonna be able to keep his glasses on?"

"You know, kid, you're nuts."

Inside the police sign-in room Manny spoke to Lieutenant Cummings. He told him about my collar and the crew that come with No Nose to watch the proceedings. Cummings picked up the phone and, in a few clipped sentences, alerted the court officers. He then got two of his men to go into the courtroom through the judge's chambers. I might add, two big men. The O'Brien brothers. They told the judge what was believed to be going to happen. The court officers had everything else covered.

Finally court resumed after the lunch break. Manny and I sat in the front row which was designated for the police and attorneys. I sat sideways so I could eyeball the gallery behind me. Manny did the same. I figured since I didn't have eyes in the back of my head, this was the next best thing.

The court started filling up with uniformed court and police officers. Sergeant Jimmy Riley and Lieutenant Cummings had a solid line of blue right across the rear of the courtroom and another line down the side wall on the side where No Nose and his entourage were seated.

Finally the judge came out. The case was called. I went into the holding pen and took custody of them from Corrections. I brought them in front of the judge. Their attorney had spoken to them in the holding pen so he was there as was the Assistant District Attorney (ADA).

The court officer read the charges. The judge reviewed their yellow sheets and then asked the shark skin suit wearing attorney, "Do you want to be heard?"

"Yes, your Honor," and for the next ten minutes be extolled the virtues of his two clients (his representation of them was just for the arraignment). After the arraignment, the "boys" would get two high-profile attorneys who specialized in "wise guys."

Mercifully, the judge finally held up his hand and signaled, the windy shark skin suit, that he had heard enough. Turning in the direction of the ADA, he asked, "Do the people wish to be heard?"

"Briefly, your Honor," and everyone let out a sigh of relief.

After he finished, the judge looked down at the prisoners and announced, "Based on the arresting officer's affidavit and the lengthy arrest records and inordinate amount of convictions, I'm setting bail in the amount of one million dollars each. Pick a date for a hearing." Shark skin suit asked, "Your Honor, is that cash or bond?" The judge looked out into the gallery and announced, "That's one million in cash and the District Attorney's Office will verify that the money is not from the proceeds of any crime, put 'em in, Officer."

So I did. Mikey and Tommy were not happy campers. "You don't know who you're up against, Cop."

"You better watch your back, Cop." Now, I didn't care about that, but I got a little annoyed, no, a lot annoyed, when Tommy said, "Hey, Cop, I know where you live."

By this time, I had taken off their cuffs. I turned sideways, grabbed him by the hair, pulling his head up and with the heel of my hand hit him right in the Adam's apple. Tommy Tough Guy went to his knees. "Listen, you piece of shit, I know where you live too, but if I ever see you or one of your no-necks or no-nose friends or relatives anywhere near me or anyone I care about, I swear to God you will watch me kill your mother just before I kill you. Do yourself a favor, believe me." I turned to Mikey Toronto. "Keep a leash on your mutt 'cause rabid dogs have to be shot."

I left the holding cell area and walked through the courtroom out into the main hall. Manny was by my side and there was a phalanx of court and police officers. "Hey, Manny, is this for real? I mean, if everybody knows that No Nose is such a bad guy, then why isn't he in jail?" "Witnesses disappear, jurors are bought off, air-tight cases get holes in them. He insulates himself in such a way that it's hard to pin anything on him that will stick." "Oh", I said. Just before the door to the sign-in room I saw "No Neck" One and "No Neck" Two lounging against the wall. No Nose was standing between them. He was staring at me with that "if looks could kill" look. He took his thumb and drew it across his throat as if it was a knife. I walked to about two feet in front of him and took my index finger and shoved it up my nose to the second knuckle. "Don't you wish you could do that?" And I winked.

Did you ever see a guy turn purple? Well, I did. His veins were popping in his neck and a large one was pulsating right in the front of his head. It was beautiful.

We went in to sign out and Lieutenant Cummings just looked at me, with his fatherly, lopsided grin. "Kid, you are nuts." I just nodded, signed out, and my bodyguard, Manny, and I took the train back to the Six-One. I was starting to run out of gas. I mean, I was really tired. "You want to stop for a beer?" Manny asked, and much to my surprise, I said, "No. Thanks anyway, Manny, I'm whipped. I can't wait to get into bed."

"Listen, kid, just make sure that nobody is following you. Look for a tail. You insulted the hell out of that bum and he really is nuts. You're only partway there. By the way, I almost laughed my ass off when you stuck your finger up your nose."

I got to the car and did as I was told. I watched for a tail. I made a few U-turns for no reason. I went around a few blocks that I didn't have to. I checked the mirror frequently, all the way to North Arlington, New Jersey, for my three days off. Well, actually, because of the arrest, I only had two left.

I arrived without incident, and the first thing I did, after saying hello to my mother-in-law, was to reach for a can of beer in the fridge. I went into the living room, took a couple of swallows and promptly fell asleep on the couch. When I woke up, Jennifer was there as well as her sister Eileen. I could smell the pot roast cooking. The mother was a great cook.

After the dishes were done, we were all in the living room watching TV. I fell asleep again. Along about twelve thirty, the front door flew open and Georgie came flying into the living room. "Hey, Tip." (Georgie called me Tip or Trunk, depending on his mood. Why? I don't know.) "Look at this." He had copies of the early editions of the *News* and *Post*. There on the front page was me with my two prisoners. Inside on page three were two more pictures and the story. They made it sound like I had captured John Dillinger. To me it was just another collar.

Jennifer was all excited about me being on the front pages. That was until she read the story and learned about their records and all about No Nose. "These are very bad people. I mean, they're killers. They're in a gang." I got off the couch and held her in my arms. "Don't worry, hon, the gang I'm in is bigger and better. These mutts are all talk and no action."

"All the same, I want you to promise me you'll be careful."

"I will. I promise," I said. The picture caused a flurry of phone calls from Big Jim, my sisters, aunts, and uncles. But a few days later it was all forgotten and everything was back to normal. Or so I thought.

I went to work for a day tour and was riding with Manny Bogen. We weren't assigned to Manny's regular sector but were sent to the area furthest away from the Ro-Sal and all the boys. We were patrolling in Gerritsen Beach. Gerritsen Beach is a small enclave made up of single-family homes that were, at one time, summer bungalows. The bungalows were converted into all year-round homes. Some of them were enlarged to two-story homes. The area was inhabited, primarily, by cops, firemen, construction workers, and families that had lived there for years and years. The homes were well kept and the people actually seemed glad that the cops were around.

It had water on three sides with a marina for boats, from rows to yachts, moored there. It was similar to an old New England fishing town except that it was in Brooklyn. Manny and I spent the week just driving around talking and laughing. I asked him why we weren't in his usual sector and all he did was shrug and say, "Hey, I go where I'm told."

After my swing, I came back to do a week of four-by-twelves. Again we were assigned to Gerritsen Beach. I didn't think anything of it because at least I was riding and not on afoot post. We handled a few jobs involving kids congregating on the corner, some "lovers" parked in front of someone's house. The owners of a couple of double-parked cars had to be located and told to move them.

We answered one job, at about ten thirty, regarding a car being driven on the sidewalk on Gerritsen Avenue. We rounded the corner and, sure enough, there is a car going forward and reverse in front of a neighborhood saloon. I slipped on the dome light of our car and got out. The car stopped, blocking the door of the bar. I tapped on the driver's window and the driver rolled it down. "What seems to be the matter, Officer?"came the question from this beautiful-looking young woman. "You are driving on the sidewalk. May I see your license and registration, please?"

"You don't seem to understand. Every Wednesday night, my husband and all his pals from this bar come to my house for a card game. I'm tired of the house smelling like a bar when I get up on Thursday. I figure if I don't let them out of here, they won't be able to come to my house and stink it up. I don't think I'm wrong." How do you argue with female logic?

We got her to park the car and a guy came out of the bar. "Listen, Officer, I'm sorry. I mean, all she had to do was tell me she didn't want me to have the game and we woulda gone someplace else."

"I've told you a hundred times."

"I thought you were kidding."

"I'm not."

"I can tell." I felt like I was watching a ping-pong game. Finally I called a time-out. "Look," I said to the guy, "just promise the lady you and your buddies won't play and I think she'll be happy. Am I right?" So now she pipes in, "I don't care if they play, but just don't leave a mess and open the basement windows to let the smoke out." So Manny and I look at the guy and he says, "If that's all that's bothering you, consider it done, okay?" Now she says, "Okay. Can I go home now, Officer?" I gave her back the license and registration and off she went. The guy thanked us and gave a thumbs-up to his buddies looking out the bar windows. Manny got on the radio and told Central-Dispatch that the condition was corrected. Another marriage saved.

On my next to last four by twelve, I went into the sitting room and there, on the chalk board, was a note for me to see the Roll Call man. As usual, I was about an hour early for work. So I climbed the stairs to "my pal's" office. "Tomorrow you have to go to Headquarters, in civilian clothes, for an interview for a plain clothes detail." I shot him a withering look. "I swear to God this is legit. It came on the teletype. It came through the Boro right to the captain. He told me to notify you, I swear."

This all came out in one rapid sentence. I took a copy of the teletype message and went out. Manny and I turned out and I told him. He smiled and wished me luck with the interview. We stopped for coffee and I called Jackie. He didn't seem overly happy or even surprised. He just wished me luck. I called Big Jim. Now he really seemed excited for me. But, there's always a "but" with Big Jim. "You know what plain clothes work entails, don't you?"

"I kinda know. I think they go after bookies and drug pushers, right?"

"Right, and the bookies and drug pushers offer the cops money to, A, let them go, or B, after you arrest them, you throw the case." He continued, "If I ever hear of you taking any money from anyone, I will put you in jail. You got that?"

"I got it, Jim."

He continued, "Well, anyway, good luck."

After I left the roll call man, I called Jennifer and she was happy for me. "I'll iron that new white shirt I just bought you. I'm sure you'll do fine at the interview."

The night passed very slowly. No radio runs, no double-parkers, no cars on sidewalks. I could only describe it as a long, boring night. Finally I got home. Jennifer was up waiting for me. She wanted to know exactly what it meant to be a plainclothes cop. I gave her what I thought, but I really wasn't sure. I saw them at the precinct when they had an arrest, but I didn't know how they filled their day. I knew it wasn't like walking under the boardwalk like I had done in Coney Island.

The teletype message directed me to report at 8:00 a.m. at Headquarters. I went to a room on the third floor, told the uniform officer who I was, and he directed me to sit on a bench. The room started filling up with guys. I was obviously the youngest in the group. From overhearing conversations, the average time in the job was between eight and ten years. I barely had two. Anyway, my time came for the interview.

I went into the room and saw five white-haired, red-faced men sitting at a large table with stacks of personnel files all over the place. They all introduced themselves to me. I have no idea who they were. I don't even think their names registered in my brain. I guess you'd say I was nervous.

The obvious leader of the white heads looked at me with eyes that were like laser beams. "All right, why'd you apply for plainclothes and why should we consider you?" Gulp, gulp. "Well, sir, I didn't apply for plainclothes, I . . ." He held up his hand. "Then what the hell are you doing here?"

"I don't know, sir."

"What's your name again?" Oh, here it is. "Wait outside."

"Yes, sir."

I sat on the bench and all the remaining candidates were staring at me. I thought that had to be the shortest interview anyone ever had. About thirty seconds later the door opened and the white-haired guy, or was it one of the other white-haired guys, looked at me and said, "Return to your command. You'll be notified." I kinda bowed and out I went. Crushed. Ya see, I thought that all the work I'd done I was being rewarded. At the time you did four years in "clothes" and if you kept your nose clean, you automatically became a *detective*. So much for that thought. I called Jennifer, at work, and told her that I was told they'd notify me if I was accepted or not. "Well, what did they ask? I mean, what kind of questions?"

"Oh, just the usual stuff. No big deal. It was really over before it began, if you know what I mean."

"Are you optimistic?"

"Naw, I honestly like patrol. I don't know if I'd like plainclothes. I'll see you tonight when I get home. Love ya."

"Love you too."

I rode the train back to Brooklyn thoroughly discouraged. It was a nice day, but I felt like it was winter. When I got to the station house, I saw Lieutenant Priola and Sergeant Joyce talking at the desk. "Hey, kid, how'd you do with the interview?"

"They said I'll be notified" is all I could say. Sergeant Joyce asked me, "Where are you going?"

"To change into uniform."

"No, no, no, go home. You shouldn't even have comeback. When you go for an interview, you leave from there. You didn't have to come back."

"Oh." So I got back on the train and headed to Stuyvesant Town and our apartment.

A few days later I was back at work for another set of midnights. I looked at the roll call. Manny's partner was back and I was assigned to the station house. The *station house*? What the . . . I marched out to the desk and saw Lieutenant Ravalgi. "Am I being punished? I mean, why the station house. I want to work. Can't you put someone who wants to be inside and me outside?" "Hey, kid, you do what you told to do, capeesh?"

"Yes, sir."

When you are assigned inside, you make the coffee, sweep out the cells, and watch the prisoners to make sure they don't hurt themselves, and relieve the men on the TS (that's cop talk for telephone switchboard). I gotta tell you about that. Did you ever see pictures of the old telephone operator with that thingamajig on their head with this big board in front of them? The board had all sorts of wires that you plugged into little holes that sent the call to the proper extension? No? Well, I did but only in the movies.

About three o'clock Lieutenant Ravalgi calls me from the cells. "Hey, kid, come here. You got the TS." The TS was usually manned by a sergeant. Half his tour was on the TS. The other half he went on patrol and the patrol sergeant took over the TS. "Boss, I never did this before."

"Well, tonight you learn." The foot cops would call in for their hourly ringtime and you'd mark down the time and the call box number he called in from. Easy, right? Wrong.

People were calling in. I mean, real people, not just cops. "Let me talk to the detectives. I want to talk to the person in charge. I need to get a report number 'cause they stole my car. Hey, I need the cops here. There's a blankety-blank dog barking and I can't sleep. There's people fighting or arguing on the corner." Lights all over the board blinking and winking at me.

After the tenth or twentieth misdirected call, Joe the Boss had had enough. "Hey, kid, make some fresh coffee. You're screwing this up. I'll take over." Well, at least he thought I knew how to make coffee. For the entire week I was "in the house," sweeping, making coffee, watching prisoners, and learning how to work the TS. Man, it was boring. On my last tour, I was notified to report to Headquarters on the following Monday at 8:00 a.m.

The weekend flew by, and at seven thirty, I was back at Headquarters standing in front of the big cement lions guarding the entrance. I made my way up to the third floor, and at eight o'clock on the dot, I was handed a bunch of papers. "Sit over there and fill them out. Any questions just give a yell." So I sat over there and filled out the forms and the questionnaire. About twenty minutes later, I went up to the cop and gave him all the papers. He checked them and said, "Okay, you'll be notified." I thanked him and left. I'll tell you I was thoroughly confused.

I went out onto the street and headed to the little hole in the wall diner, across the street from Headquarters. I settled into a booth, ordered breakfast.

There was a Daily News on the seat so I opened it and started reading the sports pages. I left the diner and it was only about nine thirty. I didn't have to go back to the Six-One (as per Sergeant Joyce). Now, what do I do? So I went home. I woke up about two and was very hungry. I changed into jeans and a sweater and left.

On the corner of Twenty-Third and First was a place called Walsh's Steakhouse. I'd never been in there before, but it always looked inviting, so I went in. I ordered a roast beef and a beer. Halfway through the sandwich, a guy sat next to me. He nodded and I nodded.

As happens in bars, we just started talking. I measured him about six foot four. He was about ten or so years older than me. We talked, had a few more beers, and he left. He told me his name was Jim. I told him mine. "Hey, nice talking to you. I'll see you around." "Okay, Jim, nice talking to you."

The bartender came over and gave me a refill. "You a cop?"

"Yeah."

"I thought so. Jim doesn't usually talk to many people unless they're cops."

"Is he a cop too?"

"Oh, yeah. He works in Headquarters." Oh boy, now I'm paranoid. What are the chances of meeting "Jim" from Headquarters in a saloon I've never been in before, on the same day I just left there? Hmmm.

I finished out the rest of the week walking a foot post on Nostrand Avenue. I didn't even think about it but I couldn't have been further away from "the Boys" area of operation. Nothing really happened on Nostrand Avenue. It's a shopping area with a city project on the east side of the street and all stores on the west side. The east side was covered by the Housing Police Department. I had, what the old-timers called, a one-arm post.

So I'm walking along, smiling, enjoying a nice sunny day, unreasonably warm, just doing . . . Well, doing nothing but keeping an eye on things. I'm walking toward the call box, to make a ring, and this beautiful—and I mean beautiful—young girl is walking toward me. Well, I know I'm married, but this girl was movie star beautiful.

Every head (male, that is) turned to look at her. I wasn't much different. I turned but kept walking straight ahead. As I turned to look forward,

I walked smack into a street light pole. I saw stars, all right, but they weren't movie stars.

I heard this voice. "Mista, Mista, do ya know you're bleeding?" It was Doc Weinberg, the druggist. "Come in the store. I'll fix you." The post on the cap device had gone right into my forehead and a trickle of blood was running down my nose. Some of the pedestrians were smiling. Others were outright in hysterics. I was embarrassed. So "Doc" cleaned it, put a little Band-Aid over it, and smiled. "She was pretty though." He laughed. "I don't know if you're married, Officer, but if you are, remember this: Just because you're on a diet doesn't mean you can't look at the menu."

"Is that one from you or Confucius?"

"No, it's from the Talmud." He laughed a hearty laugh.

When I got home that night, Jennifer asked me what had happened. So I told her and she laughed. I told her what Doc Weinberg had said about the diet and she laughed even harder. "Did anyone at work ask what happened?"

"Oh, yeah, I told them I had a huge zit. I think they believed it."

The next day I went in and on my locker was a picture of a light pole. Man, there are no secrets. I took a lot of good-natured ribbing about my "zit."

"Hey, it's better than getting hit in the head with a bag of chicken parts, right?" More ribbing. I'll tell you something, I worked with a great bunch of guys. It is a serious job, but it's also fun.

I came back after my swing to do a week of four-by-twelves. There was a note on the blackboard with my name. "See Captain." I said to myself, "What the heck did I do now?" I knocked on the door and Captain Walsh called for me to enter. "You wanted to see me, Captain?" It was half question, half fact.

He came out from behind his desk and put his hand out. And shook mine. He pumped it a few times. "Sit down, son. Now listen to me. When you get wherever you're assigned, just be careful. People will offer you money. Don't be tempted. Don't put yourself in a position where you disgrace your family, yourself, or the job. If you ever, and I mean ever, want to discuss anything that you don't think is right, just call me. I mean this sincerely. Now, do you have any questions?"

"Sir, I have no idea what you're talking about."

"Wait a minute. You mean you don't know? Nobody notified you about the transfer? Starting Monday, you're going to the CIC course at the academy. You're going to be put into plainclothes."

I flopped back in the chair. I guess the look on my face said it all. "Captain, did I do something wrong? Are you trying to get rid of me? I mean, I went for the interview and I think I was in the room about thirty seconds. Did I screw up? I mean, I like it here. I'm just learning the job. I really don't know what a plainclothes cop does."

"Listen, son, this is a stepping stone to the Detective Bureau. It takes most cops, at least, five years to get their opportunity. Just stay the way you are. Stay away from anybody that you think might be corrupt. I'm not saying there are corrupt cops, but these bookmakers and now drug dealers, love to have a corrupt cop in their pocket. Don't you be one of them."

"In answer to your question, no, you haven't done anything wrong. As a matter of fact, you've done everything I've asked and then some. You're dedicated and honest. Just stay that way. Remember, if you ever want to talk about anything, don't hesitate to give me a call. Now, go upstairs, clean out your locker, say your so-longs and report to the academy next Monday at 8:00 a.m. Wear your uniform the first day. One more thing, go to roll call and pick your vacation. Take a summer one, if you want. You'll probably be low man wherever they send you so at least you'll have a few weeks in the summer. If he gives you a hard time, just tell him I approved it. You have time coming so why don't you take the rest of the week? Just give roll call two twenty-eights, one for the rest of the week and your summer vacation. Good luck to you, son, and God bless you."

I did just what the boss said. The roll call guy couldn't have been nicer. I stopped in the Detective Squad and shook hands all around. I waited for the four-by-twelve crew to be in the sitting room, said good-bye, and thanked them all. They all wished me luck, told me to drop back sometime.

I called Jennifer and told her what had transpired. She was thrilled for me. I was thrilled for me, but I was apprehensive. I told her that I had one more stop to make and then I'd meet her at home. I made another phone call. When I got home, Jennifer was already there. It didn't take me long to convince her to go to Pete's Tavern for dinner.

There was a nice, warm breeze coming off the East River as we made our way up to Irving Place. We just chatted and walked, holding hands. I told her that I was apprehensive about leaving the Six-One and the guys, but she just said, "Wherever you go, you'll be fine."

We settled into a table in the back room of Pete's Tavern. I ordered a beer; she a white wine. "So how did your visit with Mr. Abe go?" I then told her all about how he and Mrs. Freeman were so glad I called. He talked all about my father and mother and how much they meant to them. He talked about how Daddy would help him when people would make anti-Semitic remarks about him, how Daddy would steer customers to him to help him develop a client base.

Mrs. Freeman told me how Momma came to their apartment right after she and Mr. Abe brought Paula home for the hospital. Momma cooked dinner for them and made breakfast, lunch, and the following night's dinner. Momma fixed all the baby bottles for the night so Mrs. Freeman would just have to warm them. She couldn't say enough about both Momma and Daddy.

I asked Mr. Abe how he knew Lieutenant Miltie Bloch and he told me that they went to the same synagogue. They had been friends for years. The same with Manny Bogen. Then Mr. Abe got very serious and didn't say anything for a few minutes. I just sat there. It was if he was trying to find the right words.

Finally he reached across the table and took my hand. "Listen, son, you are going into a new area of police work. Miltie Bloch tells me there's a lot of temptation. Don't fall into the trap. I only know what Miltie tells me but . . . please don't become a bad cop. Don't take any money from anyone." I looked him in the eyes and promised I wouldn't. I really didn't know why anyone would want to give me money, but I promised him.

He then told a story that I found interesting. He prefaced it by saying that Daddy took the time to listen to people. He was interested in what people had to say. It didn't matter what their economic status was. They could be the man who sold the paper on the street or the president of *Metropolitan Life*. He would take the time to talk to them, to listen to them, and to be nice to them. He would talk to anyone. I should do the same.

It seems that there was a sports award dinner at the Central Knights of Columbus building at Grand Army Plaza and Prospect Park West. Mr. Abe went with Daddy, Jimmy, and Jackie. Jimmy was about fourteen and Jackie almost thirteen. The Rilley cousins were high school athletes at Brooklyn Prep and they were getting awards. Uncle Doctor Vin was there with his sons, Jay, Dick, and Don. They were getting the awards for football.

The war was on and Uncle Doctor Vin was in the Coast Guard and wore his commander's uniform. After the awards, the kids all went into the game room to play pool or ping-pong and the men went into the bar for some drinks. My father went right over to a man in an army uniform and started talking to him. Mr. Abe couldn't remember if he was a captain or a major. Anyway, after a few minutes, Daddy and the officer joined Uncle Doctor Vin and Mr. Abe. It turns out that the officer was none other than James J. Braddock. Braddock was the former boxing heavy-weight champ. They all stood at the bar and talked and laughed like old friends.

Daddy asked Braddock if he could introduce his boys to him. They left the bar room and Daddy called Jimmy and Jackie out into the hallway. Now it seems that they had Braddock's picture hanging on the wall of their room. So when they saw him, in person, they were speechless.

Braddock smiled and took their skinny hands into his massive hand and, looking them directly in the eye, shook their hands and thanked them for having his picture in their room. Daddy had told that to the champ. So Mr. Abe continued, and said that the last thing Braddock said to them was, and he quoted, "Remember, boys, no matter what you do in life, always be true to your family, your country, and yourself. In your case, boys, always be a Catholic gentleman."

Mr. Abe looked me in the eye and said, "I want you to always be a Catholic gentleman." I assured this wonderful Jewish man that I would.

So Monday came and I was back at Hubert Street. The Civil War Prison, now the Police Academy, the Criminal Investigation Course (CIC). I had to be the youngest guy in the class. There were men there who had so many citation bars above their shields that my puny four made me feel embarrassed. Some of the "students" were scheduled to become detectives. The rest of us were to be sent to plainclothes units throughout the city.

I found the course extremely interesting. We learned the law pertaining to gambling, narcotics, and laws pertaining to moral turpitude. I was going to raise my hand and ask what the phrase "moral turpitude" meant, but the instructor explained it. I guess he knew that not too many cops were up on their "moral turpitude" laws. It had to do with any and all forbidden sexual conduct, conduct between a man and woman, woman and woman, man and man, or even man/woman and animal. I kinda thought the last one was really gross.

Captain Walsh was right. The instructor told us that we had the option to come in uniform or civilian clothes. On the second day not a uniform was seen. The three weeks flew. It was really interesting stuff. I didn't ask many questions. I sat and listened and learned. On the breaks, we went into the courtyard and hung out just smoking or drinking coffee from the deli down the block. I listened to the stories of the old-timers and was awed by their knowledge of the city and of people in general. These guys were good. I mean, they knew what life was all about. Like, what made people tick.

Toward the end of the second week, the instructor was giving a lecture on burglary, the tools they used, and the different by-pass methods. He then asked if anyone remembered a recent collar made in Brooklyn. "It was made by a uniform cop on foot patrol. The two guys arrested were "made men" and usually pretty sophisticated. But this night, after they by-passed the alarm, they started breaking in the rear door. A neighbor alerted the cop on foot about the noise and he went to investigate and collared both of the bums."

I raised my hand and he acknowledged me. "That isn't actually the way it happened."

"Really" was his snide reply. "Well, why don't you come up here and tell us how it actually happened?" So I did, and when I finished, he said, "How do you know?"

"'Cause, I made the collar."

"Oh" was his snappy reply.

It seems that by re-telling the story it gave a sort of legitimacy to my being in the CIC program. A couple of the guys even invited me to stop for a "couple of cold ones." I accepted.

The buzz was all about "Hey, where you going?"

"Did you make a phone call?"

"Did you call your rabbi?" (Rabbi is cop speak for someone who can get you the assignment you're looking for.)

"Did you call your hook?" (Hook, see Rabbi.)

I called my brother Jackie. "Don't worry about where they send you. Wherever you go is where the job wants you to be, okay?"

"Okay" was all I said. If I hadn't told you this before, Jackie is a man of few words.

So the last day came and the assignments were posted. I was being sent to the Four-One Precinct on Simpson Street in the Bronx. "The Bronx? How the hell do I get there? I'm a Brooklyn guy. The friggin Bronx!" I called Jackie. "I don't know a damn thing about the Bronx. What the heck am I gonna do?"

"Learn" and he hung up.

Jennifer and I decided to take a ride up to the Bronx, specifically to the area of the Four-One. Man, what a shock. I have never seen such abject poverty except in movies. Yet, there was a vitality about the area. People all over the place, coming and going and going and coming.

Southern Boulevard was the main drag with all the stores. There were banks and bars, dollar shops and sandwich shops. You could see that the area was poor, but the stores were full, full of dark-skinned people, mostly speaking a foreign (at least to me) language. We drove down Simpson Street off Westchester Avenue past the station house. Across the street were pre-Depression era tenements. Four and five story walk-ups. Kids were all over the street playing street games. I didn't go into the station house because I didn't want to leave Jennifer sitting in front alone.

The station house itself was a formidable sight. It was, well, it was awesome looking. It looked like a fortress. Gray stone, massive oak doors, large windows with big shutters on the inside. On the outside, you had the ubiquitous round green globes; you see them in front of every station house. I remember as a kid Pop Walsh referring to our neighborhood station house as the Green Light Hotel.

I asked him why he called it that and he just smiled. I asked Uncle Mike why Pop called the station house the Green Light Hotel and he smiled. "When Pop and his brothers were young men, they apparently were a bit wild so the cops would grab them and lock them up overnight. This would happen in a lot of Irish neighborhoods. So when the offender's mother, father, wife, or whoever would ask where they were all night, they'd answer that they stayed at the Green Light Hotel. Simple answer. So that's how it got its name.

I was going to take a tour of the precinct to learn the streets and the different sections, but I could see by her face that she was shocked by the area. I gotta tell you, I wasn't too thrilled by my new home either. We headed back to Manhattan but were still in the Four-One area and radio cars were streaming all over the place, red lights and sirens. She still didn't say a word. Finally she got a little better when we crossed the Third Avenue Bridge into Manhattan.

"Well, that was quite an experience. It isn't North Arlington, is it?" I smiled and so did she. "Whatta you say we grab something at Pete's?"

"Now that sounds good."

We sat in the back, and after ordering, she reached across the table and took my hand. "What?"

"Nothing, I just want to hold your hand."

"Oh!"

The next morning we went to mass at Saint Emeric's Church on East Twelfth off Avenue C. It was a small church that had a very eclectic congregation. You had the old Irish East-Siders, the new Latino immigrants, the Stuyvesant Town residents, the old ones, and the new ones like us. I don't know what Jennifer was praying for, but I could guess. I was praying to St. Michael to keep me safe in this new assignment. Keep me safe from harm and keep me away from any corruption. I threw a tall order at St. Michael but I know he could handle it. At least I prayed he could handle it.

I was told to be at the Four-One at ten in the morning. I got there at nine fifteen. I approached the desk and told the lieutenant who I was and why I was there. He looked over the desk at me and just smiled. "They're not here yet, son. Why don't you go through there?" He thumb-pointed toward a door. "The plainclothes office is in the second door on the left."

So I went in, found the door marked "Plainclothes," and knocked. I waited and knocked again. No answer. I turned the knob and walked into a cramped room. Three desks, four filing cabinets, two typewriters, three chairs behind the desks, and three chairs scattered around. On the far wall there was another door, which I opened without knocking. "Hey, whatta ya doing?" There was a guy sitting on the bowl reading the *Times*. "Hey, I'm sorry, pal," and I backed up. "Shut the damn door." So I did.

Eventually the door opened and the bowl man came out tucking the *Times* under his arm. "You still here? Who the hell are you?" I was just about to ask him who the hell he was but thought better of it. "I'm Dan Stark. I've been assigned to the precinct, plainclothes," and I stuck my hand out and gave my best Ipana smile. He took my hand, shook it, and walked out. No name, no pleased to meet you, no welcome aboard, no nothing. So I sat on a chair and waited.

About ten to ten, the door opened, and a cop stuck his head in. "Come on." So I followed him past the front desk to the captain's office. I knocked and heard, "Come in." You guessed it. The man on the bowl was the captain. A very auspicious way to start off. "Sorry about that, kid. When you get to know me, you'll know that I'm a grump in the morning. I'm John Mink. I already know who you are. Do you want coffee? Help yourself." He had pointed toward a coffee pot on a little hot plate in the corner of the office. "Help yourself." So I did.

He was reading some Department forms, and putting them down, he looked at me. "So you don't like the Italians?"

"Is that a question, Captain?"

"No, it's a statement. I get the feeling you don't agree."

"Well, sir [always say 'sir'], whoever gave you that idea is all wrong. Sir, I arrested some Italian people but that was because they were committing crimes, not because they were Italian. I imagine that I'll be locking up Puerto Ricans up here. Is that going to indicate that I don't like Puerto Ricans?"

"All right, all right, kid, I get the point. Now let me tell you what I expect. I run a pretty loose ship. You and your partner will have plenty of freedom. I do expect you to produce. The primary function of the Precinct Plainclothes Unit is the suppression of gambling. The secondary function is narcotics suppression.

"Personally, I believe that the geniuses at Headquarters have it ass backward. Narco is what we should be going after and we should go after it hard. Who the hell cares if some guy wants to bet on a horse or a number? The state is gonna legalize gambling anyway." He continued, "You'll be working with Tom Healey, Bob Kearney, Rolf Zigmund, and Mike Lieb. I'll probably team you up with Healey. He has about eight years in the job. His father was a detective, good man. The tours are usually Monday to Friday from ten in the morning till six at night. Every other month you will work Tuesday to Saturday. You guys can work it out among yourselves. Sometimes you will work nights to get the after-hour joints or an occasional Sunday for the cock fights. Got it?"

"Yes, sir."

He took me into the small office and introduced me around to the guys. "Now here's the most important guy in the unit. Byron B. Blisset. Byron is the clerical man. He'll keep track of all your time and vacation. He'll give you the kites I want you to work." ("Kite" is cop speak for a communication from Headquarters or a civilian alleging some violation of gambling or narcotics.) "Oh", he added, "I don't know if you know this, but we have a huge prostitution problem, and I also want—no, I expect, a lot of arrests of the ladies of the night. So once every couple of months, you'll do nights and get as many girls as you can. Got it?" We all shook our heads. "You will use your own cars when you go out. If you go into a bar, use your own money. The same goes for placing bets. At the end of the month, I'll give you a check for ninety-nine dollars and ninety-nine cents. Some genius at the Boro feels that if you get an even hundred, then it has to be approved by some bean counter at Headquarters. So my advice is don't spend more than ninety-nine ninety-nine 'cause you ain't getting any more. If you have any questions, problems, let me know. One more thing, and I mean it, don't take any war brides. Now go to work. Tom, show the kid the ropes."

There couldn't have been a more patient teacher than Tom Healey. Oh, by the way, no relation to Frank Healy from the Six-One. Anyway, Tom got me a map of the precinct boundaries and took me on a tour of the place. One block was worse than the other. Graffiti on the buildings, sidewalks, and burned-out cars, of which there were plenty. What a hell-hole. Tom explained that there were plenty of hard-working, family-loving people in the precinct, so I shouldn't come to any judgment because they were poor.

He likened the Puerto Ricans situation to being the same as it was for the Irish when they first came to America. "You see, Dan, when our people got here, they weren't welcomed. No jobs. Signs everywhere "Irish need not apply." Even the saloons had signs "Dogs and Irish not allowed." So they moved into their own areas. They formed gangs for their own protection and security. Eventually they were assimilated into the American society. They became, look at us, cops, firemen, teachers, politicians, laborers, the whole gambit was run. This will eventually happen with the Puerto Ricans. It's already begun in the job. Next week we're getting a Puerto Rican guy. His name is"—with that, he fished out a little notebook—"yeah, here it is, Vic

Tarasco. I did a little checking and he's got a good rep. Harlem cop outta the Three-Two. Good solid guy, I'm told."

"Now, how did you find this out?" I asked. "Aw, I got friends in high places. I checked on you before you even knew you were coming here. For a young cop, you got a good rep. They say you're a little nuts, but if the shit ever hit the fan, my sources tell me you're the guy I want with me."

"Well, that's nice to hear . . . I think," I said.

The following week Vic Tarasco came to be part of our Four-One Plainclothes Unit. He didn't look Puerto Rican. Actually, he was Irish or Italian looking. He was second generation from PR (cop speak for Puerto Rican). He didn't have any accent except a New York one, if you know what I mean.

He read and spoke Spanish flawlessly. He was a great resource for us. We'd hit a place with a warrant and the people in the place would allege that they didn't speak English. "Nose habla." Vic wouldn't say a word or even acknowledge that he understood what they were talking about among themselves.

He'd come over to one of the team and whisper that one of them said that he was glad that he put the numbers or drugs or guns and the money in a pot in the oven or behind the refrigerator or under the loose floorboard under the radiator. We'd wait and continue to look in the obvious places: under the bed, under the mattress, in the shoebox. Eventually one of us would accidently find the hidden spot. It worked well every time, thanks to Vic.

Everyone on the team had young children except for Tom and me. He and Eleanor, his wife, had been married for almost eight years without kids. We hit it off right away as did our wives. After work we'd all go out together. On our days off we'd meet in Manhattan and have dinner at some out-of-the-way restaurant in Greenwich Village or we'd go to Little Italy, Chinatown, or Pete's Tavern. We took a trip up to Cape Cod where we saw the Kennedy compound, stayed in an inn in Hyannis Port, and even attended Mass in the same church that the president went to.

The president was in Hyannis Port so we decided to go to the ten o'clock mass because he was going to be at the noon mass. So in we go and this older priest walks right up to Tom and me, and with his New England accent says to us, "Now, don't lie to me, lads. I can tell you were both altar boys and I need your help today. Good lads and thank you."

Now, I have to admit I had put on a few, well, maybe more than a few, pounds and it all settled in my behind. I was wearing a pair of slacks that did fit when I bought them, but now they were kinda snug. (In the old days, before mass was said in English and the priest faced the congregation, the altar boys knelt throughout the mass or stood at the appropriate time, and they and the priest had their backs to the people.) Or, in my case, my backside to the people.

So Tom and I agreed to "volunteer" to be the altar boys. The good father then informed us that the Kennedy clan, minus the president, his wife, and parents, would be at the mass. All I could picture was my pants splitting and me being arrested by the Secret Service or the FBI for mooning the attorney general and his wife and the rest of his family. Well, anyway, my pants didn't split and I remembered most of the Latin. Actually, the good father said he was impressed by our responses and the way we handled the tasks of the altar boys. So we survived the mass. The girls got to see the Kennedy sisters and the attorney general, Bobby Kennedy, up close. When I told them about my fear of mooning the clan, they howled. I mean, it was comical, but not hysterical. When we got back to work, Tom didn't waste any time telling the story but he added that I did split the ass of my pants. "Hey, it made the story better" was his wise-ass reply. I love cop humor.

One day I went into work and Captain Mink motioned me into his office. "I need you to go to . . ." and he told me the location. "Take plate numbers of as many cars you can that double-park in front of the bodega there. Here's ten bucks. Go into the locker room, get some pylons, a hard hat, and a pair of overalls, stop a Con Ed truck, given them the ten, then open the manhole, put the cones around you so nobody drives into the manhole. You should be able to hear when a car pulls up. When you do stick your head up, get the plate number and then duck back into the hole. Got it? Any questions?

"No, sir, it seems simple enough."

"Good, give it about two or three hours. I'll get Healey to get another Con Ed truck to pick you up and close the manhole cover. Hey, kid?"

"Yes, sir?"

"Bring a pad to write the plate numbers on." I just nodded, but I thought to myself, "Whatta ya think I'm stupid or something?"

So I did as I was told. Got the overalls from the storage room where we had different types of jackets and coveralls and hard hats and UPS uniforms, Sanitation uniforms, and other things to be used for undercover assignments to disguise ourselves. I got four traffic pylons or cones, or whatever the heck you call them, and stood on the corner near the Con Ed garage a few blocks away. The Con Ed guys were happy to help. The ten spot helped their enthusiasm, I'm sure.

Anyway, I'm in the hole about forty-five minutes and every once in awhile I'd look up. No cars were stopping. Every time I looked up, there were three guys sitting on milk crates in front of the bodega, just looking in my direction. I remembered from the CIC training that they said when you are working an undercover assignment, you will *think* that the subjects have "made you" (cop speak for they know you're a cop), but it's just your imagination.

Well, imagination or not, nobody was double-parking in front of the store and those three guys were just sitting there looking at me. *Me!* About an hour and a half after I went into the hole, I heard a car stop so I popped my head up. "You Stark?" said the cop in the marked radio car from the driver's seat. "Whadda ya doing? I'm working undercover. You want them to make me?" "The captain says for you to close this hole and get your ass back to the house. I gotta tell you, pal, he ain't too happy." And he just put the car in gear and drove off.

I climbed up to the street, struggled with the two hundred-pound cover, got it into place, and started to pile the pylons into each other. Then I noticed. Oh my God! Am I in deep trouble! It seems that in BIG BLACK letters on the yellow cones were NYPD painted on by someone who had nothing better to do. Oh my God, am I in deep trouble!

I walked about twelve blocks to the station house lugging the cones, switching them from one shoulder to another. Those damn things are heavy by themselves, but when you have four stuck together, well, they weigh a ton. Hey, don't laugh; it wasn't funny.

So I got back to the station house, changed into my clothes and sat by myself in the little office for about an hour. Finally the phone rang. I picked it up, and before I could even say hello, the voice on the other end said—no, bellowed, "Get in here now." *Click.* All I could think of was the line from the poem "The Charge of the Light Brigade": "Into the valley of death, etc., etc." Well, I won't go into the conversation, but all I can say is that Captain Johnny Mink had some command of the English language. He must have used the "F" word forty different ways, all directed at my intelligence, my ability, my future in the police department, my worth as a human being, as a man, and six hundred reasons why I shouldn't be allowed to breathe the air of the planet Earth. "Now get outta here and do some work." I think he even called me a moron. I thought to myself, *Well, that went well.*

The lieutenant on the desk just looked at me and shook his head. The sergeant on the switchboard actually called me a dope. The cops that were around were just laughing out loud.

So a couple of weeks went by without incident. We made collars of all sorts: prostitution, numbers, bookmakers, drugs, and street crap games, when things got slow. Mink seemed to be pleased with our work. A few times he even took us to an Irish bar in the Four-Three Precinct and treated us to lunch, with a few beers thrown in. But, invariably, he'd bring up the manhole story. Everyone got a good laugh out of it. Everyone but me, that is. One thing about Mink, he really didn't hold the mistake against me.

On a Friday afternoon, Mink called me into his office. "All right, kid, here's a chance to redeem yourself. Next week I want you to go over to . . ." And he gave me the location. "There's a barber shop that is supposed to be taking action, with a side line of selling dope. I don't care how you do it, but I want observations on how many people go in, how long they stay, if they have anything in their hands when they come out. You know what to look for by now. If they don't get a haircut, then why are they going in? It's a clear view into the place and you can see if they go into the back room. If they go into the backroom, they're either placing bets or buying dope. Got it?"

"Yes, sir, I do."

"Okay. Now have a nice weekend."

"Thanks, boss, you too."

All weekend long I couldn't think of anything else but the assignment. I had told Jennifer about the cone caper but she already knew. "Eleanor called me. Tom told her." Big mouth Bozo, I thought to myself. We went to their house on Saturday night and he couldn't resist re-telling the story. He had a panache for adding to it. I have to admit, it was funny. I mean, if it weren't me that it happened to, I probably would have thought it was hysterical.

So I go back to work on Monday. Tom and Vic had court appearances and the rest of the team were doing a later tour. I went into the back room and put on the overalls and hard hat. I got another Con Ed truck (this time I only gave them five dollars)to drop me off across the street from the barber shop. I had driven past the shop on my way home on Friday. There was a fire hydrant right across the street from the place. The street was cobblestone with a little bit of black top on it. I had gotten a four-foot metal rod with a hook on the end and a large metal handle on the top. Construction crews and Con Ed used it for pulling open manholes. I figured I'd use it to pull up a section of the cobblestones near the hydrant. Good idea, right? Wrong!

I got to the location about ten. I had a large piece of chalk and a bag with a sandwich and a soda in it. I chalked off the area near the hydrant. I made a big display of measuring so far out and so long on either side of the hydrant, all the time casting an eye at the shop.

Then I proceeded to start pulling up the cobblestones and neatly stacking them at the curb. I was there about, almost, two hours. I had a nice neat pile of ten-pound cobblestones all stacked. In all the time I was there, I didn't see one person go into the store. As a matter of fact, I didn't see one person come out of the store. Hmmmmm . . .

A radio car pulled up as I was sitting on the stone pile asI was finishing my sandwich. "You Stark?"

"Yes."

"Captain says to put the street back together and get into the house." And he drove away.

My arms, legs, and back were killing me, but about an hour later, I was finished. I made my way back to the house. The lieutenant on the desk just looked at me and shook his head. The sergeant shook his head and pointed to the captain's office.

Now, let me tell you, I was confused. I knew I had the right location. I knew I had the perfect cover (cop speak for disguise). I was trying to figure out how it was my fault that nobody was going in or out. I knocked and he barked a "Come in."

"Whose side are you on? Their side or ours?"

"I don't understand, sir. What'd I do wrong?"

"Today is Monday. Barbershops are closed on Monday. Get out of my office." Ever since I was a kid, I knew that. Geez, maybe I am a moron.

The lieutenant on the desk was still shaking his head. The sergeant called me a dope. And, yes, the cops that were around were just laughing out loud. In spite of me, the team made enough observations and we got enough "probable cause" to apply for a search warrant. Had a judge review it and sign it. We executed the warrant on a Thursday (not a Monday) and got two loaded guns, one hundred twelve glassine envelopes of heroin and thirteen hundred numbers (policy slips). We also confiscated $4,860 in cash, plus we arrested four people. Not bad work at all. The bonus was that Captain Mink was happy.

So one humid day, Tom and I are just patrolling around and we see a foot cop stop a car under the El train on Southern Boulevard. "Pull over and we'll keep an eye on this. There's four guys in the car. Maybe the cop might need some backup."

So I double-parked about two car lengths behind the suspect vehicle. The uniform cop goes to the driver's side, takes the operator's license and registration, and goes to the front of the car. Tom and I got out. I guess we both realized what was going to happen. The driver started to back up little by little. It was as if the scene was in slow-mo. Tom yelled just as the car accelerated. The cop got hit. I fired a shot at the car, I thought.

The next thing I heard was glass shattering. I apparently hit a plate glass window just right to make it shatter and explode. The car veered right into the El pillar. Tom ran to the cop. I ran to the car. In seconds, radio cars were all over the place. Now, you have to remember, we didn't have cell phones or radios. So one of the citizens called in. Tom was right. These were some very good people living and working in the neighborhood.

After the scene calmed down, Captain Mink arrived. The foot cop had a broken leg and he was rushed to Lincoln Hospital. The car was stolen. And all the occupants, except the driver, had felony warrants outstanding. So they all got arrested. Mink surmised that the force of the car hitting the El pillar caused the store window to shatter. "Right, kid?"

"Right, Captain."

He never mentioned the shot. But he knew. How? I don't know. I do know that Tom didn't tell him. But he knew. The window I broke was in a vacant store so nobody got hurt or cut or anything. Good ol' St. Michael. He had his hand on my shoulder. Too bad he didn't have it on my gun.

The next few weeks were busy. The summer brought out the people in droves. The streets were filled with kids playing the street games kids play everywhere. Hydrants were open day and night, but the humidity just hung in the air. There were fights all over the street. The uniform guys really had their hands full. No matter what tour we were doing, the cells were always full of people screaming, cursing, fighting, and sleeping. The smell in the cell area was, sometimes, overpowering. But the minute you walked into the house, the adrenalin started pumping.

One bright and hot day the three cops who were the Community Affairs officers were around the corner at a block party that the precinct was running for the community kids. The idea was to show the neighborhood that we, the police, were their friends. We were there to protect them and to help them.

About two in the afternoon, I was standing in front of the desk talking to Lieutenant Gittens. He was a huge black man with a smile that would light up Broadway. Tom and I had made a drug arrest and I was getting some vouchers from the lieutenant.

The station house doors flew open and the three community cops came running in at full gallop. Now, I told you that there were shutters on the inside of the windows and the cops started slamming them shut. They locked the station house door. Then I heard the unmistakable sound of gunshots. I might not be the sharpest tool in the shed, but when I saw the lieutenant and the TS operator drop to the floor, I ran behind the desk and crouched next to Gittens.

There was a base radio and the phone on the desk. Gittens had grabbed the phone and was calling the Boro office. The TS operator was calling Central Dispatch. I grabbed the base radio and started transmitting Ten-Thirteen calls. "Central to Four One base, where's the Ten-Thirteen?"

"At the station house."

"Ten-Four" was the calm voice at Central. Shots were ringing out. Cops were shooting out through the little slits in the shutters. The "community people" were shooting into the house.

The desk phone was ringing and Gittens snatched it from the cradle. "Who's this? AP, what's it like up here? I'll tell you, it's like effing Fort Apache.

That's what it's like," and he slammed the phone down. The whole assault lasted about ten minutes, but it seemed like ten hours. Miraculously there was not one reported injury from all the outgoing or incoming gunfire.

It seems that the three cops, who were in civilian clothes, were mingling with the crowd. Some nitwit threw firecrackers into the crowd. A little girl about four fell down. The Puerto Rican cop picked her up in his arms. Apparently when he bent down to get her, his gun became exposed for all to see. Some a-hole yelled, "The cop shot the kid." The crowd turned as one and started toward the trio of cops. The Puerto Rican cop took the kid and threw her into the oncoming mutts and the three of them ran for their life to "Fort Apache." To this day, if you go past the old Four-One, you can still see the pockmarks in the granite facade from the bullets fired at the house. Another exciting day in the Bronx beautiful.

Fortunately, for the next five days it rained. Rain, snow, and cold are the cops best friend. The mutts don't like inclement weather. This gave the community and the cops a little time to cool off. After work, we stopped at a local bar called the Don Q Lounge. It was primarily a safe haven for cops. It was off limits to the local lowlifes. The Puerto Ricans that came in were all working class stiffs who just wanted a couple of beers before going home. Just the same as us.

The team, except for Bob Kearney, were all there and we talked sports and other nonsense. Finally Vic kind of whispered, "Ya hear about Kearney? The captain called him in just as I was leaving. Mink didn't look too happy and neither did Bob." Then like a bunch of old women, we gossiped about Kearney. Zigmund was the first to complain. "I'm supposed to be teamed up with him and he's never around. Most of the time I make my observations on my kites by myself. Then at the end of the month, he always comes scrounging around for me to help him get collars."

"He comes to me too," I said.

"Me too," from Tom.

"Me too," from Vic.

Mike Leif got up from the table and went to the phone booth. When he came back, his face was bright red. "That son-of-a-bitch. You know what he's doin'? He's getting all of us to help him and now he's leading, not only the precinct but the entire Boro in collars. And the son-of-a-bitch never goes to court."

"Who'd you call?"

"I called a buddy in the Boro office. That sneaky bastard. I make two collars and put his name on one of the arrests. I take the collar to court but the Boro just sees the arrest report, not the court affidavit. He's doin' it to you guys too. So he gets credit for ten collars a month and never does any work. This gives him more time to spend with his Puerto Rican girlfriend."

"He violated Mink's rule. He took a war bride."

I looked up from my beer. "What? What Puerto Rican girlfriend?" was my question. "You didn't know? Where the heck do you think he goes all day? She treats him like a king. Waits on him hand and foot. We're out looking for collars and he's up there in her apartment, studying for the sergeant's exam and getting taken care of by her. He's not only screwing her but he's also screwing us."

The door to the Don Q opened and in walked Captain Mink. He stopped at the bar and grabbed a pitcher of beer and came to the table. "Drink up, fellas, it's on me." So we all helped ourselves and for a long few minutes sat in silence. Finally Mink said, "No more sharing collars. Got it?" We all nodded as he drained his glass, put it down, nodded to all of us, and left.

Now, coincidentally, the whole team was to go to Kearney's house for a barbecue on the coming Saturday. We had been out with Bob and his wife Dorothy numerous times. Jennifer got along with her as did the other wives. Tom was the first to ask what we were going to do about the barbecue. We all agreed that it wouldn't be fair to Bob's wife, Dorothy, and the kids if we didn't go. So we agreed we'd go.

They lived in the ass end of Long Island. I told Tom that we'd pick up him and Eleanor and go in one car. We got to the house and were met at the door by Bob's wife. Oh, she couldn't have greeted us more warmly. There was one exception. That was, the way she greeted me. Talk about a cold reception. She hugged Eleanor and Jennifer, gave Tom a kiss on the cheek, and gave me a curt, icy hello.

The day went well. Nobody mentioned how Bob was screwing us but Dorothy kept giving me the cold shoulder. Eleanor was the first to pick up on it. "What did you do to get Dorothy mad at you?" I pretended that I didn't know what she was talking about. Jennifer jumped in. "Yeah, I noticed that she's a little cool to you too." Talk about an understatement.

Finally I took Bob on the side. "Hey, what's with Dorothy? She's acting like I pissed in her oatmeal. What's going on?"

"I hadn't noticed," says he.

"Bullshit," says me.

"All right," says he. "I came home one night and I had lipstick on my neck and collar. She spotted it and I told her that you had locked up a pros [cop speak for 'prostitute'] and that you took her lipstick and put it on me kidding around. I told her I tried to wash it off but I guess I didn't get it all."

"Why the hell did you tell her it was me? I wouldn't do that. These broads have all sorts of disease. I don't even like talking to them, let alone search their pocketbooks. She is really ticked at me and it's obvious."

"I'll tell you what to do," says he. "Just tell her you're sorry you did it and I bet she forgets all about it. Whadda ya say?"

I had a burger and a couple of beers. I looked at Bob playing with his kids and the other guys' kids. He was leading them in a three-legged race. They were all laughing. Falling down. Laughing. Getting up. I didn't know what to do.

I finally went over to Dorothy and took her on the side. "I can tell you're annoyed at me and I'm sorry for what I did to Bob. It was only a goof. I'm really sorry."

"Do you know how many diseases he could have gotten from your little stunt? I mean, he could have gotten sick. He could have brought something home and passed it on to me, or the kids. What were you thinking?"

"I really am sorry" was all I said. I couldn't stop thinking about Bob and his Puerto Rican girlfriend and all the things he could pick up from her, but I didn't say a word about it. Not even to Jennifer. After that, we didn't socialize.

The summer was coming to an end. Kearney had gotten transferred to some detail in Headquarters. He eventually wound up as a chief in what was later called Internal Affairs Bureau (IAB), but now it was still called the PCCIU.

So Tom and I are just tooling around the precinct looking for . . . ? I don't know, I guess something out of place. Anyway, we spot this guy moping down the block. He head is going left, right, left, right. He's looking into cars. He's trying car handles. I swear, if he could have, he would have swiveled his head three-sixty. Oh yeah, it was hot as hell and he had on a heavy army field jacket. We watched him go into a building. So we gave him a minute or two and followed.

We weren't in the business of catching car thieves or burglars, but we both agreed that crime is crime. We had made enough bookmakers and policy and drug collars, so why not make a burglary collar?

The building was an old Bronx five-story walkup. I told Tom I'd take the stairs to the top floor and he'd check the doors on the floors on the way up. I took the stairs, three at a time. I got to the top floor, fully out of breath. I saw him when he saw me. He threw the TV set that he was carrying right toward my head. I ducked, pulled out my gun. "Don't move."

I could hear Tom lumbering my way and I shifted my eyes toward the stairs. The junkie was on me in a flash. He grabbed my gun hand with his left hand and I felt him scratch my face with his right hand. I tripped him and we both crashed to the floor. I could smell his body odor. I could even taste his sweat. It tasted like metal.

I started gagging on his sweat. I had my finger on the trigger and he wrapped his finger around mine. The metallic taste in my mouth was overpowering. I was focusing on the hammer of the gun and struggling to get my thumb up to stop it from firing. I was losing the struggle. St. Michael, if I ever needed help, now's the time.

I was losing the battle when Tom kicked my gun hand. The junkie let go and I rolled away. I struggled to my feet, and leaning against the wall, I couldn't do anything but watch Healy cuff the junkie/burglar to the hallway radiator. Tom, for a big guy—all right, a heavy guy—was at my side in a flash. He gently took the gun from my hand and helped me to sit on the hallway floor. He took his handkerchief and put it in my hand and lifted both to my face. "Put pressure on the cut."

"What cut?"

"Don't talk, just put this on your face." I did. He entered the burglarized apartment and I could hear him on the phone calling for assistance.

Before he got back to my side, I could hear the sirens from the street below. Everything seemed to be going in slow motion. I thought it was funny that Tom was taking off his shirt and pressing it to my face. I tried to talk but it felt as if my tongue was falling out of my mouth. Then I saw the blood on the front of my shirt and on the floor. "Oh, dear God, please tell me I didn't shoot this guy."

The next thing I remember was being, kind of, roughly pushed into the backseat of a radio car with Tom holding something red up to my face. We got to Lincoln Hospital and I was . . . I can only describe it as being plopped onto a gurney and pushed into the ER.

I tried talking but nothing was coming out that sounded like words. Anyway, a few hours later I woke up with Captain Mink and Tom (wearing a different shirt) staring down at me. "Geez, kid, is there a day that's gonna go by that you don't screw up?" He was smiling when he said it, so I know I wasn't in trouble.

It turns out that the burglar/junkie had cut me with a potato knife. Now, you ask: What's a potato knife? Well, I'll tell you. It's a thin blade sharpened on both sides. The scratch I thought he gave me was actually the knife cutting into my face. Oh, yeah, I got fifty stitches to boot.

The medics wanted me to stay overnight but I didn't want Jennifer to have to come to the hospital. They gave me a tetanus shot and told me how to clean the wound. I signed a gazillion releases and Mink drove Healy and me back to the house. I called Jennifer at work and told her that I had a little cut and a big bandage on my face but there was nothing to worry about. Vic drove me home in my car and Tom followed in his. I still had the metallic taste in my mouth. It wasn't junkie sweat. It was the taste of my own blood. "Vic, we gotta get some beer." He understood what I said, but he told me later it sounded like, "Bic, be botta bet sum ear." We stopped, got the beer, and went into the apartment. It was tough to drink with this big bandage on my face, but I managed.

Vic and Tom left and I fell asleep on the couch until the gentle touch on my shoulder let me know that Jennifer was home. After the initial shock of seeing the big white bandage, she relaxed and wanted to know how it happened. I simply told her that "It's not a big deal. I'm really fine. In a few days this thing will clear up and you'll forget all about it." She looked at me with her eyes brimming with tears and tried to smile. "I think you'll probably have a scar. Would you like something to eat?"

I went back to work about three weeks later with a nice red scar. It healed pretty good but a scar is a scar. During the three weeks off, I sat in the park in Stuyvesant Town just soaking up the sun and reading. I had a nice tan but you could see the red slit. I mean, I'm not vain or anything but I was a little self-conscious about it.

One bright sunny day I walked over to Walsh's Steakhouse for a sandwich and a beer. Again, at the bar was Jim, the cop who worked at Headquarters. He gave me a big hello, bought me a beer, inspected the scar. "It gives you character. So how you doing up there? In the Bronx?"

I don't know why, but I just got the feeling that he knew more about me than I wanted him to. "I like it up there. It's a busy shop and the cops all work together. The bosses are good too. The only problem I have is eating. I eat that Spanish food and I can't kiss my wife for two days." He laughed and we had another beer. "Okay, I'll see you around." And he patted me on the back and left. I asked the bartender again, "Where does he work, at Headquarters?"

"I don't know. As I told you, he doesn't talk to many people here. I guess he likes you."

So the summer was over and I settled back into the work routine. September turned to October and October to November. It was an unreasonably warm month for November. Vic and I went out to a location that I had been betting in for the past month. It was a little coffee shop in the Hunts Point Market area. Besides selling coffee, sandwiches, etc., they dabbled in policy and horses and sold beer without a license.

The owner was a heavyset, very jovial black lady named Minnie Means. Her "husband" was a tall, very thin, black man named Jerry Paul. So, anyway, I go in and played a couple of horses with her and some policy numbers with him. We, Vic and I, identified ourselves and arrested them. "Damn, I knew you was a cop. I said to mah man, 'You see that white boy? He ain't no trucker like he make believe. He be a cop.' That what I said to mah man. Ain't that right, lover?" She then let out a whoop and slapped her ample rump.

One of her workmen was left in charge and we drove them to the Four-One. All the way in she was yakking and laughing. Poor Jerry failed to see the humor in the situation. So we parked, and as we're walking to the house, Mike Leib comes out, "Hey, Dan, someone just took a shot at your Irish pal, did ya hear?"

"Who? What the hell are you talking about?" But he just kept walking. All I thought about was Tom.

We went before the desk and the normally busy area was as quiet as a tomb. Everyone was gathered around the radio Lieutenant Gittens had at the desk. Then the announcement: "It's official, President Kennedy has been assassinated. The president was pronounced dead at 1:00 p.m. Dallas time at Parkland Memorial Hospital." The lieutenant just let the tears roll down his cheeks. There wasn't a dry eye in the station house.

I went through the motions of the booking process. Took the prisoners to night court in Manhattan. Their yellow sheets came back with multiple convictions for gambling. Minnie had a couple of assault charges and her "man" had a gun conviction. Normally, the judge would have set some bail, but everyone was in a zombie-like mode. He was releasing everyone without bail.

I had called Jennifer earlier and told her to go right over to her mother's from work. We had planned on going there anyway. I told her I'd meet her there when I finished at court. I gotta tell you, the whole city was in a state of shock. It was a surreal time.

I was off Saturday, Sunday, and Monday so we thought we'd just hang out with her family all weekend. In reality, we were all glued to the TV, watching the widow, the children, the brothers, and the sisters. Our hearts, as were the hearts of all the world, were aching for the president and his family. Lost in the shuffle was the death of the brave Dallas patrolman J. D. Tippett. We prayed for his family too.

I cheered when Jack Ruby killed Oswald. I mean, I didn't do flips or anything. I just, at the time, was glad the bastard that ended Camelot suffered and died. I know, I know, it would have been better for the nation to know Oswald's motive, but at that time, I was glad old sleazy Jack shot Lee Harvey.

We watched the coverage on the TV all weekend. We all went to Mass together and prayed as one for the president, his family, and our nation. We prayed for the new president, Lyndon Johnson. We also prayed for ourselves. My prayer, as always, included that God bless us with a family. After a few weeks, things were almost back to normal in the nation. It's not that the tragedy was forgotten but the old adage was true, "Life goes on."

I'd received a call from Manny Bogen telling me that the Six-One was having a racket (cop speak for a party) to celebrate the retirement of Hugo Pulzone at the Palms Catering Hall on Emmons Avenue. If I was interested at going, I should let him know as soon as possible; they needed a head count.

Hugo was a nice man that the job was forcing to retire because he wa shitting the mandatory age of sixty-two.

The racket was on a Thursday night. Most cop rackets are on the Thursday of payday. I put in to take the following day off. I told Jennifer that I'd stay at Jackie and Muriel's house after the party. I knew they wouldn't mind. I suggested she go to her mother's for the night, but she told me that she'd be all right at the apartment. So all was set.

It was just about a week before Christmas, and as I said, life goes on. We were all in a party mood. It was nice to see the men I'd worked with. There were a few speeches and Hugo was given a bunch of plaques for his wall. These acknowledged his cases and his service to the city and the community at large. There was a speech by Captain Walsh, Lieutenant Bloch, Sergeant Joyce, and a couple of ribald remarks by some of the older cops. All in good taste because Hugo's two sons were there.

After most of the other bosses left, the cards and dice game started. Some of us headed to the bar to toast and thank Hugo. About an hour later, somewhere around midnight, I decided not to get to Jackie's but head home. I called Jennifer to tell her so she wouldn't get nervous if she heard me coming in. I could tell she was glad even though she said she wasn't worried about being alone.

I walked to the parking lot with the wind whipping off Sheepshead Bay. I turned the collar of my coat up and was kinda quick stepping toward my car. "Hey, kid, hold up." I reached inside my coat and put my hand on my gun. I kinda recognized the voice but I wasn't sure.

"It's only me." I turned slowly and saw the figure emerge from between two garbage dumpsters in the lot. It was the ex-cop who told me about the goings-on at the Ro-Sal. I relaxed a bit as he walked toward me. "I was hoping you'd be here tonight. I heard you'd been transferred and I didn't get a chance to thank you." This was the first time I'd seen him sober. But he looked sickly to me.

I put my hand out to shake his and he took it. "Good evening, sir. How are you?"

"I don't have much time so I just want to thank you."

"For what?" I asked. "For being kind to me. A lot of people just looked at me and all they saw was a drunken bum. You treated me with respect. You never made me feel . . . well, feel like a drunken bum. You talked to me and you listened to me. For that, I wanted to say thanks."

I didn't know what to say. I stood there looking at this broken, sickly man. I was at a loss for words. "You're welcome" was all I managed. "Can I give you a ride somewhere?"

"No, thank you. But I just want you to be careful. You know the people on Avenue X are still mad at you. No Nose, his son, and grandson are still very angry. You know that the trial is coming soon." I nodded. "Just be careful around the courthouse. Will you promise me, son?"   "Yes, sir, I'll be careful." I put my hand in my pocket, and he held up his in a stop manner. "No, thanks, son. I have enough for what I need." He then turned and walked away.

I figured that I had the day off, so why waste it. I drove Jennifer to work early and we had breakfast together. I went back to Stuyvesant Town, found a parking spot, and promptly went back to bed. Again, about two, I walked over to Walsh's for a burger and a couple of beers. Jim the cop wasn't there. I settled in at the corner of the bar. The bartender gave me a copy of the *News* to read.

There on the front page of the afternoon edition was a banner headline: MOB HIT IN BROOKLYN BAR with a picture of the Ro-Sal with bodies being carried out. The story went as follows:

> A rub-out of a notorious gangster, his son, and grandson took place in the mob hangout, the Ro-Sal Lounge on Avenue X in Brooklyn. Sources tell the *News* that Michael "No Nose" Toronto, his son Michael/Mikey, and his grandson Tommy were gunned down as they sipped expresso at a rear booth. The three died instantly. They were each shot once in the head at close range and were pronounced dead at the scene.
>
> Witnesses could only describe the shooter as a white male who was known in the neighborhood as a derelict who told people he was an ex-cop. None of the witnesses could supply any further information. Of the twenty or so patrons, at least ten said they were in the men's room at the time they heard the shots.

The story went on to list the record of No Nose and his family. It told about the coming Dad and Lad trial. Oh, well, I guess I won't have to go to court on that one.

I knew I should call someone and tell them about the encounter with . . . with who, though? I mean, I didn't even know his name or anything about him. All I knew was that he told me he was an ex-cop who had gotten jammed up and was bounced from the force. Jackie would know what I should do.

I called the Safe and Loft Squad and asked the detective on duty to have my brother call me at home. By the time I got to the apartment, the phone was ringing. "What's up?"

"Jack, are you in your office?"

"Yeah."

"Can I buy you a beer when you're finished?"

"Okay, but why aren't you at work?"

"I put in for the day last week. I had some shopping and banking I wanted to do today."

"All right, I'll meet you in front of the building. I get out at four."

"I'll be there."

I got to the Safe and Loft office. It was housed in an old warehouse on Broome Street right behind Police Headquarters in Little Italy. There were other units housed there too. BCCI for one and a bunch of others supports bureaus. I found a good spot to park and waited across the street. When he came out, I waved to him and he waved back. "What happened last night? Muriel said you were gonna come over. She had the couch all made for you. The kids were disappointed you weren't there when they got up for school."

We walked into a little old bar on Broome Street. "What's the matter? You got a problem?"

"I don't know," and I told him about the ex-cop. He sat for a while nursing his beer. I had two more by the time he finally spoke. "Did you encourage him to kill those guys? I mean, in any way? Did you ever talk to him on the phone? Did you ever go to where he lived? Did you ever tell anyone about him? I mean, anyone at all?"

"No! You're the only person that I'm telling. I don't even know his name let alone where he lives."

"Okay, now listen to me. Do not tell anyone about this guy. I mean, not now or ever. Do you hear me?"

"But, Jack, don't you think I should let the Six-One Squad know? It might help them find him. Maybe they can get him some help or put him in a hospital or something. I don't know." He looked me in the eye and just said, "There's a lot you don't know. Just do as I tell you. Let it drop. Now, you gonna buy me that beer or not?"

About a week later I went into the Four-One Precinct and Captain Mink motioned me into his office. *Oh, boy, this cannot be good,* I thought to myself. Tom and Vic were already inside. I felt a little better until I saw the looks on their faces. "What's up, sir?"

"I got transferred" was all Mink said. I flopped in a chair. We all just sat there looking at him. "Hey, I'm not dead. I just got transferred. I'm going to go to the Tenth on the west side of Manhattan."

He took a deep breath. "Look, fellas, I called the three of you in to tell you thanks for all your good work, in spite of you, Stark." But he was smiling when he said it. "Seriously, you guys did fine work and I just wanted to thank you. The new skipper will be here in the morning and I want you guys to give him the same effort you gave me. Dan, stick with these two. You've come a long way and you'll be a good detective someday. Tom, Vic, keep an eye on the kid for me. Now, who wants to volunteer to help me lug all of my personal crap to my car?" We all got to our feet and grabbed for boxes.

That night it seemed like the whole precinct was at the Don Q Lounge. Mink was beaming. He gave a little speech of thanks and did something I've never seen before or since. Without mentioning any names or circumstances, he simply said, "Some of you guys have had a bumpy road with me. You've had allegations concerning your personal and professional lives made against you. You all know I've kept files on you. Well, those files no longer exist. I've destroyed them. If you screw up now with the new boss, it's your fault. You are starting off clean with him. Clean up your act. You're getting the chance to start anew. Don't blow it. Men, I want to thank each and every one of you, warts and all. Now, let's have a drink."

The new captain, Philip Sherman, came in and he just addressed all of us. He said that we should just continue with what we were doing. He complimented Mink's stewardship and he didn't anticipate making any major changes. About two months later, we all were transferred to different units. I was sent to the Third Division in mid-town Manhattan.

In those days, part of the duties, besides making gambling, prostitution, and drug arrests, was to inspect the cabaret licenses of the performers in the various mid-town nightclubs and the Dime-A-Dance Hall. The big name clubs were fading fast, but you still had Lou Walters Latin Quarter, the Copacabana, the new Peppermint Lounge, and of course, the famous Toots Shor.

Our job was to make sure that the entertainers had cabaret cards that were up-to-date and valid. I got hooked up with a big guy named Bernie Rice. Bernie was a wrestler type who took great care of himself. You know the type, lifting weights, running, all that sort of healthy crap. He was a handsome-looking Jewish kid from the Bronx.

Overnight we went into the second floor office at the Seventeenth Precinct and the inspector, Joe Nakovics, is sitting there waiting for us with Lieutenant Sullivan and Lieutenant Risley. "Hey, Stack," says Nakovics, "I'm gonna hang with you and Rice tonight. We're gonna hit the Latin quarters about ten to check the showgirls' cabaret cards, okay?" Like I'm really going to say, "No, it's not."

"Sure, boss."

"Good. You and Bernie get some dinner and meet me back here around nine thirty, okay? ("No, it's not and I'm not hungry.")

"Sure, boss." I guess I should have noticed the smiles or smirks on everyone's faces, but I didn't.

So we meet and now the chief was with us, Stanford Garfuss. "I'll just take a walk with you guys, okay?" ("No, Chief, I don't want you to come with us.")

"Sure, boss," Bernie and I said in unison. Garfuss was a short man and it was comical to see him next to Nakovics. Nakovics was a huge, second generation of Russian decent. When I say "huge," I mean huge. Height six-four and not an ounce of fat on his two hundred forty-pound body.

We're walking down the street side by side and the denizens of mid-town, the street hustlers, the three-card Monte men, the "psst, buddy, ya wanna buy a watch" hustlers, just faded into the alleyways or hugged the wall of the buildings. Bernie and Garfuss were together talking about the Shomrin

Society and their upcoming dinner dance. The Shomrin Society is the fraternal organization of cops of the Jewish faith.

So we finally get to the Latin Quarter. We go through the stage door entrance. I'm introduced to Lou Walters. "So you're new in the division?"

"Yes, sir."

"Well," he continued, "you'll find everything in order in my place. You can come in any time you want." Then he whispered in my ear, "Even if you're not working." Then he smiled and winked. He handed me a shoebox and pointed to a door. "You can use that room to talk to the girls." So in I go with my little entourage and inside were Lieutenants Sullivan and Risley. Nakovics tells me, "Make it simple, kid. You take out a card with their name and photo. You ask them their date of birth, look at the picture and their face to match it. We don't tolerate people working in these places who aren't licensed. Got it?"

"Yes, sir," says I.

I sit behind the desk and asked Mr. Walters to please send in "Sally La Tour." All the bosses and Bernie are lined up against one wall facing me. They all had these shit-eating grins on their faces. So the door opens. I'm looking down at the card studying the picture. "Miss La Tour, what's your date of birth?"

"Excuse me?"

"Your date of birth, you know, your birthday."

"Excuse me?" I finally look up and there is this Amazon, naked, except for a feather headdress, woman in high heels standing in front of me.

I guess the look on my face and the fact that I turned red as a stop light was enough. Everyone in the room was hysterical. Mr. Walters actually had tears in his eyes from laughing. "Sandy," Mr. Walters said, addressing the chief, "it never gets old. We get them every time."

Nakovics put his paw on my shoulder and gave a friendly squeeze. The friendly squeeze almost broke my collarbone. "We got you good, kid. Welcome to the Third Division. You should have seen your face. It was great. We do this to all the new guys."

"Really? May I ask why?" This brought another round of laughter. "'Cause it's fun," was Garfuss's reply. I didn't think so at the time.

Bernie and I made our arrests and he felt the same as I did about narcotics. In plainclothes there was a kind of rating system. Gambling and prostitution were called majors and narco collars and ABC violations were classified as minors. I forget the numbers, but I think if you had six minors in a month, that equaled one major. But, you could only do that, maybe once every three months or so. If you did it more frequently, the boss would call you into his office, and depending on the boss, he'd either try to help you or chew you out. Bernie and I never got chewed out. Well, except until about two months after we partnered up.

We were just strolling up and down Eighth Avenue in the Forties. It was a nice winter night, clear and just enough cold to let you know Old Man Winter was still around. I spotted a guy I went to the academy with in front of the firehouse on Eighth and Forty-Seventh. He had left the PD and joined the Fire Department. I introduced Bernie and we all started shooting the breeze. Across Eighth, I saw a cop in uniform hurrying along the avenue. He went up about two steps into a bar and the next we saw, he came flying out the door. He landed in a heap on the sidewalk. I told the fireman, "Call the cops. Tell them we need help," and Bernie and I took off dodging traffic to get across the avenue to the bar.

The cop was moving and moaning on the sidewalk. Bernie stopped to help him. I ran up the steps, through the open bar door. The next thing I saw was what looked like a blacksmith's anvil coming right at my face. The next thing I remember is that I was sitting on a chair and somebody was waving something smelly under my nose. I pushed his hand away and started to gag. The bar was jammed with uniforms and detectives. At the rear of the bar was this huge man lying on the floor. He was cuffed and his legs were tied together with rope.

Even though he was hogtied, he was still struggling and cursing. "Bernie," I asked, "how's the cop?"

"He's fine. They took him to the hospital. How are you? You were out like a light."

"What the hell did he hit me with?"

"He hit you with his fist."

"His fist! My God! How the hell big is his hand? I mean, he broke my nose."

"Yes, he did," said Bernie.

I found out later that the "big guy" that hit me was a one-time movie actor who had gone on the skids and was now a construction worker working as a dock builder. His main starring role was that of a gangster. So every time the movie was on TV, he'd get a load on and terrorize the bars and the people along Eighth Avenue. Now, as to why we got "chewed out?" Well, I shouldn't have just run into the bar without assessing what I was going into. They, the bosses, were right but they lumped Bernie into my mistake. I didn't think that was fair. So, I opened my big mouth to tell them how I felt. Just then, Inspector Nakovics came in and all the precinct bosses clammed up. Again, he put his massive hand on my shoulder but it was very gentle.

"I'll take it from here, gentlemen. He is in my command. I'll get the message across." So the two sergeants, one lieutenant, and two captains all left. I guess I was wrong, but the fact that I was trying to help a cop in uniform who got knocked on his backside should have been enough for a pat on the back, not an ass chewing.

"Listen, son, I know you had good intentions but your tactics were all wrong. You should have known better. What did you learn from the marines and the academy? You look and assess what the terrain looks like. Got that?" I nodded yes.

The inspector continued, "Good. Now, if anyone asks you, you were chewed out by me and you learned your lesson, right?"

"Right, sir."

So all's well that ends well. Bernie and I continued to make our arrests and handle all the kites (cop speak for letters that alleged vice, gambling, or narcotics violations) assigned to us.

Bernie had Shomrin business and was going to be off for a week. I took five days off. Jennifer and I, with Tom Healy and Eleanor, took a quick trip to Washington DC just for fun. When I came back to work, we were scheduled to do a ten at night to six in the morning. When I got to the plainclothes office, Bernie was already there looking through his kites. I had one that was about three months old. The allegation was that the Copacabana had organized crime members gathering there. Also, they were selling alcohol to minors. And last but not least, they were serving intoxicated people.

Now, in those days, the Copa was one of the premier nightclubs in the city. People from all over came to New York and just had to go to the Copa. All the big show biz names headlined at the Copa, including Sinatra himself. I even went there after my high school prom. Did we drink? Yes. Were we underage? Yes. But a kite is a kite. We waited until after eleven o'clock and the lieutenant, "Nutsy Jim" Braverman, wasn't anywhere to be found. "Hey,

Bernie, let's go over to the Copa so I can make a few observations and close this thing out."

So off we went. The doorman, "Carmen, the Ape," tried to stop us, but we showed our shields and told him we were from the Division and were on official business. Reluctantly he let us past the velvet rope. He was muttering about our parents not being married or something like that. So in we go. I really forget who the headliner was, but we got a table in the rear and sat. After about a half hour or so, I saw this guy and a beautiful girl at a table near us. The guy was a lot older than the doll he was with, and it was obviously he was crocked. Bernie saw this too. "Isn't it nice to see a father take his daughter out for a night on the town?" Bernie cracked. I laughed. Just then, the doll got up and the "father" pulled her down into the chair. He reached over and gave her hair a pull.

This got our attention. A waiter appeared and put a shot and a glass of water in front of the guy. He downed the shot and chased it with water. He snapped his finger and another waiter brought another shot. The girl got up, as if to leave, and he pulled her down again. This really got our attention. He then smashed her across the face. Bernie and I got up, and with our shields out, we approached the table. Drunken face saw us and stood up, knocking his chair over. The Copa girls were dancing. The music was loud. The cigarette and cigar smoke was hanging in a blue haze all through the room.

The "father" tried to grab me and I hit him with a short left that smacked him further off balance and he knocked over the table and he hit the floor. He spilled the drinks on the table. One of the waiters grabbed Bernie around the neck and he decked that guy. A few of the busboys tried to grab us. Bernie and I kept yelling that we were cops.

The Copa girls kept dancing. The patrons kept drinking and smoking. They were oblivious to the fight going on in the rear of the room. Telling you now, it was kind of comical. Somebody called the cops and about six uniformed cops came in and restored order. I had the "father" in cuffs. The "daughter" was crying. The busboys and waiters were bleeding and the Copa dancers were still dancing.

When the situation calmed down, we all, the "father", the "daughter," two waiters, and two busboys, moved into an alcove at the foot of the stairs. I finally looked at the uniform guys. I saw the collar brass had the precinct numbers nineteen on it. "Whadda you guys doing here?" I asked.

"Whadda ya mean? It's our precinct. Where are you guys from?"

"The Third Division Plainclothes."

"Well, as of two days ago, the division boundaries were changed. This joint is now in the Fourth Division." Bernie and I looked at each other and simultaneously uttered, "Oh shit!"

We brought our catch to the Nineteen Precinct and the desk officer, rather sarcastically, suggested that we contact one of our bosses. So I called the Seventeenth and asked the desk if they had heard from Lieutenant Braverman. The answer was no. I had him give me Inspector Nakovics's home number.

The conversation went something like this: "Sir, I hate to bother you with this but . . ." When I finished, he told me to take out my shield. "What's it say?" I read off my shield number, 15945. "No, what's it say on the top?"

"City of New York Police, sir."

"Right. Last time I checked, the Copa was in the city of New York. Book 'em or give them summonses. Wait for me at the office when you finish. I'll be in early." Click.

We gave a bunch of summonses to the offending parties, wiped away their blood, and sent them on their way. "Father" and "daughter" became lovey-dovey again.

Because the drinks the waiter served was now part of the Copa floor, I had no evidence that they had actually served the drunk any alcohol. I gave the waiter a summons for serving an intox person anyway. Bernie gave the others summonses for disorderly conduct and everybody was happy.

Well, not everybody. The owner of the Copa, Julie Podell came bursting into the squad room. He was with Carmine, "the Ape." Podell was an obnoxious punk, squat built, fat little man. His voice was squeaky and high pitched. The son-of-a-bitch came in like he owned the place. He was demanding to speak to the man in charge. "Do you know who I am? Do you know who I know?"

Finally I had enough. I escorted him into an empty office and told him where to go. I told him I didn't give a rat's ass who he knew. In essence, I blasted the hell out of this sputtering, red faced, loud mouth. Then I told him and Carmine, "the Ape," to get the hell out of the house.

About six in the morning Nakovics came into the office. "Why did you go to the Copa?" I explained about the kites. I explained that Bernie and I had been off for five days. I explained what we saw and what happened after we tried to stop the old guy from smacking the girl. I explained that I just wanted to close the kite out and the Copa people exacerbated the situation. I ran out of things to explain, so I just shut up.

The inspector looked at Bernie and me for a long minute. "Okay, I'm satisfied you didn't know about the division change. Don't worry about it. By the way, where was Braverman?" The door opened and in he came. "I'm right here, boss. What's up?" Bernie and I ran out of the office. We didn't want to be around when you know what hit the fan.

The following night I reported to the office, and to my surprise, Chief Garfuss, Nakovics, and Lieutenant Sullivan were there. I said to myself, "Self, this can't be good." The chief was the first to speak. "You're going to have to apologize to Podell, the owner of the Copa. You know that, don't you?"

"No, sir, I don't. And for what, if I may ask." So he answered. "Well, he's a kind of well-connected person in the city. He knows a lot of high-placed people. He's not really happy with the way you treated him last night. So he wants an apology, okay?"

"Not really," I said to myself. Out loud I asked, "Is that an order, Chief?"

"If it is, will you obey it?" To this day I hate people who answer a question with a question. "Think about it because he is coming here in about fifteen minutes and he's going to have someone from Mayor Lindsey's office with him.

Tick tock. Two seconds went by. "Chief, I didn't do anything to apologize for, so if I may speak freely?" He nodded his assent. "He and his keeper, from the mayor's office, can kiss my ass." I saw the vestiges of smiles on the assembled. Or maybe I thought I did.

Podell swaggered in and promptly took a chair behind one of the empty desks. I took a chair behind another empty desk. He wore a big pinky ring that looked like it came out of one of those machines. You know, the thing where you put in the coin and then manipulate a crane-type thingie? You know what I mean?

Anyway, he starts banging the ring on the desktop and, with his finger, motions me to come across the room to him as he pointed to the "witness" chair at the side of the desk. I sat there listening to the ring knocking. All the bosses left the squad room and went into another office. The one they chose had the two-way glass. They could see us but we couldn't see them.

So after about thirty seconds of the ring knocking and the ordering gestures, to come to him, I flipped him the bird. In his squeaky, high-pitched voice he screamed at this stooge from Lindsey's office. "I want his job! I want his job!" His face turning colors and the ring knocking getting more furious. I walked out.

Inspector Nakovics met me in the hall. "Meet me over at Jilly's." I nodded and left the station house. Jilly's was a little bar on the west side. It was sort of famous because Frank Sinatra and his "Rat Pack" buddies frequented the place.

I was greeted at the door by Mike Patrick, the maitre de cum bouncer. "Whatsa matter? You look pissed." I told him what had happened and what I did. He just looked at me and laughed. "Come on in. Let me buy you a beer." He took me to a table in the back and a waiter appeared with a bottle of Bud.

Jilly came over and sat down. "Mike told me what happened. You know that Podell is a piece of shit. I won't even let him in here. Frank hates him. He screwed Frank a few years back. Listen"—and he pulled his chair closer and in a conspiratorial whisper said, "I don't tell many people when he's coming in, but he's coming in about an hour. I'd like you to meet him, all right?" (No, it's not all right. Why would I want to meet one of the most famous people in the free world?) "That would be great, Jilly. I'd love to meet him."

"Done deal, pal."

Nakovics and Bernie came in with Lieutenant Sullivan and sat at the table. Drinks were delivered and finally Nakovics spoke. "You're going to be transferred. It's going to take a few weeks, but the chief isn't going to let you get hurt. Just for the record, you and Bernie didn't do anything wrong. The fact that you weren't notified about the division boundary change isn't your fault. The fact that Braverman wasn't available is not your fault." Jilly came back over.

"Didya tell them?" I shook my head no. So he told the group and we settled in. About three rounds later, in walks Frank and Sammy Davis. Now, I have to admit, I'm a celebrity freak. I mean, I get a kick out of seeing people from TV and movies. Don't get me wrong, I mean, I don't drool or anything and I don't ask for autographs. I just get a kick out of seeing them up close.

Eventually Jilly brought Sam and Frank over to our table and introduced us all. Sinatra knew Inspector Nakovics. Nakovics just waved a hello to him. "Hi, Inspector, how the hell are you?" "Fine, Frank."

Apparently Jilly had told Sinatra about my run-in with Podell. "Hey, kid, you really flipped that old bastard the bird?"

"Yes, sir, I did." He slapped me on the back. "Good for you. I shoulda punched him out years ago. Hey, we're gonna eat, why don't you guys join us?"

I'll tell you, I don't think I've ever laughed so hard in my entire life. Sammy Davis, Jr. was a riot. Sinatra and Jilly were nonstop with jokes. Along about two, Sinatra got up, went behind the bar, put a tape into the machine, and started singing.

I don't know how he did it, but Mike Patrick got rid of the tourists and the gawkers at the bar. He had pulled a shade down that covers the front window. Just the regulars were there and only a select few that would be allowed in.

Sinatra sang about six songs. All his signature saloon songs. Then Sammy Davis got up and accapella did "What Kind of Fool Am I." Jilly put a tape in, and Davis danced and sang to Mr. Bo Jangles. For me it was a night to remember. I was tempted to call Jennifer, tell her to jump into a cab, and join us. Now I wish I had. She would have enjoyed it.

About four, the impromptu party was breaking up. Nakovics came over to me and gave me one of his famous hugs. I thought my lungs were going to collapse. "Dan, you did a good job for me. I put you in for lost time for tonight and the rest of the week. You go home, relax, and don't worry about Podell. Wherever they decide to send you guys, the chief and I will put in a good word for you. Downtown caved in, but that's the world of politics. You'll be all right. If you think I can ever help you, let me know. You have all my contact numbers. I hope you enjoyed your party." "Thanks for everything, boss. As Frank would say, 'It's been a gas.'" He laughed and so did I.

Sinatra came over to us and put his hand out. "Geez, I wish I had seen the look on that slob, Podell's, face when you shot him the bird. Here's my card. It has all my contact numbers on it. If you need me, call. If I'm not around, call my pal Jilly. He can always reach me."

With that, he shook my hand, slapped me on the back, and out the door he went. What a night. I mean, really, what a night!

I tried to get into the apartment without waking up Jennifer. I guess it was about five-thirty. She stirred. "You're home early."

"Can you take the rest of the week off without any trouble?" I asked.

"I have to go in today and the next day. My boss has meetings and I have to be there. Why, what's the matter?"

"Nothing's wrong. I'm going to be transferred in about two weeks so the boss told me to take some lost time."

"After the meetings I should be able to take off. Where do you want to go?" I told her we'd figure out someplace.

She got up and put on a pot of coffee. I told her all about being with Sinatra and Sammy Davis. I showed her the card Sinatra gave me. I glossed over the "meeting" with Podell. The words were just pouring out. I was like a talking machine. Finally, Jennifer said, "You get some sleep. I won't call you. In fact, I'll turn the phone off so you won't be disturbed."

She went to work and I went to sleep. About seven-thirty I felt this gentle touch on my forehead. There she was smiling. "Well, sleep beauty, did you have a good nap?"

"As a matter of fact, I did. Where do you want to go to eat? I'm famished." She looked at me with her beautiful blue eyes and her perfect smile. "How about we go to Pete's Tavern? I know you like the place." So we did.

The next morning I woke about ten-thirty. There was a note on her pillow. "Thanks for last night. It was great." I smiled. "Yes, it was," I said to myself. I sat around, had a cup of coffee she had pre-made. I watched a little TV. I cleaned up our small kitchen, when I heard a knock on the door. It was my brother Jackie.

"Dan, why won't you answer the phone? I've been calling you since last night. Have you seen the papers?"

I was still in a happy state from last night. "Hi, and good afternoon to you too," I said with a smile. "I guess we didn't put the ringer on since the other day. What's up?"

He shoved the paper into my hand. "Look at page three."

"Sit down, Jack." He did. I opened the *Daily News* to page three and halfway down the page was an old photo of a cop in uniform. I started to read.

"Shooter of mobster and his family located shortly before he dies," by Pat Toomey. The article outlined the shooting of No Nose Toronto, his son, and grandson at the Ro-Sal. I skipped a few paragraphs and read, "Isodore Goldstein, a former police officer, confessed to the slayings of the alleged mobsters shortly before he died in a hospital in Pittsburgh, Pennsylvania.

"Goldstein, who was dismissed from the force ten years ago as a result of a corruption probe, was deserted by his family and was forced to live on the streets. Goldstein did odd jobs in stores, bars, and restaurants. People in the Sheepshead Bay area told a reporter that he was harmless and usually under the influence of alcohol. They knew him as Izzy.

"After the shootings, Goldstein disappeared from the neighborhood. Police are baffled as to a motive for the killings or how he wound up in Pittsburgh. A group of Jewish businessmen have pledged to bury Mr. Goldstein. Attempts to locate any relatives have not been successful. Police say the cause of death was from cancer."

The article went on, "Detectives Frank Healy and Walter Gannon flew to Pittsburgh after receiving a call from Mr. Goldstein. Goldstein told them where he was and that he wanted to confess. Police describe Goldstein's statement as 'a death-bed confession.' Police would not disclose the motive for the slayings, nor would they discuss the contents of the confession. A police spokesman said the case is closed and the Kings County District Attorney agreed."

I put the newspaper on the table and plopped into a chair. "That's a shame. He wasn't a bad guy. I wonder what made him shoot the mutts." Jackie looked at me long and hard. Finally he said, "Do you know why you were put into Plainclothes with no little time on the job?" It was my turn, so I looked at him. Finally I said, "Because of all the good work I did in Coney Island and in the Six-One, right?" Wrong.

For the next half hour, he told me that No Nose was trying to get the mob bosses to permit him to have me killed. The powers in the mob are hesitant to approve a hit on a cop. Then he added, "Even if he is young and sometimes stupid." He continued and told me that a cop from our neighborhood was in a card game with some half-assed wise guys. They didn't know the guy was a cop. One of them started talking about the request from No Nose to the bosses and the card player mentioned my name as the intended target. Jackie looked at me. "Sit down, Dan. I tried to tell you that those people play for keeps. Do you remember what Uncle Mike told you?" He didn't wait for an answer. "He told you, and me when I went in the job, when it's over, it's over.

Remember? Well, you kept it going with the sticking of your finger up your nose and then asking Toronto if he wished he could do it."

I started to protest but he held up his hand. "It doesn't matter now why you did it. It doesn't matter if you were right or wrong. Your guardian angel, Goldstein, ended it for you. The mob bosses were happy because they don't have to decide about you. So you're safe now. You really don't know how close you came to making Jennifer a young widow."

I got up and went to the sink and poured myself a glass of water. Suddenly my mouth was dry as a bone. After a few minutes, I sat down. "Who's the off-duty cop?" He looked at me and smiled. "It really doesn't matter. What does matter is that he told me and I told my boss and up the chain it went. So that's why you got into Plainclothes and sent to the Bronx. Out of sight, out of mind, as they say. Come on, I'll buy you lunch." I said a silent prayer of thanks to St. Michael and a special one for Izzy Goldstein.

We walked over to Walsh's and sat at the bar. The bartender, Mickey, came over and I introduced Jackie to him. "Hey, you just missed Jim the Cop. He was asking for you. Wanted to know if I'd seen you around." Jackie asked who Jim the Cop was and I told him. "He's a real big guy who works in Headquarters, I think. He and I just shoot the breeze when I see him in here."

After lunch, Jackie left me and I walked back to the apartment. I couldn't stop thinking about what he had told me. I wasn't scared or even worried about myself. I was just worried about Jennifer, I guess.

After she came home from work, she cooked up a beautiful pork-chop dinner with all the trimmings. "So where are we going to go?" I hadn't even thought about it. Quoting from the movie *Marty*, I said, "I don't know, Marty, where do you wanna go?"

"Anywhere you are is fine with me." So we flew up to Boston to do the tourist bit. We went to all the revolutionary war sites. We toured the USS *Constitution*, the Old North Church, Quincy Market. We drank and ate, in more than a few Irish pubs. We laughed and made love a lot. When we got home, we settled back in our work routine.

Bernie and I realized that we'd be transferred in a week or so, but we were still on the hunt for arrests. About five-thirty one morning, I stopped the car in front of the Paramount Theatre. We were planning to get a final cup of coffee before quitting time. I got out to cross over to Nedicks when this rather scantily-clad colored girl approached me. "Hey, handsome, do you and your friend want some action before you go to work?" Bernie heard this and got out of the car and leaned against the door. "Whadda you have in mind?"

Now, when you make a prostitution arrest, certain things have to be articulated. For instance, I can't just say "okay, let's go." The pros has to tell you what kind of sex act she's going to perform and how much it's going to cost. Once she, and in some cases she/he, says the magic words, you can make the arrest. Got that? Okay.

So we're talking. She's not coming right out with the magic words but getting close when all of a sudden, a thin colored guy parks behind my car and comes storming over to our happy little trio. "Sister, what's the matter with you? Can't you smell pigs in the morning ? Get on your way, girl."

The guy was dressed like a construction worker complete with a tool belt that had a fine red hatchet in one of those circle thingies attached to the belt. Oh, I didn't mention that he had his hand on it. Well, he did.

"Hey, pal, why don't you just mind your own business?" Bernie says. I turned to him just as he's yanking the hatchet from his belt. "Hey, Geronimo, take it easy," I said just as he grabbed the handle and was starting to raise it. Bernie hit him with his right shoulder and sent him sprawling across the hood of his car and the fine red hatchet hit the sidewalk. Miss Morning Delight took off like the proverbial bat outta hell down Seventh Avenue. How the heck she ran so fast in her high heels, I'll never know. I scooped up the hatchet and Bernie had Geronimo pinned against the hood of his car.

Well, when we all calmed down, it turned out that he wasn't Geronimo or Cochese or even Tonto. He was a reverend. Yep, a reverend who, I guess, only moonlighted as a construction worker during the week so he could make the payments on his Cadillac.

On weekends, from his storefront cathedral in Harlem, he dispensed his brand of fire and brimstone. I figured he even took up his own collection. "I wants to hear a silent collection. I's don't wants to hear no clinking on the plate. Praise the Lord."

I got his driver's license and it said Reverend Nelson D. Riches with the address of his Harlem cathedral. We gave him some traffic summonses and sent him on his way. We didn't put the tickets down as part of our Plainclothes activity. Oh, yeah, I kept the hatchet as a souvenir.

So here I am back in the Boro of Churches, Brooklyn. I found a spot near the Seven-Eight Precinct on Sixth Avenue and Bergen Street. I climbed the stairs, went up the desk officer, told him who I was, and with a thumb motion and head jerk, indicated toward the stairs.

I climbed to the third floor and saw a door with a cardboard sign taped to the wall: 11th Div. Plainclothes Office. I guess this must be the place. So in I go. I get the quick up-and-down look from the assorted crew in the room.

"You the new guy?" says a voice from a room within a room. I looked toward the doorway and spotted an arm waving me forward. "I'm Lieutenant Sam Duke. You Stark?"

"Yes, sir."

"Now listen to me. There's no need for the sir business. We're kind of informal around here. If we were in uniform that would be different, okay?"

"Yes, sir—er, okay."

He told me to follow him. He introduced me to several men, some in uniform, some in civies. We went into another office, which was in the office that was in the main office. There were two men standing, and seated on the couch was Jim the Cop.

Hey, a face I recognize. "Hi ya, Jim. What are you doing here?" Jim stood up and put his hand out and introduced me to Jimmy Gebhardt and Joe Sheldorfer. Smiles and handshakes were exchanged, but they all had kind of weird expressions on their faces. I looked around at the group but didn't say anything.

Jim the Cop went behind the desk and sat. "Sit down, fellas." Oh boy, Jim the Cop was a little more than a cop, I deduced. "Stark here is going to be working with you two guys. He comes highly recommended and knows Brooklyn. So make him feel at home." He looked at me. "Dan, welcome aboard." He turned to the lieutenant. "Sam, get him a locker and somewhere to sit." Then back to me, "We'll talk again soon." We all got up, and being the last one, I closed the door. I looked back at the door, and on the fronted glass window was stenciled: "Commanding Officer 11th Division". Another good start.

"So, Stark, I guess you know the inspector pretty good," says Lieutenant Duke. The other guys, Jimmy and Joe, are just watching and waiting for my answer. They were looking at me with the old fish eye.

"Well, to tell you the truth"—I hate starting a sentence like that—"I really don't know him at all, actually. I mean, I know him but I don't know him. Does that make sense?"

So my new lieutenant and partners shook their heads in tandem. At the same time, they all said, "No."

Lieutenant Duke just said, "Elucidate."

"Well"—I hate when someone starts that way—"I've seen him in the neighborhood. I really didn't know he was a boss. I thought he was just a cop."

The old jaundice eye was given to me, but that was all I was going to give them. I wasn't about to tell them that I knew him from a saloon. It wasn't any of their business if the inspector drank or where or how often. Now was it?

So I settled in, so to speak, learning the confines of the division. It was a very eclectic area that encompassed factories, homes, poverty, prostitutes, and a whole area of organized crime members. There was the Six-Eight, Seven-Two, Seven-Six, Seven-Eight, and the Eight-Four Precincts in the division. Nice homes, nice people, crummy homes, and bad people. The Eleventh Division was a microcosm of our world. Years later, Eastwood summed it up: "The Good, the Bad, and the Ugly."

The work was actually enjoyable. Gebhardt was a real character, always with the one liners. Joe was serious but enjoyed a good laugh. Lieutenant Sam was hot and cold. Some days he was your best friend and other days he could be a royal pain. You never knew which way he would be when he walked through the door.

About two months after I was assigned, Sam pulled me into his office for a chat. "So, Dan, how do you like our merry band of crime fighters?" Before I could answer, he continued, "Just between us, how well do you know the inspector? I don't buy the 'just neighbors business.' You can tell me."

"Lieu, I just know him from the neighborhood. I was getting a cup of coffee in a diner and I sat next to him and we started to BS. He came out and asked if I was on the job. I asked him why he would ask that, and he said 'cause he was and what else would I be except a cop or fireman. It was the middle of the week in the afternoon. Who else would be off but a cop of fireman? So I told him where I worked and he told me he worked in Headquarters. When he left the diner, I asked the counterman about him.

He told me that all he knew was that he was a cop who lived in the neighborhood. I didn't know he was a boss until I got here."

I figured that was it, but Sam "Baby" pressed on. "So you never knew him before, right?" "Hey, Lieu, I told you how I met him and that's all there is to that." I was starting to get annoyed and trying not to show it. But enough is enough. "Are we finished now?" He nodded and I left.

The following week we were getting another plainclothes cop from Bed-Sty section of Brooklyn. Nobody knew anything about him except his name was Steve Brown. Duke was looking out the window at the police parking area when he spotted this beautiful-looking Pontiac convertible pull to the curb. A few minutes later in walks Steve Brown.

He was a six-footer with a wide, bright smile and sandy brown hair with emerald green eyes.

"Hi, I'm Steven Brown. Who do I report to?"

"I'm Lieutenant Duke. Is that your car? The convertible down there?"

"Yes, it is." Duke looked at him in an accusatory manner.

"Yeah, well, sell it."

"Sell it! I just bought it."

"It doesn't look good for a cop to be driving next year's car."

Brown looked at Duke. "Can I ask you a question?"

"Go ahead."

"Do you own a house?"

"Yes."

"Well, when you sell your house, I'll sell my car. Not that it's anybody's business, but I'm single and I live in the house my parents left me. And it's mortgage free."

Duke gave Brown one of those "if looks could kill" looks. I, along with everyone else, walked away from this staring contest.

It turned out that Brownie was a very capable and experienced cop and was one of those guys who could fit in anywhere. He turned out to be one of Lieutenant Duke's favorite go-to guys.

One day my "pal Jim" calls us into his office. We all sit and he holds up a sheet of paper. "I just got this direct from the PC's Office." (Cop talk for Police Commissioner.) "And it's marked 'Immediate Action.' It seems that some of the mayor's big-time supporters are complaining about homosexual activity taking place right near their front doors. You all know where the Promenade is in Brooklyn Heights?" He continued, "I need one team to work from eleven to seven in the morning and see if you can make a few arrests for soliciting."

He looked at Joe, Jim, and me. "I want to thank team three for volunteering. Make it a Friday night into Saturday morning. Thanks, fellas. You know how to deal with the female pros, so it's the same drill only with guys. They have to tell you what the guy will do for you and have to give you a price. Once that's done, you make the arrest."

So it turns out that I got the short straw. I drove Jennifer to her mother's house Friday after work, grabbed a little nap, and went to work about a quarter to ten.

Gebhardt had three matches in his hand. Joe picked first, Jim second, and I got the short one. So that meant I was the one to sit on the bench on the Promenade and wait to get picked up by some homosexual.

I didn't mind the pros, but the thought of me, macho me, being picked up by a guy. This was one I wouldn't share with Jennifer or her brother Georgie.

So long about twelve-thirty, we piled into Joe's car and went to the promenade. I found a park bench and plopped down. Now, the view from the bench was great. The Promenade is a wide concrete expanse that is built over the Brooklyn-Queens Expressway. It's so thick that you can't hear the noise from the constant stream of traffic below. The view is great. You look right over to the Manhattan skyline across the East River.

It was a beautiful, clear night and Manhattan was in all its electric glory. The majestic Empire State and Chrysler buildings, the rectangular shape of the United Nations to the north, all the skyscrapers in lower Manhattan, and the shell of the soon-to-be crown jewel of the city, the Twin Towers of the World Trade Center.

So long about a half hour after I got there, I was in the midst of a daydream when I became aware of someone else on the bench. I looked at him, and he looked at me and smiled. I smiled back. He edged closer, so I edged closer. He edged more and I edged over more. He's smiling. I'm smiling. Then all of a sudden he scoots back to the far side of the bench. I looked behind me and I spot a marked radio car slowly driving on the Promenade. It passes by and then backs up. The driver lowers the window, "Hey, Stark! How ya doin'? I heard you got transferred to the Division Plainclothes. Whattya doin' here?" My smiling guy broke the record for getting to the street exit.

The uniform cop and I went through the academy together, Mike Sylvester. "I'm working, Mike. What the hell do you think I'm doing here?" Jim and Joe came out of their hiding spots and joined us. "Geez, Dan, I'm sorry. We got word that the fags were doing their thing here. They told us to give it special attention. Geez, I'm sorry." We chatted a little longer and they left.

I resumed my position on the bench and nearly fell asleep. I came back from my little nap to see a guy, about three hundred pounds, waddling down the Promenade. "This is gonna be fun," comes a voice from the bushes.

The same drill took place. The large man smiled. I smiled. He hefted his frame closer and I moved closer. I just didn't have any patience for the small talk, so I just said, "I hope you won't hurt me." And he said, "I'll be very gentle. I'll treat you like you're a little doll." Me! A little doll! Okay.

For about a week after, Jim and Joe told anyone who would listen the story (embellishment, of course). I was called Doll Face.

Plainclothes work, actually, can become mundane. You go into a bar, watch the occupants, and see who is approached the most. After about three or four guys approach one, the one guy, invariably, would get up and walk into the men's room or go into the kitchen. He'd write down the three bets and then return to his spot at the bar.

This scenario became a bit boring. One of us would go into the men's room, find where the guy stuffed the "work" and eventually make a jump collar. After making several observations, over several days, you'd follow the guy into the bathroom and "jump" him when he had the "work" in his hand.

There was a humorous aspect at times. Like the time we went into "Crazy" Joey Gallo's "social" club. It was a storefront on President Street not far from the docks. Periodically we'd go in and just roust everyone in the place. The caretaker was Gallo's cousin, a midget. He was a funny guy.

Gallo himself was a murderer. He also controlled loan-sharking, drugs, and gambling in his slice of Brooklyn. Because he was nuts, he was given the sobriquet of Crazy Joe.

Anyway, back to the midget. One day Jim the Cop calls us in and tells us that he wants us to shake up Gallo's club. He gave us pictures of guys who had arrest warrants outstanding and told us to lock them up if they're in the club. Okay was the reply. About two in the afternoon, we hit the front door. There were about eighteen bozos and the midget in the club. "Up against the wall" was the command. As it had been rehearsed, they all left their cards on the table (no money, just matchsticks for currency) and assumed the position.

Joe had the pictures so he's going down the line looking at the faces. Jimmy and the door and I were about five feet away from the group holding my gun at my side.

All of sudden, I hear this growling and I feel a tugging on my trousers. I look down and there's this mangy, dirty, junkyard dog biting on my cuff. The dog looked to be a cross between a collie and a German shepherd. It was so dirty; it was hard to tell.

"Armando," I said to the midget, "get this mutt away from me."

"Hey, Stark, whatta ya want. He's a police dog. He likes his own kind." Have you any idea how hard it is to keep a stern face when you want to laugh? And you have a gun in your hand?

Jimmy started first, then the midget, then the guys on the wall. Joe came to the rescue. "The guys we want aren't here. Let's go." We left with laughter pouring out of the club. I actually thought it was pretty funny too.

The months were flying by. We made collars for everything. I told you before that Plainclothes was to suppress gambling, prostitution, and little emphasis on narcotics. We took everything we saw—burglars, street robberies, gun collars, assaults. Everything including our required gambling and prostitution. Out team lead the borough in arrests and we had a 99 percent conviction on all our gambling arrests. That was not too shabby.

A few times I was offered money to dump a case, but the offerer (if there is such a word) regretted the encounter. Big Jim's prediction was right. They will offer you money to dump the case or copy the betting slips you seize. That way a bettor can't claim that he or she bet the number that hit or the horse that won. Once the word got out that the bookie or the "bank" had been raided, the bettors all swore that their horse won and they played the winning number. It was a headache for the boys.

One bright, sunny day we all assembled in Jim the Cop's office. He started off by clearing his throat. "Men, I . . . I, in . . . oh, hell, I've been transferred. I want to thank each and every one of you for the job you've done here, and I'm sure you'll continue to do it for the new boss."

Steve Brown interrupted. "Boss, where you going?"

"I'm glad you asked that, Steve, even though you interrupted my speech." He was smiling when he said it. "I got word, last night, that I'm being promoted to chief and I'm going to Manhattan South Detectives." We all broke out in spontaneous applause. He bowed and his smile got wider. Holding up his hand to quiet us, he added, "You are all invited to dinner at Two Toms at six tonight. On me."

We all assembled in the "new" boss's office. Lieutenant Duke introduced us one by one. He was a tall, thin, distinguished-looking man with just a touch of gray at the temples. He wore a dark blue suit with a blue shirt and red-and-blue striped tie. He looked more like a college professor than an inspector of police.

He sat down behind his desk and we all either sat or lounged against the walls. "My name is Georgie Murphy. It will take me a week or so, but I'll remember everyone's name. So please bear with me. I'll be calling you in, one by one, in the next week or so. It will be a get-to-know-you meeting. Nothing heavy, just a hello-and-how-are-you're-doing type of meet." He looked around the room and smiled a big white-toothed smile. His blue-green eyes had a type of twinkle in them. I immediately liked him.

About three days later, it was my turn. I went in and he came from around his desk. He dragged a chair around to the front and positioned it so we were facing each other. I waited until he was seated and he gestured for me to sit. "So tell me about yourself." I did. After about a half hour of non-stop verbal resume, I ran out of things to say. "Interesting story, Dan. We have a lot in common. I'm one of nine children too. I also lost my parents when I was young. My predecessor spoke glowingly about you." I gave a little smile and a nod. "Well, I hope to be able to say the same when someone asks me about you sometime down the line. Are you satisfied with the team you're in? If not, I'll switch you to another." Without a bit of hesitation I said, "Inspector, I am very happy with Jim and Joe. I know I've learned a lot from them and I'll continue to learn. The other guys you have here are all top notch too. But if I have a choice and it's okay with you . . .," as an afterthought I added, "And them, I'd like to stay with them."

"All right, Dan. If you feel the need to talk, just come on in." He stood and I stood. He put his hand out and I shook it. As I was at the door, he said, "Just keep up the good work."

"I will, sir." And I closed the office door.

After about six months things were going fine. Jim, Joe, and I were in the office catching up on our paperwork. The lieutenant came in. "Listen, guys, we got a hot one that has to be looked at. Everybody and his brother has tried to make bets in this bar but to no avail. I want you guys to give it a shot. We'll see if you have any luck." He dropped a stack of papers on the community desk and walked out.

We did all the usual background checks: Who owned the building, who held the mortgage, how many apartments, who lives there, how long has the bar been there, who owns the bar, where does he or she live. All the mundane things that, down the line, might make or break a case.

On the days off, Jennifer and I would get up when we wanted, ate when we wanted, went to the movies or just sat home and read. Or, we'd go to North Arlington and hang out. Life was good, and fun too.

I went into work one morning and grabbed Joe and Jimmy. "Listen, I got a bright idea over the weekend about the Bergen Bar kites." That was the name of the place. It was on Bergen Street and Fourth Avenue near the taxicab garage. Johnny Most owned it. His real name was Mostrangelo but the wise guys called him Johnny Most.

Our background check told us that "Most" had never been arrested but was a fringe wannabe. Made men frequented the place as well as the neighborhood people and off-duty cabbies.

Jimmy says, "Okay, Doll Face, what's your bright idea?"

"What if I walk down there in uniform? I mean, just the uniform trousers. Go down, grab a sandwich, read the racing form and nurse a couple of beers. I do this for two or three days and make observations. I'll pick out who the bookie is and see where he puts his bets. Maybe after a week or so, maybe I can get a couple of directs in with the guy." Jim asked, "What if they ask you your name and where you work?"

"I thought this out too. I'll give them a phony name but tell them I work at the Seven-Eight and I'm on limited duty. We'll leave a message at the switchboard that if anyone asks for Officer Tommy Malloy, they just take a message. This way they'll know I'm legit and just a cop that likes to eat, have a few beers and likes the ponies. Whatta ya think?"

We ran the scenario through the lieutenant and the inspector. They both approved. So, the following Monday I walked down to the bar and grabbed a stool by the window. My shadows, Joe and Jim, were parked across the street where they could keep an eye on the bar and me, through the window.

"Whatta ya have?"

"Give me a Schaeffer. What kind of sandwiches do you have?" I took the *Daily News* out of my jacket pocket and immediately opened to the racing section. I drained the beer and nodded to the barkeep for another. I went back to scoping out the horses. The sandwich was wordlessly put in front of me. I ate and studied the racing pages.

After about an hour and a half, I left the bar. Other than "whatta ya have," no other word was spoken to me. I saw the bookie at a table in the corner, but he paid me no mind. People did approach him, but I didn't see any money exchanged, nor did he write anything down. He went into the bathroom about every twenty minutes. When I left the bar, I went to the pay phone on the corner. With my back to the bar, I called Jennifer. I held the paper out and I hoped it looked like I was placing bets.

I walked the three blocks back to the station house. Joe and Jimmy told me that some guy came out of the side door of the bar and followed me to the precinct. They, in turn, followed him back to the bar. It looked like the plan was working.

I repeated the routine the next three days. Then, on the fourth day, "Whatta ya have?" Introduced himself. "I'm Johnny Most. I own this place. You new around here?" I took his proffered hand. "Tom Malloy. Yeah, I guess you could say that." I went back to my sandwich, beer and racing form. When I left, I went to the corner phone and called Jennifer while ostensibly appearing to place my bets.

When I got back to the station house, the cop on the T.S.(cop speak for telephone switchboard) called out. "Hey, Dan, I got a call for Tom Malloy. I told the guy I'd take a message but he hung up."

"What exactly did he say, if you remember?"

"He said, 'You got a Tom Malloy working there'?"

"I said yeah, but you weren't around but I'd take a message. He hung up."

"Thanks a lot. I really appreciate it." I went upstairs to the office and let the lieutenant know.

The next day we had a scheduled search warrant on one of Joe's kites. We made four collars, seized a ton of work and about five thousand in cash. Joe and Jimmy took the collars to court. The Inspector didn't want me near the court until out little play was over. You never can tell who knew who in the world of gambling.

We were off Saturday, Sunday and Monday. I put in a twenty-eight (cop speak for a day off request form) for Tuesday. Jennifer and I were going to take a ride to the Amish Country in Pennsylvania. Why? Why not! Early Saturday we set out map in hand. It was a beautiful day, which stretched into a beautiful weekend. One thing though. Do you know how hard it is to find a Catholic church in Amish land? But we did.

We got back to the apartment, and as we were unpacking, the phone rang. It was my brother Jackie. "Where did you go now? I've been trying to reach you all weekend."

"Why, is something wrong?"

"No, everything's all right. I just haven't heard from you in awhile."

"Are you working now?" I asked.

"Yeah, I get off at four." I told him to hold on and turned to Jennifer, putting my hand over the mouthpiece, I said, "Jen, I'm going to meet Jackie when he gets off and have a few beers. Then I'll come home and we'll go to Pete's Tavern for dinner."

"Sure" was her reply. "Jack, I'll meet you near the office and I'll buy you a couple of beers, okay?"

"Great" was his reply.

We went to a little joint near his office. It was smoky and crowded with off-duty cops. Finding a spot at the bar, we settled in and caught up on all the news about his family. He asked about the Amish country and I told him how nice they were and how simply they live.

After a few rounds, he turned serious. "You know you should think about saving some money. I mean, God willing, when the children come, you don't want to be in the boat that I'm in. You should think about saving. I'm not saying don't go out. But instead of going to dinner four or five times a week, cut it down to two and these little trips cut back. I'm telling you from experience. Kids cost money. Now's the time to save. End of sermon. I'll let you buy me another beer and then I have to go."

"Okay" was all I said.

So I went back to my assignment and my new best friend. Johnny Most greeted me with a big smile. He placed a Schaeffer in front of me before I asked for it. "How's it goin'? I haven't seen you for a couple of days."

"Yeah, I haven't been around." I went back to my beer. I took out the paper and turned to the racing page. I motioned for another beer and ordered a sandwich. "So do you work around here?"

"Yeah" and I didn't offer anymore. Most walked away. After about an hour, I left, called Jennifer, and went back to the station house.

This kept on going for about another two weeks. Most would talk, I'd grunt a few grunts, and tell him a little more about myself. One fine day he started talking sports and then casually drifted into the sport of Kings. I told him I liked the ponies but "You know, being a cop and all, some guys are reluctant to take my bets."

"Yeah, I see what you mean. You want another beer? It's on the house."

"Thanks." I think my act was being believed.

Monday came and I donned my uniform pants and today I put on the uniform shirt with 78 brass on the collar. I put a windbreaker on and let the numerals show. Johnny Most had already asked, and I answered, that I was on light duty recovering from a radio car accident. "All I do is move papers from one desk to another. Nobody even knows if I'm there or not. It's real boring."

The two of us were now chatting like old friends. Sports, politics, and of course, racing. Suddenly, and without preamble, he motioned to the bookie at the table. "That's Jimmy Green. He takes all the action around here. I see you placing your bets on the phone. I checked you out. You're all right. Jimmy'll take your action."

Most took me over to him and introductions were made. Green gave me the up-and-down look, but he kept looking right at my face. After a few, long seconds, he said, "Okay, kid, whattaya like today?" I gave him the bets and put my hand in my pocket to get some money. Most said, "Don't do that. Just leave your bet on the bar like it's a tip. Jimmy takes the action. I handle the money. You understand?"

"Yeah, I got it."

So for two more days I went back and bet with Jimmy Green. I left the money for the bets on the bar as I was told. On the second day, Joe went in and ordered a beer and watched Most take the "tip" money and put it in a drawer at the far end of the bar. So now we had the operation down.

Green took the bets and Most took the money. Green wrote the bets down in the men's room and stashed them somewhere in there. We applied for, and were granted, a search warrant. I was to go in and bet with marked and recorded money.

So on a beautiful Thursday, I went into the bar as planned. I followed the same procedure and so did they. Green still looked at me as if he was studying my face. I finished my beer and sandwich and headed back to the house.

As planned, about ten minutes after I left, Joe and Jimmy, Steve Brown and three other guys hit the place. They recovered the money and a bag full of bets. He hid them under the sink in a false wall area. Everyone was pleased. Everyone except Johnny Most. He was, what would say? Pissed off at me or maybe himself. I didn't know, nor did I really care.

I had changed back into street clothes by the time they came in from the bar with the prisoners. I took Jimmy Green into one of the offices to get his "information" for the arrest process. "You got us good, kid. I just want you to know there's no bad feelings. One thing, though, I know who you are and you're not Tom Malloy. I figured it out a little too late."

"Really? Who am I?" His answer shocked me.

"I was out of jail about six weeks when my mother got sick and died. I was in, 'cause I pulled a stickup and grabbed some food ration and gas ration stamps. This was during the war. Anyway, after a three-year bit, I was just pullin' petty jobs, ya know, petty stuff just to get some walking around cash. So now my mother dies and I ain't got enough bread to bury her. I hadn't been home long enough to gain any credit and most of my crew were still in jail or dead. So the day after she dies, there's a knock on the apartment door. I open it, and who's standing there but your father." I opened my mouth to say something and he held up his hand. "Yeah, kid, it was your old man. He was my mother's insurance agent. See, Mom had a policy but she didn't have the money to keep it up. Your father carried her. He heard she died and he bought me the money. It was about a thousand and a half. He didn't want it, but I paid him back the money he laid out. He never once said a word about my life. Ya know, kid, I did time for murder, robbin', and all sorts of stuff. He never mentioned it, though. I know you was a kid when he died, but I just wanted you to know he was a great guy. So was ya mother Celie." I looked up when he said that. He smiled. "I used to take action in the bar on New Utrecht and Sixty-Ninth."

"Guggelmetie's," I volunteered.

"Yeah. They would come in with all you brats and sit in the back and have pizza."

"I remember", I said. "I was sad when he died and then a few years later she died. It musta been tough."

"Let me ask you something, all right?"

"Sure, kid, shoot."

"How do you know I'm their son?"

"That's an easy one, kid. You got your father's eyes and his smile. You look just like him. You got his eyes and his smile. I used to ask the guys whatever happened to youse kids. One is a Fed, your other brudder is a bull and lives in the old house. I think your sisters went to Jersey. Am I right?"

"Yes, sir, you are, and thanks for the trip down memory lane. But, you know, this doesn't change anything about the arrest."

He actually looked offended. "I'd never put you in that position. I wouldn't disrespect your father and mother. That hurt, kid. I wouldn't ask you for any help. Your old man helped me enough. You do what you gotta do. Unnerstan?"

"Yes, sir."

After the arraignment, I couldn't wait to get home to tell Jennifer the whole story. She sat and listened, never taking her eyes off me. When I finished, she had tears in her eyes. All she said was, "I really wish I had known them."

"Yeah, that would have been nice. I know they would have liked you." She smiled.

Her brother Jack and Margaret had returned home from Kansas and had settled in a town near North Arlington. Jack asked me if I would like to play golf with him and Georgie and another guy. I told him that I had never played before but I'd like to give it a try.

As luck would have it, I went into the office early on Monday and the clerical man, Pete English, grabbed me by the arm and steered me into his office. "Best offer by the end of the day." Propped up against his desk was a golf bag with a full set of clubs with plastic wrap covering the heads. "Never been used. My brother-in-law bought them and then had a heart attack. My sister wants them out of the house so he won't be tempted to play. When he does, his blood pressure sky rockets."

As I said, I never played golf, but I saw Bob Hope handle a putter when he would be on TV so I grabbed the putter from the rest of the clubs and I saw that it was shaped like an upside-down T. I took a couple of swings and put it back. You know what I mean. The shaft fastened to the middle of the club head with the putting part on either side of the shaft. Got the picture? Good!

So I offer Pete twenty bucks for the bag, clubs, and balls. The end of the tour came and I was the highest bidder. So now I'm in possession of a brand-new set of golf clubs. I promptly threw them in the trunk of my car. About two weeks later, the day of my initial foray into the world of golf had arrived.

We met at about eight in the morning at a course in Belleville, New Jersey. Jennifer took off and so did I. So the night before we stayed at her mother's. I got to the course on time and we all met at the first tee. Georgie, who was a pretty good golfer, was cracking jokes. Jack introduced me to his wife Margaret's brother, also named Jack, and we all just were BS-ing and waiting to tee off. Our tee time was set for ten after eight.

At about five after eight, Jack looks at my brand-new never used before, heads still encased in the plastic wrap clubs. He took the driver from the bag. "Hey, Dan, I didn't know you were left handed."

"I'm not" was my reply.

Jack went on a tirade about us having to tee off in three minutes and mumbled something about me being stupid, and, in the same breath, something about golf etiquette and not holding up the players behind us. "Jack, calm down, I'll go to the pro shop and rent a set. No big deal. You start without me and I'll catch up."

He ran to his car which was in the lot about twenty feet away and came back with a bag full of clubs. "Here, these are right-handed. Be careful, they're matched."

"Oh, good," I said while thinking, what the hell is he talking about? I took the driver, and while standing on the cart path, I took a few swings to loosen up the old body. Well, I guess I shouldn't have been doing that on a paved path. You see, sparks came up when the club hit the path.

Jack went ballistic, and Georgie and the other Jack were laughing so hard they had tears in their eyes. I struggled through the day, and at the end, Jack swore a blood oath never to play golf with me again unless the course had a windmill and little tunnels.

With the clubs, still never having been used and the heads still encased in plastic, in the trunk of my car, I told Pete English my tale of woe. "Pete, you kind of neglected to tell me that the clubs are for a lefty." With the big, ever present, smile on his face, he just said, "I didn't? I'm so sorry." You couldn't get mad at a guy like that. He told me where they were bought and it so happened that it was a large sporting goods chain called Davega Sporting Goods. There happened to be one right near the office. I walked in with the bag and clubs and proceeded to tell the salesman my story. After he stopped laughing, he took my bag and gave me a duplicate. "Brother, that is one for the books. Nobody could make that up." He continued to laugh. Oh, yeah, I checked all the clubs to make sure they were right-handed.

Jennifer and I were eating out less frequently. I had told her what Jackie had told me and she agreed that saving was a good idea.

Don't get me wrong. We didn't become hermits or anything like that. We . . . well, we . . . oh, hell, we practically stopped going to dinner altogether. And, as far as trips went, the furthest we traveled was to North Arlington. But (it was a big "but"), the good news was that we were banking practically all of Jennifer's salary and were trying to get by on mine.

I still had money for my beer and cigars and still bought her flowers every payday. I had started doing that when we first started dating and I just kept it up. I know it pleased her.

The only thing that would please her more would be if we had a baby. C'mon, St. Michael, give us any help you can.

The time was flying by. I had passed the three and a half-year mark in clothes. Another six months and I'd be eligible to go into the Bureau (cop speak for the Detective Bureau) and get the gold shield of a Third Grade Detective. Nice!

No rhyme, no reason, Jimmy, Joe and I got called into Inspector Murphy's office. "Sit down, fellas. You guys are all being transferred. Dan, you're going to the Sixth Division in Harlem. Joe, you're going to Queens Boro Office. And, Jim, you're going to the Eighth Division in the Bronx. Why? I don't know. You are all nearing the, alleged, magical date of four years in clothes. So maybe that has something to do with it. I really don't know. How about we all meet at Jack O'Connor's Club Car for a little farewell drink. Oh, yeah, the transfers aren't official until this coming Monday. I'd advise that you put in for your vacation picks, because the one you pick here, as I'm sure you know, follows you to the next command. I'll see you at five at the Club Car."

Jack O'Connor's Club Car was a bar and restaurant situated right above the Atlantic Avenue terminal of the Long Island Rail Road, or, as it was commonly referred to as the LIRR. It was actually a club car, from the old LIRR, that Jack had acquired and built a successful business around. He bought the property on both sides, but the centerpiece was the club car itself. Nice atmosphere, good food and reasonable prices. I had taken Jennifer there once when we, Jimmy, Joe and I, took our wives there. She liked it.

While we were there with Inspector Murphy having our farewell drinks, I had an idea. So I called Jennifer and ran it by her. She liked it. We had made plans to have Gramma Walsh, Jackie and Muriel and Jimmy and Barbara over to Sty Town for dinner in the near future. Uncle Jack, the priest, was home on leave. I figured it would be nice to go out and eat. Why not the Club Car. It would be convenient for everyone. Jimmy and Barbara lived about two blocks from Jackie and Muriel and Gramma Walsh lived in Bay Ridge. This way they wouldn't have to travel to Manhattan, find parking and probably have to walk three or four blocks to get to our apartment. They could all meet and take the subway right to the Club Car. From Grandma's apartment it was about a ten-minute ride. From Sixty-Ninth Street, it was a ten-minute cab ride to Grandma's and then they could all hop (well, Grandma couldn't hop. I mean, she was eighty or close to it) on the subway or continue in the cab. I figured we'd treat and it would save Jennifer the hassle of having to cook and clean up after.

The arrangements were made, but we had an extra guest. My cousin, Donald Rilley. The priest was in Brooklyn visiting both Jimmy and Jackie so he came. Uncle Jack was in his navy uniform and Donald was wearing his priest suit.

We all arrived at about the same time and were escorted to our table by Jack O'Connor himself. I liked Jack. He was an outgoing Irish man with a quick wit and a ready smile. He immediately turned the charm on Grandma and she was loving it.

We all settled in and started chatting away. Grandma was (as usual) holding court. She regaled us with stories of her childhood, early marriage years, what my (our) mother was like as a youngster and just things that she had seen and lived through.

In true cop fashion, Jimmy, Jackie, and I were seated without backs to the wall, the fair ladies across from us and the two priests at either end. From our vantage point we could see the entrance, the bar area and the whole of the dining room. Halfway through the meal three guys walked in, talked to Jack and were led to a table across the room from us against the wall. The three promptly placed themselves against the walls with a full view of the dining room. Cousin Father Don was the first to say something. "You can spot cops a mile away." Jennifer asked, "Why do you say that?" "Look at the way those three are sitting backs to the wall and their eyes looking all over the place. Now, turn around and look at the guys in the far corner behind you." In unison, the three of us said, "Don't turn around." She didn't but Grandma did. "Don, can't you tell the difference between gangsters and cops? Those guys are hoods."

She hit it right on the head. The trio were pretty bad guys. They were into everything from bookmaking to hijacking to mob hits. Jerry (Bank), Hugie (Apples) and Carmine (the Snake), quite a deadly trio. They weren't doing anything but sitting there chatting with each other over drinks. "Big" Jim changed the subject and the trio was forgotten. Yeah, right, forgotten my foot. Jimmy, Jackie and I were constantly watching them until another man entered the dining room and sat down with them. When he arrived, I relaxed and enjoyed the company and the meal. We were just having dessert when the trio, now a quartet, got up and left.

Jack O'Connor came over to the table and offered to buy us an after-dinner drink. We all accepted with Grandma being the first. The waiter delivered the drinks and I asked for the check. "The bill has already been paid, sir, including a generous tip. Thank you."

I motioned for O'Connor and he ambled over. "Jack, I want to pay. I really wish you hadn't done that." "I didn't. Jimmy Green paid. He said it was a present from your parents. I don't know what that means, but that's what he said. He paid when he left with Carmine and the boys. Tell me what he meant."

Jack pulled up a chair, motioned to the waiter to bring another round of drinks and listened as I told the story about Daddy and Jimmy Green's mother and my arresting him.

O'Connor knew about the arrest and he explained that he had a very diverse clientele. He had the commuters who stopped for a couple before catching the train to the burbs. You also had judges, defense lawyers, prosecutors, gangsters and cops. When you were in his place, it was like Switzerland, he said. It was neutral territory. Hey, who was I to argue? If it worked for him, that was all that mattered.

Nobody said anything about the Green story until Grandma finally spoke. "Your father was one of a kind. He'd give you the shirt off his back.

Uncle Jack started talking about him and how he influenced him to go into the priesthood. "He knew I had a vocation before I did. He said to me, 'Jack, just follow the Lord ad your heart and you'll be fine.' That's what he told me and that's what I did. He was quite a guy."

Then Donald talked about Daddy. Then Jackie, then Muriel because she knew him from Mountain View. Then Big Jim started telling his stories. Jack O'Connor sat with us and was enthralled by the stories and the fond remembrances. He also kept his waiter busy running drinks for our table.

On the cab ride home, Jennifer turned to me and touched my cheek. "Did you enjoy yourself? I know I did. All those stories about him and all of you growing up. I really feel like . . . I wish I could have met them."

The following day was Saturday. I got up early (none the worse for all the beer I had at the Club Car, I might add) and told Jennifer to hurry up and get ready because I wanted to take her somewhere. I made coffee and toast and we ate it on the run. "Where are we going?"

"You'll see."

I pulled through the arched gates of Calvary Cemetery and went directly to their grave sites. "Mom, Dad, this is my wife Jennifer. Jennifer, these are my parents." She smiled, bowed her head and made the sign of the cross. After a couple of minutes, she lifted up her head again, made the sign of the cross and looked at me with eyes brimming with tears. We walked back to the car in silence holding hands. Finally I said, "That was nice that you said a prayer form them." She looked at me, smiled and said, "I wasn't praying for them. I was praying to them."

"What a girl", I thought.

Harlem! What do I know about Harlem except that the colored people live there. I also know that it was a poor neighborhood, and where there's poverty, there's crime. I talked to my brother Jackie about the place and he gave me some advice. "Treat people the way you'd want your family treated." I put that one in the back of my head in the good advice locker.

Jackie, when he came on the job, was assigned to the Two-Five on foot patrol. It was a rough neighborhood but he made friends with the residents, very quickly. That's not to say he didn't see his share of action. But, unlike me, he rarely talked about it. If he hadn't been active and made quality arrests, then he wouldn't have been made a detective.

I pulled into a spot in front of the station house. With a few butterflies in my stomach, I crossed the wide street. The building itself was in the middle of the block on One-Thirty-Fifth between Eighth and Saint Nicholas Avenue. It was gray and stood tall in a sea of tenements, burned-out buildings and stores of every type.

It was nine in the morning when I got there and already you could feel the pulse of the neighborhood. Adult males and females lounging on stoops. Kids running all over. But what struck me was the way they looked at me. The all looked like I was . . . oh, I don't know. I was some part of an occupying army. The looks I was getting was not the looks the Negroes gave in the movies. You know what I mean. The son of Charlie Chan or the Uncle Remus Negro. Smiling all the time or dispensing wisdom to the youngsters. Their looks were, I felt, looks of hate.

I have to tell you about my limited experience with colored people. I was a freshman at St. Francis Prep, and we freshman were attending a welcome mass in the chapel. So it's time to receive Communion, and out of the corner of my eye I see this colored kid get out of the pew and get in line to receive. Now, to say I was surprised would be an understatement. I was shocked. I didn't think Negroes could be Catholic. You have to understand. I grew up in a predominately Italian neighborhood with a sprinkling of Irish. The only coloreds were Mr. and Mrs. Green who lived near the corner of Sixty-Ninth and Seventeenth Avenue.

They were "old" people who were retired. I use to carry Mrs. Green's packages for her from the Ralston's Grocery Store. She'd give me a nickel. One day I asked Mr. Green why he was so dark. I think I was about eight. Momma and Daddy were there. I guess they were embarrassed, but Mr. Green, not missing a beat, put his hand on my head, bent down to eye level with me, and with a big smile on his face said, "Boy, I didn't eat my vegetables when I was your age." And he laughed and laughed.

Daddy had another Negro friend, a Mr. Jim. I don't remember who he was, but he was at our house a lot when Daddy was alive. Mr. Jim, I remember, had a funny way of walking. I remember he had a big shiny car, and when we'd go to Mountain View for the summer. Mr. Keegan would take some of us up and Daddy would go with Mr. Jim, the luggage and one or two of us kids. The year Daddy died, I distinctly remember we were all lined up in the living room. Daddy would close his eyes and randomly pick two lucky passengers to go with Mr. Jim and him.

Now, Jimmy and Jackie were out of it because they were still in the service. Cele, Peggy, Kathleen, Patty Ann, Mary and I (Virginia Ellen was too young) were all lined up. Daddy turned his back to us, and then turned around and pointed (with eyes allegedly closed) right at me. Me and only Me! He announced that due to the large amount of baggage, there was only room for one extra person in the back seat. I was in heaven. Me, just me, and Daddy and Mr. Jim.

On the way up, I sat in the back wedged in between suitcases and pillowcases all filed with clothes. Mr. Jim and Daddy would talk, and every once in a while, laugh about something. Mr. Jim had a deep voice and I remember very bright eyes. They were dark brown in color.

On the way up, I leaned over into the front seat. "Mr. Jim?"

"What's up, son?" in his deep baritone that I could feel in my toes.

"Why do you walk so funny?" Daddy turned and glared at me and I shrank back into the pillowcases. Mr. Jim put his hand on my father's shoulder. "I got hurt during the war and lost my leg, so the government gave me a new one." I didn't say another word. I didn't understand what that meant, but that was all right. It didn't look like Daddy was mad at me. He just sat there shaking his head.

The car came to a stop and I woke up. We were in Mountain View. Not Hoffman Grove, but the town itself. We were right near the Erie Rail Road Station but in the parking lot of the Cozy Tavern. "Come on, let's get a cold one and I'll get some for tonight." Mr. Jim just said, "You go in and have one, Lester. I'll wait with the boy." "No way. We'll all go in. Reluctantly Mr. Jim got out of the car. Enthusiastically I jumped out. The Cozy Tavern. Wow!

Daddy went in first and I was right on his heels with Mr. Jim bringing up the rear. The inside was dark and had a . . . well, a kind of sweet smell to it. (Years later I found out it was the bar smell of sweat and stale beer.)

Daddy pointed to a table and motioned for me to be seated and he continued onto the bar. Off to the left of the bar was aside room with a shuffleboard table and a pool table. Mr. Jim was limping past my table when this big fat, dirty-looking man in bib overalls came toward the bar.

"Hey, who let the crippled nigger in here?" With his left hand, Daddy grabbed the fat guy around the throat and bent him backward over the bar. It all happened in one fast motion. In a voice as cold as the winter, Daddy said, "For your own safety, I suggest that you keep your mouth shut, pick up your change and leave while you're still alive." I could see him tightening his grip on the bib man's throat. Do you understand me?" All the man did was nod. And just like that, it was over with. The guy leaving and not ever looking back.

The bartender came to Daddy. "Thanks, Mr. Stark. That clown is . . . well, I don't have to tell you what he is. What can I get you two and the boy?" About an hour later, we left for Hoffman Grove. Daddy and Mr. Jim were smiling and laughing. The patrons in the bar kept buying them drinks and shaking both their hands. Everybody was happy, at least until we get to the bungalow and saw Momma.

Mr. Jim pulled the car off the road and into the side yard. Momma was on the back porch with her arms akimbo. "Traffic?" was all she said and Daddy just smiled. About a half hour later, he had her laughing.

After dinner, Momma, Daddy, Mr. Jim, Gramma and Pop Walsh headed up to Arnie's for a night of "social activity," as Daddy called it. I was well asleep when they came home. I was on one couch/bed on one wall in the front room and Mr. Jim was on the other. I woke in the morning when I heard him start the car. I ran out and gave him a big hug and thanked him for the ride. Momma gave him a kiss on the cheek, and Daddy pumped his hand and patted him on the back. And then he was gone.

Daddy called to me and we sat on a bench under the big tree on the side of the bungalow. "Dan, there are a few things I think I need to explain to you. First of all, I'm sorry you saw me lose my temper. What that man called Mr. Jim is a terrible insult. I want you to promise me you'll never call anyone that word." I promised. "Secondly, you should know what happened to his leg. During the war he was in Europe driving a truck. His unit would bring supplies right up to the front lines. One night he was the first truck in a convoy. Do you know what a convoy is?" I shook my head yes. "Good. Anyway, his truck rolled over a land mine and the Nazis opened up on them with machine guns and rifles. Mr. Jim was thrown out of the truck into a big snow bank. He got a crate of hand grenades out of the second truck and began to blow up the other trucks in the convoy so the enemy wouldn't get the supplies and use them against the Americans. Of course he made sure that none of his men were in the trucks.

"While he was running from truck to truck, he was shot in the back and then in the leg. He and five other truckers were captured. They didn't give him immediate medical help. The leg got infected and some Nazi doctor cut it off. From what I was told, by a couple of the men that were prisoners with him, they gave him very little anesthetics and that he was awake when they were cutting off the leg. They told me he never begged for any painkillers. He didn't want to give the Nazis the idea that an American soldier would accept anything from the enemy. He is one brave man." Daddy said this in a tone that showed he was in awe of his friend, Jim.

"So, now you see why I got angry at the loud mouth bully and did what I did? There are still jerks around that think that white people are superior to the Negro people. Don't you believe it, son. No, son, don't you believe it for a second."

As I headed up the stairs, I heard a young man say to his pal, "Just what Harlem needs, another white-ass Nigger thumper." I turned and looked right at him, but he was already walking away. I kind of wondered why he'd say that when he didn't know anything about me or how I felt about the coloreds. Talk about being prejudice. That guy was as prejudiced against whites, the same as the Klan was against coloreds. St. Michael was gonna have to work overtime.

In the months to come, I saw, firsthand, racism but it was usually the coloreds toward the whites. Oh, yeah, I saw and heard white cops call people "nigger" but they (the white cops) were just plain assholes. The colored cops used Nigger as a greeting: "Hi, Nigger, whasup?" Or, in a command: "Up against the wall, Nigger!" Or, as a wish for the future: "Man, I wish I could nail that nigger's black ass to the wall with a good felony collar." The word was adaptable to any situation. A black girl walking by could evoke a "man, look at that fine-looking Nigger!" I personally found the word abhorrent. I never used it. Every time I heard it, I remembered the Bar Bully from Mountain View and the look in Mr. Jim's eyes.

I climbed the stairs to the plainclothes office. It was your typical PD-type office. Neutral desks, mismatched chairs, a bench along the far wall and offices inside of offices. Guys were coming and going. Constant chatter. Typewriters cracking. Prisoners in the cage swearing, singing or just talking. Telephones were ringing on almost every desk. This was one busy shop. There was electricity in the air.

For me it was a kind of homecoming of sorts. Manny Bogen stuck his head out of one of the offices in an office. "Dan, over here." I walked toward him and he motioned me inside. Seated behind a desk was Inspector Ray McDermott. Seated on a couch was Lieutenant Vic Rohe from the academy. Excuse me again, now Captain Vic Rohe. There were handshakes all around as well as the obligatory smacks on the back. Rohe told a few of my transgressions from my police academy days. McDermott recounted the tale of the peddler summons I gave to Sidney Cooper's buddy.

The days and weeks turned into months and I settled into the routine of Harlem. They didn't assign steady partners because somebody felt that friendships could lead to corruption. I still don't see the logic but that was the way it was.

I really never had any exposure, socially that is, to black guys. As a side note, back then they were referred to as colored or Negro. So it was very interesting to learn that these guys had the same needs, wants and aspirations as the white guys. A lot of them were single, all of us were relatively young. Of course, I was the youngest. But we all worked as a team. One day with

Johnson, the next with Handwick or Washington. It was fun. Even though they had different personalities, the conversations and the work ethics were the same as mine. We talked about family, sports, politics, and the job.

I was still making narcotics collars along with the gambling and the street prostitutes. We'd raid after-hours joints or illegal "juice joints" on the weekends. Juice joints were apartments where you could buy wine and liquor mostly on Sundays when the sale was prohibited.

Once in awhile things could get a little hairy. There was the time when I was with Henry Crabbe. If you didn't know him, you'd think that he was just what his name implied, a crab. In reality, Henry was well-educated, a family man and he had a terrific sense of humor. He had no patience for, as he put it, "these lowlife welfare animals." He would go nuts when we'd stop a large, young, Negro kid, and Henry would ask, "How come you're not working?" And the large, young Negro kid would reply, "I gots me the asthma. I gets the check from Social Security." Henry would go crazy. You could see the veins popping. The guy would probably have felt better if Henry had punched him.

So one sunny day we were just wandering through the streets in Henry's old Chevrolet station wagon. We parked right near a school when he saw a guy he knew that dealt drugs. "Drugs are going to kill my race" was one of his expressions. I slouched down in the seat and was watching the action through my binoculars. A big kid, very tall, approached the dealer and we saw the transaction.

Henry jumped out of the car and I followed. The dealer was the first to spot us and he took off down the block with me on his tail. Henry took off after the kid. I chased the other guy down the stairs into an alleyway leading to the courtyard of a five-story tenement.

I caught up to him and we fought. He got in a few good shots to my head and I gave back to him what he gave to me. I felt he was winning, so I took out my black Jack and hit him right in the throat. This ended the confrontation. I cuffed him and recovered a bag with two hundred neatly sealed glassine envelopes containing heroin.

Now, you have to remember, this was before cell phones and portable radios. Plus, I really didn't know the address where we were. I guess getting punched in the head will do that to you. I started toward the alleyway to go back up to the street when the courtyard started filling up with young colored folks. The alleyway was blocked by another sea of black angry faces.

"Let the brother go," started to ring in my ears. "Let the brother go." I took out my gun, backed up to the wall with my prisoner. I wrapped my left arm around his neck and put my revolver against his head. "I am a police officer and he's under arrest. What's the matter with you people? This guy is selling H (cop talk for heroin) to your kids. Don't make me shoot."

"Let the brother go."

At a fifth floor window I saw movement of the blinds. I kept my eyes on the dealer while trying to figure out what a nice Irish-Catholic boy from Brooklyn was going in this alley in Harlem when I heard the sweet sounds of wailing sirens. Right on, St. Michael! Before I knew it, the courtyard was clear except for a bunch of guys in blue suits. God, I love this job.

Henry and I met back at the office where I was processing the dealer and Henry was lecturing to the grandmother of the big kid. And he was only a kid. It turns out he was fourteen. He had never used any drugs but was goaded into buying them for his friends. It turned out that he wasn't a bad kid, just a kid in a man's body. Maybe there was hope for him. Who knows? But he was cut loose and sent home with Grandma. The next day, I stopped at a liquor store and bought a bottle of Scotch and a bottle of Rye. The owner was in his wheelchair and he greeted me with a big smile. Actually, I never saw him frown. "Hey, Dan, I hear you had a scare yesterday."

"It was kind of hairy, I have to admit that."

"Well, for what it's worth, coming from me, I appreciate it when you guys take these guys off the streets. Drugs are killing our neighborhood."

"Thank you, Mr. Campanella."

"Dan, when are you gonna stop with the Mr. and just call me Roy?"

"Probably never, Mr. Campanella," and we both laughed. Oh yeah, the store owner was Roy Campanella, a great athlete, a Brooklyn Dodger and a great man. Tragically, he was paralyzed from an auto accident and was relegated to the wheelchair.

After a little more talk, I went back to the block where I had made the arrest. Making sure I wasn't seen, I entered a tenement two buildings away from the arrest scene. I went to the roof and climbed over to the building that looked into the courtyard. I went from the roof to the fifth floor and knocked on the apartment door. "What you want?"

"I want to thank you for yesterday. I have something for you."

"Go away. I don't know what you talking 'bout."

"Well, thanks just the same." I placed the bag with the bottles in front of the door. I rustled the bag so it made noise and I gently clinked the bottles on the tile floor. As I walked away, I heard latches and locks being opened. I heard the door creak open. I saw a black hand and arm reach out and pick up the bag, and as the door was closing, I heard a voice say, "You welcome. Be careful, son. Thanks for what you be doin'."

Remember when I was in the Third Division and Bernie Rice and I had the run-in with the "Reverend" Nelson C. Buckes? Well, he came up again. About six months after the stand-off in the courtyard and the release of the kid that Crabbe caught, there was a police-involved shooting. It went like this: An off-duty white cop was walking down the street with a radio under his arm. (Yeah, I said a radio, okay?) He was bringing it to a repair shop. (Yes, people did bring radios to a repair shops to be fixed. We really didn't throw them away and just buy a replacement. We had them fixed.) But I digress.

The off-duty cop was about a block away from his apartment when he was surrounded by a group of about ten young Negro boys. The biggest one in the group produced a knife and demanded the radio. The cop identified himself as a police lieutenant and tried to push his way through the crowd. They blocked his path so he tried to go around them to no avail.

The big kid with the knife lashed out at the lieutenant and cut through his jacket into his forearm. The lieutenant drew his revolver and backed away. The mob hemmed him in and he had his back against the window of a laundromat. With nowhere to go, he again identified himself as a cop. Again to no avail. The kid with the knife came at him with the knife raised above his head. The Lieutenant fired one shot. The kid fell and the mob dispersed.

Somebody called the cops. The Lieutenant holstered his weapon and putting the radio on the ground, he went to aid the kid. As he knelt down, next to the supine figure, a black hand reached over his shoulder, pushing the lieutenant forward. The black hand snatched up the knife before the cop could react.

The radio cars screeched to a halt and the ambulance was close behind. The first cops on the scene sent out a call for the sergeant and the detectives. The uniformed cops covered the body with a sheet and cordoned off the immediate area. The medics took the lieutenant to the ambulance where they discovered that his forearm was cut open. At the hospital, it took twelve stitches to close the wound. Witnesses were canvassed, both Negro and white, with few exceptions, told in detail what they saw and how the lieutenant tried to avoid the confrontation. The fact that the knife was gone was compounded by the fact that the radio was also taken.

As the reports started to be broadcast over the radio and television stations, half fact and half fiction came out of the news people's mouths. As a for instance, reports on TV showed a picture of the dead kid, which was taken when he was about ten years old. A sweet, innocent face with a gap-toothed smile and big brown eyes. In reality, the kid was six foot three inches and a hundred and eighty-five pounds. He was the same kid that Henry Crabbe had released to his grandmother six months ago. So much for giving a second chance.

I was off that day sitting home when I saw a special bulletin on the TV:

"After a police shooting, of an unnamed youth in Harlem, there are reports of scattered, sporadic looting and demonstrations taking place. A march is being led by Bishop Nelson C. Buckes, a community activist. He is going to stage a protest in front of the Twenty-Fifth Precinct Station House to demand the arrest of the officer who murdered the Harlem child. We will keep you informed as developments happen. We'll have full coverage at the eleven o'clock newscast."

I almost threw a shoe at the TV. These news people, obviously, never heard of the "facts before acts" school of journalism. They didn't have the facts, but they acted before they had them. Reports, such as these, would only inflame those in Harlem that already hated the cops and give an excuse for others to go on a shopping spree. Translated, that means breaking into liquor stores or TV appliance stores or just cause as much vandalism as possible. It was like a holiday for them. Happy Smash and Grab Day!

I called the station house and asked for Captain Rohe or Inspector McDermott. The TS operator (cop speak for the guy answering the phones. TS means telephone switchboard in case you forgot.)

After about twenty rings to the plainclothes office, I got put through to McDermott. "Boss, it's Dan Stark. How's it going up there? Do you need me to come in?"

"No, we got it covered. There's some looting going on and a few assholes trying to make this a racial thing, but stay by your phone in case we have to suit up. At this point, the geniuses downtown don't want any cops in civilian clothes on the street. If things change and we have to put on the 'bag' [cop speak for uniform], you'll be notified."

"Listen, boss, why I called, is to tell you about this so-called bishop leading the group to the Two-Five. "What do you know about him?" McDermott asked, his voice sounding really interested. So I told him the story about the confrontation Bernie Rice and I had. I also told him that the guy, the bishop, probably had warrants because of the summonses we issued. Neither Bernie, nor I, ever went to court and the chances of him—sorry, I mean the bishop—having paid the fines were slim to none.

"Dan, this is good. Let me do some checking and I'll get back to you. If you and Jennifer go out tonight, call the office once in awhile to see if we got mobilized."

"Will do, boss."

About two in the afternoon, I heard someone at the front door of the apartment. I got up to see and in walked Jennifer. "What are you doing here?"

"I live here," she said. "Oh," was my only response. "My boss let me out early because there were reports that there was going to be a mob coming down to the Wall Street area, because of the shooting. You heard about the shooting, didn't you?" I told her it was on the TV and that they might be calling people in if riots broke out. She grunted.

Well, I don't know what happened, but the Tactical Patrol Force, (TPF) was mobilized and they augmented the precinct uniform cops. The TPF was a mobile unit that flooded high-crime areas to put a lid on street gangs and other miscreants. They lived out of the trunks of their cars. They'd fly into a precinct, kick ass, put the fear of the law into the bad guys and then go on to another hot spot.

It wasn't that the precinct cops couldn't control the streets, but they had to do their regular jobs. They couldn't dedicate their entire tour to one or two, hard-core tough guy blocks. TPF came in and just rousted everyone on the target blocks. The guys in the unit were mostly hand-picked for their size, ability, and willingness to kick ass. The majority of them were well over six foot tall. When they got off their bus and onto the target block, it looked like . . . like . . . I don't know, but it was impressive. Those guys scared me!

So it seems that the reverend or the bishop, or whatever the hell he was, did have warrants for his arrest for failure to appear to adjudicate the summonses he had received from Bernie and me.

Inspector McDermott "invited" Bishop Buckes and a couple of other "community organizers" into the Two-Five to discuss the situation and help bring the looting and unrest to an end. Peacefully, of course.

Now, you have to remember, I wasn't there, but I heard that McDermott confronted the bishop and told him, in no uncertain terms (interspersed with street language), that if the good bishop didn't get his flock of followers off the streets, he, the bishop, was going to get the shit kicked out of him and then be arrested for the traffic warrants.

The bishop, flanked by two colored police captains, stood on the steps of the Two-Eight and, in his best preacher voice, extolled the police and the fine job they were doing. He pleaded with the crowd to disperse peacefully and "Trust in the Lord God Jehovah to ensure that justice with triumph". Well, I guess the "Lord God Jehovah" and his friggin' flock didn't listen to the good bishop. His little march started six days of rioting. Harlem became a war zone. Bottles and bricks rained down from every rooftop onto and at the cops below. St. Michael, protect us.

Everybody was mobilized and put in uniform. They issued us helmets to replace our regular hats. There was only one problem with the helmets. They were white. Now, imagine you're a brick thrower on the roof and you see a white helmet standing in front of a liquor store or clothing or appliance store. "Bombs away . . . let'er rip . . . kill the pigs." The helmets were the old civil defense World War I type that you see Jimmy Cagney and Pat O' Brien wearing in The Fighting 69th movie.

Everyone was working twelve on and twelve off shifts. TPF sent their entire unit into the war zone. The precincts brought cots in so the guys that lived out of the city could get some rest.

Fires were started, and when the rubber men arrived, they were pelted with bricks and bottles as they tried to save a building. They, I mean the miscreant assholes who were fomenting the racial hatred and violence, started a new chant, "Burn, baby, burn." How stupid were these people?

They were burning buildings, cars, and businesses of the hard-working Negro people who lived and worked in Harlem. These were decent, industrious people. People with families. They didn't want or need this "urban war" played out in their neighborhood. They were being victimized by a small minority of agitators who had their own agendas. "Burn, baby, burn" my ass.

To add insult to injury, *LIFE Magazine* did a story about the bishop. At the end, you'd think he was up for sainthood. In reality, he was just a BS artist who had a good speaking voice. He was nothing but a punk, a two-bit con man. He took from his people and laughed all the way to the bank. Yet, the flock loved him. Go figure!

As quickly as it began, it ended and things got back to normal, at least as normal as life in Harlem could be.

One Saturday morning, Jennifer said, "Let's go for a walk in the park and people watch." I don't know about you, but we love to people watch. Anyway, I got us two coffees and buttered rolls from the deli on Fourteenth Street and Avenue C. We went into the park behind our building and got us a bench near the playground. I started babbling about some funny thing that somebody at work had done or said. She listened and laughed.

"You really love your job and that's good." It was early, about ten, but there were kids and parents at the monkey bars and the see-saws. The sun was warm on our backs, and I was enjoying relaxing and just people watching. Without a preamble, she leaned over and whispered, "I'm pregnant. You'll have three things you can love."

I guess I let out a whoop, because people stopped pushing the swings and looked over at us. I gave her a big kiss and then another. Now they were staring at us. I didn't care. I was as happy as could be. She had a grin from ear to ear. We both sat on the bench hugging each other.

I should have realized that something was up because she just seemed to be in a better mood lately. I mean, she was usually in a good mood, but she was, I don't know, she was different. She was on the phone, a lot more often, with her sister and mother. I'd walk into the room and she'd start to whisper. She told me that she didn't want me to get any hopes up. She wanted to wait until she (the doctor) confirmed that she was really pregnant. Man, was I happy.

The riots were now a bad memory and the political finger-pointing game was afoot. The politicians were blaming (who else) the cops. The papers were blaming (who else) the cops. TV and radio also jumped on us. It wasn't an easy time to be a white cop in a colored neighborhood.

The majority of the hard-working, family-rearing residents would silently show their support by giving a little wink, a smile, or a simple nod of the head. The mutts would walk past the uniformed cops and deliberately try to provoke him. They'd walk past with another mutt and one would shove the other into the passing cop. This tactic was wearing thin, but the brass warned the cops that "if you start something that escalates, you're in deep trouble. Walk away. Don't do anything. We don't need another riot. You're just there for window dressing."

Enough was enough. The cops solved the problem, much to the chagrin of the brass. It was a simple solution. The footman would get the names and IDs of the troublemakers, pass them along to his PBA delegate. The delegate would contact another delegate, usually from another borough.

The wheels were in motion. One dark night the troublemaker would be walking. No, more like strutting, and suddenly, out of nowhere, he was surrounded by eight or nine Negro and white guys in old clothes. He, and anybody with him, were dragged into an alleyway and had the shit punched out of them.

While conscious, they were told that if they continued to harass the cops, they'd be lucky if they wound up in the hospital. The implied threat of death just hung there. When the message was delivered, the cops would go to where they'd left their station wagons and return to the Bronx or Brooklyn.

You don't believe me? Believe me! 'Cause it happened. It happened in reverse also. When the Bronx or Brooklyn guys had a situation, the Harlem guys would pay back the favor. Believe me, I know.

I had about six months left before the four-year stint in clothes was supposed to be over. Then I'd get the Gold Shield. I'd be in an exclusive club with the likes of Uncle Mike, my brother Jackie, Frank Healy, Wally Gannon, and a whole bunch of great cops and good men. I was pumped.

I was pumped more about the thought of being a father. I'd be in another club. One with the likes of Daddy, Uncles Bill, Mike, Richie, Tom, Steve, and my brothers Jimmy and Jackie, just to name a few. I didn't realize that when the baby came, life would change a lot. It would change for the better, if that was possible, 'cause things were going great now.

Our unit continued to make the requisite number of policy (numbers) and bookmaking (horse betting) arrests, and I continued to make narco collars. Everyone knew that drugs were ruining neighborhoods one block at a time. But because it hadn't hit the white, middle/upper class neighborhoods, the department heads didn't think it was a problem. "What the hell. It's only in the colored areas. Let them be."

To me, that kind of thinking was just plain wrong. These people deserved to be able to walk the streets without fearing some junkie was going to knock them, or their grandmother or aunt, down and rob their pocketbook for a few lousy dollars. So I just grabbed the junkies anytime I could. So did a lot of the rest of the unit. Plus, we'd, sometimes, get valuable info from the junkie about their suppliers or apartments or other locations where "sheet writers" (cop speak for numbers taken at a fixed location) were "taking action" (more cop speak for accepting bets.)

The fall and winter passed oh so slowly for Jennifer. She was getting larger and, if possible, more beautiful. She literally glowed. We spent most of my days off over in North Arlington where her mother and sister Eileen doted on her. It was a warm and cheery time. We had taken my brother Jackie's advice and were banking most of her salary. That isn't to say we didn't splurge on a Broadway show or a dinner at Pete's Tavern once in a while. But the lion's share of her pay went into the bank.

We had decided that, because her doctor was in Kearney, she'd go to the West Hudson Hospital also in Kearney. She was going to work until two weeks before her due date, which was July 4. Hot dog! We were gonna have a real Yankee Doodle Dandy baby. I told her that, if she wanted and her mother agreed, we'd stay in North Arlington until after the baby was born. She said okay.

I was paired to work a week with Joel Washington. Joel was dark skinned and had the kind of face that fit in anywhere. He had a great sense of humor and he loved to talk about his family. He'd been on the job for about eleven years and had seen his fair share of street action.

Coming out of the station house we saw, or, more correctly, one of the drug addicts I had arrested about a year ago saw us. He made a beeline toward us. You could see he was looking for a handout. Ever since I arrested him and he did his ten days, for possession of heroin, he kind of latched onto me. "Ya know, Stark, you did me right. You didn't push me around. Ah don't forget kindness. By the way, could you let me hold five bucks? I'll get it back to you."

This guy usually knew when I had money so I'd give him two or three dollars. I never gave him what he asked for. He was a kinda poor soul type. He would always swear that he wasn't going to use the money for drugs. Yeah, right!

This particular day he says to me, "How you like to hit a location that does a ton of business every day? It's West Indian Dave's main spot."

"That would be nice." Joel nodded his head in agreement.

He gave us an address about a block and a half from the station house.

Joel and I watched the location for about two hours. It was a four-story tenement walk-up building. The informant told us it was the rear apartment on the second floor.

Finally, we left the area and drove to a few locations that Joel had open kites on. We sat, made observations, and logged them into our memo books.

About three, we went back to the address and observed the similar activity from the morning. Men and women entering the building, and after a brief period, come out and leave the area. At one point there was a backup out onto the front stoop. Man, this guy was doing some business. The yard behind the building had two burned-out cars in it and the building behind was a burned-out shell. All I could think of was the mantra, "Burn, baby, burn." I kinda "junkie" walked into the backyard for a look. One of the burned-out cars was right near the fire escape. The ladder was about eight feet from the ground just hanging. So I hopped onto the roof of the derelict car and grabbed the bottom rung of the fire escape ladder, pulling myself up. I got to the second floor and looked in the window the informant told us about. Sure enough, there was a guy sitting at a desk and a young Negro man, about twenty or twenty-one, standing near the door. The doorman was built like a weightlifter. I mean, he had muscles on his muscles.

I watched for about fifteen minutes as the young guy would look through the peephole and let a customer in to place a bet. The last one in was Joel Washington. He nodded to muscleman and gave the guy at the desk twenty dollars. He turned and left the apartment. I climbed down onto the roof of the car and met up with Joel a few blocks away.

We called the office to tell at least one of the bosses what we had and what we observed. Joel had written down the serial number of the bill he had given to the sheet writer, plus he wrote 6D on a corner of the bill. Get it? Six D for the Sixth Division. That was the area designation.

There wasn't one boss available so I asked the switchboard operator to give me anyone in the Division office. After about twelve rings, Zack Pickett finally answered. He sounded like he had a mouthful of food and he did. "Whatta ya want? I'm having a sandwich."

Zack was a nice guy, kinda average and not too quick on the uptake, if you know what I mean. He had two speeds, slow and reverse. Born in Georgia, he somehow wound up in New York and eventually on the police force.

"Zack, this is Dan and Joel. We're looking for a boss. Is anyone around?"

"Nah, they all got called to something at some place."

"Zack, take a message for me to Lieutenant Ingulli, please."

"I told you I'm having a sandwich." With that, he hung up the phone.

Joel and I decided that we would go back to the location. The plan was that he'd go in, bet again, and when they opened the door to let him out, I'd go in and we'd make the collar. I brought along my ten-pound sledge hammer just in case they made Joel as a cop. If he was inside and I was outside, how would I get in? Simple. I'd use the sledge hammer as a door key.

I went to the far corner of the block and entered the corner building. I went up to the roof and crossed over all the roofs to our target building. From the roof I made my way down to the second floor where Joel was waiting. He knocked. He entered. He played again. I heard the locks being opened, and as soon as I saw the door cracked, I put my shoulder into it and it swung back whacking the muscleman in the head.

Joel had his shield out, as did I. The sheet writer had a bundle of slips in his hand and was trying to open the window, I guess, to throw the evidence out. Joel grabbed him and that ended that idea.

Mr. Muscles was coming right at me and I wasn't too happy about that. But, then again, neither was he. You see, he had a four-inch split in his forehead. I guess it happened when I hit the door and the door clocked him in his massive head.

I wouldn't say he was growling, nor would I say he was yelling. It was more like the sound you might hear Big Foot make. He was coming straight at me with his arms outstretched like Frankenstein. I reacted calmly and with extreme professionalism. I hit him right in the nuts with the business end of my sledge hammer. While he was rolling around (and I believe feigning pain), I managed to cuff him.

We walked the two of them the block and a half to the station house. I stopped at the desk to tell the lieutenant what we had and that we were going to take them up to the office for processing. Mr. Muscles was muttering and I think he was trying to put some voodoo curse on me. It sounded like he was talking in tongues. Not nice tongues either. Kind of like curse tongue.

We put them in the cage and left the handcuffs on them. It was tough enough getting them on Sasquatch the first time. I didn't want to go through that again. The paperwork was finished and they had to be fingerprinted. The sheet writer was very cooperative, but Mr. Muscles was . . . well, let's say . . . pissed off.

Joel went downstairs to the desk and recruited six of the biggest cops in the precinct to help. The print area was small and with all the monsters in the area, it was near claustrophobic. But Mr. Muscles got the idea and he behaved. Thank you, St. Michael, and a bunch of very large cops.

At night court we wrote up two separate affidavits. In my guy's, I charged him with the possession of gambling records, acting in concert with another to accept illegal bets and resisting arrest. I told the ADA that necessary force was used to effect the arrest. No, I didn't say I hit him in the nuts with a ten-pound sledge hammer. Why? Cause he didn't ask.

I left court and headed to North Arlington for my two days off. When I got there, Mrs. McDermott said I had gotten a phone call and I was to call work as soon as I got the message. I had given the North Arlington number to Captain Rohe, Inspector McDermott, and Lieutenant Ingulli. This could not be good.

I was right, it wasn't. I got the lieutenant on the phone. "Lieu, it's Dan. What's up?" What was up was that on Monday at 8:00 a.m., Joel and I were to be at the PCCIU office in the Fifth Precinct in Chinatown. Bring our memo books. No further info was given to the division. Inguilli told me to be at the Sixth Division office at 6:00 a.m. Rohe, McDermott, and the newly arrived chief, Wolfgang O'Leary, would be waiting to talk to us. The call ended with Lieutenant Inguilli saying, "Have a nice weekend, Dan." Yeah, right!

Monday couldn't come fast enough for me. I had a nice weekend and, as usual, the hours were filled with jokes and food and good times. But Monday was on my mind. Jennifer knew I was distracted and asked me if there was a problem. "No, everything is going great." I lied.

I got to the office about a quarter to six and it was hot already. I climbed the stairs and ran into Manny Bogen. He'd worked at night and was process-ing two prostitutes he'd arrested. Joel was already there, as were the bosses. After pleasantries, Inspector McDermott told us to tell about the arrest of the sheet writer and bodyguard. When we finished, they grunted. I thought I saw them grin when I told them how I was able to cuff Big Foot. I gave all the details.

Chief Wolfgang O'Leary cleared his throat and said, "I called a friend downtown and the suits have been asked to look into the collar. Now, how many total bets did you recover?" Joel told him it was 1,237 bets and exactly $3,428 in cash including the two bills with the 6D on them.

O'Leary said that we weren't being accused of taking money and his people downtown didn't know why PCCIU was looking into the arrest. He assured us he'd find out.

He was a tank of a man. Square build, crew cut and a face that said, "Don't mess with me unless you want your ass kicked." With a name like his, I guess you had to be tough.

"Here's what's going to happen today. You'll go down there, sign in, sit on the bench in the hallway, nobody will acknowledge you. About noon someone will open a door and tell you to go to meal (cop speak for lunch) and be back in an hour. You'll sit there until four and somebody will tell you to sign out and return tomorrow. Tomorrow, in the morning, there will be more of the same. After meal, you, Dan, will go into one room, and Joel, you'll go in another. At four, you'll be released and told to come back on Wednesday.

"Wednesday, you'll both go to your separate rooms. The door will be opened periodically and a head will look in and you'll hear, 'Yeah, that's him.' This will go on all day.

"Thursday, the same with the exception that some suit will come in, offer you a soda or coffee and say, "You know, Joel, Stark hates colored people. He's saying it's all your fault.

"Dan, some other guy is gonna do the same to you and tell you that Joel really hates white guys and that it's all your fault. Don't fall for it, it's all bullshit. I know this 'cause I worked for three years in the unit.

"All I'm telling you guys is to tell the truth and bring a good book cause it's boring. Finally, on Friday, they'll start with the threats and the good guy/ bad guy team. They may or may not bring you back a second week. That depends on what they think you've done. I should know soon why you were called down there. I'm assuming it's about your latest arrest."

We were just getting ready to go downtown and the phone rang. Captain Rohe answered and handed it to Chief Wolfgang O'Leary (God, I love that name). He mumbled and grunted his thanks. "Gentlemen, it appears that Big Foot is related to one of our esteemed Harlem politicians who thinks his nephew was flaked" (cop speak for having evidence planted on him). In other words, he was being framed. "So in order to placate him, the PCCIU is going to investigate. Joel, how many plays was that?"

"One thousand two hundred thirty-seven sir." Chief Wolfgang O'Leary's face reddened. "This is total bullshit. You guys are the ones being framed." On that happy note, we traveled downtown.

Books, newspapers and coffee in hand, we climbed the age-worn and slightly slanted stairs to the top floor of one of the oldest police facilities in good old New York. Some guy in a suit pointed to a large police blotter. "Sign in." We did. He took the blotter and went down the narrow hall and disappeared through a door that creaked open and creaked again when it closed. We sat there, read the papers cover to cover. Then we started on the books.

Noon came (time flies when you're having fun) and just as Chief O'Leary had said, some guy said, "Be back in an hour." We were. We continued reading and at four we were dismissed and told to return on Tuesday at 8:00 a.m.

The script was followed exactly as we were told. After meal, we were sent to separate rooms. At four, we were told to come back on Wednesday.

On Wednesday, Joel and I decided to place our chairs with our backs to the doors of our separate accommodations. So when the door was opened, whoever was supposed to be identifying us saw only our backs and the back of our heads. Yeah, that's him, my ass. I know, I know, it was childish but it made us chuckle.

Thursday, same, same. Again, as O'Leary had said, some Bozo came in all friendly. "Hi, pal, ya want a coffee, soda or somethin'?" I guess he was trying to sound illiterate and the college ring on his finger was as a result of some social promotion program. "Naw, youse guys have been great. Tanks." I then went back to reading. Oh yeah, I was reading *The Complete Works of Joyce Kilmer.*

Jennifer was becoming increasingly suspicious of my going out in a suit and tie. Finally, one night when we were in Grandpa's room she asked, "Is everything all right at work?"

"I arrested some politician's nephew and they [I didn't say who they were] want to make sure we have all the bases touched. So, for a week or so, Joel and I have been assigned to a special unit." (How was that for some fancy footwork?) "All right. Now I feel better. Maybe when I'm not so tired you can tell me about it." Before I could say anything, she was asleep.

There was just a sliver of moonlight coming through the window and it was resting on her face. I propped myself up on my elbow and just stared at her. "Man, am I a lucky guy," I said out loud. All thoughts of the PCCIU, Harlem, the poverty, the drugs, the politics, the overall meanness of people to people, was completely washed away. I bypassed St. Michael and went right to his boss. "Thanks, Jesus. Thanks for all you've given me. No matter what happens with the job, as long as you let me have her, I'll be fine. Amen." Then I fell asleep.

Friday came and I met Joel in front of the precinct. I gave him a big hello and a pat on the back. "Hey, take it easy. Don't you know I was told you hate my kind?" We both had a good laugh as we went up to our eight-hour cells.

About ten, the door to my cell (sorry, I mean room) opened and in walked a man I can only describe as Mr. Wrinkles. From his face to his suit, he was Mr. Wrinkles.

"Don't get up", he said.

"I had no intention of getting up," I said.

"Don't you know who I am?" he said. "No," I said. Out of caution I didn't say, "Nor do I care."

"I'm Deputy Inspector Jules Sussman." "May I see some ID, please?"

"What? What did you just say?" I know, I know, I shouldn't have said that. But what the heck. I was sitting there all week 'cause some politician's relative got arrested for a crime he was committing and made a sucker's holler cause he got caught. I was pissed.

"I said, 'May I see some ID, please'?"

"Oh, you haven't changed one bit. You were a punk-ass wise guy when you were in Coney Island. Now you're still a punk." He was saying all this as he produced his shield. I won!

"Thank you. Now, what can I do for you, Deputy Inspector?" In the job, a deputy inspector or deputy chief or a deputy commissioner are never referred to as deputy inspector, deputy chief, or deputy commissioner. It's always inspector, chief, or commissioner. The slight to protocol was not wasted. He started turning red. "You don't remember me."

"Is that a statement or a question, sir?" I threw the "sir" in, just for the hell of it. He turned a little more red.

"Damn you! If you want to be a smart ass, go ahead." I almost said. I said I almost said, "thank you." but I didn't. "But you're just living up to the stereotype of the Irish."(What the hell did that mean?) "You bastards think you run this job, but you'll see, the days of the Irish are over. My people run it now. You'll see."

I don't know what I was supposed to see, but right then and there, I didn't see. He continued, and now his veins in his neck were starting to pulsate, "You came up to me and asked me if I had a light. You arrogant son-of-a-bitch. Me. I was a lieutenant then and I swore I'd get you. I know you were living in Jersey. You got away from me that time but not now. Now I got ya!" I was going to correct him and say, "No, you're wrong. It's now I go you, not ya," but I let that slide.

The more he spoke, the angrier he got. He looked like what I pictured Captain Quigg to look like. You know, the guy in Herman Wouk's book *The Caine Mutiny Court Marshal*. Veins popping, eyes bulging, spittle airborne. It was beautiful to watch. You just had to be agile to avoid the spittle. The best was the white froth at the corner of his mouth. It was beautiful.

His harangue/soliloquy continued with his anti-Irish speak. "You drunken, Irish mutts, you think you run the job? No, no, no. We do. Ya got that?" I didn't know if I was supposed to answer, so I didn't. "With your bagpipes and your dresses, you lead every parade. You drunken mutts. Think you run this job?" This was getting kind of redundant so I said, "Deputy Inspector, sir, what the hell are you talking about? I'm an American of Irish decent. I'm not Irish nor am I drunk. What the hell are you talking about?"

It was surreal. It was as if I hadn't spoken at all or if I wasn't even there. He just continued babbling about the Irish in the job and how they were finished, how "his people" were finally in charge. Then it hit me what he was talking about. He was talking about Jewish people. It took me awhile but I figured it out when he screamed, "It's our time. The time of the Jew. You disrespected Chief Cooper when you gave his uncle that ticket, when you . . . and that band of thieves that McDermott ran, were almost arrested."

By this time I was biting my tongue to keep from laughing. I really didn't give a rat's ass about his anti-Irish crap. We were raised to be Americans first and Irish second. Sure it was great growing up listening to Irish music, and as a cop, marching in uniform on Saint Patrick's Day. But my favorite holiday was the Fourth of July.

So the little peddler six years ago was Sydney Cooper's uncle. What a bunch of phonies. The do-as-I-say mentality was applied to the workers, not the PCCIU. I wondered how many other "uncles" were running around that Cooper and his minions had given passes too.

Sussman was continuing his bluster and I was barely hearing him. I kind of have this ability to tune people out when I'm really disinterested in what they have to say.

That ability had kicked in and I was thinking about Jennifer and the baby. Through the fog of my disinterested state, I heard more anti-Irish, drunken fools . . . drunken cops . . . disgrace to the uniform . . . bits and pieces.

Then I heard Jesus' name mentioned. Now his face was purple and I started to focus on what he was saying. "It's now our turn, the Jews' turn. You get it! You bullshit Catholics are out, with your bullshit saints," and that was followed up . . . Well, I won't even tell you what he said about the Blessed Virgin Mary, mainly because it was too despicable. Now he had my full attention.

Look, as I said, I'm American. I could care less about some Bozo's opinion of the Emerald Society or Irish music or traditions. But when you start attacking my religion, that's another story.

He kept up this tirade of anti-Catholic slurs and downright blasphemous statements. Now he got up from his chair and leaned across the table and pointed his finger right about two inches from my nose. (I hate when someone does that to me.) He continued with the most obscene statements about my religion that I've ever heard. He finished by saying "Off the record, I'm gonna put your Irish Catholic ass in jail if it's the last thing I do. You'll learn that the Jews are in charge."

I slammed the chair back. It hit the wall and toppled over. "On the record," I said, "if you don't take that Jew finger out of my Irish Catholic face, I'm gonna break your arm and stick it up your Jew ass." He was now backing away toward the door as I started to come around the table.

(Look, as I said, say whatever you want about me or the Irish, but don't attack my faith or my family. It could be hazardous to your health.)

The door opened and two suits came in and Sussman backed out. "You'll pay. You'll pay." I have never seen anyone as scared as that wrinkled little turd. I picked up the chair and sat. At noon, I got up and walked out and went to lunch. I didn't wait for my jailer to give me permission. I showed them.

One thing you have to understand is that cops didn't have the protection they have now when it comes to being interrogated. The Patrolman's Benevolent Association (PBA) were not pro-active when it came to safeguarding cops' rights. If the truth be told, they rarely, if ever, fought against the bosses. Their mentality, as a union, was "Hey, kid, take your lumps and move on." Hopefully now it's different. Or at least I would like to believe it is. There really wasn't anyone I could go to to complain about his remarks about my religion.

Back at the command, I told the bosses what had transpired and I could tell they were pissed. McDermott took particular offense at the remark about him and his "band of thieves." I heard him mumble, "That little shit."

Wolfgang O'Leary put his hand on my shoulder. "If you're worried, Dan, he wasn't wearing a wire. If he was, he never would have flipped his lid the way you described. He's a coward! But he is connected. You have made a real enemy. But I guess you know that." Geez, thanks, boss.

Joel and I received subpoenaes to go to the Grand Jury on the collar. Now, this in itself was unusual because gambling offenses were usually knocked down to a misdemeanor and the policy guy paid a fine. I should have realized something was up.

Jennifer had taken her leave from work and was getting anxious to have the baby. June was two days from ending. "I don't want to wish my life away, but I wish it was over," she said on more than one occasion. Who could blame her? I didn't tell her this, of course, but she was BIG. I just kept telling her how beautiful she was. And I wasn't telling a lie.

We went down to the big courthouse on Centre Street. It was a massive structure with a much storied history. For some reason, Lieutenant Charlie Ingulli "just happened" to be in the lobby. "I have some time to kill so I'll go up to the Grand Jury with you guys." On the ninth floor were the Grand Jury rooms.

A Grand Jury is made up of twenty-four ordinary citizens from all walks of life. All ages, twenty-one and up. All colors, all different beliefs. Once you go and are sworn, the assistant district attorney asks you questions related to your arrest. No one else besides the jurors, the ADA, the stenographer, and the witness are in the room. No defense attorney. No defendant. Just you, the ADA, and the jury. The juror cannot ask the witness questions directly. They have to tell the ADA the question and then he or she decides if the question is relevant to the matter at hand. Got all that? Good.

The three of us went into the waiting room, and who do you think was there waiting? Mr. Wrinkles, and two other, equally unimpressive-looking, suits. I ignored them because I saw my brother Jackie sitting on one of the church-type pew benches.

I introduced him to the lieutenant and Joel, and then Sussman came over. "Stark, come up to the desk." Almost as an afterthought, "Oh, you too, Washington." The ADA introduced herself as Maggie something or another. Pleasant looking with short white hair and the bluest eyes I've ever seen.

"I have to advise you that before you testify, you have to sign this Waiver of Immunity. That means that I can ask any questions about anything you've done, even if it doesn't pertain to this particular arrest." Before she could finish, Sussman said, "And if you don't . . ." Maggie, what's her name, shot him a withering look and he shut up. Chief Wolfgang was right; he is a coward. "If you refuse to sign, you will be subject to disciplinary action from the department, which could include suspension or even dismissal. Do you agree to sign and answer all my questions truthfully?"

I didn't hesitate. I took a pen from my suit jacket pocket and signed. Without even looking at him, I held out the pen and Joel took it and he signed.

What the hell was she going to ask? I thought. The shot I fired into the sand in Coney Island? Or when I dragged the wrong Lombardi into the alley? Or a couple of dozen other or's. Who knows? Well, I figured I'd find out soon enough. C'mon, St. Michael.

I turned around and saw Sussman talking to Jackie. When he walked away, Lieutenant Ingulli went over and sat next to him. He talked and Jackie talked. Then Jackie got up and went out of the Grand Jury room. The court officer called my name and in I went to what I perceived to be an inquisition.

Honestly, it wasn't bad at all. The ADA was all business just like the show Dragnet where Sergeant Friday wanted "just the facts." She wasn't interested in, oh, for instance, who the informant was, or how we knew him, or had he ever given me any substantial information before. Just the facts. You know, to this day, I can't figure out why she never mentioned the fact that I hit the guy with the sledgehammer. I don't know if she even knew. Or he was embarrassed too and didn't tell. I still don't know.

After about a half hour of recounting the events, she asked the jurors if they had any relevant questions. Only one did, and she asked me, "Officer Stark, what were you wearing when you climbed the fire escape?"

"A T-shirt, shorts, and sneakers, ma'am."

"So you weren't wearing a suit?"

"No, ma'am."

"Thank you. Please wait outside."

I left the jury room and sat next to Ingulli and Jackie. Joel was on the other side. ADA Maggie called Joel into the room, and about fifteen minutes later, he came out. Sussman looked perplexed, annoyed, surprised, or all of the above. He went over to ADA Maggie and, very animately, was making wild gestures with his hands and his face reddened. I turned to Jackie and the lieutenant. "Watch this, he's gonna turn purple and you'll see spit coming out of his mouth." I no sooner said it when ADA Maggie put her hand up and, loud enough for all to hear, said, "Inspector, please stop spitting."

The green light went on over the Grand Jury room door. This signaled that the jurors had reached a decision. Maggie went in, and about a minute later, she came out. I really wouldn't want to play poker with her. I couldn't read her face.

She went to the clerk's desk, filled out a form, put the form in the case folder and then turned to all of us. "Thank you, gentlemen. You'll be notified as to the Grand Jury's findings."

Sussman piped up. "Wait just a minute. You're telling me I have to wait to find out if the Grand Jurors voted an indictment against these two officers? Is that what you're telling me!" "Yes" was all she said and she gave him an icy stare. "You know the law, Inspector. The Grand Jury proceedings are secret and sealed. They are not released until they are unsealed by a judge."

"This is bullshit! We always find out. I have never had to wait." Again, with the icy stare and an iceberg sound to her voice, she said, "You might want to rethink or even rephrase what you just said, Inspector. It is a crime to release or receive secret Grand Jury decisions before they are unsealed. You didn't just tell me, in front of witnesses, I might add, that there have been times when you've broken the law by receiving Grand Jury decisions prior to a judge releasing them."

He was caught flat-footed (no pun intended as a reference to cops, you know Flat Foot.) "What I mean, meant . . . no, that wasn't what I . . . really it . . . what I . . ." She let him squirm a little more and then said, "I think you meant to say that in cases involving cops your office gets notified first. Even before the cop does. Is that fair to say?"

"Exactly what I meant" and out the door he scurried in his wrinkled suit and wrinkled body with sweat covering his wrinkled brow.

I looked over at Mike, the court clerk for the Grand Jury, and he winked and gave me a thumbs up as he held the case folder with the name of Washington and Stark. He then held up thefolder with "Big Foot's" name and gave a thumbs down. This meant there was No True Bill against Joel and me. But "Big Foot" had been indicted for felony possession of gambling records. The sheet writer had already copped a plea to misdemeanor possession of gambling records and paid a fine. His case was closed. Thank you, St. Michael.

Eventually I found out that there was a sit-down in District Attorney Frank Hogan's office prior to our Grand Jury appearance. Present at the meeting were Chief O'Leary, Chief Seamus Morgan, (he was from the Boro), Inspector Ray McDermott and Lieutenant Ingulli (his mother was an O'Rourke and his father's mother was a Conroy). District Attorney Hogan was a legend in law enforcement circles. Tough, firm but very fair.

He listened to the assembled group who told them that they believed Sussman was railroading me because of a personal animus. They also believed that Sussman was possessed with a virulent hatred for the Irish Catholics . . . Based on the No True Bill vote, I guess the days of the Irish weren't over.

Oh, yeah, remember when Ingulli talked to Jackie and Jackie left the room? The lieutenant asked Jackie if he was on or off duty. Jackie said he was working but was taking his meal hour early to be with me. Ingulli told him to call his office and cover his ass because Sussman was going to call and check. He did just that and he put in for the rest of the day off.

Ingulli was right, Sussman, it seems, when he left the jury room, called the Safe and Loft Squad and spoke to Inspector McGuire. He asked McGuire why Jackie was at court. McGuiretold him it was none of his business. "But, just for the record, Julie, he took the day off." What a piece of crap. He couldn't get me so he tried to get Jackie. Unbelievable.

I was looking forward to the baby. All the other crap I put behind me. I remember distinctly it was July 3rd when Captain Rohe called me into his office. "Sit down, Dan. I have some bad news for you." My heart sank. "Is Jennifer all right? What about the baby?"

"No, no, no, nothing like that. I mean work bad news."

"Captain, I really don't care about work. Geez, you scared the hell out of me."

"Sorry."

I went home to North Arlington and was greeted by Eileen. "Georgie and Momma just took Jennifer to West Hudson. They left me a note. I just got home from work." She was working for the PBI in Newark. "Give me a minute and I'll go with you."

It was a long night. She was in great discomfort. About midnight a nurse came out and told us all to go home. By this time, Betty Ann had joined us as well as Aunt Rose.

I was back at eight the next morning. I called work and explained to Lieutenant Ingulli and he approved the time. "Hey, Dan, call us with the good news. "Right, boss. I will. And thanks for all your support." He grunted and hung up the phone.

On the Fourth, the rockets glared red and the bombs burst overhead. (Actually, they were Fourth-sponsored fireworks.)But no Fourth of July baby. Jennifer was in discomfort and the doctors were talking about a "C" Section. They asked her if she wanted that and she declined. They didn't want to let her go home because "You're almost there. It won't be long now." I went home about midnight, still no baby. Still a lot of pain for Jennifer.

I got up at about a quarter to seven on the Fifth, took care of business, dressed, and tip-toed downstairs. Mrs. McDermott was in the kitchen. I gave her a kiss on the cheek. She handed me a cup of coffee. "Mrs. McDermott, is she going to be all right? Is the baby going to be okay?"

"They both will be fine. Don't worry."

She continued. "Are you going to go up to the hospital now?"

"No, I was going to go to mass at that big church near the hospital." She looked at me and said, "That's Saint Cecelia's." Now I was definitely going there. How could I not? I don't believe in omens but Momma was telling me [remember her name was Cecelia], "Come on, my little man, come to me. Everything will be fine."

I know that church wasn't named after Momma but it should have been. Mrs. McDermott put on her hat and the both of us went off to visit Momma's church.

When we got to the hospital, Jennifer's doctor greeted us and we were ushered into the new momma's room.

Jennifer was propped up and she even had lipstick on. She was holding the most beautiful baby in the world. I know, I know, every parent thinks their baby is the most beautiful that was ever born. But, in this case, it was true. Oh, yeah, she was a girl. We decided that if the baby was a girl, she'd be Janet. Jennifer loved that name. Her middle name was to be Elizabeth after Jennifer's mother. I know my Momma would approve.

We moved out of Stuyvesant Town within the year because we needed a bigger place. The following September, Kathleen Cecelia was born. The year after that, Tara Ann was born. Two miscarriages past and Erin Patricia was born. When Jennifer was expecting the last one, some of the guys at work would ask, "What are you hoping for? I bet you want a boy this time." My standard answer was, "As long as they're both healthy, I really don't care. But if I had a say in the matter, I'd want another girl."

"Aw, that's BS. You want a son, admit it." Ever the practical one, I'd reply, "We have a three-bedroom house. Where the heck would I put him?" They'd all laugh and some would actually agree.

As the song goes, "Thank heaven for little girls. They grow up in the most delightful way." And, you know, they did! Well, that's about it. You asked me to tell you about myself and my life and that's part of it. There's a lot more to tell, if you're interested. But, tonight is meatloaf night. If you don't get there early, all the best pieces are gone. You know, I just love meatloaf.

Oh, what was the bad news that Captain Rohe had for me? It was that he was told by a friend, in Headquarters, that I was going to be flopped (cop speak for taken out of my plainclothes assignment and put back into uniform). I'd have to make detective another way. Right now, I just want to get to that meatloaf.